THE FREEDOM FLEET

THE FREEDOM FLEET

FREEDOM FLEET BOOK 1

DANIEL ARENSON

This novel is a work of fiction. Names, characters, places and incidents are either the product of the author's imagination, or, if real, used fictitiously.

PROLOGUE
The Shadows of Our Past

Toliman Space Station
Alpha Centauri
4.46 light-years from Earth
September 1, 2207

Of all the terrors in the universe—black holes, marauding aliens, supernova explosions—nothing terrifies the wise more than the cruelty of man. And no hearts are crueler than those that beat, black and wretched, in the hearts of the Third Reich officers.

Commander Ishmael Jordan knew his history. He knew the evil mankind was capable of. His own ancestors had been carried to America in chains, slaves for the plantations. Yes, Ishmael knew all about the dark heart of man. But he knew it only from books. From films. From nearly forgotten tales.

Tonight, this night in 2207 so far away from home, Ishmael Jordan would learn this truth on his own flesh.

The night began like a thousand others. Had it been a thousand nights already? Ishmael thought so. He had been here for nearly three years now. It was a prestigious post—commanding a space station orbiting a distant star. But sometimes Ishmael felt like an animal in a cage. A thousand days and nights without breathing fresh air, without feeling grass beneath his feet, without seeing blue sky. Yes, he had his family here. And the officers under his command. He was far from alone. But he felt trapped.

It wasn't natural spending so long in space. Oh, his uncle could do it, of course. The famous Larry Jordan, last commander of the starship *Freedom*, would often spend years in space. And not just stuck on guard duty at Alpha Centauri. No. Uncle Larry—the war hero, the legend—had battled alien empires! What was Ishmael Jordan in comparison? True, Ishmael had star insignia on his shoulders. He had the respect of his crew. Most would consider him a successful officer. But Ishmael had big shoes to fill. And somehow his own achievements seemed paltry compared to the legendary deeds of Uncle Larry.

Stop that, he scolded himself. *You sound like a boy. You're a senior officer. The commander of a space station. You're no longer that frightened kid from the slums of LA.*

Ishmael raised his chin, shoving those memories down. He looked around the Operation Center. Ops was the beating heart of Toliman Space Station, its command and control facility. The circular chamber spread around Ishmael like a solar system. He stood in the center like the sun. Around him, reminiscent of rocky planets, floated spherical screens. The globes showed stats from across the station—one globe for the engine room, one for the docking bay, and so on. Farther out, like gas giants, stood bulky workstations for Ishmael's officers. Most of those officers were off duty tonight. Only the night crew stood in the shadows, monitors illuminating their faces with pale blue light. They reminded Ishmael of the faces of sleepy moons from a child's picture book. The machinery hummed, the coffee machine percolated, and the dim lights buzzed. Only the odd yawn punctuated this music of the night. Ops always felt so different after hours. The bustling chamber became a dreamlike planetarium for ghosts.

Of course, there was no day or night aboard a space station. Not one in deep space like Toliman. But the lights were programmed to brighten and dim, mimicking the circadian rhythm of Earth. So the crew still spoke of day and night. At the end of the day (literally and figuratively), they were biological beings, not too far removed from their ancestors of the wilderness. They needed at least some mimicry of Earth. Nice as dimming lights were, Ishmael would have given his second leg to hear birds, to feel grass, to see the blue sky.

He had already worked the day shift, but he couldn't sleep, so he remained on duty throughout the night. Over the past few weeks, an unease had been growing in him. Memories resurfaced in his dreams. Memories of losing his parents in the terrible Spider War. Memories of losing his leg. They haunted his nightmares. Perhaps it was these thousand days in space. A thousand days without feeling the sun on his face, without hearing leaves rustle, without smelling a flower or feeling the rain. It was getting to him. Peeling away the scabs he had built around his soul. Exposing the infection.

Stop, he told himself.

He turned toward one workstation. "Major Cross, have you completed the diagnostic of our telemetry array?"

The major looked up from her workstation. The monitor's blue light softened her sharp features. Part of the night crew, Major Mary Cross was a mousy officer with a tight brown ponytail, nervous lips, and gray eyes that seemed too large in her gaunt face. Ishmael always found night crews to be a little shy, a little awkward, creatures of the night who only emerged from their burrows in the safety of darkness.

"Almost done, sir," she said. "The scan is ninety-eight percent complete. All sensors working properly, sir."

"So far," Ishmael said.

Major Cross frowned. "Sir?"

"All sensors are working properly *so far*. You haven't scanned the last two percent yet."

"Of course, sir," Major Cross said. "But the gamma quadrant sensors have never shown any issues. We can safely assume that—"

"Never assume, Major Cross. Out here at Alpha Centauri, we're the farthest outpost of humanity. A beacon in the dark. We are all that separates Sol from the vast darkness of space. We are Earth's guardians, Major Cross. Her first and finest line of defense. And so, unless proved otherwise, we will never *assume* things are well."

She nodded. "Of course, sir. Completing diagnostics of final telemetry arrays now."

Ishmael turned away. Hands clasped behind his back, he faced the towering viewport that dominated Ops. Dammit, his stump hurt. The prosthetic was chafing him again. He gritted his jaw, ignoring the pain, and stared at the vista ahead.

Space. The vast darkness of the soul. Alpha Centauri was a triple star system. The station orbited Toliman, one of those three suns. From Earth, all three stars of Alpha Centauri morphed into one dot of light. Throughout human history, druids and shamans worshipped Alpha Centauri. Navigators followed the celestial lamp as they sailed the oceans. The Egyptians revered the light. And they never knew its true nature. Not one star—but three orbiting one another.

It was sometimes hard to believe, but only five years ago, humans couldn't reach the stars. Spacetime portals, discovered during the brutal Spider War, had let the first explorers leave Sol. Until three years ago, Toliman Space Station hadn't existed. It seemed like forever. But in the grand scheme of history, this was all brand-new. The frontier of space, science, and human exploration.

It was funny. Alpha Centauri was only 4.46 light-years from Earth. Anyone looking from Earth now would see Alpha Centauri as it had been four years ago. No station. No humans.

Beyond reach. Just the same star those navigators had gazed upon in the ancient days.

And there outside the viewport—the vast distance. The infinite void. The universe.

Billions of stars shone. Beyond them, visible thanks to the wonders of modern telescopes, shone countless galaxies. What unknown horrors lurked there? A few years ago, humanity had dipped its toes into this cosmic ocean. And got bitten. The rahs, arachnid aliens from deep space, had stung humanity. Stung them hard. Millions had died. Ishmael had lost his parents and his leg. But humanity shoved the aliens back! Humanity learned from her foe's technology. And now Ishmael was here. Light-years from home. Guardian of a nascent empire. And ahead spread the great abyss, a pit swarming with hidden monsters.

"Sir?"

Major Cross's voice pierced the shadows. Ishmael spun toward her. Her large eyes peered over her monitor, reflecting the blue light. Mousy she might be, but those eyes seemed almost feline. A cat's eyes shining in a dark alleyway.

"Major, is the diagnostic sweeps complete?" Ishmael said.

She squinted at her monitor. "It's weird."

"Major, talk to me, not to yourself," Ishmael said.

She glanced up at him. Her eyes gleamed again, startlingly bright in the shadows. "Sir, there's . . . an anomaly."

Ishmael frowned. "An anomaly?"

"It must be a mistake. A hardware malfunction in one of the telemetry telescopic satellites."

"Send the data to the main systems screen," Ishmael said. "Let's take a look."

With quick, slender fingers, Cross tapped a few buttons. Hallucinatory monitors constantly floated through Ops like soap bubbles. One expanded now, showing a stream of data. The lines of green characters scrolled furiously. Ishmael stroked his chin, trying to find patterns in the barrage of data.

"It almost looks like . . ." He squinted. "Like spacetime is warping."

Other crew members looked up from their workstations. The science officer knocked over his cup of tea.

"That's what I thought too, sir." Cross nervously fiddled with her uniform's cuff links. "I assume it's a warped lens on the satellite."

"Never assume!" Ishmael said. "Give me a live visual of that sector of space. No alphanumeric data. Just the video stream. Primary viewport."

Warped space, he thought. *Could be a rah portal.*

Spiders seemed to scuttle down his spine and gnaw on his stump. He suppressed a shudder. Famous Uncle Larry, commanding the starship *Freedom*, had destroyed the rahs. Nobody had heard from the alien arachnids since. Those spiders were crushed. Of course it was just a bad lens.

The visual finally came on-screen. The telescope filmed a sector of space off the station's starboard docks. Sirius and Betelgeuse shone side by side like dueling boxers. Orion's belt glowed beneath them while Gemini oversaw the celestial tableau. From here at Alpha Centauri, the night sky seemed remarkably like the one viewed from Earth. Even here, at another star, one barely noticed a difference in the constellations. To a man, 4.46 light-years was a vastness beyond imagination. On the cosmic scale, it was barely any distance at all.

And then, as Ishmael watched, Sirius and Betelgeuse seemed to . . . draw apart. The two luminous boxers seemed to be retreating from each other.

"What the hell?" Ishmael muttered. "Is anyone else seeing this?"

Other stars began to move too. Orion's belt expanded as if the ancient warrior were gaining weight. All of spacetime seemed to be rippling outward from a central point. Of course the stars weren't moving (at least not any more than usual). Something was bending the light. A sphere of spacetime, perhaps no larger than this station, was twisting and warping the image.

"A portal?" Ishmael said. "AP, give me some data! Can you analyze what Telemetry is seeing?"

He turned toward the astrophysics station. Major Akira Minatozaki, the science officer on duty, looked up. Tea stains darkened his blue uniform. The two departments worked closely together. Telemetry handled satellites, telescopes, and data collection. Astrophysics made sense of it.

Major Minatozaki was a middle-aged man with a goatee and round glasses, an anachronism in this age of ophthalmological gene therapy. But then again, the docs could grow you a new leg today too, and Ishmael still wore a prosthetic. He wasn't the only one who feared modern medicine, it seemed.

"Sir, this will sound strange," Minatozaki said, "but whatever we're looking at . . . it's not a spacetime portal. Space and time aren't warping at all."

"Nonsense," Ishmael said. "Look at the stars, man! Something is bending the light."

"I can't explain it, sir," Minatozaki said. "Yet."

Ishmael pursed his lips. "Get me an explanation as soon as you can, Major."

The Japanese officer nodded. His fingers danced over his keyboard, collecting and analyzing data. "Working on it, sir."

Ishmael wrapped his fingers around the railing that surrounded his circular workstation. The command station was elevated like a small round dais. By design, the commander must see all stations in Ops, and everyone must see him. But Ishmael always felt a little vulnerable up here. Like an old-time sailor in a crow's nest, exposed to the storm.

Could it be them? he wondered. *The rahs? Are they back?*

Memories of that old war resurfaced. The aliens scuttling through his starship. Slaying spacers around him. Jaws closing around his leg and—

Stop. Focus. Your crew depends on you. Be strong.

Ishmael turned again toward the telemetry station. "Major Cross, run a sweep with our gravitational wave detection."

The young, mousy major tapped a few buttons. She blinked those large, luminous eyes of hers. "The data confirms it, sir. There is no spacetime portal."

The starlight kept warping. A dark sphere materialized in the heart of the anomaly, swirling the starlight around it. Ishmael imagined a drain opening in space, the starlight forming a maelstrom around the pit.

"So what the hell is that thing?" Ishmael said. "Astrophysics, give me some theories, dammit."

Major Minatozaki gulped. "Sir, it almost looks like . . ." The nebbish physicist dropped his voice and mumbled something.

"Say that again, Major Minatozaki," Ishmael said.

"It almost looks like a . . ." The bespectacled man gulped. "An opening to another universe."

Ishmael blinked. "A *what?*"

Minatozaki blinked rapidly, cleared his throat, and smoothed his uniform. "Of course, it's all only hypothetical, sir. Parallel universes have never been directly observed. Unless you consider the so-called *Otherworld* of modern hopscotch drives, though many physicists believe that's more like a reflection of our universe than a true parallel universe. But you did ask for theories, sir, and according to theoretical studies recently conducted at the Orionlabs at—"

"Yellow alert!" Ishmael said, interrupting the scientist. "Station guards at all airlock doors. Get our starfighter pilots into their cockpits, ready to launch. I'm not taking any chances." His voice dropped. "Whatever this is, we'll be ready."

"Yellow alert, aye!" cried Major Benedict Watts, the tactical officer on duty. The tall, rawboned soldier stood at the back of Ops. Until now, Watts had hidden in the shadows, merely watching. Observing. Always on alert. Now yellow lights flashed, bathing his gaunt features, and his hand reached toward his sidearm.

Floating monitors showed pilots racing toward the hangar bay. One of those pilots was Colonel Valentina Jordan, commander of the starfighter fleet. No matter how high she climbed the ranks, to Ishmael she would always be little Tina, his baby sister. He watched her on an orbiting screen. Tina glanced up toward a floating camera, made eye contact with Ishmael, then ran onward.

This wasn't a red alert. No klaxons were blaring. Yet. Across Toliman Space Station, most people were still asleep, blissfully unaware of the anomaly. Telepathic signals woke a few guards from their slumber. They leaped from bed, pulled on their uniforms, and ran to guard the airlocks. The bar shut down. A few civilians, up late drinking, returned to their quarters and locked their doors. All standard yellow alert procedures. The station tensed up like a muscle. Waiting. Ready for trouble.

Three hundred Alliance soldiers served here, along with their families. For a thousand days, they had lived out here in the darkness, forming a community. A tribe. A family. For a long time now, Ishmael had resented his post. He had felt trapped here, so far from home. Now, under threat, Toliman suddenly felt like home. A home he must protect.

And then something emerged from the portal. Yes, a portal it must be. Whether to another time, place, or universe, Ishmael did not know. But a portal this was, and something was flying through.

Ishmael stood straight at his station, gripping the railing, staring.

Gasps sounded across Ops. But Ishmael refused to let his face betray his fear. He must remain strong. For his crew. For his family aboard. For his planet far behind.

It was a ship. A warship. A *huge* warship. At first only the prow emerged from the portal. And stars above, that prow was something from the mind of Hell's twisted engineers. Cannons thrust out, their bores so wide one could fly a starfighter inside. Gears the size of Ferris wheels spun, moving the gargantuan guns. A figurehead topped the prow, depicting a two-headed black eagle the size of an Egyptian temple, wings spread out.

The ship kept emerging, revealing more and more cannons. The warship seemed to never end. Thousands of guns lined her beams, and armored plates covered her hull. Soon a full mile of starship had emerged from the portal. And still she kept coming. Dear Lord, how could any machine be so large? This warship dwarfed any ship Ishmael had ever seen. She dwarfed this entire space station. Finally the stern emerged from the portal too, revealing blazing red engines. Stats raced across the screens in Ops. Ishmael could barely believe the data. Stern to stem, this ship was over two miles long. She was the size of New York's Central Park.

She was twice the length of the starship *Freedom*, which Uncle Larry had commanded, famous for being the largest ship in Alliance history. And this new terror was far, far bulkier and heavier.

The monstrosity ahead wasn't just a dreadnought. It was something larger, fiercer. A super-dreadnought. A thing that should not be. Was this an alien ship? It had to be. No humans could build such a machine. Was a name painted onto the side hull? Ishmael couldn't see from this angle.

"Telemetry, switch main viewport to astro satellite C12," he said.

Major Mary Cross nodded. "Aye, sir, switching view now."

The towering screen switched to a new video feed. The camera was orbiting the station a megameter away. Normally, C12 satellite let Ops view Toliman Space Station's exterior. Useful for scanning for hull damage or space barnacles. But tonight the camera turned toward the gargantuan starship, filming the intruder from the side. Ishmael got a good look at the invader's starboard. The armored hull stretched for two miles, bathed in the light of Alpha Centauri B, also known as Toliman's star.

Ishmael felt the blood drain from his face. Just like it had once drained from the stump of his leg. The terror gripped him like the jaws of that long-dead spider.

"Dear God," whispered Major Cross. She clutched the crucifix that hung from her neck.

The starlight shone on a towering sigil upon the strange ship's hull.

It was a swastika.

*****

"What the hell?" Ishmael muttered under his breath. He stared at the strange warship in disbelief.

A warship sporting a swastika sigil. Not a Buddhist or Hindu swastika either. This was a clockwise swastika, nesting within a white circle upon a red field. Symbol of Nazi Germany. And it was *massive*. Each of the swastika's arms was like a city block.

The starship's name appeared below the swastika, each letter the size of a church. *BARBAROSSA.*

"What kind of ship is this?" Major Cross rubbed her eyes. "A Nazi ship? I thought we defeated those guys three centuries ago."

"We did," Ishmael said. "My ancestors fought in that war."

"All our ancestors did," said Major Minatozaki. He stared at the ship with dark eyes. "My own ancestors fought on the wrong side of that war. I'm not proud of our past."

"And it looks like the past just caught up with us," Major Cross said.

Ishmael's stomach soured. How could this be real? For years, Ishmael had served in the Freedom Fleet, the space force of the Alliance. Before commanding a space station, he had flown warships. He knew every ship in the fleet. No Alliance starship was anywhere near this large, nor would it display such a foul symbol. The Alliance was about democracy, humanity, and freedom. No, certainly this was no Alliance ship.

Could it be something from the Red Dawn then? No. Preposterous. The Russians, the Chinese, the North Koreans, and their allies—they perhaps held no love for the Alliance and her democracies. But they absolutely *loathed* fascism. If the Reds hated anything more than capitalism, it was Nazism.

Maybe the Desert Thorns had built this juggernaut? The Middle East and North Africa were wealthy, and their union was powerful. They certainly could afford to build something this big. But no. Ishmael ruled that out too. Desert Thorn ships were small, sleek things, while this was a crude monstrosity.

And surely this was no alien vessel. Ishmael had fought alien vessels before. They were lumpy, misshapen things, oddly organic. Only humans, it seemed, loved to build in straight lines. So where *did* this ship come from?

"We've got a mystery on our hands," Ishmael said. "Comms!"

"Aye, sir?" said Celestia, the communication officer on duty. Her chrome body gleamed. Celestia had a human brain, but the rest of her was mechanical. She stared at Ishmael with cold, glowing eyes. Those eyes were little cameras set in her metal skull. They held no emotion, no soul. Yes, Celestia had a human brain, but emotions relied heavily on chemicals from the biological body. Cyborgs like Celestia, emotionless under any amount of pressure, were rare and desired officers. Especially at times of war. They combined human intuition and a robot's logic.

"Activate our CWG, Celestia," Ishmael told her. "We're going to generate a communication wormhole. Just long enough to reach Earth. Doesn't have to be any fancy wormhole. Whatever's quickest to weave. We only need to send HQ a quick message. Show them what we're looking at. Keep them in the loop."

"Aye, sir," said the cyborg. "I'll open a level B5 ultraviolet-class wormhole. Should be up in only three minutes. Enough to send Earth the images and—"

"The enemy ship is aiming its cannons!" cried tall, lanky Watts from his perch at the Tactical station. The security officer's fists tightened. The yellow lights gave his gaunt features a jaundiced look.

"Shields up!" Ishmael barked. "Red alert! Tactical, lock torpedoes on the enemy ship but wait for my orders. Comms, open a hailing frequency to the enemy ship."

Yes, an enemy ship. That was what they were dealing with, it seemed. A tremble ran through Ishmael. Those cold, familiar spiders scuttled down his back.

Shove the fear down, he thought. *Crush the memories. Be strong. In charge. These people need you. Your family needs you.*

Red lights flashed across Ops. A siren sounded throughout the station. Citizens waited behind locked doors. Soldiers leaped from bed, grabbed their weapons, and ran to their posts. In the hangar bays, the fighter pilots fired up their engines. They were just waiting for the order to launch. They were like crouching tigers, ready to pounce.

"Hailing frequency open, Commander," Celestia said. The cyborg's voice was fair and ethereal. A voice like bells echoing through a city street at dawn. "I'm still working on your wormhole to Earth. For now, you may speak to the enemy ship."

Ishmael stared at the super-dreadnought. He clasped his hands behind his back.

"*Barbarossa*, this is Commander Ishmael Jordan from Toliman Space Station. We're ready to defend ourselves if necessary. Disengage your cannons and—"

"Incomi—" Major Watts began.

White light flashed, flooding the Ops room.

Blasts rocked the station. The deck swayed beneath Ishmael's feet. He grabbed the railing for support. Smoke filled Ops. A monitor exploded. Sparks flew. The klaxons wailed like wounded animals.

"Damage report!" Ishmael cried. His voice was hoarse. He coughed out smoke.

Major Watts tapped buttons and pulled up screens. He spoke with his grainy voice. "They targeted both our wormhole generators, sir." The security chief coughed and waved aside smoke. "Both primary and backup."

Celestia nodded. "Confirmed, sir." The cyborg sounded completely calm. As if she were discussing the weather. "The enemy destroyed my wormhole."

"What about the third wormhole generator?" Ishmael said. "On the satellite?" He coughed. "And somebody turn off that damn siren!"

A young systems officer tapped some buttons, silencing the wailing alarm.

Watts checked and pursed his thin lips. "Gone, sir. The third one too."

Ishmael nodded. "They cut off our phone lines to Earth. They knew what to attack." He turned toward Comms. "Celestia, before the enemy destroyed our wormhole generators, did you get that message to Earth?"

The cyborg tilted her head. Her chrome body was charred and cracked. Among everyone on Ops, she had suffered the worst of the blast. Thankfully, cyborgs could feel no pain.

"I think so, sir. For a second or two, I was transmitting. Though I can't be sure. Earth never had time to ping us a confirmation." Her metallic head twitched. Sparks flew from a crack in her skull. "We're offline now. Cut off from Earth. I—" One of her camera eyes collapsed. The lens clattered against the deck. "I am . . . damaged." Her voice trembled—a rare display of emotion. Maybe cyborgs could feel after all.

"Hang in there, Celestia," Ishmael said. "We'll get you repaired soon." He turned toward Tactical. "Watts, fire torpedoes! All cannons! Take that ship out."

Toliman Space Station was a guard outpost, not a full fortress. It didn't have the mighty firepower of a frigate or dreadnought. It could not unleash devastation like the great warships of the past. Like the one Uncle Larry had commanded. But they were not defenseless. And Ishmael Jordan vowed to make his uncle proud. Like famous Uncle Larry, he would fight.

I fought a battle years ago and lost half my entire crew, he thought. *Not to mention my leg. I won't lose again.*

"Firing torpedoes, aye!" cried Major Watts from Tactical.

Toliman Space Station rocked as her cannons fired. On the monitors, Ishmael watched the torpedoes streak forth. Each of those torpedoes was the size of a sperm whale. Chemical explosives filled them, and spinning drills tipped their warheads. These were missiles designed to drill through the mightiest hulls, burrow into enemy ships like worms into flesh, and unleash pure destruction. Each one cost more than what Ishmael Jordan would earn in his lifetime. Hell, probably more than what the *entire Ops crew* would earn in their lifetimes. And Ishmael had just fired ten of them. Well, the admiralty could send him the bill.

The torpedoes' engines blazed. They raced toward the Nazi warship like barracudas on the hunt. Ishmael smiled thinly. He still had no idea who the hell flew that titanic ship. But he wouldn't shed any tears over its destruction.

The torpedoes streaked toward *Barbarossa* and—

Ishmael inhaled sharply.

Lasers fired from *Barbarossa*'s hull. Ten red beams hit ten torpedoes. A mere twelve megameters from *Barbarossa*'s hull, the torpedoes detonated.

All of them.

Explosions lit space. White light flooded Ops. The viewports dimmed automatically. Toliman Space Station shook under waves of radiation, its shield sparking and trembling. Scattered fires blazed across Ops, illuminating cracked machinery, smoke, and blood splatters.

"Did we hit anything?" Ishmael cried, squinting in the light.

The flare of explosions dimmed. Everyone stared at the viewport.

"Negative," said Major Watts from Tactical. Blood dripped from a gash on his forehead. "The enemy's laser defense system took everything out. They—"

"They're hailing us!" Celestia cried from Comms. The cyborg was definitely showing some human emotion now.

So this is what it takes to crack a cyborg's shell, Ishmael thought. *Looming death.*

Ishmael frowned and tapped his temple. Inside his skull, his MindLink thrummed. The neural implant made Ishmael hallucinate an interface that floated before him, translucent like a hologram. MindPlay Operating System allowed him to control his implant's many functions. He loaded the communication app, ready to accept a telepathic call from *Barbarossa.*

Nothing. Nobody was calling. Odd.

A thought struck him. Ishmael tapped a button on the floating interface, running a scan for nearby MindLinks. Every implant aboard Toliman Space Station appeared as a little green icon. When Ishmael looked at his crew, he hallucinated their MindLinks glowing inside their skulls. It was like having x-ray vision. When he looked down, up, and to the sides, Ishmael could see hundreds of lights. A sea of them like stars, shining through the walls. He was hallucinating the MindLinks of crew members across Toliman Space Station.

He looked through the viewport at *Barbarossa.* He should see the enemy starship light up with MindLinks. A ship that big? There should be thousands of glowing icons there—thousands of spacers with neural implants. But nothing showed up. Nothing! As if *Barbarossa* were a ghost ship. Was nobody aboard? Was AI running this massive warship? Were they jamming the signals? Or maybe . . . No. It couldn't be. But Ishmael must consider the possibility. Maybe *Barbarossa*'s crew simply didn't have neural implants. Nothing to show up on the scan.

Incredible. Like people from the pre-telepathic revolution.

"I'm not getting any telepathic calls," Ishmael said. "They're not on MindWeb?"

Celestia shook her head. The cyborg was regaining some of her composure. "Negative. I'm detecting no MindLinks aboard the *Barbarossa.* They're hailing us by radio, sir."

"Radio!" Ishmael exclaimed. "What, not smoke signals?" He laughed nervously.

Who used radio these days? MindWeb had been developed in America, an Alliance nation. Since then, it had spread across Earth and her colonies. Every officer today—whether Alliance, Red Dawn, or Desert Thorns—had a MindLink surgically inserted into their skull. In the military, telepathy had become as commonplace as email. Hell, as commonplace as talking.

No MindLinks on that ship ahead, huh? Ishmael thought. That was strange indeed.

The Ops crew was silent. Everyone turned to stare at the central viewport. Major Watts and Major Cross had to wave smoke aside. The hailing frequency was still coming in strong, flashing red on-screen. The phone was ringing.

Ishmael hesitated. Should he answer? Should he refuse the call? For now, neither side was firing any more lasers or torpedoes.

They must think we're helpless, Ishmael thought. *But we still have some surprises up our sleeve. We still have our starfighters. With my sister leading the wing.*

Yes, his sister. She served here. And Ishmael's wife and children were aboard too. He must defend them. Should they die, should war sweep over the Jordan family again . . . Should the terrors return, and the blood, and the grief, and—

Enough! Ishmael scolded himself. *That war is over. Those days are gone like your leg. Focus on the now. Focus on the threat at hand.*

The radio call was still flashing on the screens. His crew looked at him, awaiting orders.

"Very well," Ishmael said. He spoke loudly, trying to project confidence for his crew. A confidence he did not feel. "Comms, take the call. Main viewport. Let's see who we're dealing with."

*****

The telemetry monitors kept displaying the *Barbarossa* from different angles. The massive ship loomed above the station like a spider over trapped prey. Meanwhile, the central viewport accepted the call. The towering screen displayed a view from inside *Barbarossa.*

Ishmael clenched his jaw and balled his fists. Around him, crew members muttered and cursed. Even Celestia seemed shaken; the cyborg slightly narrowed her remaining eye, a sign of shock.

"Well, they're Nazis all right," Major Cross muttered from the telemetry station.

Barbarossa's bridge looked like something out of an old World War II movie. Red banners hung across the bulkheads, proudly displaying swastikas. The domed deckhead featured a mural of a black eagle, wings engulfing the bridge. A portrait of Hitler hung below the eagle's talons. The words EWIGER FÜHRER were etched into the golden frame.

Eternal leader, Ishmael thought, remembering his German. Well, Hitler had died centuries ago. It seems nobody had bothered to inform those anachronistic goons.

Barbarossa's crew stood on the bridge, hands clasped behind their backs. They looked like Nazi officers all right. The long black coats. The hats with metal skulls badges. The swastika arm bands. Yet these were no relics from the past somehow transported into the present. No, that portal was no time machine. These were modern men. They carried advanced firearms (possibly plasma-shooters). And they stared with bionic eyes that shone like coals. Each and every *Barbarossa* officer was missing an eye. Scars circled the bionic implants and sometimes stretched across half the face; they had lost their eyes to traumatic injuries. All those bionic eyes stared as one, burning across the distance and piercing Toliman Space Station. Ishmael could almost feel those gazes burning his skin.

"*Barbarossa!*" Ishmael barked. "You are in Free Alliance space. I am Commander Ishmael Jordan. Who are you? On whose authority do you attack us?"

One of the Nazi officers stepped closer. He was a tall, beefy man. Even his elaborate uniform could not hide his muscular frame. He looked fortysomething (about the same age as Ishmael), his jaw wide, his eyes startling blue. Scars ran across his left cheek, eye socket, and forehead. A red bionic eye peered from the deep nest of scar tissue. An iron cross shone between his collarbones, and braided insignia topped his shoulders.

Surreptitiously, Ishmael connected to MindWeb. With thoughts alone, he pulled up a telepathic article on Nazi Germany's military ranks. Bingo. The insignia showed up. The Nazi officer was a grand admiral.

"*Mein Gott*," the admiral muttered. "The führer was right. This universe does exist." He stared at Ishmael from the viewport and grimaced. "Disgusting! They still have subhumans."

Likely, the officer was speaking entirely in German. But Ishmael's MindLink had recognized the language and began to translate into English. For effect, the software gave the words a German accent. And those words sickened Ishmael.

His fury rose, burning through his fear. "Wherever you came from—turn back! Or we will send you back."

On the viewport, another Nazi officer stepped closer to the camera. She was a young woman. Barely more than a girl. Her blond hair spilled out from under a military cap with a skull badge. Her eyes widened—one blue real eye, one red bionic eye.

"Look at them, Papa!" she breathed, cheeks flushing. "Subhumans! Real *untermenschen*! And they wear clothes and everything. Oh, can I have one as a pet?"

The admiral ignored the girl. He stared at Ishmael through the screen, and a small smile twisted his thin lips. "We will promptly be boarding your station, Commander Jordan. I suggest you cooperate. Or your punishment will be swift, brutal, and efficient." He turned toward a lower-ranking officer. "Release the Wolfjägers!"

The video image cut off.

He hung up on us, Ishmael thought.

The viewport once more showed *Barbarossa* floating in space, facing Toliman Station. And Ishmael saw it happen. The Nazi dreadnought opened her airlocks and disgorged armored dropships. Their hulls displayed paintings of snarling wolves leaping over swastikas. Ishmael had never seen that particular ship design before, but he knew troop transporters when he saw them.

This was an invasion.

*****

They were coming. Invaders. Enemy warriors.

The spiders scuttled through the hall. Jaws closed around his leg. Ishmael screamed as the beast bit down, as—

No. No! No memories now. No panic. He must fight.

"Sir, I recommend firing our port grapeshot guns at those incoming bogeys," said Major Watts. "They'll beef up our point-defense system. Do you approve, sir?"

Ishmael looked toward the Tactical station. Watts stood there, gripping the railing, his face gaunt and hard.

"No," Ishmael said. "Concentrate artillery on that super-dreadnought. Let's see if we can overwhelm her missile-defense system with grapeshot, then hit her with another torpedo volley. This is like a boxing match. We'll have to lower our guard to get in some punches."

"And the incoming dropships, sir?" said Watts.

"My sister will take care of that." Ishmael tapped his temple, summoning MindPlay. "Tina, do you hear me?"

He hallucinated a small image of his sister. She floated before him, sitting in a cockpit. Her starfighter, an Eagle F-77, was still stationary, just waiting to deploy. Ishmael knew how the technology worked. Cameras in the hangar bay were filming her. They transmitted the video to MindWeb servers. Meanwhile, the MindLink device in Ishmael's skull downloaded the video, then sent electrical signals into his brain. His brain, reacting to the input, hallucinated his sister (a tiny version of her, at least) floating in the air here in Ops. The data transmitted across the entire chain within an instant.

Of course, Ishmael could simply telepathize with Tina, speaking directly into her mind. He didn't need to hallucinate her. But he wanted to see his dear sister. She was eight years younger. He remembered her as a little girl, watching him leave to officer school, vowing to become an officer someday too. Just like her old brother. Well, here they were. Two senior officers. Him—commander of a space station. Her—leading an Eagle starfighter wing.

Our famous uncle began his career as a fighter pilot, Ishmael thought. *She's so much like him.*

"Ishmael, I'm here," she said.

"We have incoming bogeys. Launch all your starfighters! And take them out." He hesitated. "Tina, I . . ."

He wanted to tell her more. To tell her he loved her. To say sorry for so many things he had done. But there was no time.

Tina understood. She saluted him. Staring into her eyes through MindWeb, he returned the salute. And perhaps she understood. Perhaps, without needing telepathy, she heard it all.

The space station's airlock dilated. And out flew twenty Eagle starfighters. Their full complement.

The Wolfjägers rumbled closer. The Eagles flew to meet them. And the two fleets clashed in battle.

* * * * *

Space erupted with dogfights. Ishmael watched from Ops, feeling helpless. All he could do now was watch.

We're alone out here, he thought.

Just one space station. A handful of Eagles. A few guards.

That was all. Cut off from Earth. Facing . . . whatever this was. It still spun Ishmael's mind. An evil from the past. A warship from an impossible future. What was going on? Ishmael could not even guess. This all felt like a bizarre dream.

Major Minatozaki's words echoed through his mind.

"A portal between universes, huh?" Ishmael muttered.

Minatozaki was cowering behind his workstation. He peeked over the monitor like a frightened gopher. One of his spectacle lenses had shattered. The nebbish scientist nodded.

"So it would seem, sir. They came from . . . somewhere else. Some other reality. That portal did not warp spacetime. It was not a wormhole. It warped the quantum realm of probabilities."

The dogfights continued outside. Eagle starfighters and Wolfjäger dropships fired their missiles. An Eagle exploded. The pilot's MindLink vanished off the hallucinatory map. Ishmael stared, face hard. A blue icon—gone dark. A life—lost. A soldier under his command—gone. A hole pierced his soul.

From her Eagle starfighter, Tina fired a missile. It streaked toward a Wolfjäger, and watching from Ops, Ishmael dared to hope.

But then a shield flickered to life around the German dropship. A force field—around a ship so small! Force fields required massive reactors. You needed a ship the size of a frigate to generate them. Yet there one shone—around a mere dropship! Tina's missile exploded. The Wolfjäger flew through the explosion and rumbled onward, unharmed.

Ishmael looked back at his astrophysicist. "Quantum realm of probabilities? What does that mean?"

Perhaps that was inconsequential now. But Ishmael wanted to understand. Where had these enemies come from? How did they have such technology? Without knowing his enemy, how could he fight it?

Minatozaki wiped sweat and blood off his forehead. With effort, he composed himself, gulped, and spoke. "Sir, imagine every decision you make branching off into two directions. Like a tree sprouting branches. You choose to eat lasagna for lunch? One branch grows to the left. You decide to skip lunch and hit the gym? A different branch grows to the right. Over time, with thousands of decisions, you craft a sprawling tree. A huge redwood of our lives. We all do this. All humans. With every decision, the trees of probability bloom and fractal and—"

"Get to the point, man!" Ishmael barked. "This is a battle, not a lecture hall."

Minatozaki wiped blood off his forehead. "Theoretically, it's possible to bend branches in this sprawling tree. To warp the tree. To bring two distant branches close together, then link them with a portal. Parallel universes."

"One in which I ate lasagna, the other in which I hit the gym," Ishmael said. "The skinny me and the fat me meet. Chaos ensues."

"Yes, sir. In this case, we're seeing beings from another universe."

"A universe where Nazi scum took to space," Ishmael muttered.

This all felt like a bad dream. Would he not wake up?

Another universe. Was it true? A universe in which the Nazis had somehow won the Second World War? Or perhaps resurfaced after the war and reclaimed their power? A universe in which they flew starships? Ishmael could not believe it. It all seemed so surreal. And yet there they were, right before him! Real dropships. Full of real goddamn honest-to-goodness Nazis. And they were carving through his Eagle Fleet.

Ishmael could only stare as another Eagle starfighter exploded.

And another.

Inside every starfighter—a pilot. An officer he knew. An officer he had dined with. Trained with. A friend.

The Wolfjägers kept firing. Another Eagle exploded.

Only sixteen starfighters remained. Their missiles flew, bombarding the Wolfjägers. But the German force fields withstood the assault. The bulky, armored dropships were moments away from the space station now. On the monitors, Ishmael saw the station guards at the airlocks. They stood waiting, pale, guns drawn.

Another Eagle exploded.

And then *Barbarossa*'s gears wheeled. The broadside guns of the juggernaut turned, aiming at the fleet of starfighters.

Terror flooded Ishmael.

"Tina!" he cried. "Get out of there! Scatter!"

She looked at him over MindPlay's hallucinatory interface. "Ishmael . . ."

"The *Barbarossa* is about to fire!" Ishmael cried. "Tina, get out of—"

The guns of *Barbarossa* fired.

A full broadside blasted out.

Missiles slammed into the remaining Eagles. All fifteen of them. At once. Warheads exploded, unleashing not fire, not light, but strange black smoke. Like demons of living tar, the clouds devoured the Eagles, guzzling their energy, then crushing the starfighters into charred ruins.

Ishmael had never seen anything like it. What kind of ghostly weapon was that?

Whatever it was—it worked. The starfighters floated away, frozen husks like crushed tin cans. Nobody could be alive inside those crumpled chunks of metal. And indeed, MindPlay confirmed it. On the hallucinatory map of the battle, fifteen MindLinks, implants in the brains of pilots, went dark.

Ishmael stared at the screen, frozen in shock.

They were dead. All of them.

"Tina?" Ishmael telepathized, sending the word over MindWeb.

But her once-luminous icon was grayed out. Her starfighter was gone. Tina was gone. The bastards had taken her from him. They had taken his sweet little sister. And by God above, they would pay. Ishmael clenched his fists, and his eyes burned with tears of grief and rage.

A *thud* shook through the space station. Then another thud and another. Viewports rattled. The deck shook. Ishmael swayed on his feet, holding the railing for support. He wanted to let go. To fall. To fall and fall into a dark pit and never emerge.

"Sir?" came Major Watts's gruff voice through the smoke. "Sir. The enemy dropships. They've reached the station."

Ishmael took a deep breath.

Don't fall apart now, he told himself. *Keep standing! Stay in charge. Tina is gone. But there are still a thousand people aboard this space station who depend on you. Your wife and kids still need you.*

Ishmael turned toward a floating screen. One telemetry satellite was still online, filming Toliman Space Station from a megameter away. Ishmael could see it happening. The Wolfjägers were thudding onto the station, snapping themselves into place. They were like wolves locking their jaws around a bison's flesh.

Drills emerged from the Wolfjägers. They began drilling through the airlocks.

Tina. My sister. Gone.

Then the airlocks broke open, and the horrors of hell flowed into Toliman Space Station.

* * * * *

The Nazi troops stormed into the station.

More and more kept emerging from the Wolfjäger ships,

firing their rifles, and charging into Toliman. From his post at Ops, Ishmael stared at the monitors, watching it happen. Dozens, scores, then hundreds of enemy troops barged through the airlocks.

They wore black cloaks over crimson body armor. Their helmets resembled German helmets from the Second World War, modernized for space. A steel visor was one augmentation, protecting the face from vacuum and enemy fire. The steel was forged to resemble a skull. Eyes peered from the shadowy sockets. One blue eye. One red eye, bionic, seeking prey. Every soldier here had those same mismatched eyes, one real, one artificial. Swastikas adorned the soldiers' arms, but more prominent was the sigil on their chests. Two lightning bolts were engraved into their breastplates, filled with crackling electricity. Here marched warriors of the Waffen-SS. Nazi Germany's elite unit of killers, revamped for the modern age.

Ishmael knew their history. Back in the twentieth century, those bastards had brutalized Europe, murdering millions in death camps. They were shock troops, torturers, executioners, and sadists. The SS. Few names in history evoked such terror and disgust. For a long time, they had been just that. History. Yet now they rose again from Hell's past. And hundreds of them were charging through the corridors of Toliman Space Station.

The SS raised bulky assault rifles. Each gun was engraved with a wolf sigil above the word *Lugerheulen*, perhaps the name of the manufacturer. When those guns fired, they indeed sounded like howling wolves. The sound was eerie, echoing, disturbingly organic. Blasts of black smoke flew like condensed little storm clouds.

The rounds slammed into Toliman's guards. The dark, smoky bolts ripped through limbs and torsos. Blood and bits of bone splattered the halls.

The surviving guards did not flee. They were soldiers of

the Free Alliance, strong and proud. Even as their comrades fell around them, mutilated beyond recognition, Toliman's defenders fought onward. They fired their Mordecai guns, unleashing bolts of red plasma at the enemy.

But the red fireballs scattered against the Nazi body armor. Sparks washed harmlessly off the black cloaks. The Waffen-SS kept advancing through the fire, moving deeper into the station. Once more their Lugerheulens howled. More black bolts slammed into guards. The brave soldiers fell, smoking holes in their chests.

Ishmael could only watch from here in Ops. Watch on the screens. Helpless to stop it. He wished he were there, fighting with his men! But all he could do was watch them die.

Gunfire kept blazing, lighting up the security video feeds. On the MindWeb maps, more and more lights kept dimming. More and more soldiers—fallen.

Soldiers under my command, Ishmael thought. *Soldiers who depended on me.*

He inhaled sharply, his sidearm still holstered at his side. His fingers itched to draw the weapon. He ached to run out there. To join his men. To fight and die with them if he must. With sheer force of will, he stayed where he was. His post was here.

He wasn't the only one struggling to stay put. Across Ops, a few officers drew their sidearms.

"I'm going out there," Major Watts said, taking a step away from his Tactical station.

"I'm joining you!" said Major Cross. She was pale, and her voice shook, but with a surprising show of courage, the mousy officer drew her weapon and left the Telemetry controls.

"Stay at your posts!" Ishmael said. "You are officers of Toliman Space Station Operations Center. You are officers of the Free Alliance! You will man your posts and do your duty. Major Cross, work on analyzing the enemy's force fields. I want to know their composition. I want to know how to break through them. And I want to know what the hell those smoky weapons of theirs are. You're the telemetry officer, Cross, responsible for collecting and analyzing data. So build me a report on that enemy ship and its tech."

The mousy little officer nodded. "Yes, sir."

Ishmael turned toward Comms. "Celestia!"

The cyborg turned toward him, one eye gone. Sparks still flew from a crack in her chrome skull. "Sir?"

"Work on restoring our communication with Earth," Ishmael said.

Celestia tilted her head. "But without wormhole generators—"

"I don't care how—get a wormhole open. Repurpose whatever tech we have. Build me a whole new generator if you must. You'll figure out a way." He turned toward Tactical. "Major Watts, begin to organize an evacuation of the women and children. Get them into our escape shuttles and—"

"Without the ability to generate wormholes, they'll starve to death in their shuttles," Celestia interjected. "It would take them ten thousand years to reach Earth. I told you, sir—our wormhole generators are dead."

"Celestia, dammit, then give me some ideas!" Ishmael shouted.

The crew all froze and stared at him. Mousy Major Cross started and paled.

Hold it together, Ishmael, he told himself. *Don't lose control. Don't fall apart.*

His sister was dead. So many of his men—dead. The nightmares of the war—here again.

Stop. Hold it together.

He closed his eyes. The words of an old poem resurfaced in Ishmael's memory. *If you can keep your head when all about you are losing theirs . . . yours is the Earth . . .*

He opened his eyes again. He spoke to his crew in a calmer voice. "We need wormholes. Small ones to call Earth. Big ones to fly evacuation shuttles through. Without wormholes, we're dead. Maybe we can reconfigure our warp shields to generate those wormholes. Warp shields rely on the same basic technology as wormhole generators. Maybe they can be rejiggered."

The cyborg nodded. "Aye, sir. That's a good idea. I'm on it."

Ishmael turned toward the physics department. "Major Minatozaki, help her."

The physicist nodded and pushed up his sliding spectacles. "Aye, sir. I'm on it."

Ishmael turned toward Tactical again. "Major Watts, you have your orders. Get the civilians ready for evacuation."

The lanky tactical officer saluted, then rushed out of Ops.

Ishmael took a deep breath. *Good. Stay calm. Stay in control. Command! Even as the battle rages—lead!*

He glanced back toward the floating maps of Toliman Space Station. Across the schematics, more lights were dimming. More guards were falling. More lives—snuffed out.

The defenders of Toliman kept firing their guns. But the plasma could not burn the Nazi armor. And the Waffen-SS troops kept advancing through the fire like machines. Yes, they must be machines. How could men march with such precision? How could mere mortals withstand such a barrage? Their bionic eyes pierced the smoke and shadows. Their Lugerheulens kept howling, ripping men apart.

It didn't even take them fifteen minutes. And the SS troops slew the last Alliance guards . . . and marched deeper into Toliman Station. Toward the crew quarters.

Toward the women and children.

Toward my family, Ishmael thought.

*****

From Ops, they watched it happen.

The horror. The atrocity. All right there on-screen. Live, HD terror.

Major Watts was still trying to organize an evacuation, but corpses blocked the corridors to the airlocks. Seven hundred civilians were trapped. The enemy came marching from every side. Down every corridor. Through every hatch.

No way out.

Trapped. Trapped in the jaws of the Third Reich. And the teeth were sinking in.

The wolves of war howled. Those shadowy black rounds flew, rippling the air. The astral coals ripped through civilians. They tore the leg off a woman. Blew open a boy's head. Carved out the innards of an old man.

They fell.

Three civilians. Then ten. Then dozens. All across the station maps, lights were going dark.

And they were the lucky ones. The dead were the blessed.

Ishmael watched, tears in his eyes, unable to look away from the fate of the living.

The Waffen-SS grabbed women. Girls. Some only children. Stripped them naked, had their way. They tossed babies into the air for target practice. They hung boys from hooks, drew blades, and dissected them alive. As they tortured, mutilated, and defiled, they laughed. Their laughter echoed through the bloody halls. One man lifted a heart overhead, howled, raised his visor, and took a bite. Another man kicked a severed head to his friend. A child's head. They kicked the head back and forth, singing soccer chants.

This wasn't just a mission for them. It was sick, perverted joy. This wasn't about conquest. It was sadism.

Earlier, Ishmael had wondered if they were machines. No machines could be so cruel. Machines were merely cold and efficient. Only humans carried such evil inside them.

And the Nazis were moving closer, ever closer, to the quarter where Ishmael's family lived.

"I'm going out there," Ishmael said. He cocked his handgun and left his post.

"Sir!" cried Major Mary Cross. She hugged herself and trembled. Tears filled her large feline eyes. "You told us . . . You said not to abandon our posts."

"The station has fallen," Ishmael said. "All we can do now is fight as we see best."

"Then we must fight here from Ops!" she said. "I can weld shut the doors. I can barricade the entrances. We can stay safe here until rescue comes. I—"

"I won't let them defile my wife!" Ishmael said. His voice cracked. "I won't let them torture my children. Major Cross, Ops is yours."

He took a step toward the door. On his way, he glanced up at a floating monitor. It showed the cargo bay. An escape pod was leaving, carrying refugees from the station. The shuttle flew for only a few seconds before the *Barbarossa* opened fire. The shuttle cracked open, spilling children into space.

Were my own children in there? My boy and girl?

Ishmael's throat constricted. Gripping his gun, he stepped closer toward the door.

Before he could exit Ops, the door dilated, revealing two figures.

Within a split second, Ishmael took in the long black coats. The swastikas. The skull visors.

He opened fire.

His plasma bolt slammed into the taller figure. He was a towering officer, a giant of a man. The beast must have stood seven feet tall. Ishmael scored a direct hit to his helmet. For all the damned good it did. The flames washed off the gleaming, skull-shaped visor. The metal charred but didn't so much as bend. It must be some advanced alloy. Plasma bolts would have ripped through normal steel. The huge man paused. With a beefy, gloved hand, he brushed sparks off his visor.

The second figure was smaller. Barely half the size of the towering, beefy male. She was a young female, judging by her graceful form. A visor hid her face too, shaped like a grinning skull. The other Nazis sported visors shaped like stern, glowering skulls, yet hers grinned the maniacal grin of death.

The female raised her Lugerheulen and fired.

A shadow-bolt slammed into Ishmael's hand.

Two of his fingers tumbled into the distance, wrinkled and wreathed in smoke.

Ishmael roared. His gun fell from his mangled hand, hit the deck, and discharged another blast. The bolt hit a viewport hanging above. The screen shattered, scattering glassy shards everywhere. Ishmael could no longer see the horrors across his space station. A good thing perhaps.

Both Nazis at the door—the towering male and slender female—fired their Lugerheulens. The guns howled. Ishmael winced, expecting to fall. At least he would die in battle. With honor.

But the shadowy rounds flew around him. With perfect precision, the bolts plowed through his Ops crew. Through the heart of Major Mary Cross at Telemetry. Through the head of Major Minatozaki at Astrophysics. Through the chrome skull of Celestia and into her human brain. Through the chest, throats, and faces of everyone else in the room. The commanders of this space station. They fell at their posts.

His crew.

His friends.

Gone. All of them.

Commander Ishmael Jordan stood alone, clutching his mangled hand. Shadowy particles clung to the stumps of his fingers, stanching the blood. Perhaps he was the only survivor of the station. He stood before the two figures at the door and raised his chin.

"Go ahead," Ishmael said. "I'm unarmed. Gun me down like the savages you are."

Slowly the two figures removed their helmets.

Ishmael recognized them. They had spoken to him from *Barbarossa*'s bridge. The Nazi grand admiral and his daughter.

"Good evening, Commander Ishmael Jordan." The tall, beefy admiral was speaking German, but MindLink translated it into accented English. "I am Wolfgang König, Grand Admiral of the Weltraumwaffe, the space fleet of the Third Reich. I realize this must all be confusing for you. Not to worry. Things will become quite clear to you soon."

Ishmael frowned. He stared at that broad, square-jawed face. A pale, scarred face with one bionic eye.

I've seen him before! he thought. *I know this man from somewhere. But where?*

"I've set the station to self-destruct," Ishmael said. "Get the hell out. Or die here with me if you prefer."

The burly admiral laughed, though no mirth reached his eyes, not the bionic one or the blue one. "Quite amusing, Commander Jordan. We are aware that your station is incapable of self-destructing. We are not interested in destruction, Commander. We could have bombed you to pieces from a distance. We are merciful. We are willing to continue your work. Once we've purified this station from the . . ." He grimaced, looking around at the dead. "Impurities."

The admiral's daughter stepped closer to Ishmael, holding her helmet under her arm. Her long blond hair cascaded down to her shoulders. Like every other Nazi invader, a scar ran across her cheek, taking one eye. The bionic eye narrowed, focusing on Ishmael. A crooked smile spread across the girl's lips. It was just as deranged as the smile on her skull-shaped visor.

Ishmael noticed an interesting detail. Upon his armored chest, Admiral König bore the sigil of a flying black eagle with two heads. Presumably, that was the symbol of the Weltraumwaffe, the enemy's fleet. That corps did not exist in the history books. The girl, meanwhile, sported the lightning bolts of the SS upon her chest. The Sig runes crackled with real lightning.

She's just a girl, Ishmael thought. *Probably no older than my daughter. Yet she bears the rank of colonel on her slender shoulders.*

"Look at him, Papa!" the girl breathed. "Look at his skin. The color of mahogany. The Eternal Führer told us they were subhumans, but this one is strong. Like an animal."

She reached out to caress Ishmael's cheek. He grabbed her wrist, keeping her hand away.

The girl laughed. "Yes, look, Papa! He has spirit!" She turned toward the admiral. "Can I keep him as a pet?"

The admiral's face twisted in disgust. He spat. "Don't touch that thing, Eva. These creatures are infected. Now sterilize your hands."

"But—"

"Do as I say."

The girl harrumphed, pulled her hand free, and retreated. She retrieved a bottle of hand sanitizer from a hidden compartment on her suit. As she rubbed the liquid over her hands, she kept glancing at Ishmael, her real eye full of curiosity.

"So fascinating!" she whispered.

Ishmael took a step closer to the towering admiral. From the corner of his eye, he could see Mary Cross lying on the deck, chest blasted open. In his memory, he still saw his little sister, flying out to battle, her starfighter crumpling like a tin can. Blood oozed around his boots.

No panic now, he told himself. *Remain in control. Your wife and kids might still be alive.*

He stared at the German admiral. Ishmael Jordan was a tall man, but Admiral Wolfgang König towered above him. The brute wore thick body armor, but there was no hiding the powerful physique beneath. He was the size of a rearing grizzly bear.

"I thought we wiped you Nazi scum off the face of the earth long ago," Ishmael said. "What rock did you crawl out from under?"

Admiral König laughed. "I will ask the questions here, Commander. I kept you alive for one reason. One alone. To interrogate you. You will tell me everything you know. About this universe. About the defenses of Earth. About this so-called Alliance I heard your men squeal about as they lay dying. You will reveal every bit of information to me. And maybe, at the end, I will be merciful. Maybe, if you cooperate, I will eventually let you die."

Ishmael bared his teeth. "Go ahead. Torture me if you must. You've already taken everything from me. I won't speak. I won't tell you a goddamn thing."

He spat on Admiral König's boot.

The admiral stared down at the glob of spit. Then he looked back up at Ishmael. And kicked.

The steel-tip boot drove into Ishmael's stomach. He doubled over, gasping. His arms wrapped protectively around his belly. The stumps of his fingers ripped open, leaking blood.

Ishmael groaned. Then laughed. "So we begin already, huh? Like I said, you Nazi scum, I ain't telling you a goddamn thing."

König pulled a handkerchief from a hidden compartment in his armor. He polished his boot. "Oh, but you will tell me everything, Commander. We have ways of making you speak. I did not want to do this. Unlike my beloved daughter, I do not relish torture. But you leave me no choice." He turned toward the door. "Soldiers! Bring in the commander's family."

Still doubled over, Ishmael stared at the doorway.

Soldiers of the Waffen-SS entered the room, their skull visors hiding their faces. Their armor clanked. With powerful gloved hands, they dragged them into the room.

A woman. A boy. A girl.

No, Ishmael thought. *Oh God above, no.*

* * * * *

Long, long ago, when Ishmael had been but a boy, he had visited Uncle Larry aboard the starship *Freedom.* Back then, Uncle Larry had been the XO of the ship, not yet her commander. And back then, the *Freedom* had been a mere museum ship. A floating tourist attraction. The Third World War had ended long ago, and the Alliance had emerged victorious. The Spider War against the aliens was still years away. And so, during those years of peace, the famous battleship floated in deep orbit. Instead of starfighters, her hangars contained gift shops and restaurants. Instead of missiles, her ammunition bays housed arcade games and buffets. The spacers aboard, once proud fighters, now acted as hosts for loud, noisy tourists from Earth.

Even as a boy, young Ishmael had found the garishness disturbing.

"Uncle Larry, they should restore the *Freedom* to how she was," the boy said. "A ship of war! Of battle! A ship that blows up enemies! You fought, right? In the Great War before I was born? It must have been glorious!"

His tall uncle had knelt, bringing himself to eye level with that young, naive boy. Uncle Larry put a hand on his shoulder.

"War can be glorious, Ishmael. But it's also full of horror, pain, and death. I've seen things I'll never speak of. It's far, far better that this ship remains a museum than fly to war again."

The boy considered. "But I want to fight in a war someday too. To be like you."

"You don't want to be like me," Larry Jordan said, then seemed to gaze into the distance, and ghosts flitted across his eyes. Then he snapped back to reality and patted Ishmael on the shoulder. "Come now! I'll take you to see the observatory. There'll be fireworks off the port bow tonight."

Later in life, Ishmael had often thought about that day aboard the starship. About that lesson. And he had learned that lesson well. When the spiders invaded, he got his war. He saw his share of terror. Those nightmares still haunted him.

But never, not in all that time, had anything terrified Ishmael like this.

The Nazis had his family.

Ishmael trembled, fists clenched.

They had his family. His wife! His boy! His little girl! They held them in their filthy hands.

Admiral Wolfgang König inhaled deeply, nostrils flaring. "Ah, the smell of fear! I savor it." He took another whiff, his eyes closing. "Marvelous fear. The purest emotion in the universe."

"Let them go, you son of a bitch!" Ishmael howled.

Eva burst out laughing. "Hear how he yells, Papa! What a glorious beast."

Wolfgang nodded to Ishmael. "We will let your family go, Commander. Don't worry. We will send them peacefully into the afterlife." He took a step closer, and his eyes narrowed. "*If* you tell us everything about Earth's defenses. How many warships does Earth have?"

"Don't tell him anything!" Hannah cried.

Ishmael looked at his wife. She gazed back, eyes wide and teary. An officer slammed a gloved hand over her mouth, muffling her cries. Other Nazi brutes tightened their grips on Ishmael's children.

Wolfgang sighed. "Commander Ishmael, must we drag this out? You may cooperate now. And we'll spare everyone so much pain. Yes. My sweet daughter, innocent though she looks, can cause *so much* pain."

Eva grinned. She tapped buttons on her armored suit. Hidden compartments opened. Rods extended, displaying knives, needles, pliers, a small blowtorch, and vials of acid.

"The tools of the trade," the girl said. She drew a curved knife and twirled it around her finger. "I think I shall begin with some simple slicing. Good old lingchi to get the juices flowing."

Ishmael opened his mouth to speak. He hesitated. His throat locked up. Eva froze, knife raised.

"Yes, Commander?" Wolfgang said. "You were going to say something? To tell me, perhaps, how many ships serve in Earth's fleet?"

He could check the station records, Ishmael thought. *He doesn't need me to speak. He's enjoying this. The son of a bitch is enjoying this!*

Ishmael spat again.

Wolfgang wiped the spit off his chin.

"Very well, Commander. You've made your choice." He nodded to Eva. "You may begin."

Eva licked the blade. Her eyes glinted. "With pleasure. I think I'll start with the woman. Then move to the children."

And Ishmael broke that day.

He had not broken when battling the spiders in space. Not broken when the jaws ripped off his leg. Not broken as his starship fell apart around him. But today he broke.

Today he wept.

He tried to stop Eva. To save his family. But the guards grabbed his arms, held him back. He tried to close his eyes. Not to see it. But Wolfgang grabbed his eyelids, pulled them open, and forced him to see.

To see the blades slice. To see the tools of the trade work.

"Please!" Ishmael begged. "I'll tell you. I'll tell you everything! If only you let them go."

Wolfgang laughed. "Let them go, Commander? No. That was never an option. But I *will* kill them. I will show them that mercy. Now how many ships are there?"

And Ishmael told the man everything.

About the Alliance Fleet. Its numbers. Its structure. Its commanders. Everything.

"Now let them die," Ishmael whispered. "Please. Kill them. Please make the screaming stop."

König nodded and patted him on the shoulder. "There there, Commander. You did a good job like a good boy. And so you will get your reward." He looked over his shoulder. "Eva? End their suffering."

The girl paused from her work. She pulled back her bloody tools and pouted. "But I was just getting into it!"

"Eva!" Wolfgang glowered. "We are not bloodthirsty savages. We keep our word. Exterminate them." He stared at Ishmael's family and grimaced. "Whatever . . . is left of them, at least."

Eva sighed. "Fine! But you never let me play for long enough."

She approached Hannah. And Ishmael remembered his wedding day. Remembered her smile. Remembered the light in her eyes. Back when she still had eyes.

Eva slashed her blade. Hannah fell. And it was a mercy.

The admiral's daughter licked her blade, smacked her lips, and approached the children.

Ishmael remembered holding the babies in his arms. Teaching them to walk and talk. Cradling them in his arms.

The blade slashed twice. And it was a mercy.

Ishmael fell to his knees and raised his head, exposing his neck.

I'll be with you soon, my family, he thought as tears ran down his cheeks. *We'll be together, and nothing will hurt.*

He kept waiting, but the blade of mercy did not slice. Ishmael blinked.

"Well?" he said. "Do it! Kill me!"

The admiral and his daughter merely stared at him. Eva snickered.

Ishmael growled, wrenched himself free from the guards who held him, and charged at the pair.

"Then I'll die in battle!" he roared.

Wolfgang raised his arm and balled his fist. A bracelet-gun fired. A pulse of energy slammed into Ishmael, shoving him back. He hit the deck, trembling with electricity.

"No, Commander," Wolfgang said. "You will not. Only warriors get to die in battle. Not filthy animals. You do not deserve the mercy of death."

He turned and left the Ops deck.

Eva blew Ishmael a kiss, winked, and then swaggered out of the room.

Their faceless Nazi troops marched out after them, leaving Ishmael on his knees. He knelt among the corpses. Of his officers. Of his family. The hatch slammed shut, sealing him in this tomb. A man buried alive among the dead.

A few viewports still hung from the beams, buzzing and displaying video streams. The Wolfjägers detached from the station. Navigating through the debris of battle, the dropships flew back toward their mothership.

Ishmael pulled up a MindWeb map, showing the life

signals of everybody aboard the station.

Of a thousand souls, only one light still shone. His own.

As the great *Barbarossa* turned away, Ishmael Jordan tossed back his head and howled.

Part I
The Storm Unleashed

CHAPTER ONE
Home on the Range

Nebraska
Alliance Territory
Earth
September 2, 2207

James King was an old man with stiff joints, a creaky spine, and a bad temper. But this late-summer morning he was at peace. He was doing what he loved best—restoring an antique starfighter.

Not just any old starfighter either. *His* old starfighter. The legend. The Golden Eagle herself. Beams of light shone through holes in the thatched roof, illuminating the ravaged machine. She stood in the center of the barn—dented, scratched, and charred. Half her hull was missing, and the cockpit's canopy had shattered long ago. Most of her components lay scattered across the straw floor. No, she was not much to look at, his dear old Goldie. Not in this state. But by God, she had been beautiful once. And King would bring her back to glory.

Johnny Cash songs played in the background from a beat-up record player. Another antique. A few cows shared the barn with King and his starship, munching on hay, tails flicking. Sometimes King swore the cows actually listened to the music, that their tails flicked to Cash's chugging locomotive beat.

"I hope you enjoy your breakfast," King rasped at his cattle. His voice always sounded like gravel. Ever since the injury, at least. "I spent all of yesterday gathering hay instead of working on my girl."

The cows kept chewing, ignoring him. Ungrateful girls.

Ha! The famous war hero—making hay! Talking to his cows! He snorted. Yes, old James King had become something of a cowboy in recent years. The gray-haired, gruff admiral had shed his uniform. Instead, he wore jeans, flannel, and a cowboy hat. He spent his days farming, tinkering, and whittling. Building things. Enjoying his retirement.

But a part of him still yearned for the stars. A part of him missed the freedom of flight. He ran a wrinkled, callused hand across the Golden Eagle's hull.

"We had some glorious times together, didn't we, girl?" He patted her like a loyal hound. "I'll get you back up there. Don't you worry." His voice dropped to a whisper. "I'll get both of us back."

He reached for a box of nails, then grimaced. His spine *creaked.* His sciatica flared across his leg and hips.

"This used to be easier in the old days," he muttered, finally grabbing the nails.

He grunted, rubbed his lower back, and reached for his electric hammer. His spine let out another creak of protest. As a young man, he would be crawling under, climbing over, and running rings around the hull. The job would be done by now. But at sixty-eight years young, James King was a little slower. He couldn't lean quite as low. Or climb quite as high. Sometimes just a simple task—say, kneeling to lift a fallen tool—was a challenge. But with enough aspirin and a good dose of Ben-Gay, he would get the job done, consarn it.

It's not only my age, he thought, knuckling the small of his back.

It was also the war wounds. The wound across his neck, a memento from the infamous Katyusha of the Red Dawn, still hurt all these years later. The injury to his back, the gift of a rah torturer, had never healed properly either. Worse were the scars inside. Pills could dull the pain in his body. The pain in his mind was a trickier beast to tame.

Well, King had learned that brooding made things worse. He returned to his work. Something was wrong with the starfighter's landing skids. He adjusted a few joints and clasps, then began banging in nails.

A voice sounded from the barn door, as soft and warm as the beams of sunlight between the rafters.

"You just can't let go of your true love, can you?"

King looked up to see Kim Fletcher-King. His lovely wife.

Now there's a sight for sore eyes, he thought. Whenever he saw her, his aches faded, and warmth filled his scarred old heart.

Kim was a bit younger than him. Okay—a lot younger. At fifty years of age, she was a radiant woman, a beam of sunrise taken human form. Like him, she wore jeans and a flannel shirt, but no hat hid her long golden hair. She cradled a cup of coffee in her hands.

"I thought *you* were my true love," King rasped.

She walked closer to him, straw crunching beneath her boots. "Oh, I know I'll always be second place. Space is your first and true love." She kissed his cheek, then winced. "Like sandpaper. I miss when you used to shave every morning."

"The little joys of civilian life," King said.

Kim stroked his stubble, then frowned and stared at the Golden Eagle. Her eyes widened.

"Are you using nails? On a *starfighter*?" Kim guffawed. "What are you building—a cabinet?"

King grumbled under his breath. "This is what I get for marrying an engineer. Constant criticism whenever I build anything."

Kim rolled her eyes. "Oh please, this isn't about me being an engineer. You don't need a doctorate in engineering to know that, well, you don't cobble spaceships together with nails!"

"Hey, nails get the job done!"

Kim blinked. "Jim! This is a precise machine, each part calibrated to the exact micromillimeter, designed to slide together like the scales of a baby snake, then be secured with microscopic quantum-clamps." She knelt under the hull. "See, if you had just assembled the . . ." She frowned. "Hey, you're right. These pieces don't quite snap together."

King snorted. "That's the difference between engineers and grumpy old captains. You design machines to be perfect. We troubleshoot all the problems later."

Kim pulled off his cowboy hat, mussed his hair, and hugged him. "Good morning, Jim. Fresh coffee is brewing. Come share a cup with me on the porch. You've been here since before dawn. You deserve a break."

King wanted to argue, to insist he was good to work until lunch. In truth, this wasn't work. This was relaxation. But hell, a coffee break with his beautiful wife sounded even better. He held out his arm, and she took it. Arm in arm, they walked out the barn.

The glory of Nebraska spread around them. Grasslands sprawled toward low hills topped with pines. Golden wheat rustled in the fields, and the horses nickered in the corral. Not a cloud marred the blue sky. For decades, King had flown above that sky. It seemed far fairer from below. He inhaled deeply. Even after three years of retirement on Earth, he still never ceased to marvel at fresh air. What a luxury!

He walked with Kim toward the wooden cabin. Their home. He had built the house last year with his own two hands. Well, one real hand. One prosthetic shaped like a medieval gauntlet, the gift of the Spider War. Like many veterans, King had not come home in one piece. He was cobbled together, a broken man held together with nails and crude welding. Maybe that was the true reason he kept working on his starship. Why he was so determined to get her back in shape. Because he wasn't just trying to fix the Golden Eagle. But to fix himself.

"Maybe I need to know that broken old things can still fly," he said softly.

He stepped onto the patio with his wife. She poured two mugs of coffee, and they sat on their rocking chairs, gazing out upon the glory of God's country. This was good. This was peace. He had a home, a beautiful wife, and a good cup of joe.

So why the hell did he feel so restless? Why had he felt restless these past three years? Was it because he had been an admiral, a war hero, and they put him out to pasture? No. He had chosen this retirement. He had enough of wars for two lifetimes. This was good. This was peace. This was . . .

Another man's retirement, he realized.

Yes, that was it. He could dress up as a cowboy. He could play at being a farmer. But at the end of the day, he was a soldier. Always would be. As a fighter pilot, his call sign had been Bulldog. And a bulldog needed some good bones to gnaw on. Or his teeth dulled.

"Oh!" Kim said. "By the way. I invited my brother over for dinner. You don't mind, do you?"

King raised his eyebrows. "Ben has time for dinner? I thought he was so busy commanding his new starship they just feed him through a tube."

Kim laughed. "Feels like that. I haven't seen Ben in weeks. If you're not feeling social . . ."

"I like Ben," King said. "It'll give me a chance to beat him a few more times at gin."

The clip-clop of hooves interrupted the quiet morning. King raised his head, staring toward the sound.

A lone rider was approaching the cabin, making his way up the winding dirt road. His black cowboy hat shadowed his face, and dust stained his long brown cloak. When he reached the patio, the tall, dark rider tugged the reins. His horse reared and kicked the air, and the rider let out a whoop.

"Stop showing off!" King growled. "You're an old man. You're gonna fall off your horse and break your hip."

The rider dismounted. Not as fast as he used to. He removed his hat, revealing close-cropped white hair, dark skin, and gleaming eyes. His teeth glinted as he grinned.

"Old man? I'm only sixty-six. Younger than you, Grampa." He barked a laugh.

Larry Jordan had a deep, velvety voice. While King spoke with a rasp, the lingering curse of his neck injury, Jordan had a voice to woo angels. Back in the fleet, his call sign had been Phantom. Partly because he could fly a starfighter like a ghost. And partly because, every Christmas, he would croon songs from his favorite musical, *The Phantom of the Opera.* ("Is it because you're so ugly you should be wearing a mask?" King had once asked his friend. They had been bantering since then—almost half a century now.)

"I had to suffer you for fifty years in space," King muttered. "I finally got rid of you, and you had to retire at the cabin next hill over."

Jordan shaded his eyes, scanning the hills. "You mean that cabin way yonder? The one larger than yours? That's actually built properly?"

King snorted. "It'll collapse this winter. Ain't got more than three years in her, that one."

"It'll outlive us both, old man," Larry said softly, and this time his voice wasn't bantering. It was sad.

King waved dismissively. "We're gonna live forever. We were both commanders of the starship *Freedom.* We're a special breed, us. Invincible."

Both old men raised their eyes to the sky as if seeking her.

But the starship *Freedom* was gone now. She had flown into the heart of a distant star, and in her dying fury, she had taken out an alien empire. King missed her. They all did.

"She sure was a grand old lady," Jordan said.

King nodded. "The best there ever was."

Kim gazed up at the sky with them. She squinted. "What are we looking at here, boys?"

"Memories," King said.

For a long time, the three of them had served up there. Fought up there. James King—first a starfighter pilot, then starship commander, and finally admiral, leading the fleet from *Freedom*'s bridge. Larry Jordan—commander after him, the final leader of the great dreadnought. And Kim Fletcher—ship's engineer and professional miracle worker.

"You know what?" Kim said. "I don't miss it."

King raised an eyebrow. "I thought you loved the *Freedom*, Kim."

"I did. With all my heart." She slung her arms around him. "But the *Freedom* is gone. She's in the past. And once all you can do is look at the past, you forget to live for the future. And we still have a bright future."

Yours longer than mine, King thought, more aware than ever of their age difference. Of his own aging, weakening body. He had thought himself old when turning sixty. Now, at sixty-eight, each birthday cut him like a blade. How much future did he have left? Oh, he might linger on for another twenty years. But how many *good* years remained? Years of vigor before senescence beat him down? Years when he could still work, fix things, build things, ride his horse. Years of real life. Not many. Not nearly enough. He had lived a full life, but now, approaching the end, the ride seemed so short. So unfairly short.

Maybe he should take that new drug everyone was talking about. What was it called again? Rejuvamin? Rejuvenex?

Something like that. They said it made you ten years younger. King shook his head, banishing the thought. It also killed one in every ten people who took the damn thing. Not worth it. Not at all. He still had a few good years left, dammit. And he'd make the most of them. Down here on Earth. Under the sky. With the people he loved.

"What say we go for a ride?" King said. "The three of us. I want to see the crater."

Jordan raised an eyebrow. "The crater, Jim? A bit morbid, don't you think?"

"You know I go every year. I want to see it." He walked toward the corral. "I'm riding over there. You two coming?"

Jordan heaved a theatrical sigh. "I suppose so. Without Kim and me to watch over you, you'd probably fall into the crater. And break your hip." The old phantom climbed back into the saddle, tugged the reins, and his horse reared and kicked the air.

"Show-off," King muttered, walking through the corral.

After retiring and building his cabin, he had bought a couple of horses. King had grown up on a Nebraska farm, and he had spent his youth horseback riding. Then he spent half a century in space. Flying starfighters. Flying frigates. Commanding dreadnoughts. And finally commanding fleets. But in his heart, he still felt like a farm boy. It still felt right to ride.

King approached his horse, an aging stallion named Buck. His brown coat was going gray at spots. For years, Buck had worked as a stud. He was too old now for that sort of work. And so King had bought him, deciding to give the old stud the retirement he deserved.

"Ready for a ride, Buck?" King patted the horse and spoke softly into his ear. "Yeah, I know, old boy. You're not as fast as you used to be. You're tired and creaky. We got that in common. Let's go show the world what we still got. They put us out to pasture. But there's still some fire in our bellies."

He climbed into the saddle and lowered his hat's rim, shadowing his eyes. His trusty sidearm, a pistol that fired good old-fashioned bullets, hung from his hip.

"You almost look like a real cowboy!" Jordan called from the dirt road. "The costume is very convincing."

King snorted. "Says the boy from LA dressed like the Lone Ranger."

"Oh, it's been a long time since I've been a boy, old man," Jordan said. "Of course, not as long ago as your childhood. When was that? Back in the steam era?"

"I wish," King muttered. "I was born in the wrong time."

Yes. A time of starships clashing. A time of war among the stars. Of alien terrors. Of death in the darkness. Things had been simpler back in the old days. Rugged men like him could have made a name for themselves. Could have thrived. Oh, he had achieved great heights for a man of his generation. Not many men made admiral. But he would have given it all away for a simpler life. A lifetime of memories from a farm, not the bridge of a starship at war.

Well, that was in the past. Perhaps Kim was right. He couldn't wallow in memory and regret. He still had the here and now.

Kim mounted her own horse, a golden mare. The engineer had become an excellent rider these past three years. After losing the *Freedom*, Colonel Kim Fletcher had retired from the military alongside the boys, though she still worked as a civilian engineer. While King puttered around the farm and tinkered with his starfighter, Kim spent most of her days in space, working for NovaTech Industries. The same corporation that had invented the Talaria Drive, ushering in a new era of space travel. Today NovaTech was working on scientific research past the orbit of the moon. Something to do with parallel universes. Most days, Kim was there working alongside the physicists, building machines for their experiments. King always joked that someday his wife would open the portal to hell.

Well, right now they were both in heaven. Kim had the day off. She was back on Earth, and they were riding. These were good times. His favorite times.

These are the best days of my life, King thought.

But were they? Were they really? Yes, he had his best friend, his wife, his horses, his ranch. But part of him . . . Well, part of him missed the life of a soldier. The glory of battle. The camaraderie one could only feel under fire. Oh, war was hell, King knew that. He had fought two big ones, and those had been the worst days of his life. Yet in some ways—the best days too.

The three horses trotted down the dirt road, leaving the cabin behind. The sound of beating hooves, the rustling fields, the whispering wind, the creaking of the saddle—they wove a song of soothing meditation. King took another deep breath. This was life. This was freedom.

They rode across the wilderness of Nebraska. The farms, forests, and rolling hills filled King with pride. For his state. For his country. For his planet.

We came so close to losing you, Earth, he thought. *But you're safe now. You're healing. And you're beautiful.*

But even here in God's country, they could see the scars of war. King had defeated the rahs three years ago. The land had not fully healed. Burnt trees still littered the landscape. Soil and rocks still filled riverbeds where the water had boiled away. Farmlands lay fallow, and even now, you could still come across some skeletons among the wildflowers. But the flowers were growing again, and saplings sprouted where once mighty conifers had soared. New life rose from the ashes of tragedy. As it always did.

* * * * *

The *Barbarossa*
Alpha Centauri
4.46 light-years from Earth
September 2, 2207

The *Barbarossa*, flagship of the Weltraumwaffe, was the largest starship ever built by man. In this universe or the one it had emerged from.

The bridge sprawled, a command center the size of a cathedral nave. Banners hung from the mezzanines, displaying swastikas. Officers stood at command posts, while armored troops stood in neat rows, skull helmets hiding their faces. A military band waited on a mezzanine, ready to play songs of war.

A portrait of Hitler loomed above, overlooking the bridge. The Eternal Führer had died centuries ago, of course, though he still ruled the Third Reich from beyond the grave. All subsequent führers (including Wolfgang's father, the current chancellor) were mere stewards of Hitler's legacy.

Wolfgang took a deep, satisfied breath. Standing on the bridge, he admired a floating schematic of his ship. The *Barbarossa* stretched over three kilometers from stern to stem. Wagner-class nuclear engines blazed deep within the ship's core like miniature stars. Thirty thousand troops served aboard—officers, spacers, and shock troops of the Waffen-SS. Hundreds of cannons lined the hull, ready to fire torpedoes, lasers, and umbrionic demolition. Plates of armor coated the *Barbarossa*, and a shimmering force field surrounded him. Yes, *Barbarossa* was a him, not a her. Starships were normally female. Yet *Barbarossa* was so mighty they referred to the ship as *him*. How could such a warrior be female?

They built you for this mission, Wolfgang thought. *The terror of the stars. And you are glorious.*

Wolfgang took another deep, satisfied breath. The

Barbarossa. After a decade in the shipyard, the juggernaut was flying. The ship had crossed the great void between universes, fought his first skirmish, and was ready to conquer. It was the honor of Admiral Wolfgang König's life to command this glorious flagship.

Of course, great things were expected of him. He was the son of the führer. He was not descended from the Eternal Führer, of course. Adolf Hitler, founder of the Third Reich, had left no heir. With blood, butchery, and brutality, the König family had claimed what the Eternal Führer had built. In that glorious year of 1982, they had won the War of Succession, crushing the other claimants to the Third Reich. For generations since, the König dynasty had expanded Hitler's empire. From Europe and America to all continents of Earth. From Earth to the moon and planets. From the solar system to the stars. And now to here. To this parallel universe. To this nightmare where the Third Reich was no more, where Deutschland was but a shell of itself, and where subhumans swarmed across the galaxy like rats.

"We will purify this universe," König vowed. "We will exterminate the *untermenschen*, the communists, and all the rest of them. Here too will our glory reign."

Standing beside him, Eva yawned and covered her mouth. The girl stretched. "I still wish you let me keep that black captain as a slave."

König snorted. "Leave him in his tomb among his dead."

Father and daughter turned toward Toliman Space Station. The station loomed on the viewport, tilted and cracked, shedding debris with each spin around its axis. Half the decks had been blasted open. The station reminded König of some decrepit ballerina, pirouetting lazily as she cracked and crumbled, shedding dust and chunks of chalky flesh. But in Ops, while all others lay dead, the swarthy captain still lived. The last survivor of a thousand souls.

Eva raised her eyebrow. "If he escapes and seeks revenge . . ."

Wolfgang burst out laughing. "Are you afraid of an animal? You are an Aryan woman! The granddaughter of a führer! Act like it."

She growled, bared her teeth, and tapped buttons on her armor. Hatches slid open. Her blades, pincers, and pliers emerged on little hooks. "I tortured them, Papa. I tortured them well. Do not call me a coward."

He snorted. "Torturing women and children. Ha! Such courage! You've never faced enemies in battle, Eva."

She bristled. "I fought aliens!"

"But not men, and men are the most brutal killers in this galaxy. Until you face a true enemy on the field, your mettle cannot be known. Soon you'll face men in war, Eva. Yes. I've trained you all your life. Soon we will see your heart."

She raised her chin. "I've seen many hearts. And eaten them. They're all the same. Just meat."

Wolfgang shook his head. "No. Not the hearts of soldiers. You carved out the hearts of cripples, traitors, and weaklings. You will see, Eva. Glorious battle looms." He turned his head. "Ah! And here come our friends."

He gazed at the multiverse portal, which hovered in space fifty-odd megameters away. Another ship was emerging, her cannons pointing the way. The prow was painted crimson, sporting a mural of a two-headed black eagle. Here flew the *Nachtkaiserin*, the Empress of the Night, the dreadnought that had subjugated the Orion rebellion. Then came another ship, a starfighter carrier, her bays heavy with mechanical predators. She was the *Siegessterne*, the ship that had savaged the rahs and shattered their hives. They kept coming. One ship after another, each glorious, each the victor of many battles.

Wolfgang König had fought in most of those battles

himself. He had crushed alien worlds. Had wiped out entire species of squirming, sniveling alien life. He had even crushed the arachnid rahs (aliens that had fought Earth in this universe too, it seemed).

But Wolfgang König had never fought other men. Oh, he had dueled them with blades, of course. In the Third Reich, you could only earn your commission by fencing other men. Not until you both took and lost an eye could you join the ranks. But those duels were just for sport. An eye for an eye, that was all. This would be *true* war. War against other human empires. Like the Great War that Hitler had won.

Except in this universe, he had not!

It was still hard to believe. Wolfgang gazed through the portal. Between the emerging ships, he could see the stars shine back in his universe. A universe of glory. A universe in which Nazi Germany had developed the atom bomb first, wiped out the Soviet Union, crushed America and Britain, and took to space. But something happened back then. Something went wrong in 1944. A secret experiment, carried out deep in the labs below Berlin, cracked the universe in two. To this day, nobody knew what the experiment had been. Only that it had split reality itself.

And now Wolfgang flew in that parallel universe. A perverse universe. A universe in which Hitler had lost the war. In which the Third Reich had lasted a measly twelve years. A universe in which *untermenschen*—subhuman creatures, inferior to Aryans—had spread like a disease. It sickened him.

How did the portal work? Wolfgang wasn't sure. His stepmother, the dreaded Anneliese Heisenberg-König, had tried to explain it to him. It was her invention. At first, she had spoken a language of mathematics and advanced physics. It might as well have been Chinese. (Once the most widely spoken language in the world, Chinese was now a relic for linguists to waste time on. Wolfgang had read multiple books on Hitler's Chinese

Purification Campaign of the 1970s.)

"Explain it so I can understand it," Wolfgang had told his stepmother, interrupting her stream of numbers and nonsense.

"As to a child? Very well." Anneliese had laughed, eyes shining with mockery. "Universes are like branches in trees, splitting off in different directions. My machine will pull two branches together, letting you hop from one branch to another." She stroked his cheek. "Better, stepson dearest?"

That was technical enough for Admiral Wolfgang König (or the Night Wolf, as they called him). He would leave the science to Anneliese. He was a soldier, plain and simple. He had conquered alien worlds. Now he would conquer his greatest prize—Earth itself!

As he stood on *Barbarossa*'s bridge, lost in thoughts, Wolfgang kept watching the ships emerge from the portal. Soon enough, three hundred German warships floated at Alpha Centauri.

"Won't the subhumans notice?" Eva asked. "If they're watching from Earth."

Wolfgang noticed a chunk of dried blood on his uniform. He winced and flicked it off. "Don't be daft, Eva. Earth is over four light-years away. They won't see this for another four-and-a-half years."

Eva glared at him, fists clenched at her sides. "But if the space station managed to open a wormhole, to warn them—"

"We destroyed their wormhole generators with the first volley," Wolfgang said. "But you're right, Eva. Maybe we were slow. Maybe Earth got early warning. Can you imagine their reaction?" He barked a laugh. "To see the glorious *Barbarossa* emerge from nothingness, a shadow of their past?"

Eva shrugged. "They probably forgot all about us. In this universe, the Third Reich has been gone for centuries. When's the last time you thought of the Austro-Hungarian Empire? The Qing dynasty? The Golden Caliphate?"

"I think of them most days," Wolfgang said.

"Well, most people aren't like you, Papa. Not in this universe." Eva laughed. "Here they're weak. Decadent. They forgot their history. Forgot *us*."

"We'll remind them of our superiority," Wolfgang said. "It's time."

At first, Wolfgang had expected his stepmother to open the multiverse portal on Earth, allowing the ground forces to storm through. Or at least in space right above the planet. But, Anneliese had explained, that was impossible. Connecting two universes on Earth—the very planet where they had split—risked the two realities bleeding together.

"Our universe is a juicy steak, while theirs is spoiled meat," Anneliese had explained. "We can't risk cross-contamination."

They must open the portal several light-years away. And so Anneliese had chosen Alpha Centauri for the portal. Fine with Wolfgang. He was grand admiral of the fleet. Attacking planets from a distance was what he did best.

Who could have expected to find a space station here at Alpha Centauri? Let alone one manned by subhumans? Well, it had been a delightful surprise. The place had given Wolfgang and his crew a chance to whet their appetite. The main course still awaited.

Briefly Wolfgang debated waiting another few hours. Should he let more ships emerge before attacking Earth? Tens of thousands of warships flew in the Weltraumwaffe, the grand space force of the Fatherworld. They would quickly overwhelm this pathetic parallel Earth. What was it Commander Ishmael had said? According to the subhuman, two powerful unions ruled Earth now. America, Britain, India, and other democratic nations formed the Alliance. Russia, China, Brazil, North Korea (yes, there were two Koreas in this universe), and other "equalist" nations (they sounded a lot like communists to Wolfgang) formed the Red Dawn. A third pact, the Desert Thorns, yielded significant power too. In this universe, Earth was fractured into groups. Between them, they commanded only six thousand starships. Ha! That was it? In full force, the Weltraumwaffe would bulldoze over them. Like wolves in a chicken coop.

But that meant waiting. The portal was a bottleneck. It took time to move ten thousand starships through one by one. And Wolfgang was loath to give up the element of surprise. Yes, perhaps Eva was right. Perhaps Toliman Space Station had managed to warn Earth before *Barbarossa* destroyed their wormhole generators. What would Earth make of it? Wolfgang imagined them receiving the message—an image of a glorious dreadnought proudly bearing the swastika. Wolfgang chuckled. Imagine them trying to make sense of that!

Eva is wrong about one thing, he thought. *Even in this universe, they will not have forgotten the Eternal Führer.*

It would take the subhumans some time, Wolfgang imagined, to make sense of the warning from Alpha Centauri. To get over the shock of seeing a shadow from the past. To get their act together. At first confusion would reign. But soon the subhumans would recognize *Barbarossa* as a threat. After all, subhumans were prey animals, and they would quickly recognize the threat of a dominant predator. When the penny dropped, they would begin to prepare a defense of Earth.

And so Wolfgang made up his mind. He would charge to Earth now with his vanguard and begin the blitzkrieg. While the subhumans still ran around like headless chickens, he would rain death upon them. Then, when the rest of the Weltraumwaffe emerged and took position, they could join Wolfgang for a second wave of assaults.

With mere thoughts, he accessed the computer system

within his bionic eye. When Germans were young, they had both eyes. But once they turned ten, they began to fight with real blades. A proper Aryan fought a duel every week. Most fought every day. Only once you lost an eye in battle could you get your *adlerauge*—a bionic eye, proof of courage.

The adlerauge. The Eye of the Reich, as they sometimes called it. The bionic eye let you control systems, communicate telepathically, and gaze into the hearts of men.

("During the Great Struggle for Freedom," they would say, "we used Enigma machines. Now we have Eyenigmas!" The joke was supposedly funny in English. Wolfgang didn't speak it and didn't get it. If you asked him, anyone on the Fatherworld who still spoke English was a traitor who should be summarily executed. Once he inherited the throne, he would crack down on those rogue languages. Far too many Aryans still spoke them in secret. If Chinese went extinct, why not English?)

Using his adlerauge, Wolfgang contacted the captains of his vanguard. By sending the right electric signals down his optic nerve, the bionic eye produced an artificial image in Wolfgang's brain. He hallucinated the captains of his vanguard—three hundred officers—standing before him.

Eva would not see them. Nor the other crew members. Adlerauges could share hallucinations across a team, but Wolfgang kept this one on private mode. To everyone else, the bridge would seem normal. They would see *Barbarossa*'s usual bridge officers, guards, and military band. But Wolfgang saw the bridge packed with starship captains. In the flesh, they were aboard the bridges of their own ships. In his mind, they stood before him as loyal soldiers.

Wolfgang raised his hand in salute. "Hail Hitler, the Eternal Führer!"

"Hail Hitler!" they cried.

Many believed that the Eternal Führer still lived. In some

state, at least. That his spirit still reigned over the Third Reich and kept watch over his underlings. Wolfgang paid lip service to the notion. It had become something like a religion, one even an admiral dared not criticize.

"It keeps the people united," Father had told him once.

"They should be hailing our name—the name König!" the younger Wolfgang had said.

"Beware vanity," the chancellor cautioned. "The people worship ideas, not men. And when he became a spirit, the Eternal Führer became an idea."

"The people will worship me when I lead!" the younger Wolfgang vowed.

Yes, he had been an idealist back then. Too proud, too cocky. But he had learned wisdom. Learned to wield legend and myth as weapons of control. Wolfgang was in his forties now, more sensible, less hotheaded. Now it was Eva who was young and impetuous. He must temper his daughter. Teach her wisdom. Like Father had taught him.

Ideas control men like reins control horses, he thought, watching the captains salute their "Eternal Führer." He held these reins tightly. Yet a part of Wolfgang König still rankled. Were they following *him* to battle? Or the ghost in the portrait that hung above him? Always that ghost hovered over his shoulder.

Father won't live forever, Wolfgang thought. *When I'm führer, I will not control men with reins. I will use a whip.*

"Prepare your warp engines," Wolfgang told his captains. "We fly to Earth at top speed. In our ships, we have the firepower to destroy the planet. But we will not. That is *our* world. Our Fatherworld. A world that has been perverted and defiled—and can still be saved. We will purify Earth of the subhumans, and the glory of the Aryan race will shine across the multiverse!"

"Hail Hitler!" they cried.

Ah yes, Hitler again. Yes, Wolfgang must endure that

ghost for a while longer. He was in this for the long game. When he was done, they would be hailing the name of König, Führer of Two Worlds!

Three hundred ships fired up their *Überlichtantrieb* engines (another invention from the cunning mind of *Stiefmutter* Anneliese). Warp nacelles shone red, bending spacetime around the ships, forming warp bubbles. The technology was still new. Only seventeen years old. It was hard to believe sometimes how new warp engines were. When Eva had been born, humans could not travel to the stars. Now ten thousand ships of the Weltraumwaffe could travel faster than light.

Such quick adoption of technology was far from unprecedented. Wolfgang knew his history. In 1903, the Wright brothers invented the first airplane. Just a few years later, the Red Baron flew alongside thousands of other brave German pilots in glorious war. In times of war, technology moved fast. War was the great enabler. War was the mother of invention. War was the father of glory. And the Third Reich was always at war. It was the guiding principle of their society—constant aggression, constant conquest. With this will and might, they had conquered the world. Then conquered alien worlds. At times of no external enemy, they fought each other, staging great battles between their fortresses. Peace was for the fat, the weak, the decadent. For the glorious—only war!

"Charge!" König cried.

"Charge!" Eva shouted, fist raised.

The bridge orchestra burst into a vigorous rendition of *Flight of the Valkyries*. Back in Hitler's Struggle for Freedom, the great war that conquered the world, Wagner's heavenly notes would accompany the troops to battle. Thus it remained today, centuries later. Another ghost that forever flew above their battles.

"Onward to glory!" Wolfgang cried, and the warp engines

roared.

The ships blasted forth, leaving behind streaks of red light like rivers of blood. Three hundred ships, the vanguard of the Weltraumwaffe, raced across the darkness. Alpha Centauri shrank behind them. The system's three stars morphed into one light. The light flared but then dimmed, becoming smaller and smaller. Ahead another light brightened. The light of Sol. The sun. And there beside her—a blue planet that meant so much. The Fatherworld. Earth. Wolfgang reached out and clenched his fist as if grabbing the little blue world.

CHAPTER TWO
Does Their Glory Exceed That of Ours?

Nebraska
Alliance Territory
Earth
September 2, 2207

Three horses traveled across the wilderness. Three riders held the reins, gazing from under the rims of their cowboy hats. They had been riding all morning (taking only brief breaks to let the horses graze). Finally they reached their destination.

The crater.

It spread before them, as large as a city. Ground zero. The place where the alien beams had slammed into the world. The place where Omaha had once stood.

The three riders paused on the edge of the crater. They gazed down into the pit.

"Four years," King said. "Four years since that terrible day."

He remembered coming here the first year. Seeing the melting rocks and scattered fires and pits of bubbling lava. The city had become a festering wound. Half a million people—wiped out in an instant. Another million had died moments later, victims of the flaming shock ring that rippled across the state. But even this horrific wound was healing. Grass, shrubs, and flowers now filled the crater. And where Omaha had fallen, several villages had popped up.

"Humans are stubborn like this," King said. "You can beat us down. But we keep getting up."

"At your age, you ain't getting anything up," Jordan said. The famous Larry Jordan, final commander of the starship *Freedom*, looked like an old cowboy, wearing dusty jeans and a big dark hat. He gave King a smirk.

"I could get my boot right up your backside if you don't shut up," King growled.

Kim rolled her eyes. "Will you two grumpy old men give it a break for once?" Her voice softened. "This is a sacred place."

The three sat in their saddles, gazing into the crater together, silent.

The breeze rustled the grass. The birds sang. A horse nickered.

"How much longer do we have to sit here?" Jordan said.

"Shut up and show some respect, goddammit," King said.

Jordan leaned sideways in his saddle and smacked King with his hat. "That's for blasphemy. Listen to your wife. This is a sacred place."

Yes, the cussing. A bad habit from King's decades in the military. One he couldn't seem to kick.

They sat in silence for a moment longer, gazing into the crater, at new life rising from death. The fall and rebirth. That was the story of Nebraska. And it was the story of Earth. A world King had dedicated his life to defending. A world that had burned and could now heal.

Jordan broke the silence. "That's odd. Have you noticed that MindWeb is down?"

King glowered at his old friend. "A sacred place, and you're checking the football game on MindWeb?"

Kim frowned. "He's right. This is weird. I can't access MindWeb either."

King grumbled, not wanting to activate his MindLink. He

rarely turned the damn thing on. Throughout his service, he had vowed to remove the neural implant the instant he retired. Well, three years later, the damn thing was still inside his skull. He kept saying he'd schedule an appointment, have the doc carve his skull open, remove the cursed device, and bolt him back together. But he needed brain surgery like a hole in the head. Easier to just keep the implant turned off. To pretend it wasn't there.

All soldiers today—whether they served in the Alliance, Red Dawn, or Desert Thorns—had MindLinks implanted in their skulls. Many civilians had begun getting their own version of the implants installed. The MindWeb had begun with a simple goal: Allow soldiers to communicate telepathically in battle. But over the years, it had grown into a beast. It now dominated human society.

The MindWeb had various components. A MindLink device (a neural chip the size of a postage stamp) let you summon MindPlay, a hallucinatory interface that floated before your eyes like a hologram. With MindPlay, you could hallucinate friends across the world, talk to them in real time, even touch them. Kiss across continents? You got it. And there was more. Every day, they added new features. Last year, the software had introduced MindSoul. Have a bunch of photos, videos, and recordings of dead loved ones? Just upload them to MindSoul, pay a small (and recurring) fee, and hallucinate the dead! You could speak to Grandma again—a fairly convincing hallucination of her at least. She could even bake you hallucinatory cookies. And there was entertainment too. Endless hours of entertainment. Instead of watching movies like in the old days, now you could hallucinate the movie all around you. Why watch James Bond when you could *become* James Bond? Why go surfing, skydiving, or swimming with sharks when you could simply hallucinate yourself doing it? Much safer. For two centuries, the internet had dominated human society. Then came MindWeb—far more immersive. A dive from reality into the endless realities in the mind.

Well, if you asked King, the whole thing was a bunch of nonsense. He had tried a few of the hallucinations. They all felt fake. Too clear. Too perfect. Nothing like the grit of real life. And what the hell was the *point* of extreme sports if they were safe? At most, when Kim was sleeping, King might use MindPlay to stream Johnny Cash songs directly into his mind. Even those sounded better on his beat-up, vintage record player.

So, most days, King simply kept his neural implant turned off. That was one of the nice things about being retired. In the army, they made you keep it online 24/7. In case they must call you to battle. You never really unplugged in the military, not even in your sleep. King often missed space. But he did not miss that.

"I've never seen MindWeb go down," Jordan said. All trace of banter or joviality left his face. "I can get onto MindPlay OS. But no farther."

"It's as if the satellite networks are gone," Kim said. She peered at the sky, squinting, as if she could see the satellites at daytime.

King harrumphed. "If you ask me, it's a good thing that—"

"Jim!" Kim cried. "Look!"

King looked upward.

A dagger of ice seemed to plunge through him.

Explosions filled the sky.

It was nothing dramatic. Each blast was barely larger than a shooting star. King could not hear the explosions. They did not shake the clouds or sky. Those blasts were in space. High orbit, by the looks of it. From here on Earth, anyone might have missed it.

Jordan sat nearby on his horse, squinting at the sky. He scratched his white stubble. "It's gotta just be a fireworks display in space. Some military gala we weren't invited to."

"I don't think so," King said. "That's a battle. Our fleet is fighting in high orbit." That icy dagger twisted in his gut. "Earth is under attack."

* * * * *

The three riders galloped across the plains. They leaned forward in the saddles as if that could lend their horses more speed. Clouds of dust rose behind them. The sky burned.

Earth. Under attack.

King narrowed his eyes, gripping the reins. He hated not knowing. Being cut off. Begrudgingly, he even tapped his temple and turned on his MindLink. And he hadn't done that in months. But like Jordan and Kim, he couldn't connect to MindWeb.

The bastards took out the satellites.

But who were the bastards? Who the hell was attacking Earth? Aliens? Other humans? AI gone haywire? Dammit, King hated not knowing.

Back at the ranch, he had an old-school radio. It was an antique. One of the machines he liked tinkering with. A few other enthusiasts still used radio across the country, sharing news and gossip. A hobby for old-timers. With MindWeb down, the radio network would bring him news.

"It's the rahs again," Jordan telepathized, speaking—or at least thinking—directly into King's brain. "It's gotta be the rahs."

Even with MindWeb down, telepathy still worked at short range. Within a mile, MindLinks could connect peer-to-peer, no satellite connection necessary. As they galloped, it was easier to telepathize than talk. The clattering hooves, roaring wind, and snorting horses would have drowned out their voices. King could sense the minds of Jordan and Kim nearby, share his thoughts with them. He tried to reach farther, to call his son, his granddaughter, his old commander. Nothing. Without a

MindWeb connection, he could only detect nearby brains.

MindWeb. The Neural Network. The Realm of Thoughts. The Cognitive Kingdom. It had many names. MindWeb connected humanity into a massive hive mind. If MindWeb were online, King could speak to the military, watch video feeds from satellites, check the news. And most importantly—call his family. He had always preferred being cut off from the hive mind. Now King was desperate to return.

"We crushed the rahs years ago," King muttered and spat out dust. He was telepathizing, but he still liked *speaking* the words while thinking them. "We stepped on every last one of those spiders."

Kim galloped between the two men, leaning forward in her saddle. She telepathized to them both. "It's Katyusha. Mark my words, it's that crazy bitch."

King shuddered.

Ketya "Katyusha" Petrova. Premier of the Red Dawn, a union of Russia, China, North Korea, and an array of their vassal states. King brought her image to mind. Katyusha was a haughty woman with pale skin, a black bob cut, and an imperial smirk. In King's memories, she wore full regalia, medals glinting on her chest. She stood with her chin held high, one fist on her hip, the other raised in triumph. An old woman who looked young. A woman who kept cloning herself, growing younger bodies, and transplanting her brain into them. Every time she turned thirty (which she considered over-the-hill), Katyusha pulled a younger clone from the lab, visited the doc, and a few whirs of the bonesaw later, she was comfortably nesting in a twenty-year-old body again. Like that, she maintained eternal youth, parasitizing herself over and over. But with every brain transplant, she lost a little more of her sanity. If you asked King, her bizarre experiment had rendered her an abomination, a copy of a copy, each a little more *off*. She had become a caricature of herself, a self-perpetuating self-parody.

The old wound on King's neck blazed in pain. Whenever he thought of her, it hurt. It had been decades ago, but the memory flared to life, vivid and raw. Himself—a young man. Katyusha—rampaging across the red sands of Mars. Slaying his father. Then turning to King and lashing her knife. It was all so real. The grief. The pain. The blood on his neck—

"No," King rasped, shoving aside that memory. "Katyusha is our ally now. She helped us defeat the rahs. We have peace."

"Peace?" Jordan snorted. "More like a ceasefire. A very uneasy ceasefire. Kim might be right. This could be Katyusha attacking again."

"Could be something entirely new," King said. "Some alien species we don't know about. Maybe friends of the rahs, come to avenge their buddies. Once we reach the cabin, we'll know. The radio will tell us."

"Thank God for you old geezers and your radios," Jordan said.

King snorted at his white-haired friend. At sixty-six years old, Jordan was only two years younger.

"You better believe it, whippersnapper," King rasped. "If not for radio, we—"

A blast of light blazed across the sky. A *boom* shook the air. Debris came hurtling down from space, etching paths of flame across the sky. A fireball crashed into a distant hill. The land shook, and a cloud of dust and plasma bloomed like a flower woven of living flame. The horses neighed and kicked the air. King clung to his saddle. At his age, the last thing he needed was to fall off a horse.

"Easy, Buck, easy." King stroked his horse until the animal calmed.

"They're bombing Earth!" Kim cried. Her mare was rearing beneath her. She struggled to control the horse.

"No," King said. "Not yet at least. That wasn't a bomb. That was a piece of starship. Kinetic energy."

"I hope it was a piece of the enemy, not of our fleet," Jordan said.

God, King hoped so too.

"Hyah!" he said, digging his heels into Buck's sides. The poor horses were exhausted. But all three galloped onward, spooked by the strange lights in the sky.

The horses thundered across the grasslands and over the hills. They crested a hilltop, rode between trees, and descended toward a valley. There, across the fields, King saw his cabin.

The icy dagger twisted again in his belly.

A dropship stood by the cabin. A big, armored one.

Someone had come to visit.

* * * * *

As the horses galloped, King squinted, trying to get a better look. His cabin was still distant. What dropship was this? Military? King looked for symbols on the hull. But sunlight glinted off the dropship, obscuring any details.

One thing he could see. The ship was roughly the size of the cabin. Not a starship then. This ship was too small to brave interstellar space alone. The vapor trail across the sky was still fresh. This was a shuttle, and it had just descended from a mothership.

Were they friends or foes? King hated not knowing. Could it be the Alliance here to recruit him? Or at least debrief him on the attack? That was possible. But he wasn't picking up any MindLink signals. At this range, he should be detecting the MindLinks of any Alliance soldier.

Could they be the enemy? Whatever enemy this was? Well, if so, they must have seen the three riders by now, and they weren't firing. A good sign perhaps. The trio galloped closer.

As they approached, more details became visible. King saw several men outside the dropship. They stood near his wooden cabin. A gust of wind billowed their long black coats, revealing crimson body armor. Red lights shone from their helmets. Laser scopes? From here, they almost looked like blazing red eyes.

"I don't like this," Kim telepathized.

Jordan stared at the strangers with narrowed eyes. "Me neither." Even when speaking in their minds, the phantom had a deep, velvety voice. "Those aren't Alliance men."

King wished he had brought his binoculars. As he rode, he gripped the butt of his pistol. From the corner of his eye, King noticed Jordan doing the same. Kim was unarmed, and she rode a little closer to King.

"If they wanted to shoot us, we'd be dead by now," King telepathized. "Let's see who the hell these are."

They rode along the dirt road between the cornfields. Dust flew from under the horses' hooves. With the clouds of dust and glints of sunlight, they couldn't see much, only the blurred figures of men in black cloaks, red eyes shining.

Demon eyes, King thought. That icy shard burrowed deeper through him.

But alongside the fear, a cold determination filled James King. He had been a soldier for fifty years. He had fought in World War III against Katyusha and the Red Dawn. He had fought in the Spider War against the rahs. He was a soldier through and through. Dealing with monsters was what he did. What he had done for half a century. Three years of retirement could not change that, could not soften a man who'd been hardened in the forge of war. As he rode, he drew his pistol. Ready to do what he had always done. Whatever it took.

King reached the cabin first, tugged the reins, and Buck

came to a halt. He leaned forward in the saddle, eyes narrowed, and waved away dust. And he saw . . .

His heart jolted. No. Impossible. How could this be real?

His hand drew nearer to his gun.

Jordan and Kim reached him and held their horses. They let out low curses.

As the dust settled, they got a good look at the men ahead.

Nazis. Goddamn Nazis.

The strangers wore swastika armbands. The lightning bolts of the SS shone on their breastplates, and their helmets sported visors shaped like skulls. Each goon stared with one normal blue eye, one blazing bionic eye.

"Nazis," King growled, fingers inching closer to his gun. "I hate these guys."

Six of them stood outside the cabin. There might be more inside the dropship. Maybe even inside King's home.

One of the SS men stepped closer. "*Guten Morgen, freunde!*" the man said. *"Ich bin Scharführer Anselm Vogel."*

King's MindLink popped up a hallucinatory window. GREETINGS! I'VE DETECTED A NEW FRIEND SPEAKING GERMAN! WOULD YOU LIKE ME TO TRANSLATE TO ENGLISH?

Yes, dammit, King thought.

The stranger's words repeated in his mind, this time in heavily accented English. "Good morning, friends! I am Scharführer Anselm Vogel."

Scharführer, huh? King thought. A student of history, he recognized that rank. It was common back in Nazi Germany. One of their noncommissioned officer ranks. No modern military still used that rank.

"Never heard of you," King growled. "Did you just crawl out of one of those ridiculous holes of yours? Crawl back in."

Vogel laughed. "Crawl from holes? I do not understand.

Ah! Must be some English idiom my adlerauge cannot translate." He pointed at his prosthetic eye. "These are remarkable pieces of German engineering. But they do struggle with inferior languages."

King had heard of white supremacist chapters across the country. Some lived in holes—literally. When they weren't marching and waving their little flags, they dug bunkers and stored weapons. They vowed to fight equalist spies from the Red Dawn. And to fight aliens, who they claimed were roaming the world in human skins. They appealed to lots of folks. Folks who still remembered fighting the Red Dawn and the alien spiders. The problem wasn't that those goons hated equalists and aliens. Hell, King hated them too. He had fought his share of both. It was that the neo-Nazis hated *everyone.*

King glanced at Vogel's grunts. They sported the insignia of *oberschütze*. Low-ranking killers. King recognized that rank too. It also dated back to Nazi Germany.

This was all very odd. The neo-Nazis who tunneled under Nebraska were just lowlifes. Inbred morons who didn't have proper uniforms, just ragged armbands they sewed themselves. *These* men were different. They wore expensive battle armor and fine leather cloaks. They carried guns of a design King didn't recognize. And their dropship was a serious piece of military machinery, not just some crop duster painted with swastikas. And these men were *tall.* Each one could have been a basketball player. At over six feet, King was a tall man, but these brutes towered above him.

What the hell is going on here?

King glared at Vogel.

"Get the hell off my ranch!" he said. "Does your robot eye understand that, punk?"

Vogel tilted his head and squinted. "You really do look like him. They warned us about this happening. Fascinating."

"What the hell are you talking about?" King growled.

Vogel ignored him. The tall Nazi commander walked toward a wooden barrel full of apples. Harvest from King's orchard. Vogel took an apple, hefted it in his gloved hand, then brushed it against his robe. He raised his visor, revealing a pale face with a wide jaw, thin lips, and a scar along the left cheek. The bionic eye peered from the scar tissue like a raw, red wound.

Vogel took a bite. The apple *crunched.* "Ah, excellent! Honeycrisp? From your orchard over there?"

Jordan's horse nickered and sidestepped. The white-haired commander glanced at King.

"Jim, who the hell are these goons?" Jordan telepathized.

"I don't know," King thought back. His own horse was nervous. Buck nickered and stamped his hooves.

King looked at Kim. His wife gazed at him, fear in her blue eyes. Her blond hair spilled across her shoulders, touched with the morning light. God, he loved her. He loved her more than the sun and the world.

"Kim, get out of here," he telepathized. "Ride to the hills. If these goons cause trouble, we'll hold them off."

Sitting straight in her saddle, Kim raised her chin. "I won't leave you."

King growled. He wanted to slap her horse and send the mare fleeing—with Kim in the saddle. But he knew she'd just wheel the horse around and come back. Colonel Kim Fletcher had fought at his side through the Spider War. She wouldn't escape now and leave him in danger.

Vogel finished his apple. He had eaten the core too, crunching the seeds between his teeth. After swallowing the last mouthful, he tapped his temple. His bionic eye cast out blue beams of light. A holographic notepad materialized before him. With his gloved fingers, the scharführer scrolled through the translucent pages.

"Let's see, let's see . . . the names of the day . . . Ah! Here we are." Vogel smiled. "We are searching for one Admiral James King, an old white man, a traitor to his race. And one Commander Lawrence Jordan, an old subhuman." He peered at King and Jordan with his good eye. "You seem to match the descriptions. You will have to come with me. My commanding officer wishes to speak to you."

King snorted. "Tell him to come down here then."

Vogel laughed. "Our commander is a woman, Herr King. The blessed Eva König herself, heiress of the Third Reich! You are honored. Not many get to meet Frau Eva." Vogel gestured at the dropship with the barrel of his gun. "Into the Wolfjäger. All three of you."

"I'm not going anywhere," King growled, his raspy voice scraping across his wounded throat. "But you are. Get the hell off my property, you goddamn piece of Nazi filth."

Vogel sighed, lowered his skull visor, and turned to his men. "Very well. Arrest them. We'll take them to Frau Eva in chains."

King drew his pistol. From his saddle, he stared down at the Nazis, squinting to see under the blaring sun. "Hold it right there, fellows. You don't want to lose your heads."

The SS troops froze. Their bionic eyes turned toward their commander, casting beams through the dusty air.

"Herr King!" Vogel said. "Do not cause trouble. These men are trained soldiers of the Waffen-SS. Professional killers."

"I don't give a damn who you think you are." King spat. "You came onto my property. You came here with guns. With threats. With that filth on your armbands. I give you to the count of five to get the hell off my land. Or by God, I'll gun you down like the mad dogs that you are."

The Germans looked at one another, then burst out laughing.

"One," King rasped.

The Nazis stepped closer, raising electric handcuffs. Sparks flashed across the metal rings.

"Two," King said. He pulled back the hammer of his single-action firearm.

The Germans aimed their guns at his head.

"Lower your pistol, Herr King!" Vogel said.

"Three," King said. And fired his gun.

* * * * *

King was a lover of all things old and outdated. Even in the twenty-third century, he listened to Johnny Cash on vinyl records. He communicated with other old men on ham radio. He read paperback novels. Actual paper made from honest-to-goodness trees. He often spoke of being born in the wrong era. In line with his anachronisms, he carried an obsolete pistol. It was an old-school revolver. A replica of the Colt Peacemaker, the famous pistol of the Old West. It had a manual hammer and room for six rounds. In an era of plasma weapons, it was an antique. A real cowboy gun. King loved it.

His first round streaked toward the nearest Nazi. One of the low-level thugs. The bullet flew through the helmet's eyehole, shattered the bionic eye, and drove into the brain.

The man collapsed, blood spurting.

At once, the other Nazis opened fire. Their rifles howled like wolves, discharging strange black rounds that left trails of smoke.

King leaped from the saddle, dodging the barrage. In midair, he cocked back the hammer, fired again, then slammed sideways onto the ground, banging his shoulder and hip.

Another SS soldier crashed down dead, a bullet in his eye.

The surviving four Nazis kept firing.

Buck neighed in terror and turned to flee. Blood speckled the ground. The horse was hit!

King rolled in the dust, dodging more of those strange smoky rounds. What the hell *were* those rounds? Behind the barrel of apples, he rose to one knee. The enemy's smoky projectiles plowed through apples, splattering hot juice. Aiming over the barrel, King fired his third bullet.

Once more, he hit a man in the eyehole. The Nazi collapsed.

Three pistol rounds fired. Three Nazis dead.

Three enemies remained. And King had three bullets left.

Meanwhile, Jordan was firing too. But he wasn't able to hit any eyeholes. His kept hitting the Nazis' body armor. His bullets fell, crushed, to the ground. Jordan was an excellent pilot—as good as King. But bless the man, he had never been a great shot.

The barrel of apples exploded under the enemy fire. King ran at a crouch through flying wooden chips and bits of apple. The mess distracted his enemies. King reached the patio, aimed his gun over the railing, and another man crashed down.

A smoky round slammed into the railing beside King. Bits of wood flew every which way. Splinters drove into King's arms and cheeks. He stood his ground and fired his fifth bullet.

A fifth Nazi collapsed.

That left one. Scharführer Anselm Vogel.

Jordan was firing everything at the man. Bullets slammed into Vogel's armor. Sparks flew. The Nazi advanced through the storm of bullets. But he was ignoring Jordan. He was stepping toward King.

"We heard you were a war hero once, Herr King!" Vogel said, armor sparking under Jordan's bullets. "I see your strength. We could use a man like you."

King aimed his pistol at Vogel's face.

"Not in a million years, punk."

He fired.

He was aiming at Vogel's eye. But he missed.

He missed! His bullet hit the skull-shaped visor two inches away from the eyehole, doing Vogel no harm.

King was out of ammo. He stood, glowering at his enemy, refusing to run. Vogel stomped closer, his steel-tipped boots crushing apples.

"Ah, I see you are out of bullets, Herr King." Vogel tossed aside his gun and balled his fists. "We can fight now like gentlemen. With honor."

King thought Vogel had him at a slight disadvantage. The man was thirty years younger, half a foot taller, and clad in body armor.

"What would you know about honor?" King said.

"I know that when an honorable man says he will count to five, he will not count to three," Vogel said.

The Nazi swung his fist. King moved aside, dodging the blow.

"Yeah, well, I got impatient." King tossed a punch.

Vogel took a step back, laughing. "Ah, you have studied the art and science of boxing, I see. But with age, you've slowed down. Like an old bulldog who lost his bite."

King studied his opponent. Vogel had his visor down. The steel skull leered. That visor was bulletproof. Maybe if King could grab the visor, lift it . . .

He leaped toward Vogel, making a lunge for the visor.

Vogel reached out and caught King's wrist.

Staring into King's eyes, Vogel squeezed. Tighter. *Tighter.* Something cracked inside King's wrist. He growled in agony. Through the pain, he wondered why Jordan and Kim weren't helping. He soon got his answer.

"Jim!" came a cry from nearby.

King glanced to the left. More Nazi scum had crawled out from their dropship. Five men surrounded Jordan and Kim. Both commander and engineer were still on their horses. Then the SS opened fire. Rounds slammed into the horses, and Jordan and Kim crashed down into the dust.

Jordan—his best friend. Kim—his wife. On the ground, maybe hurt, and the Nazis aimed their guns, ready to kill humans alongside horses.

"Watch them, King!" Vogel laughed, squeezing harder, crushing King's wrist. "Men! Before you kill the woman, have your fun. We'll make sure Herr King enjoys the show."

King howled.

He swung his left fist.

The prosthetic fist. The steel fist like a medieval gauntlet.

The blow shattered Vogel's visor. Shards from the steel skull drove into the Nazi's face, carving through the nose, the cheek, the remaining eye.

Vogel fell, clutching his ravaged face, screeching. Blood spurted between his fingers.

"You cheated!" he cried. "You used a metal fist!"

"For a metal face." King stepped over bloodied apples, knelt, and lifted Vogel's gun. A wolf logo was engraved onto the gun above the word *Lugerheulen*. When King placed his finger on the trigger, the gun hummed and purred.

Hearing the sound, Vogel froze. He stared up at King with his remaining eye, the bionic one.

"We were fighting man to man," Vogel said.

"You're not a man," King growled through clenched teeth. "You're a dog. A rabid dog who crawled out from the cesspool of history. A dog who invaded my land. Who ordered his men to rape and murder my wife. And this is what I do to dirty dogs like you. I gun you down."

He pulled the trigger.

The Lugerheulen howled. A shadow-bolt slammed into Vogel's head, pulverizing the skull.

At once, King spun toward the left. Jordan and Kim stood back-to-back among corpses. Only two Nazis still lived. Jordan fired his handgun, finally hitting an eyehole. The man crumpled. During the battle, Kim had grabbed the rifle of a fallen SS soldier. She fired. The wolf-gun howled, and the final enemy collapsed.

She looked at King, the rifle in her hands. A gust of wind tossed back her golden hair, revealing a pale yet determined face. Fear filled her eyes, but pride too. She was an engineer by trade, never taught how to kill, but aboard the starship *Freedom*, they had flown through hell and back. And Kim Fletcher-King had emerged a warrior. As strong as any King had ever known.

King's boots sluiced through blood. He stepped toward his wife and pulled her into his arms.

While the couple embraced, Jordan looked around the scene. The corpses of their enemies lay in the dust. Jordan shook his head and whistled softly.

"Ten men," Jordan said, awe filling his baritone voice. "We killed ten armored men between us."

King snorted. "Bunch of punks."

"Still, not bad for two old geezers," Jordan said. "Two old geezers and one lovely young lady, that is."

"You old flirt," King said, holding his wife a little closer.

Yes, two old geezers, King thought. Two old geezers who fought the Red Dawn and the spiders. Two old dogs who still had another fight or two in them.

A plaintive mewl sounded from the distance.

King spun around. Was one of the dead actually just wounded? King still held Vogel's Lugerheulen. He raised the strange howling gun, scanning the scene.

The mewl sounded again, followed by a snort. That was

when King noticed it. Two of the horses had run off. But the third horse—Buck—lay in the grass.

King walked toward his fallen friend.

Buck looked up at him and whimpered. Blood matted the grass. The Nazis had fired several rounds into the old horse. One of Buck's legs was mangled, and he had taken a round to the gut. The horse kicked his back legs, but soon he weakened and could only lie there. Suffering.

King stared at the old stallion. He thought about the good old times. Rescuing the horse. Nursing him back to health. Riding him across the fields and farms, along canyons, through the woods and under the sprawling sky. He remembered all those hours talking to Buck, telling him secrets King could tell no one else.

You were there for me, old friend, King thought. *When I was in pain, you were there. And I know what I must do for you.*

There was no use drawing it out. That would only make things worse.

King aimed the Lugerheulen.

"Jim!" Kim put a hand on his shoulder. "Jim, you don't have—"

"I do," he rasped. "Look away, Kim."

She nodded, turned away, and covered her eyes.

When the job was done, when they were walking back toward the cabin, Jordan put a hand on King's shoulder.

"You okay, Jim?"

"No." King's neck blazed with pain. "No, Larry, I am not."

Another blast shook the sky. Chunks of starship came crashing down, etching trails of fire.

"Leave the bodies for now," King said. "Let's get inside, fire up the radio, and figure out what the hell is going on."

CHAPTER THREE
Weapon of War

Nebraska
Alliance Territory
Earth
September 2, 2207

As James King climbed onto his porch, the pain hit him. At first—a sharp pain in his lower back. Next—dull aches in his legs. After that—throbbing agony in his wrist. And of course there was the familiar pain in his neck, Katyusha's gift that kept on giving. Ah, those old aches. Those old friends. Every year he aged, more joined the party.

During the battle, adrenaline had washed away those unwelcome guests. Now, like gophers, they reemerged from hiding. The aches surged through his body, twisting his muscles, crushing his joints, and banging against his old bones. When King had been young, nobody had warned him how much being old *hurt*. Especially when you carried this many war wounds.

"War is a young man's game," he muttered.

Was that what this was? War?

A weight seemed to press down on King. Dammit, he had fought two big wars already. Had he not earned some peace? Even now, at sixty-eight, he was still fighting.

He glanced up at the sky. They were still battling up there. MindWeb was still down. And King decided to finally find out what the hell was going on.

He stepped into his cabin, holding the Lugerheulen in

both hands. Just in case any more Nazi scum were hiding in here. He swept his eyes across the living room. The cabin was rustic, a memory of the past here in the twenty-third century. Swords hung above the fireplace—one an authentic Napoleonic saber, the other a real Samurai sword from feudal Japan. Leather-bound books lined the shelves, while a deer's head peered from the wall. Antique naval instruments stood on the windowsill by the telescope. King was a lover of old things. Items from the past. Items from before MindWeb, the aliens, the technology of these times. Bless her heart, Kim tolerated his collections. Sometimes he even caught her admiring the naval instruments, tinkering with them to figure out how they worked.

"The coast is clear!" King telepathized to his wife and friend. Jordan and Kim had gone into the Wolfjäger, the enemy dropship, to search for more hostiles.

Jordan's voice spoke in King's mind. "Same here. No more bad guys in the Wolfjäger. I think we got 'em all." The phantom hesitated. "Jim, this ship is weird. There's a portrait of Hitler in the cockpit. And skulls. Real human skulls on the dashboard. What the hell is going on here?"

"I'm gonna find out," King said.

First things first, King went to his gun safe. After discarding the Lugerheulen (holding the Nazi weapon sickened him), he reloaded his Peacemaker, then holstered the antique revolver. A good old American gun. Much better. Next King grabbed his Trogdor T-7, a modern plasma pistol. It was the smaller (much smaller) civilian version of the Mordecai rifle the space marines used. As much as King hated new tech, he had to admit—a Trogdor packed a punch. With his Peacemaker, King must fire through the eyeholes of those skull helmets. But a Trogdor might just burn through the German armor. King slid the plasma pistol into his second holster.

Fully armed, King stepped into his den. Originally, he had

built the house without it. But a year ago he had expanded his home, adding a private space. "Your man cave," Kim called it. King spent most of his time outdoors—riding, tending to his cattle, living the cowboy life, a childhood dream finally come true in retirement. But every evening, he escaped into his den for some quiet study and retrospection. Those had become his favorite hours. He would light a pipe, read history books, work on his memoirs, build his little ships in bottles, and tinker with his radio.

He sat at his desk with a *creak*. Sitting down wasn't too bad at his age. Getting back up was the problem. He switched on his antique ham radio. Ah, good, reliable tech! The current generation just relied on their neural implants. They wanted to telepathize and hallucinate everything. Ha! What was wrong with an old-fashioned speaker and screen? That was something *real*, dammit. Something actually hitting your ears and eyeballs, not just hallucinated inside your skull. Some of the kids today didn't even eat real food anymore. They just gobbled down tasteless multivitamin biscuits and hallucinated whatever flavor they wanted.

Yes, King had heard the counterarguments. His son kept yammering on about it. *Everything* was a hallucination, Bastian would claim. Always had been. Colors? Those only exist in the brain. Nothing but light waves in specific patterns hit your eyeballs. It's the brain that hallucinates the color. Sounds? Not real. Outside the brain, they're only vibrations in the air. It's the brain that hallucinates sound. So how were MindLinks different? They just simplified things. Bypass your ears and eyes and go straight to the brain! Send little electric signals, get senses. Just a fancier way of doing it.

Well, King still didn't like it. Like many of his generation, he clung to the old ways. To communicate, King and his fellow ham radio enthusiasts used the OCN. The Original Comms Network. Or, as Bastian called it, the Old Codger Network.

King fiddled with the controls. Small monitors lit up. Outside the cabin, the antennae thrummed. Ah, good old OCN! The network was still online. Instead of relying on satellites like MindWeb, the OCN used big, clunky antennae down on Earth. Mostly ones raised by amateurs like King. Whoever was attacking Earth—they were smart enough to knock down the satellites. And not thorough enough to attack the outdated tech. With MindWeb down, King could not contact the admiralty. He could not contact his army buddies—some of whom were retired, many who were still in service. Worst of all, he could not contact his family. But with the Old Codgers Network, he wasn't completely isolated.

King lifted the receiver. He adjusted some dials. "Bulldog here. Anyone out there? What the hell is going on?"

Bulldog. It had been his call sign as a fighter pilot. He now used it as his ham radio sobriquet.

"Bulldog?" came a voice over the speaker. "This is Badger. Where have you been?"

A monitor lit up, showing an old man with round glasses, thick sideburns, and bushy eyebrows. He indeed looked like a badger. King didn't know his real name. But they had been friends since King had retired and began tinkering with ham radio.

"Horseback riding," King said. "The whole sky's burning. Have we got eyes up there?"

Badger didn't know King's real name either. None of the hammers did. They didn't know his past. Didn't know he had been an admiral, had commanded fleets in war, had flown to the stars and battled alien empires. They didn't know he was James King, *the* James King, supposed hero of Earth. To Badger and the others on ham radio, he was just Bulldog, the cranky old cowboy from Nebraska. The one with the old horse and scar across his neck.

Badger nodded. "Yeah, Wombat down in Australia got his telescope streaming a live feed. He's sending a second camera up now in a weather balloon. Says he needs to get closer for a better look."

"Wombat!" King said, adjusting dials. Static came from the speakers. "Wombat, you there?"

The Old Man Down Under, also known as Wombat, appeared on a little screen. He was a diminutive octogenarian with boundless energy. His head was bald, but great tufts of white hair grew from his enormous ears, and his eyebrows stuck out an inch from his face. King often felt old, but he could be Wombat's son.

"G'day, Bulldog!" said the little old Aussie. "How's the missus?"

"Lovely as always, Wombat." King couldn't suppress a smile. "Badger tells me you got Emma pointing at the sky. Mind if I take a peek?"

Emma was Wombat's beloved telescope, a gargantuan machine the size of a starfighter. Emma even had her own cockpit. Wombat was sitting inside that cockpit now, pushing levers and spinning wheels, aiming and focusing the telescope lenses.

"Eh, what's that, young fella?" Wombat flattened the tufts of hair in one ear. "You wanna look through Emma? Well, sure! But you might wanna wait until Betsy is online. She's my small scope, ya know. Sent her up in a hot-air balloon! Gotta get higher up for a good view. Less atmospheric interference. Now if the bastards at the Orbit Control Department would ever grant me a license for an orbital camera, I could—"

"Wombat, can you stream Emma's feed to me?"

"What's that, young fella? Eh? You wanna take a look now? Oh, all right, I'm streaming you a feed. But you really might wanna wait for Betsy."

King smiled. Not many things made him smile. But the Old Codger Network did. "I'll be sure to check out Betsy's beautiful work when she's ready. For now, stream Emma over."

Wombat nodded and faded from the screen. Instead of seeing a little old Australian man, King was now peering into space.

His chest constricted. The scar tightened around his neck as if Katyusha were slicing him again.

War.

War flared around Earth.

Not just a battle. Not just trouble from some local white supremacist punks. But war—massive war, total war. The enemy was bombarding Earth with the might of empires.

And who was the enemy? King could only see part of the sky from here. And what he saw chilled him. Hundreds of starships—*enormous* starships. Starships the size of dreadnoughts—and even larger. Starships with swastikas on their hulls. Their cannons were booming, bombarding targets in orbit and on the surface.

"What the hell?" King muttered, barely able to believe his eyes. Only great powers like the Alliance and Red Dawn should be able to unleash such firepower. "How did the goddamn Nazis get a fleet? I thought we defeated those bastards centuries ago."

His den door opened. Kim stepped into the study. She had pulled her hair into a loose ponytail, and she carried a sidearm on her belt. Kim rarely carried. If she was armed, this was serious.

"Jim, we should get outta here," Kim said. "The men we killed were looking for you. More will come."

King nodded. He shut off his radio. "Where's Larry?"

"He's still in the Wolfjäger. He's got the engine running."

"Well, tell him to get the hell out!" King said. "He can fly that beat-up tin can of his. The one he calls a shuttle."

Kim took his hand. "Jim, we should fly in the Wolfjäger. Yes, in a Nazi ship. They knew our names. They're looking for us. We must go undercover."

King stared into his wife's eyes. "Kim, what the hell is

going on here?"

She touched his cheek. "I don't know. We'll head to Washington. Try to get in touch with the admirals there."

King remembered what he saw on Emma's camera. The enemy bombarding targets on the surface. He hadn't seen what they were targeting. He wasn't sure he wanted to know.

"If Washington is still there," King muttered. He thought for a moment, then shook his head. "No. We're not heading to Washington. We're soldiers. And we're heading to battle."

* * * * *

King stomped across the yard between the dead men, heading toward his barn.

"Jim!" Kim hurried after him. "Jim, we're no longer soldiers! We retired."

"Well, I'm officially coming out of retirement," King said. His boots crushed bullets and little chunks of flesh, the gruesome remnants of the battle. The stench filled the air. That familiar old stench of war.

Yes, he wanted to know what was going on. More than anything, he missed the wisdom of George Godwin, High Commander of the Alliance and King's mentor. But with MindWeb down, King had learned all he could. For now, that was enough. The Alliance was fighting a battle up there. He knew many of those captains. Had known them throughout their careers. He must be up there, fighting at their side.

He shoved the barn doors open, revealing the Golden Eagle. His old starfighter.

It . . . was not in good shape.

In fact, a good portion of its "shape" was strewn across the barn floor.

King knelt and lifted a chunk of hull. "I'm taking the

Golden Eagle."

Kim blinked. "Jim, she's an antique!"

"So am I," he growled, slapping the piece of hull onto the frame.

"She's falling apart!" Kim cried.

"So am I!" he said, connecting a piece of wing.

"Jim, you can't be serious." Kim grabbed his arm. "We have the Wolfjäger outside. We can fly to battle in that. Confuse the enemy. And—"

"Larry can do that if he wants." King knelt and lifted another piece. "I'm taking Goldie. Kim, this starfighter won the war against Katyusha. She won the war against the rahs."

"*You* won those wars!" she insisted.

He caressed his wife's cheek. "Kim, I love you. If I don't see you again after tonight—know that I've loved you with the flame of a thousand erupting galaxies. Now, before this galaxy blows up too, help me put my starfighter together."

Thank God above, King had married a military engineer. She was used to fixing things in the rush of battle. Aboard the starship *Freedom*, Colonel Kim Fletcher had saved the dreadnought from destruction—along with thousands of souls aboard. More than once.

And she saved me, King thought. *Saved me from despair and loneliness. From the pit of memories and booze. She still saves me every day.*

A thousand exploding galaxies? Nonsense. That was a mere spark compared to the fire of his love.

Kim nodded. She kissed him, wiped tears from her eyes, then pulled a wrench from her belt. "Let's get this old bird into the air."

They worked in a mad fury. Right now they weren't interested in elegance, just getting the damn thing working as fast as possible. So they cut corners, welded crudely, and Kim even let King use his hammer and nails. Without Kim helping, King would have struggled for days. With the best engineer in the galaxy working with him, they got the job done in no time. There she stood before him, cobbled together, covered with fresh welding and new bolts. His old S-35 Eagle starfighter.

"They no longer build 'em like this," King said.

"Thank God." Kim wiped her brow.

There was one more thing to do. King had kept his old flight suit and helmet. They hung in the barn closet. When King pulled them on, they smelled like the starship *Freedom*. Like memories. Like the old days, flying starfighters with his friends. Many of those fellow pilots were gone now. Some had fallen in the war. Some had simply died of old age. But Larry "Phantom" Jordan was still here. And so was Jim "Bulldog" King.

"Still fits," he said, zipping up.

He stepped toward his starfighter, pulled down the folding ladder to the cockpit, then paused. He turned around. Kim gazed at him, eyes soft.

"I always hated it so much when Evan went to battle," she said softly. Evan Fletcher, a brave marine who had lost his legs in the Spider War, was her son from her first marriage.

"I always felt the same about Bastian," King said. His son from his first wife. Brigadier Bastian King was a proud officer, a big bear of a man, larger and stronger than his father. But to James King, Bastian would always be that little boy. You never stopped worrying about your kids. No matter how old they got.

"Now I feel that way about you." Kim embraced him. "Godspeed, Admiral James King. Go get 'em."

He kissed her lips, climbed into the cockpit, and gave her a salute and wink. She returned the salute, and he pulled the cockpit canopy shut.

"You almost done smooching in there, old man?" Jordan telepathized. He was probably still in the Wolfjäger outside the barn, but his voice sounded loud and clear in King's mind.

"I'm done," he said. "Let's go show the young pilots a thing or two."

"They'll get to fly with legends," said Jordan.

King fired up the engines. The Eagle hummed and purred. No parts fell off yet. That was a good sign. Even so, the cows got spooked and made a ruckus. Slowly, trying not to startle them too badly, King taxied the Golden Eagle out of the barn.

The starfighter stood on the grass under the sprawling Nebraska sky. The sun was setting, and in the darkening sky, King could see more details of the battle. The slender slivers of racing ships. The streaking lines of missiles. The blasts of lives cut short.

Nearby stood the Wolfjäger. The armored dropship was significantly larger than King's starfighter. The Eagle was no larger than an old Thunderbolt, America's workhorse fighter aircraft of World War II. Meanwhile, the Wolfjäger was big like a Heinkel He, the dreaded German bomber that had ravaged London during the blitz of 1940. The modern ships looked different than those twentieth-century machines, and they could fly in both air and space, but King, a student of history, couldn't help but see the parallels.

Jordan looked at him from the Wolfjäger cockpit. "For old times' sake." He saluted. "Godspeed, Admiral."

Fsrom his own cockpit, King returned the salute. Then he shoved down the throttle and soared into the sky.

* * * * *

As the Golden Eagle soared through the clouds, a strange tingle ran through King. As always before battle, he was afraid. King had fought countless battles, and that fear never went away. Back in the war against Katyusha, King had learned that every sane soldier, no matter how high-ranking, no matter how strong, was afraid before a battle. When you stopped being afraid, they said, that was when you knew—you had lost your sanity. Judging by his fear tonight, King was still very sane.

But there was something more here. An itch beyond fear. Something *similar* to fear but not *quite* the same. Something that electrified his bones and lifted his heart.

Excitement.

He had missed this. Missed flying. Missed fighting. Missed being *alive*.

He burst through the clouds into the stratosphere. The setting sun glinted across his cockpit. Higher and higher he rose until he leaped from the atmosphere. Back into space—the vast blackness where he had lived most of his life.

Below spread the glory of God's own Earth. Above and all around, the battle raged.

Hundreds of enemy warships surrounded Earth. They were true behemoths. The largest starship in human history had been the starship *Freedom*, the dreadnought King had once commanded. Stern to stem, the *Freedom* had measured a mile long. But now King saw many starships the same size. Or larger. One enemy ship—a true leviathan—would have dwarfed *Freedom* like a sperm whale swimming by a shark. *Freedom* might have been Jaws, but that Nazi ship? That was goddamn Moby-Dick. It was the enemy flagship. Had to be. The monstrous vessel loomed like a goddess, her hull engraved with her name: *Barbarossa.*

Her? No, King decided. That ship was male. Back in World War II, the Nazis refused to consider their largest ships female. They had referred to the *Bismarck*, the mightiest warship they ever built, as male. To them, females were weak. Most likely, they did the same with their starships.

The Freedom Fleet was in the air—the great armada of the Alliance, comprising thousands of starships. In this battle, they had the numerical superiority. But they had been caught with their pants down. The hulks of many Alliance ships tumbled through space, their hulls blasted open. Several were still spilling out the corpses of their spacers. Shattered satellites, both military and civilian, hurtled through deeper orbit. Well, that certainly explained why MindWeb was down.

As for the surviving ships—they were struggling. The Freedom Fleet, the proud space force of the Alliance, kept trying to reform the lines. They must solidify good, defensive formations—dreadnoughts in the center, frigates and warships defending the flanks. But the enemy was firing relentlessly, not letting the Alliance catch its breath. Torpedoes kept blasting the armored flanks, spilling out strange, smoky clouds that ripped hulls open. The Freedom Fleet, despite numerical superiority, could barely hold the Germans back. The formations were crumbling. Too many ships were falling. Too many spacers were dying.

King looked down at Earth. The surface wasn't faring much better. The war spread across the ground too. From up here, King could see several mushroom clouds rising from North America. As he had feared—one seemed to be coming from Washington. The enemy knew just where to hit.

This is a fiasco, King thought. *They hit us hard. They brought us to our knees. Whoever they are.*

What about the Red Dawn? Was Katyusha fighting this war too? King scanned space, trying to make out red ships. He had fought the Red Fleet before, and he knew its power. Dammit, without MindWeb, he couldn't see much. To the naked eye, starships were hard to identify. Normally MindWeb displayed stats and magnified the view. Well, King had earned his wings in the days before MindWeb. He could fight without it.

Jordan's Wolfjäger flew up beside him. The heavy machine dwarfed the smaller Eagle.

"Jim, are you seeing all this too?" Jordan said. He was close enough for telepathic range, connecting peer-to-peer instead of over MindWeb. "It's absurd! How can this be real?"

"I keep thinking it's all a bad dream," King said. "But I can't wake up. This is real. Somehow."

"But humanity defeated the Nazis!" Jordan said. "Our ancestors wiped them out centuries ago. Oh, a few holdouts remain even in the twenty-third century, but no more than some splinter groups with basic rifles. Not *starships*."

King grunted. "It's almost as if . . . they came from a parallel universe. A universe in which Hitler had won the war, then led Nazi Germany into the space age."

"Parallel universes?" Jordan said. "Those are only hypothetical."

"Not if you ask my wife," King said. "Kim knows the physics of parallel universes inside and out. I don't. But one thing I do know. In this universe or another, the Nazis are bad hombres, and I want to kill 'em."

Jordan nodded. "We can agree about that. Let's go kill some Nazis. I'll try to infiltrate their fleet in my Wolfjäger and hit them from within."

"And I'll fight my way toward an Alliance capital ship," King said. "I can help the young starfighters. And might get within peer-to-peer telepathic range of somebody who knows what the hell is going on."

"Godspeed, Bulldog."

King nodded, his throat feeling tight. He thought of the decades he and Larry "Phantom" Jordan had fought side by side. They were more than just old friends. They were brothers-in-arms. And he thought of Kim, the love of his life, waiting below on Earth. He thought of his son and grandchildren, forever beloved. He would give the world to know they were safe. Yes, James King had a lot to fight for.

"Godspeed, Phantom," he said softly.

The Eagle and Wolfjäger flew higher, branching into

separate paths, drawing a Y-shaped blaze of light.

*****

As Jordan flew into the distance, King lost contact with his friend. The two MindLinks dropped out of peer-to-peer range. Direct telepathy was fine on the ranch. But not very practical when it came to the vast distances of space. With MindWeb, the entire fleet could be in constant communication. But the neural satellites were currently hurtling down to Earth in balls of fire.

The eggheads in the big capital ships were probably working on a solution. Warships could provide their own private MindWebs without relying on Earth infrastructure. That was what the Freedom Fleet used when flying into deep space. But if any private nets were up and running, King couldn't see them. Ha. Maybe they had never added his profile. He was, after all, retired.

Well, not anymore.

He yanked his joystick, swerving around a hurtling chunk of satellite. He flew into higher orbit. An Alliance capital ship was flying above—the FAS *Patton.*

The *Patton*! King knew that ship well. She was a large, powerful starfighter carrier. A pillar of the fleet. More importantly—her commander was family. Commander Benjamin Fletcher was his name. King's brother-in-law.

Good old Ben, King thought. The two men had spent quite a few evenings on the patio, drinking beer, playing gin, and discussing philosophy, science, and history. Ben Fletcher was an excellent conversationalist, both a scholar and warrior. And tonight he was giving the enemy hell.

Patton had launched her Eagles. They were F-80 Eagles. A more advanced, modern version than the S-35 King was flying tonight. Advanced as they were, those F-80s had their hands full. Nazi starfighters were attacking them like clouds of wasps.

King stared, jaw tight. The Nazi starfighters were nasty foes. Quick. Ruthless. King had never seen ships like that before. Their angular design and black hulls reminded him of ravens. The swastikas painted onto their dark wings sickened King.

Several Alliance corvettes (small warships) and one frigate (significantly larger) flew alongside the *Patton* (larger still), assisting her in battle. The enemy surrounded them. Multiple German warships were firing their cannons. The *Patton* and her escorts had activated their missile-defense systems. The Shield of David system had emerged from the fires of the Spider War. Rails ran along modern warship hulls, quickly delivering defensive batteries to the right location. Kim herself had designed the rail system, first installing it on the *Freedom* during the heat of battle. Once in place, Shield of David batteries used artificial intelligence to launch interceptor rockets, lasers, or photon-disruptors, depending on the type of incoming projectile. Right now the system was firing its heaviest defensive rockets. The interceptors took out more of the enemy torpedoes. But some of the Nazi fire still made it through. A corvette exploded, instantly killing a hundred spacers or more aboard.

King forced down the horror.

No horror now. Fight now.

Thousands of melees were raging all around Earth. Some were great showdowns between capital ships, others mere dogfights between starfighters. The violence was everywhere, all combining into the great battle that engulfed the planet. King could have chosen any number of fights to join. But he decided to assist the *Patton.* Easy choice. Ben was there. King raced toward the starfighter carrier, determined to help his brother-in-law.

The enemy finally noticed King. At first, perhaps, they dismissed him as nonthreatening. What *was* he flying? That was an antique! But this antique had missiles on her wings. Specifically, Goldie was carrying David's Stones. Legendary missiles. The missiles that had won the Spider War. King chose a target—a German warship. She was roughly the size of an Alliance corvette, and her name appeared on the hull: *Feuervogel*.

King unleashed two David's Stones.

They streaked forth.

The *Feuervogel* activated her missile-defense system. Lasers shot out, destroying the missiles.

King had expected that. As the missiles exploded in empty space, he flew behind the explosions, hiding his Eagle starfighter.

As the German captain was blinded, as *Feuervogel*'s missile-defense system was still shooting down shrapnel, King dived toward the warship's exhaust and fired his Gatling guns.

Goldie carried two of them, one on each wing. The machine guns spun madly, unleashing a barrage of plasma rounds. The little fireballs entered *Feuervogel*'s exhaust ports, burrowed deeper . . . and detonated the fuel within.

Blasts rocked the German corvette. The exhaust ports shattered. Flames roared through the ship. A few escape pods managed to eject, and then something happened that sickened King. In the throes of death, the burning warship fired. But not at King or other Alliance ships. The *Feuervogel* fired at her own escape pods!

The torpedoes slammed into the rounded pods. They exploded, instantly pulverizing the fleeing German spacers.

King stared in disgust. During the Spider War, he had seen Katyusha fire on fleeing Russian troops. She called them cowards, unworthy of life. Were the Germans killing their own fleeing men due to a similar, twisted notion of honor? Or did they simply not want any Germans taken alive and interrogated? King didn't know. In either case, the sight sickened him.

He flew over the wreckage of the *Feuervogel*. Several German warships still separated him from the *Patton*. Dogfights swirled all around, etching spirals of light. German and American starfighters were buzzing everywhere like two warring hives of bees. As King zigzagged between the dogfights, his MindLink came within peer-to-peer range of a few pilots. The Germans were broadcasting nothing. But King picked up snippets of thoughts from the American fighter pilots.

"It's him!"

"It's the Golden Eagle. From the history books."

"That's James King inside!"

"The bulldog bites again!"

An American starfighter flew so close that King saw the pilot inside. He looked like a kid. The pilots today looked so young. King's MindPlay interface popped up. The hallucination gave him info about the young pilot. Lieutenant Ron Cross. Call sign "Hollywood." All of twenty-four years old, boasting the good looks of a Hollywood star.

"Sir!" Hollywood said. "How did you get past that missile-defense system?"

"An old trick from the Third World War," King said. "They don't teach that one in the books."

It was ironic perhaps. King had fought (and won) the Third World War decades ago. Now it seemed like the Second World War was flaring again—this time in space. He still had no idea how. He didn't need to know to fight. Right now he was no longer an admiral. Not even the commander of a ship. Not even an officer. He was nothing but a weapon now. And as a weapon of war, his only job was to kill.

CHAPTER FOUR
Rats, Ravens, and Mad Dogs

Low Orbit
Earth
September 3, 2207

The FAS *Patton* loomed ahead, a leviathan of space, pride of the Freedom Fleet. She had seen service in the great Spider War, and now she was fighting for her life. Holes gaped open on her hull. Force fields were barely holding in the leaks. Several German warships were bombarding her, and hundreds more fought in the distance. Space flared in every direction with thousands of battles. King flew through the debris, zipping around flying chunks of armor, shattered wings, and a few burnt corpses. He must get closer to the *Patton.* That warship had thousands of spacers aboard. King could not let *Patton* fall!

Not only because she was important to the war effort. Because Ben Fletcher was aboard.

My brother-in-law.

German starfighters came racing toward him. A hundred or more. King's upper lip twitched in a snarl. He was ready for more violence.

Hollywood still flew nearby, following the Golden Eagle through space. The young pilot still seemed in awe of Old Bulldog.

"Sir, watch out for their barrel rolls," Hollywood said. "Those German starfighters are wicked fast. Never seen a design like that. Rattenjägers, we heard the enemy call them."

"Rat hunters," King muttered. "They see us as rats. Let's show them who's the predator and who's the vermin."

"With pleasure!" Hollywood said. More Eagles gathered behind the old admiral and the young lieutenant.

Had Hollywood picked up any intel on this mysterious enemy? King wanted to ask. But right now they only had time to fight.

The Eagles and Rattenjägers flew closer toward each other.

King opened fire, unleashing his Gatling guns' fury.

He hit a Rattenjäger! The dark starfighter shattered, slewed, and slammed into a second Rattenjäger. Both vessels exploded. Two Nazi fighters—wiped out.

King's lip curled, forming something halfway between a snarl and a smile. Yes, a part of him had missed this. Missed the exhilaration, the terror, the terrible violence of battle. It was a drug, and he was still an addict. A part of him was still a killer. He wasn't proud of that part. It was brutal, single-minded, bloodthirsty. But that part of him—the bulldog—could be wielded as a weapon to protect the weak. Yes, King was a savage, a man who could kill without losing sleep, who could gun down his enemies and then enjoy his lunch. But Earth needed men like him. They needed killers on the wall. They needed bulldogs. When you walked down the dark forest path and wolves howled all around you, you wanted a bulldog at your side. Not a mad dog, not a rabid dog—a bulldog, loyal and brave. A dog comforting to his loved ones, terrifying to his foes. And James "Bulldog" King had vowed long ago to show his teeth only to the wolves.

Then the surviving Rattenjägers unleashed their missiles.

King sneered, barrel-rolled, and fired clouds of chaff.

Aluminum confetti fluttered into space. An old trick. All the way back from the Second World War. The modern starships couldn't do it anymore. Not the F-80s like the one Hollywood flew. They all had fancy-schmancy laser defense systems. King liked the old ways. Like a flock of glimmering hummingbirds, the chaff fluttered across space. The metal strips caught the sunlight and blazed like diamonds. It was almost beautiful.

Then the German missiles hit the chaff. The aluminum strips were just sharp and nasty enough to detonate warheads. The missiles exploded in space, blasting out clouds of black, smoky . . . *something.* What the hell *was* that black guck? Both the Nazis' cannons and handguns seemed to fire the stuff.

King would contemplate it later. Right now he was busy holding the yoke to his chest, soaring.

The Golden Eagle shot up in a straight line, hidden behind the dark clouds. Then, reaching her zenith, Goldie flipped. The starfighter swooped toward her foes, the sun at her back, firing her Gatling guns.

Below him, King saw the Rattenjägers. He saw the pilots inside, staring at him with bionic eyes. And below them, he saw his beloved Earth, so close she hid half the stars behind her. Her cities were burning. Mushroom clouds were rising from the surface. King saw his foes and what they had done. He looked those killers in the eyes . . . and made them his prey.

His Gatling guns roared. Plasma bolts slammed into one Rattenjäger, igniting its ammunition bays. The German starfighter exploded in a sphere of light and debris.

King grinned savagely. A kill!

He unleashed another David's Stone. The missile raced around a Rattenjäger, swerved, and slipped into the German starfighter's exhaust port. Another explosion lit space. Debris hurtled into the distance or crashed down to Earth, burning up in the sky.

King breathed heavily.

"Gotcha, you son of a bitch," he hissed, clenching his

metal fist.

An old familiar feeling crept through him. Bloodlust. Yes, that was a part of him too. Perhaps of every soldier. King wasn't proud of it. His bloodlust was an ugly part of him. But right now he let that red poison flow through him. He did not fear killing in this state. No—he lusted for it! He *relished* it. And when he killed, he celebrated.

No, not a part of himself King was proud of. But tonight that shameful animal let loose. Tonight the bulldog was a predator.

The enemy's smoky rounds flew toward him. King pitched, rolled, and yawed. He soared, swooped, and dodged the dark blobs. For a moment, he felt some hope. He was dodging everything they threw at him!

But then it got harder. Then the Rattenjägers fired heat-seeking missiles. Those were more serious beasts. The crimson projectiles caught King's scent and followed, as dogged as sharks following a bleeding whale. King zigzagged through the battlefield, but the enemy missiles kept stalking him, moving closer.

An idea struck him. King imagined the pursuing missiles as tin cans tied to his stern, dangling behind him. Yes, that was an intuitive way for him to grok the physics. King shoved the yoke. The Golden Eagle spun madly, slipping through the Rattenjägers' formation. Just then, King jerked the yoke madly, slinging the heat-seeking missiles (just like cans on a string) into the very Rattenjägers who had fired them.

He flew onward through the blasts, a savage grin tugging at his lips. His engine pulsed, etching blue streaks through space. Sparkling chaff fluttered around his wings, wreathing his antique starfighter in silver and gold.

"There he flies," whispered Hollywood. "Admiral James King."

"Commander of the starship *Freedom*," whispered another pilot.

"The bulldog himself."

King only caught snippets of their thoughts as he flew by their MindLinks. The other Eagles gathered closer behind him. All were the newer, modern Eagles, machines decades farther along the technological curve. Faster, stronger, their computers far more sophisticated. Compared to those state-of-the-art starfighters, the Golden Eagle was a rickety old soapbox racer. Well, he had won two wars in this soapbox. And King would make damn sure he won this one too.

"To James King!" cried Hollywood. "Rally around Admiral King!"

Together, the Eagles charged, firing their weapons at the enemy. And not just Eagles. Alliance corvettes joined the charge, cannons booming, bombarding the Rattenjägers. Together the brave pilots stormed into the Nazi horde, casting back the shadows of their past.

*****

Farther back from the Eagle charge, the FAS *Patton* was trapped between three enemy frigates. The big American ship stood alone against the German trio. In the distance, the rest of the battle spread like flaming stars in a collapsing galaxy.

King kept flying toward the beleaguered FAS *Patton.*

Ben, I'm coming.

Ben Fletcher was one of the finest officers—indeed, the finest men—King had the honor of knowing. The two had spent many hours on the porch, sipping beer while discussing philosophy, history, and science. Or sometimes just playing cards. Sometimes just listening to the crickets and distant memories. Now Ben was in trouble.

And it wasn't just Ben. It was thousands of other spacers aboard the *Patton.* King knew most of *Patton*'s officers by name. Many of the enlisted too. Some had served aboard the *Freedom* under his direct command.

In his long career, King had learned that a commander must send troops into danger. That sometimes those troops would die. But dammit, he still cared about every soldier in the Freedom Fleet. Even now, as a civilian, he cared for those he had mentored. Those who wore the uniform. Those who stood and fought to protect their families, to protect humanity.

We are the warriors on the wall, King thought. *We are brothers.*

"I'm coming to help, Ben," King whispered.

The Eagles blew more Rattenjägers aside, carving a path toward the FAS *Patton.*

A German frigate—a gargantuan machine of war—noticed the approaching Eagles. The warship yawed, bringing her cannons to bear on the Eagle formation.

The cannons boomed.

Shock waves of energy blasted out from the bores. Torpedoes streaked forth, etching white-hot lines across space. An Eagle exploded beside King. A second later, a torpedo slammed into an Alliance corvette. The starship burst apart, spilling out dead spacers.

Horror pulsed through King. He would grieve later. Those deaths would carve through his soul—*later.* Right now he must fight!

He stared at the German frigate that had killed so many Alliance spacers. Black armored plates covered her hull. Her eight prow cannons blazed red like spider eyes. Her name gleamed upon her, each letter larger than a house. Here flew the *Oldenburg*, a terror of space adorned with golden swastikas. She reminded King of an old ship of the seas rising, dripping foam and algae, to fight among the stars.

In his beat-up little starfighter, King charged onward through the battle. He must get closer to *Patton* and the other Alliance warships. Enemy missiles flew all around. It was all King could do to dodge them. Modern Eagles had computer software for dodging enemy projectiles. Human instincts were too slow, the engineers claimed. You needed the computer software to see incoming missiles and move the yoke for you, nudging your ship out of harm's way.

The software didn't work well, if you asked King. At close range, torpedoes were just too damn fast. Even for AI to avoid. At long range, the software had time to calculate vectors, yes, and it could move your starfighter for you, dodging enemy fire. But good luck scoring any hits of your own. From a distance, if you could dodge the blows, so could your enemy. And what was the point of that?

No, for battle, for *real* battle, you had to get *close*. Close enough to stare your enemy in the eyes through the cockpit. Close enough that software broke down. That was how they had done things in the old days. That was how King still fought. He relied on instinct. He sensed where the enemy would fire. He zipped around torpedoes before they were even launched. Rolling, spinning, he swerved around exploding starfighters and torpedoes, heading closer to the *Oldenburg*. The German frigate loomed above the battle like a mother spider overseeing her spiderlings.

Another Eagle exploded behind King. Another pilot—an American pilot—lost. Another young man, his whole life ahead of him—gone.

King raced closer and fired more David's Stones.

His missiles made it through! They slammed into the *Oldenburg*!

Explosions rocked the German frigate, shattering three cannons, ripping off armor plating, and punching a hole through the port beam. Around King, the younger American pilots cheered.

A few flickers of MindWeb suddenly floated in King's cockpit. The system was coming back online! King hallucinated some stats about the *Oldenburg*; the figures seemed to float above the enemy ship. The *Oldenburg*, he learned, was five hundred feet long, seventy-five feet wide, powered by a fusion core, and boasted twenty-four cannons spread across her starboard, port, and prow. No guns on the stern. This ship was not designed to flee.

"Eagles—fire!" King cried.

The starfighters charged at the *Oldenburg*, hurling David's Stones. Blasts hit the German warship, ripping through the hull. Fire spread through the frigate, and then fresh blasts hit her. *Oldenburg*'s core caught fire, and then the entire frigate burst. White light flooded the battle. A shock wave of energy blasted outward, thick with debris.

Hope flared in King. The telepathic network flickered, died a moment, then came back online again. Cheers flowed over MindWeb. They were chanting his name.

* * * * *

The *Oldenburg* was down. But two more German frigates still flew nearby—the *Weserübung* and the *Doppelschlag*. Both were busy battling the *Patton*.

"We can take them," King told his pilots. "Eagles, fly with me toward *Weserübung*. Corvettes of the Alliance, you take on the *Doppelschlag*."

A voice crackled. A hallucinatory screen came to life, showing the flickering image of a man in uniform. A blue uniform, though charred, tattered, and dusty. An Alliance uniform.

Ben! It was Commander Ben Fletcher!

"Jim?" Ben squinted and rubbed his eyes. "Jim, is that really you? In a *starfighter*?" He blinked. "Is that the *Golden Eagle*?"

Commander Ben Fletcher looked a little worse for wear. A cut bled along his cheek, and his eyebrows were singed, but he still stood straight, still in command of his warship.

King nodded. "It's me, Ben. Your very own brother-in-law. Where the hell did these Nazi bastards come from?"

"Darned if I know," Ben replied. "One moment I was getting ready to visit your ranch for dinner. I was looking forward to those ribs. Next thing you know, it's World War II all over again."

MindWeb revealed glimpses of Ben's surroundings. He stood on *Patton*'s bridge. Smoke wafted from several shattered control panels while red strobe lights flashed.

"They attacked Alpha Centauri first," the ragged commander continued. "Came out of some kinda wormhole. We got a strange warning from Toliman Space Station, then a few moments later—bang. The enemy was suddenly here. Hundreds of those warships."

"We'll let the eggheads figure it out later," King said. "For now, you and I do what we do best. Fight. We'll pin those two German frigates between us. Watch out for friendly fire, and—"

"Jim, there's a German destroyer rising below you!" Ben said.

King glanced at his tracking screens. His chest tightened. "I see her."

MindPlay identified the new arrival as the *Munich Massacre*. She was a big one. From stern to stem, the German destroyer was a thousand feet long. Not quite as large as the *Patton*. Certainly not as large as the *Barbarossa*, that monstrosity King had seen when first rising into space. But *Munich Massacre* was large enough to carry Rattenjägers in her belly. Like a mother fish releasing her offspring from her mouth, the *Munich Massacre* opened her airlocks and spewed the Nazi starfighters.

Where was the *Barbarossa*, for that matter? King scanned space, seeking the behemoth. But *Barbarossa* must be flying on the other side of Earth now. King had only glimpsed her briefly when soaring into the battle. He must have misjudged her size. Truly no warship could be that large. Unless his eyes had tricked him, *Barbarossa* was twice the length (and maybe ten times the mass) of the legendary starship *Freedom*, the largest ship ever built! Surely, in the chaos of battle, King had mistook a dreadnought for something bigger. Something that didn't even have a name.

Well, he would worry about that later. Right now he must deal with the *Munich Massacre*. The Nazi destroyer was bringing her cannons to bear on the Alliance starfighters.

"Eagles, evasive flight!" King cried.

Munich Massacre fired her guns. Streaks of blazing-white energy sliced through space. Torpedoes slammed into several F-80 Eagles, destroying the modern starfighters. Debris pattered the Golden Eagle. King's antique starfighter hurtled through space. He wrestled with the yoke, unable to steady his flight. Another torpedo flew. Desperately King fired his Gatling gun. He destroyed the torpedo only a few klicks away. The blast knocked him back in space. Debris slammed into his hull. Chunks of Goldie's fuselage ripped off, and King found himself spinning out of control.

Was this it? Would he, like thousands of others, die in the great blitzkrieg of 2207? After surviving two long, bloody wars, would he die on the first day of this new one?

I'm too old for this, he thought as his ship spun. *I can't fly like I used to.*

Another German ship was racing toward him. One of the Wolfjägers—those bulky, armored dropships. When King had seen one by his cabin, the Wolfjäger had seemed massive. It was as large as his home. Up here in space, where titans battled, the Wolfjägers seemed tiny, a honey badger racing toward battling elephants. The *Munich Massacre* (one of those elephants) spun slowly in space, bombarding the Alliance ships, while the two German frigates kept pummeling the *Patton.* Meanwhile, that Wolfjäger flew closer, closer, a predator on the prowl.

Then the little Wolfjäger opened fire.

Its missiles flew . . . and slammed into *Munich Massacre*'s exhaust ports.

Explosions rocked the German destroyer. The Wolfjäger fired again and again, bombarding the exposed ports, until *Munich*'s core caught fire.

The huge war machine burst open, scattering debris everywhere.

King regained control of his bird. He flew madly, swerving around debris. Chunks of metal hit one wing, shattering it. King tumbled, but once more, he quickly gained his bearings. His fuselage was cracked open, leaking air and fuel. His cockpit was losing pressure, and in response, his spacesuit *whuffed* and clung to his body like Saran wrap. With a confident hand, King connected his helmet to his oxygen tank, took a deep breath of his backup air, and kept flying.

Commander Larry Jordan appeared on a MindPlay screen. The white-haired man grinned from inside his commandeered Wolfjäger. "You seemed like you needed some help, old man."

"I was doing fine," King growled.

"Sure." Jordan nodded. "Just like you were doing fine that time raiding Katyusha's Siberian missile facility. I had to fly in then too to save your ass."

King snarled. "I was just about to blow that facility to kingdom come and you know it!" He took a deep breath. "But thank you, Phantom." He sent out an urgent MindWeb message to all nearby Alliance ships. "Do not fire on that Wolfjäger! It's one of ours."

He took another deep breath, letting the terror sizzle through him and burn away. Thank goodness for his old friend.

*****

With his starfighter once more flying steadily, King surveyed the battle. MindWeb was still on the fritz. King couldn't get a good picture of the entire battle; it seemed to surround the planet. Thousands of warships swirled around Earth, battling above every ocean and continent. Countless starfighters were dogfighting from low orbit (right above the atmosphere) to high orbit (as far as halfway to the moon). Could this be some trick of Katyusha? Had she disguised her Red Fleet as Nazi warships? Was she attacking the Alliance under fake flags?

No! King finally saw them. Red Dawn ships! Katyusha's fleet was fighting the Germans too. Fighting alongside the Alliance. These really *were* Nazi warships. From another universe perhaps. Or from another world where they had lived unseen for centuries. Well, King would figure things out later. Right now he would focus on killing Nazis.

Ben needed help. Both the *Weserübung* and the *Doppelschlag* were still bombarding the *Patton*. King must destroy those two German warships.

Jordan still flew alongside Goldie in his commandeered Wolfjäger. King sent his friend a telepathic message.

"Phantom, let's take out these German frigates, secure the *Patton*, and take things from there."

"All right, Bulldog, we'll play it by ear," Jordan said. On the ground, they usually referred to each other by their given names. Up here in space? They slipped right back into using their call signs. Just like the old days.

King widened his telepathic broadcast to include all

nearby Alliance ships. "All Eagles and corvettes—rally here!"

Of course, he shouldn't be giving out orders. He was retired. A civilian. But the name James "Bulldog" King still held some cachet. The pilots' formations had shattered. Their wing commanders were dead. And so Hollywood and the other young pilots—they rallied behind James King. The old bulldog. To them, he was a war hero. They didn't know about the fear in his heart.

For a brief moment, no missiles were flying at King. He glanced down toward Earth. Explosions still blazed against the surface. Mushroom clouds rose where cities had once stood. The bombardment of Earth was a vision from hell. Smoke unfurled from the surface, hiding entire nations.

My son is down there, King thought. *My grandchildren are down there. My wife is there.*

Again fury filled him. He blazed toward the enemy, guns booming, pummeling the Nazi frigates.

Under the barrage of furious Eagles, the *Weserübung* exploded. Meanwhile, good old Ben Fletcher was giving one hell of a fight. The *Patton* pounded *Doppelschlag* with brutal rakish fire, and that German ship too burst apart and crashed down to Earth's burning sky.

The pilots cheered.

Two more frigates—gone!

King took a deep breath. He allowed himself to slump in his seat. Ah, damn. His old bones were hurting again.

"All right, Ben," King said, sending a telepathic message toward the *Patton.* "We got some of the bastards off your back for now."

Commander Benjamin Fletcher reappeared on MindWeb. A small hallucination of the man stood inside King's cockpit. "Thanks, Jim. I owe you one. I recommend we make our way toward the FAS *Hughes*. We must reform the defensive flank of the Fifth Fleet. I'll send out a shuttle and bring you aboard."

King shook his head. "I'm more use out here in a starfighter."

Ben smiled thinly. "Still a fighter down to the bone, huh, Jim? But I need you on my bridge. Our fleet is falling apart and . . ."

Ben's voice trailed off.

The sunlight dimmed.

A huge ship was rising over Earth's horizon, blocking the sun, casting a shadow across the planet.

A ship? No, it was too big to be a ship. Yet there thrust out his cannons. There loomed the double-headed eagle upon his prow. There on his hull did the swastikas mock the burning free world. And, when his stern rose above the horizon, his engines blazed red, bathing the battle with light.

Here flew the *Barbarossa.* Flagship of the Weltraumwaffe.

He was even larger than King remembered. An impossible ship. A flying city. This ship made his beloved *Freedom*, the great dreadnought that had shattered a star, seem small.

Barbarossa aimed his mighty prow cannons. Those bores were the size of skyscrapers. They were so wide King could have flown his starfighter inside. When they fired, no light came out. No blinding flash of energy seared through space. Those guns fired silently, and darkness fell. A black cloak spread over the battle, darkened the sky, and blotted out the stars. Streaks of black, smoky death scuttled through the murk, angels of death riding through the storm.

The astral torpedoes flew toward the FAS *Patton*, slammed into her hull, and plowed through her innards like dark swords through flesh.

"Ben!" King cried.

God. God, no.

Explosions blazed across the mighty starfighter carrier.

Black smoke seeped from the *Patton*. Her engines caught fire. Her stern crumpled, cracked, and belched out radiation.

From the inferno, over MindWeb, rose Ben Fletcher's cry.

"Jim, get outta here!" Ben cried. "Our core is collapsing!"

Terror clutched King. Terror for his brother-in-law. For everyone else aboard the capital ship.

Already, every other starship nearby—both American and German—was fleeing the *Patton*. The starfighter carrier had become a time bomb. She was cracking open, exposing her leaking innards of molten energy. Any moment now, *Patton*'s core would go nova. For all intents and purposes, the FAS *Patton* was now a nuclear weapon. One about to blow.

"Jettison the ship, Ben!" King cried from his cockpit. "Dammit, Ben, get into an escape pod!"

Ben's hallucination flickered back to life inside the Golden Eagle's cockpit. Flames surrounded him. He gave King a salute.

"Win this war, Jim. For Kim. For all of us. Win th—"

The *Patton*'s core exploded.

The entire ship shattered as if made of glass.

The blast slammed into King, cracked his cockpit, pounded his helmet and chest . . .

. . . and he was falling . . .

. . . falling and falling through the murk, spinning, flipping, and crashing down toward the burning sky of Earth.

*****

Somewhere over the Yukon
Earth
September 3, 2207

The Golden Eagle plunged through the night sky, a bird with one wing.

To a distant observer, her fall might appear graceful, beautiful even in its tragedy, like a dying firefly still lighting the night as it glided to the snowy ground. And like that firefly, the Golden Eagle etched a trail of light through the darkness. The flames of atmospheric entry gilded her. In her dying throes, the starfighter shone with anguished grace.

Three shadows swooped through the sky, following the luminous, one-winged bird.

They too were starfighters. But not Eagles. Not American vessels. And there was nothing beautiful about them. They looked like dark ravens, eyes blazing red, twisted things that heralded death. But unlike true ravens, they were not scavengers. They were birds of prey. They were three Rattenjägers, the starfighters of the Weltraumwaffe. And they were on King's tail. Three black birds, eyes red, following a falling bird with one wing—a distant observer would view a tableau of dark beauty.

As he fell through the dark sky, strapped into the Golden Eagle, King found nothing of his descent graceful or beautiful, regardless of how it might appear to a distant observer. In here, the alarms wailed. Air roared through cracks in the hull. King's bones rattled in his body, ready to crack like his fuselage. He wrestled with the yoke, trying to control his fall. The engine was still working. He could still fight, dammit! But Goldie was missing her wing. Missing her canopy. Too much of her had burned up. She was going down.

Ben is gone, King thought. *The rest of my family might be gone too. Millions of lives are gone.*

And so he must live.

He must! To save those who still needed him. To avenge those who had fallen. The enemy had awoken something inside him. Something old and dangerous. They had stoked a dying ember into a flame. King would not let that flame die tonight.

His starfighter had lost one wing. But the remaining wing

still carried weaponry.

The Eagle fell, prow pointing downward, leaving a trail of fire. The three shadows pursued from above. King saw them reflected in what remained of his canopy. The Rattenjägers.

They opened fire.

King tugged the yoke.

Even as she fell, the Golden Eagle's exhaust ports blasted out flame, and her starboard thrusters blazed. Etching a semicircle of fire, the starfighter flipped over and faced the sky.

King opened fire.

His one remaining wing rattled as its Gatling gun fired. Bullets slammed into one of the diving Rattenjägers, shattered the cockpit, and plowed into the pilot inside. The man slumped over his yoke, his skull-shaped helmet cracked and leaking blood. His dark starfighter careened into the distance, etching a trail of red flames in the night sky.

That left two. The rat hunters kept swooping. Far above, the battle in space still flared, painting the night sky with red and black explosions like watercolor stains. But right now King's entire battle was here in the atmosphere. Against those two Rattenjägers.

And he didn't have much time. The ground was racing up toward King.

He sneered and pulled the trigger again. His Gatling gun shot out a handful of bullets . . . then fell silent.

He was out of ammo.

"Goddammit!" he blurted.

With that final burst, he had hit one Rattenjäger, perforating its fuselage. Not enough to cause serious damage. Both German starfighters kept chasing him, swooping after the Golden Eagle. And King's beloved starfighter tumbled again.

King cursed, grabbed the yoke, and tried to steady Goldie's flight. The engine was sputtering.

The two Rattenjägers opened fire. King shoved a lever. A blast of afterburner jolted the Golden Eagle across the sky. Once more, the starfighter began spinning. Without both wings, King just couldn't keep steady. He wrestled with the yoke, slowing his spin, and drew his handgun.

Bullets streaked down toward him.

King gave another burst of afterburner, dodging the assault. Goldie skittered across the air, and King aimed his handgun above. It was his trusty Trogdor.

One of the Rattenjägers was right above him. King could see the pilot inside the cockpit.

As Goldie streaked below the German starfighter, King fired his handgun.

A plasma bolt flew, slammed into the enemy starfighter, and tore through the German pilot. The Rattenjäger caught fire and tumbled into the night.

King exhaled in relief. Good!

That left one Rattenjäger. Better odds.

The starfighter raced through the night sky, chasing King's skittering Eagle. Inside the cockpit, the German pilot had a helmet like a metallic skull, one eye blazing red. He was a better pilot than the others. He barely seemed human. More like a robotic skeleton, undead and eternally hunting, forever hungry for flesh. The Rattenjäger's guns howled. Those strange, dark rounds sailed through the night.

The blasts hit the Golden Eagle.

The exhaust ports shattered. Dark fire raced through the fuselage. The starfighter tilted downward, falling and spinning toward the ground.

King cursed, grabbed an emergency handle, and tugged with all his might.

His seat burst from the cockpit, ejecting him into the night.

King tumbled through the air, head spinning, bones rattling. He grabbed a string and pulled. His parachute burst out.

The wind caught him.

The Rattenjäger was diving too fast to stop. The German starfighter kept flying downward, leaving King and his parachute high above. Seconds away from hitting the ground, the Rattenjäger flipped around and soared, rising toward King.

Hanging there from his parachute, King fired his plasma gun.

His blast slammed into the rising Rattenjäger, shattering the cockpit, then hitting the fuel tank on the underbelly.

The Rattenjäger burst into flame. The canopy shattered. The pilot inside screamed and ejected too. And suddenly, bizarrely, both men were parachuting side by side.

Normally, King might have found the moment humorous. He might have even laughed, something he did rarely. But tonight, as he glided down, he aimed his gun at the German pilot gliding beside him.

The German drew his sidearm too.

King pulled the trigger.

Nothing. His Trogdor was out of ammo too.

Damn it all to hell! He was getting sloppy in his old age. Quickly he reached for his Peacemaker revolver.

As he was drawing the antique gun, he realized something. The German pilot could have shot him by now. But instead, the German raised his visor. He was a young man. Not even thirty. He had one blue eye, one bionic one. Both those eyes widened.

"You!" he whispered. He blinked and rubbed his eyes. "It . . . it *is* you!" He raised his hand in salute. "The führer! Hail K—"

King fired.

A bullet slammed into the young pilot's forehead.

There was no honor to such a killing. King knew that. It went against the rules of war. Against his own moral code. To kill a man, to take a life so young . . . But tonight something had changed in King. Tonight the animal in him had awoken. They called him the bulldog. But tonight he felt more like a mad dog, not an honorable hound but a wild, savage thing.

He landed on icy ground in the darkness. A moment later, the corpse of the young pilot landed nearby. Just a damn kid. The German's parachute fluttered in the wind, making a sound like a wounded animal, and King wiped blood off his lips.

CHAPTER FIVE
Two Steps from Darkness

The Fatherworld
(Once known as Earth)
Nazi Galactic Empire
Before the invasion

Samantha "Stowy" Perry should be dead, and she knew it. She was one of the impure. A cripple. A subhuman. A parasite that must be purged to maintain the purity of the race. And yet, against all odds, she lived. She was thirteen years old and the bastards hadn't killed her yet.

"We're going to escape this place, Luna," she whispered to her blanket. "This entire universe. We're going somewhere that's good."

Sitting in the corner, she cuddled Luna to her chest. The blanket was old and worn, tattered at spots. But Stowy would never give her up. Luna wasn't just a blanket. She was her best friend. Someone who comforted her in the night. Someone Stowy could mumble her thoughts to. Luna was the *only* one she could talk to.

Talking. Other people took it for granted. For Stowy, it was a miracle. When she tried talking to anyone but Luna, she simply . . . clamped up. The words would not come out. She would try—oh, how hard she would try! With all her willpower, she'd order her mouth to form the syllables, to utter the words.

Just to speak! Something so simple! She knew how to do it. She whispered to Luna all the time! But if anyone else was facing her—any human, with their piercing eyes, with their powerful fists, with their mocking sneers . . .

Every time, the terror would overwhelm her. And she'd clamp up. Become mute.

She had never even talked to her parents. Not until the day they had died. The first time Stowy had spoken to her mother and father, she had spoken to corpses.

And yet, when hiding alone in the attic, or the sewers, or the ducts, or any of the other places where an impure orphan made her home . . . she could cuddle Luna to her chest, weep onto her soft fabric, and spill out all the words in her soul.

"Luna, I'm scared. Luna, I love you. Luna, we'll find a castle on the clouds."

Sometimes at night, shuddering behind pipes or huddling in trash bins, Stowy would dream of that castle on the clouds. In her dreams, Stowy would peer upward. Up past the skyscrapers draped with banners of the Eternal Führer. Up past the zeppelins with swastikas on their fins. Up past the starships of the Weltraumwaffe with their bionic officers and terrible guns. Up and up, away from the Fatherworld, away from the cruelty of the Aryan race, all the way beyond the reach of the führer . . .

And there it shone. A castle on the clouds. It was silly perhaps. There shouldn't be any clouds in deep space. Yet in Stowy's dreams, clouds floated among the stars—a vastness of clouds clumped together, forming a landscape. Atop this field of clouds rose a castle with hundreds of towers, all shimmering like mother-of-pearl. A castle the size of a city. Of a world. It was a place where the men with skull faces did not chase her. Where she was made pure. Where she could talk.

"We'll find it someday, Luna," she whispered, huddling in some forgotten alley in the slums, trembling in the rain. "Our castle on the clouds."

How many years had it been now? Since Mother and Father had died? Stowy didn't know. It seemed years ago, a different life. Sometimes she almost forgot their faces.

She didn't remember much of her early childhood. Back then, she had lived in a house. She remembered the house. Remembered the lush, beige carpet where she would sit for hours, lining up her toy dinosaurs. Again and again, she would line them up. Her parents offered her toy cars, little plastic ponies, even sweets. But Stowy would sit there all day, lining up dinosaurs. If somebody offered her a toy shaped like a modern animal—a lion, say, or a giraffe—she would shove it aside, then go back to dinosaurs.

"Why won't she talk to us?" Mother said, voice muffled through the fog of memory.

"She'll talk in time," Father said. "Don't worry."

"But if she—"

"She's not mute!" Father said. "You heard her whispering to her blanket last night. She's not impure. She can talk."

"So why won't she talk to us?" Mother pleaded.

Both figures were so fuzzy in her memory. Their faces were but a blur. They seemed so tall. Stowy was sitting on that beige carpet, aware of them. But not looking at them.

"Bob, she won't even look at us," Mother said. "She doesn't make eye contact. She doesn't talk. If they find out—"

"She's not impure!" Father roared. "Maybe with all your yammering, she just can't get a word in edgewise!"

She remembered herself a little older. A girl of four or five. Going to kindergarten.

"Why won't she talk?" the teacher said, eyes narrowed and dangerous.

Mother smiled apologetically. "She's just shy."

That day in kindergarten, Stowy sat in the corner, staring

at her lap, lining up toy dinosaurs. Others approached her. Other kids. The kindergarten teacher. She ignored them. Just shy. Not . . . the other thing. Not the *A-word.*

She wasn't sure when she first heard that word. Age seven? Eight? That night, listening through the narrow wall, Stowy heard her parents speaking in the living room. She heard that word for the first time. What she was. Why she was different. Why she was doomed.

"Bob," Mother said. "Bob, listen to me. We can't deny it any longer. She's autistic."

Father's voice broke. "I know. We must keep it secret. If they find out . . ."

Stowy peered through the keyhole to see her parents embracing. They were crying.

"We'll keep it a secret, Bob," Mother said. "We'll keep her safe. I love you."

That night, Stowy sat in the corner, stunned.

Autistic.

She was autistic! That explained everything! Joy leaped in her. She wasn't a mystery anymore. There was a reason for her eccentricities. She was autistic!

She scratched her head. What the hell did *autistic* mean?

After her parents fell asleep, Stowy crept through the house, moving from shadow to shadow. When you were autistic, you learned early how to sneak around and hide. Well, maybe not. Stowy had no idea. But she was already feeling such an affinity toward this secretive club of autistics. Her people. Were there many others? Were they also mute? Did they too have blankets?

Whether it was due to her autism or not, she had always been good at hiding. Under her bed. In her closet. Father would joke that she was haunting the ghost in her room. Sometimes Stowy would hide in his shuttle. He would fly all the way to work in space, and once he got to his asteroids, Stowy would pop up from under the shuttle seat.

"My little stowaway," he would call her. "My little Stowy."

Tonight she sneaked into the den, a dusty little room where Father came to read and think. Stowy tiptoed toward Father's bookshelf. Most of the books were in German. It was the language they were all supposed to use. But a few contraband books, tucked away behind a hidden shelf, were in English.

Father had explained it once. The Perry family lived in a province named Canada. Centuries ago, Father believed, Canada had been a colony of a now-extinct empire called Britain, not of Germany.

"Back then, we wrote English books and spoke English at home," he had whispered in German. "But don't tell anyone. Not a word. Or they'll hurt us."

Stowy pretended to zip shut her lips, lock them shut, then throw away an invisible key. Not a word. Father laughed and mussed her messy light brown hair.

She was good with languages. She could not speak, perhaps, but she could read fluently in both German, the pure language, and English, the forbidden language of the past. That night, the night she learned the word *autism*, Stowy pulled two books from the shelf. Two medical books. One written in English from Old Canada. The other written in modern times, a work in German.

Stowy opened the English book first. She flipped the pages until she reached a definition of autism. She read the first paragraph.

Autism, also called autism spectrum disorder, is a neurodevelopmental disorder marked by deficits in reciprocal social communication and the presence of restricted and repetitive patterns of behavior.

She reached the German book, an imposing tome bound in human skin. Real human skin, father had said. The title was stitched onto the cover: *THE AKTION T4 GUIDE TO IMPURITIES.*

Stowy touched the skin cover and shuddered. She opened the book and looked up autism.

A crippling condition manifesting in weakness of the mind. Autistic patients are deemed impure. Treatment: Euthanasia.

Well, that didn't sound too good. Stowy slammed the book shut and gulped.

She remembered what had happened to little Adolf next door. (About half the boys in the Fatherworld were named Adolf, it seemed to Stowy.) This particular Adolf, the pasty boy next door, had been born with six fingers on his left hand. His parents had hidden the deformity for years. Until little Adolf, insisting he was not cold, tossed off his mittens in the playground. Well, that was that for pasty little Adolf. The next day, he didn't show up at the playground.

"Euthanized," Adolf's father had explained over the garden fence that evening. "My little Dolfie—burned to a crisp. Always figured it would come to that. Poor little bugger. Should have chopped off the extra finger myself when he was born. Didn't have the heart to do it. Now he's been euthanized. Just like the Eichmann's kid down the road, the one who had dark eyes. What a shame."

"It's in service of the Aryan race!" Adolf's mother insisted, eyes flashing. "It's an honor to purge the world of our impurity."

Adolf's father bristled. "Darling, it's your own son!"

"And he was impure. We did our part to purify the Aryan race. I'm proud."

But the next day, when the Gestapo arrived to escort little Adolf's parents away, the proud woman wept.

Yes, impurity had struck the Eichmann family, cursing them with a boy with black eyes. And it had struck little Adolf with his extra finger. And now the curse had moved down the road to the Perry family. That strange family that kept their old

English surname. That kept English books hidden in their house. Whose kid was *autistic.*

The next day at school (Was it the third grade? Or the fourth?) that word kept prowling Stowy's mind.

Autistic.

She was autistic.

The teacher was saying something. Stowy just sat there at her desk in the back, silent as always, clutching her blanket. Autistic. Autistic . . .

There were others. Surely there must be others. Kids who couldn't make eye contact. Who couldn't talk. Who lined up dinosaurs and befriended blankets. Kids who'd understand her. Maybe kids she could talk to like she talked to Luna.

"Samantha Perry!" the teacher roared. "Are you paying attention?"

Everyone turned to stare at Stowy. Thirty pupils stared (if you meant the students). Sixty pupils (if you meant the pupils in your eyes). Stowy liked wordplay like that. She would whisper that pun to Luna tonight when it was safe to speak.

"Ms. Perry!" shouted the teacher. She was a matronly woman with powerful arms and stern blue eyes. "Are you dozing off again? Come to the front of your class and hold out your hand!"

Stowy obeyed. She stepped to the front of the class and held out her hand. The palm was already scarred from yesterday's blows.

Smack! Smack! The teacher landed her ruler on Stowy's hand. Over and over. *Smack! Smack!* More welts. Even some blood this time. And Stowy did not make a sound. The pain blazed inside her, and tears budded in her eyes, but not a single whimper fled her lips. The teacher beat her harder, trying to get Stowy to scream. But even in this agony, she could not make a sound.

She returned to her seat at the back of the class. The pupils stared at her. A few students snickered.

"Today," the teacher said, "we shall learn about Aktion T4, the great program to purify the Fatherworld." The teacher paced, twirling her bloodstained ruler, making little whooshing sounds in the air. "Back in 1940, Adolf Hitler, the Eternal Führer, launched the program to purify our race of the broken, the crippled, and the inferior."

"Hail Hitler!" cried the students. As one did whenever the Eternal Führer was mentioned. Stowy raised her bleeding hand in salute too, and she mouthed the words along. Like this, nobody knew she wasn't speaking.

She glanced to the two portraits that hung on the classroom wall. One portrait of Adolf Hitler—the god, the founder and eternal ruler of the Third Reich. And beside him—the current living führer, Helmut König. There was always one eternal leader and one current leader. One founder and one steward. One god and one demigod. Both photos scared Stowy. One man in black and white, his mustache small, his beady eyes boring into her. And one man in color, his mustache large and thick, his red bionic eye seeming to stare even from the portrait. It was said that the Gestapo stared through the bionic eyes in his portraits.

The teacher spoke on. About how, in the old days, Hitler had purified the world of undesirables. Of cripples. Of perverts. Of the lower races. But today, in the age of spaceflight, radiation was bringing more impurities to the Aryan race. They must all remain aware, seeking cripples, and report them to the Gestapo.

To be euthanized, Stowy thought. *Like the boys next door. Burned to a crisp.*

But that was for cripples, wasn't it? The impure. The book must have been wrong. How could Stowy be impure? Oh, she knew she wasn't perfect. Her eyes were only hazel, not quite blue.

Her hair was only light brown, not quite blond. But impure? She didn't look *too* far off from the Aryan standard. She was funny-looking maybe, but that wasn't the same as impure.

Her grandmother had even called her pretty once. "The face of an angel!" Granny had said. "If only she could talk. If only she could look you in the eyes. If only she stopped lining up those toy dinosaurs. The girl can sit there for hours with those dinosaurs . . ."

Stowy didn't think she had the face of an angel. The other kids at school called her ugly. She had, as an aunt once described it, an "impish" face. Her mouth was too wide, Stowy thought, her chin too small, her nose pugged. And her ears stuck out from her head. Like monkey ears, a boy had once told her. A doctor had once suspected that Stowy had Williams syndrome. They had even tested her for genetic abnormalities.

Nope. Not Williams syndrome. Just Stowy. An autistic girl with a weird brain and a funny face.

So Stowy kept that face covered most times, hiding it behind strands of her hair. Her ears still stuck out; not much she could do about that. At least her "impish face" remained hidden. She walked with her head lowered, her hair a mask, her eyes staring at her toes. That was how she walked around the concrete yard at recess that day. Just circling the yard, head lowered, searching for bugs on the ground. She liked bugs. If they were fast enough, they could run and hide and nobody would hurt them.

"Hey, weirdo." A boy shoved her. "Out of my way."

She glanced up between strands of her hair. It was Adolf. From her classroom. (It was yet another Adolf, not the euthanized one with six fingers. Several more Adolfs were playing a game of "Catch the Cripple" nearby. It involved chasing a cat with bound legs, pretending it was impure like Stowy, and beating it to death with rocks.)

Clutching her blanket, Stowy took a few steps away. It

was best not to fight. You survived by remaining hidden. By keeping your eyes lowered. By *not talking*.

"Hey, weirdo." Young Adolf grabbed her. "I'm talking to you."

Stowy turned around. But the boy was merciless. He grabbed her blanket. He pulled beloved Luna from her hands. And he tossed the blanket to his friend. Stowy ran from child to child, but they only laughed, tossed the blanket around, and shoved her to the ground. Finally they dropped Luna into the mud and stomped on her.

"You're a freak," a boy said. He spat on Stowy.

"You're a cripple," said a girl.

They surrounded her, laughing, kicking, spitting.

"You're impure!" Another kick.

"You're a Gypsy." Another punch.

"You're a radiation mutant." Another spit.

"We're gonna euthanize you, freak." Another stomp.

"Impure, impure!"

And that day, on the ground outside school, Stowy did something she had never done around another human before.

She spoke.

"I'm not impure. *I'm autistic*!"

The children retreated, stunned to silence. Her voice had been soft. Barely more than a whisper. But an echo seemed to ring across the silent yard.

Sniffing, Stowy lifted Luna and held the muddy blanket to her chest.

It was ironic. The one day she had talked, she had doomed herself. Doomed her parents. And her castle on the clouds rose higher beyond her reach, and the clouds became a storm.

* * * * *

That day (she was eight or nine years old; she could not remember exactly), she walked home from school, chewing on the corner of her blanket. She wasn't proud of chewing Luna, but it was a habit she couldn't break. By the time she got back to her townhouse, the Gestapo was already there.

When Stowy stepped inside, she saw it all.

Her mother on the bed, naked and bloody. The officers zipping up their pants. Her father lying on the ground, a bullet in his head. The second bullet shattering her mother. Stowy saw it all.

The officers laughed. All but their leader—a tall, stern man named Heinrich Huber. Stowy could read his name on his badge.

"Tainted DNA," Huber said. "Giving birth to monsters. Traitors to the Reich. Third one on this street. Would you believe it, boys? Must be something in the water."

Normally, Stowy would have remained hidden. But today a whimper fled her lips. She froze at once, hiding behind a dresser. But Huber's red eye scanned the house, and a grin twisted his face. He saw her! Her saw her through the dresser! When his gloved hands reached toward her, Stowy bit him. He slapped her, rattling the teeth in her jaw, and his fingers clutched her like talons.

"Gotcha!"

She closed her eyes, waiting for the bullet in her head. She wondered if she'd look like Mother. Her face gone. Stowy had never liked her face, but now she desperately wanted to keep it. But the Gestapo did not kill her. Not that day at least. They shoved a sack over her head, carried her into a shuttle, and for a long time, everything was darkness.

Stowy didn't remember much of the year that followed. She didn't like to. She kept those memories hidden. Her year in the institution was a blur.

She only remembered vague, fleeting scenes. She remembered needles stabbing her. Some needles injected her with medicine. Another needle tattooed a number onto her wrist. 52848—her new name. Above the number, the needle tattooed an inverted black triangle. Stowy knew the meaning of that symbol—the infamous *schwarzes dreieck*. The black triangle denoted her impure. Still an Aryan, but a broken one. Not quite human. She remembered trying over and over to wash the tattoo off.

She also got a tiny tattoo on her belly. Just a little blue line through a circle, crudely inked, marking her sterilized. Like all cripples. How the surgery had hurt! Impures like her did not deserve anesthesia. The wound had healed, the pain had passed, but she could never have babies. Never spread her pollution through the race.

There were other memories, even vaguer. Memories that only appeared at night. The electrodes in her head. The children down the hall who got sawed apart and stitched back together. The girls without skin. The boy with two heads (one his real head, the other one grafted on). Children who begged to be euthanized. Begged for their experiments to end.

"Don't worry," the doctor told her. She remembered his vulture face, his glinting monocle. "It's almost over, child, and then I will grant you the mercy of death."

He was a kind man. A merciful man. He would grant death to those who obeyed him, who dutifully suffered the experiments for the glory of the Third Reich. With their sacrifice, they were told, the children were providing new understandings of medicine. New ways to treat and enhance the soldiers on the battlefield. In the Fatherworld, everyone had their use. Even cripples.

His real name was Dr. Rudolph Baer. But he liked the children to call him Uncle Baer, and after administering his treatments, he often gave them treats. He would bathe a boy with radiation in the morning, take notes on how the skin peeled off, then hand the boy a chocolate. He would expose a girl to vacuum for ten seconds, watch how her skin blistered and her eyes bled, then give her a lollipop. You never wanted candy from Uncle Baer. If he gave you candy, you had suffered for it. But you always took it, and you ate it, and you accepted his hugs.

He looks like a vulture, but he calls himself a bear, Stowy sometimes thought. *He's a vulture in bear's clothing.*

That image always stayed with her. For years. A thin, balding vulture's head with a monocle, peering from inside the rotten carcass of a bear. At least vultures had the decency of waiting for their victims to die before shredding them to pieces. The good doctor kept you alive for a very long time. Sometimes Stowy felt like she was being eaten alive.

It was from Uncle Baer that she first heard of the Big Experiment. Of the multiverse portal and the worlds beyond. It was him, ironically—the cruel vulture in bear's clothing—who gave her hope. Who showed her a path to her castle on the clouds.

Uncle Baer often gave lectures at the University of Munich, speaking of his scientific breakthroughs. Not only students attended his famous lectures but also generals, admirals, and ministers. Even Dr. Anneliese Heisenberg-König, wife of the führer, sometimes came to hear Baer speak. Many considered her the most powerful, influential woman in the Fatherworld's history. Anneliese herself had a fierce scientific mind, though she preferred to put hers toward developing weapons for the wars of the Reich. Many of the Weltraumwaffe's weapons of destruction were conceived in the twisted mind of Dr. Anneliese.

When dear Uncle Baer delivered his scientific lectures, he brought some of his "nieces and nephews" (as he called them) like a carnival barker dragging along a troupe of dancing animals. He would place them on stage, displaying the children to the audience. With a long, slender blade, he would point at his beloved children.

"Look here," he might say, poking a boy. "We see the result of two treatments of skin regrowth, one synthetic, one genetic. After I bathed this boy with radiation, burning off his skin, I tried the synthetic treatment on the left side. The genetic treatment is on the right. As you can see, his left side is still severely burned, and rot has begun to spread. From this we must deduce that genetic treatment is preferable when healing our brave spacers with radiation burns."

He would give the trembling boy a piece of chocolate, then turn to a group of little ones.

"And here, ah! These precious *kinder*. The one on the left—yes, I assure you, that is a child!—was exposed to vacuum for sixty seconds. Yes, a full minute! The boy beside him? Fifty seconds. All the way down to this healthy-looking child on the right, who only endured the vacuum for a single second. Thus we can track the progression of vacuum exposure." He would give them each a lollipop. The first few could not take them.

Sometimes Uncle Baer brought Stowy along to his lectures. He would exhibit her too to the crowd.

"See this one? On the surface, she appears to be a pure Aryan child. See her elfin features! They harken back to our pagan fathers of the Bavarian forests." He would smack Stowy if she kept her head lowered. "Ah, there she is! See? Perfect form. The ideals of the Nordic race. But looks can be deceiving. For this girl's disease hides within the mind. She has what I call an *invisible impurity*. These children are the most dangerous, for they can walk among the pure, hiding in plain sight. Many still live among us."

He had her eat a cookie from his hand. And her role was over. All the world's a stage! Stowy had read that in one of Father's forbidden books, and like every actor trapped in this nightmarish theater, she played her part.

Every time he took her along, Stowy would listen to the rest of his lectures in the echoing halls of Munich University. Often Dr. Anneliese would challenge him. And Dr. Baer would debate her, getting angry inside but hiding it, for he spoke to the führer's wife. He was an esteemed doctor, beloved across the Fatherworld, and the personal physician of Führer König himself. Yet if he showed Anneliese too much teeth, Baer would be the next one skinned alive.

It was from these debates that Stowy learned about the multiverse. A reality where parallel dimensions were true.

According to Dr. Anneliese, parallel universes were real. Sometimes great events in history split the universe in two. And each part raced along a different track, branching into smaller and smaller sub-universes. The splitting events had to be grand. Dramatic on a global scale. The emergence of life from the oceans. The asteroid that purified the dinosaurs. The rise of humanity. Only great events such as those split a universe in two. According to Dr. Anneliese, the most recent "universe-splitting event" had occurred during the Great Struggle for Freedom (sometimes called the Second World War in old books). One of Anneliese's ancestors, Werner Heisenberg, had conducted experiments in nuclear power in 1944. He caused explosions so mighty they split the timeline in two.

"There is another universe," Anneliese told the lecture hall. "A universe in which the Americans invented nuclear weapons before my ancestor. A universe in which Hitler lost the war. In which my husband is not the führer. And where subhumans, cripples, and perverts squirm through our halls of power."

The audience would glance around uneasily. And Dr. Baer would laugh, crack a joke, and dismiss the notion. Sometimes Stowy saw a vein throb in his neck. He wanted to shout at Dr.

Anneliese, Stowy realized. But he dared not. So he must satisfy himself with a laugh and quip. Just hinting at but not quite showing his disdain. To the doctor, the multiverse was nonsense.

But Stowy believed. That parallel universes were real. How else could she have imagined the castle on the clouds? It must be a real place. A place in another universe. A place far above. A place she would someday reach.

*****

She didn't remember how she had escaped the lab. The clouds of forgetfulness thickened around that day.

"My, my," Dr. Baer had said that fateful day. "You've been with us for a year already, Fräulein Perry." He had checked her charts. "It looks like after a year, despite repeated shock therapy, your mind has not shown any symptoms of healing. I can therefore conclude that no known treatments of the brain can cure soldiers who return home with shell shock. Thus, I will recommend to the führer that we save expenses. Every soldier with a broken mind will be euthanized!"

Burned to bits, Stowy thought.

The vulture patted her on the head. "Good work, little Stowy. That is what your father would call you, yes? Very good work. Thanks to you, we will exterminate over ten thousand soldiers who are consuming resources without contributing to the war effort. You must be proud! Have a chocolate."

He handed her a mushy chocolate from his pocket. She ate it. She hated his warm, melty chocolates. They always tasted like bile. But she was scared to say no. So she always ate them and tried to ignore the sticky feel of sickness in her throat.

"And now," said Uncle Baer, "I will accompany you to the gas chamber, where your death will be quick and painless. You have earned this mercy."

He opened the gas chamber door, and several dead children spilled out, their skin gray. Years later, Stowy could never remember how she escaped. But she could still remember those gray faces. Still remember the thumps they made when hitting the floor. She had thought it so strange how, only moments ago, they had been alive, yet now they were something completely different, just gray sacks of meat. Just shells. Nothing that was human at all. Just . . . mass. And soon those sacks of meat would burn, and the ash would rise from the chimneys and fall upon Munich like snow.

The next thing she remembered she was running. The dark streets of Munich twisted around her. She was not from this country. They had brought her here from across the ocean. The unfamiliar streets became a labyrinth. Like the labyrinth from the book of Greek mythology in Father's forbidden library. But instead of a minotaur following Stowy, it was a vulture. A towering vulture with a monocle, peering from a bear's rancid furs.

She slipped through his talons that night. She lost the vulture in the dark warrens of Munich like a mouse fleeing into a burrow. Yes, Samantha "Stowy" Perry had always been good at hiding.

She had been nine, maybe ten? She did not remember. She did not remember her first night on the streets. Years later, she only remembered getting sick and vomiting into a garbage can. Yes, that was her only memory from her first night of freedom.

Freedom. Did she have freedom? Back in her school days, she had learned about freedom. The Eternal Führer had fought to bring them freedom. From the subhumans. From the traitors and communists and cripples. The Third Reich was free now, and the Aryan race prospered.

But not her. Not Samantha "Stowy" Perry. Not a girl with

autism. She was a cripple. A parasite. Her blood was infected. She was a wicked, filthy thing, yes, she knew that. But in her castle on the clouds, she would be cured. And that castle must rise in a different universe. She had seen it in her dreams.

They hunted for her most nights. The Gestapo prowled the streets. Their shuttles forever flew above, casting spotlights upon the city. Stowy imagined their machines as flying, mechanical eyes, giant adlerauges eternally watching Munich, seeking her. Maybe one of those Gestapo officers was Heinrich Huber, the man who had murdered her parents.

There were others like her in Munich. Other orphans who hid in the slums. Some were cripples like her. Others simply did not meet the Aryan ideal. Their eyes were too dark, their hair too curly, or their noses too large. Somebody, at some point, had accused them of carrying the blood of subhumans in their veins. And so they hid here in the streets too, children who scuttled like mice, leaping from shadow to shadow, hole to hole.

They formed little gangs, though Stowy kept to herself. She feared the other children. They were savage. Children like mice? No, more like rats with sharp teeth. Every once in a while, the Gestapo caught one, and that night, ash would rise from the chimney of Dr. Baer's laboratory. It was the ghost of the child rising to the sky, Stowy used to think. She had been so naive.

For a long while—was it a year or more?—Stowy simply lived in the gutters. She slept inside garbage bins like a stray cat. She ate the trash to survive. The spotlights of the Gestapo shuttles sent her fleeing, and whenever footfalls sounded, she slunk to the nearest shadow. She kept her tattoo hidden under a bandage; the black triangle would denote her to all as impure, a parasite to be exterminated. If ever she strayed from the shadows—perhaps to snatch an apple from a cart—she always quickly returned. She never strayed more than two steps from darkness.

Stowy had always been skinny. But now the flesh withered off her bones. Dirt covered her face, and lice rustled through her knotted hair. Her dress frayed and ripped a hundred times, threatening to fall apart. Stowy was good at sneaking and stealing. She could have stolen another dress from a clothesline, even from a store, but she refused to. This was *her* dress. As comforting to her as her blanket. So every time a new hole appeared, Stowy found a scrap of fabric, and she sewed a new pocket onto her dress. A pocket was much better than a mere *patch.* Why simply *patch* a hole when you could turn that hole into a *pocket*? Stowy loved pockets. Almost as much as she loved dinosaurs. She spent hours stalking clotheslines in the night, collecting scraps of fabric, cutting them into little squares, and sewing pockets over the holes in her dress. Before long, a hundred pockets covered the tattered garment, each sewn from different cloth. Some pockets were made from bits of old military uniforms. One pocket was made from a sock. Another from a bra. A few pockets were leather, and some came from burlap potato sacks. She collected treasures in those pockets—buttons, fallen bullet casings, a snail's shell, an interesting rock (which might, just might, actually be a piece of dinosaur bone).

She wore a striped stocking on her left leg. One stocking was all she had, and even that one was full of holes. Well, she added mini-pockets to that stocking too. She had no shoes or socks. Her beloved blanket began to fray too, despite all of Stowy's gentle ministrations with needle and thread. So Luna got a few pockets of her own, where the blanket kept her own interesting rocks, buttons, and coins. Beaten up as she was, Luna still embraced Stowy every night, keeping her safe. On the cold sidewalk, her loyal blanket pulled over her, Stowy would dream. Of those other universes. Of that sparkling city in the clouds.

At age ten—or was she eleven?—her life on the streets ended.

That winter, on a snowy night, she found an abandoned attic in the city. A family lived in the tall, narrow townhouse, but they never noticed Stowy hiding in their attic. For a while, she survived there. She learned how to catch mice and birds to eat. Though it disgusted her, she learned how to gut her little prey animals, and she cooked them on tiny fires in the alleyway behind the house. An old trick of the streets. There weren't many calories in these tiny animals, but it staved off starvation. Some nights, when she felt bold, she crept into the family's kitchen and stole scraps. That was much nicer.

And well, now she was thirteen-and-a-half. And she was still in this attic, sitting in the corner, hugging her blanket. The mice scuttled around her through the attic insulation. One mouse crawled up her dress and dropped into her pocket. Ha! That had never happened before. Did he *want* to be eaten?

Stowy patted the mouse, who remained curled up in her pocket. Involuntarily, the instincts of the streets made her mouth water. Yet how could she eat an animal that trusted her? That nestled against her chest, listening to her heartbeat?

"A new pet?" she whispered. "Do you want to be my new friend alongside Luna? Perhaps this duo can become a trio."

Talking had become easier since that day long ago in the schoolyard. She still feared speaking to humans. Talking was easier with blankets, mice, and other friends who would not hurt her. She decided to keep the mouse, and she named him Algernon.

* * * * *

A soldier lived in the house in Munich.

Hiding in the attic, Stowy came to know those who lived below her. The Brauns—the perfect example of an all-Aryan family. She heard them talk during the day. Heard them snore at night. On nights when she felt brave enough, when she tiptoed into the kitchen for scraps, she saw their portraits on the wall. The Brauns were a family of minor importance in the city. The father was a party bureaucrat, and the mother's only job was to raise soldiers. Six boys she had given birth to. The oldest, at twenty, was a spacer in the Weltraumwaffe. Oh, how they kept praising him—proud, noble Gefreiter Fritz Braun! Endlessly, Mother Braun bragged of her boy fighting a *real battle* last year against the rebels at Ganymede. Over and over, she spoke of her boy's next mission. An honorable, daring mission for only the finest Aryan warriors. Brave Fritz would fly aboard the *Barbarossa,* flagship of the fleet, to the new universe.

New universe?

That caught Stowy's attention. Lying on the attic floor, she placed her ear against the thinnest wooden board and listened. There was a crack on the floor by that board, barely a hair's width. If Stowy centered her eye right above it, she could peer down into the kitchen.

"A new universe, Papa!" Felix was saying. "Dr. Anneliese was right. They're opening the portal tomorrow. Only the bravest sons of the Reich are chosen for this mission."

"What's on the other side?" asked little Oscar Braun, the youngest brother.

"Subhumans." Felix snorted. "A subhuman infestation that spread across the Fatherworld in that universe. Only there, they don't call it Fatherworld. They use the old name. Earth. Ha! In that universe, Hitler lost the war, but we'll clean up the—"

His father smacked him. "Do not insult the Eternal Führer in my house! He knew only victories."

Felix lowered his eyes. "Apologies, Papa. You're right. If in another universe the subhumans spread, it was because Hitler allowed it. It was part of his plan. So that today's generation—so that *I*—can be tested."

Stowy rolled her eyes. She wasn't buying that. Not for one second.

Hope rose in her like the dawn between the skyscrapers. There was another universe. A good universe. A universe where Hitler was just a historical figure, not the Eternal Führer. Where untermenschen—people like her—lived freely. People like the neighbor's boy with six fingers. And the kid with eyes that were too black. People like girls who lined up dinosaurs and hugged blankets. A world on the clouds.

A world Stowy vowed to reach.

They called her Stowy because she used to stow away in her father's little starship. Her special skill was her very name. And it would bring her to her castle.

* * * * *

It had been a few years since Father had died. (When Stowy thought of that, the image of Father with his head blown open flashed before her eyes. She tried to remember him as he had been in life. A kind, mustached man. But that image of the corpse still haunted her.) During his lifetime, little Stowy would often sneak into his shuttle, hide under the seats, and stow away with him to space. She was bigger now. Not as easy to hide under the seats anymore. But she had never forgotten how to move silently, how to blend into shadows. Years of slinking through the alleyways and sewers of Munich had honed her skills. And so, that morning, when the Wolfjäger landed by the Braun family home, she knew what to do. Not-so-little-anymore Stowy sneaked inside with ease. The Brauns never suspected a thing.

Still got it, she thought, curling up inside a rucksack. She loosened the top for light and air. Here in the rucksack, stored in the crawlspace below the shuttle deck, nobody would ever find her.

Luna was wrapped into a bundle. Inside the folded blanket were Stowy's meager supplies. A shiny green apple. A beat-up, dog-eared copy of *The Hobbit* translated into German. Her sewing supplies in a cracker tin. A roll of bread wrapped in a newspaper. The hundred pockets, which she had sewn onto her dress, contained a few more treasures—crystals, coins, one of Dr. Baer's missing monocles, and other bits and bobs she had collected along the way. Those were all her belongings in the world. Algernon, for his part, rested in one of her many pockets.

The shuttle took off. Stowy sat there, hugging herself inside the rucksack. The rucksacks of other soldiers lay all around her, jostling her like a drunken crowd on Hitler's birthday. As the shuttle soared, one rucksack tumbled and fell onto Stowy. She let out a low "oof." After shoving the sack aside, she checked on Algernon. The mouse was curled up into a ball, shivering.

"I know the feeling, buddy," she whispered. She wasn't worried about anyone hearing her. The soldiers were all on the deck above, and the engines roared as the Wolfjäger soared.

It had been a few years, but Stowy had never forgotten that terrible feeling of soaring. The way the g-force tugged on your insides. Back at the lab, Uncle Baer used some children in g-force experiments, trying to see how increasing the force crushed the body. He would toss children into a wind tunnel, blast them toward the ceiling, and take measurements. Stowy had cracked more than one rib that way.

Now the Wolfjäger soared, and she rolled around in her rucksack, grunting whenever the other rucksacks thumped into her. She wondered if any other rucksacks contained autistic children stowing away to that castle on the clouds. Maybe there were many others. And maybe she was alone in the world.

But there's another universe. A place where I'll be pure.

In that glistening city atop the clouds, mice would patch up her dress, and instead of pockets, the dress would be covered with gemstones and pearls. A magical, singing brush would remove the knots from her hair. After a handsome prince kissed her lips, she would learn to talk to everyone. Oh, a part of her knew those were only fantasies. Just dreams risen from her father's forbidden books. She was no longer a little girl, and she no longer believed in fairy tales. And yet, if only *one percent* of those dreams was true, if that parallel universe truly was free of the Eternal Führer, Aktion T4, Dr. Baer with his candies, and the steel-tipped boots of the Gestapo, Stowy wanted to be there. A place where smoke did not rise from the chimneys. Where only real snow fell, not the ashes of dead children.

"A castle on the clouds," she whispered. It was dark inside the sack, but Stowy could see it. The glittering towers. The marble streets. The birds that fluttered under the starlight.

After a few minutes of rumbling ascent, the rattling abated, the noise dimmed, and Stowy had the strange sensation of floating. It felt like being trapped in one of Baer's wind tunnels again. The Wolfjäger must have just entered space. Vessels this small didn't have gravity dampeners, and the rucksacks rolled around the crawlspace. Stowy rolled with them. Objects in nearby sacks poked her. Perhaps weapons or boots.

For an hour or two, the Wolfjäger kept flying through space. Inside her dark sack, Stowy began to doze off. But then engines rumbled again. Machinery clattered. And the dropship thumped down onto a hard surface.

The rucksacks rattled. The sounds of a starship filled Stowy's ears. Not just a Wolfjäger but a real, honest-to-goodness starship, the kind that could brave the interstellar ocean. The boots of soldiers thumped. Officers shouted orders through speakers. Machines roared and thumped and clattered. A fully operational warship was a noisy place. The shuttle had entered the mothership.

The closet door banged open. Hands grabbed the

rucksacks. Including the one Stowy was in. Somebody tossed the sacks onto a cart, where they all jostled together. Stowy's sack thumped down hard, leaving her lying on her side. Ow. Above her head, the rucksack's drawstring loosened, forming a peephole of sorts. Stowy imagined herself as a baby in the womb, seeing the light of day beckon. Or perhaps like a mouse in a pocket. With one eye, she peeked out the rucksack.

The eager soldiers were exiting the Wolfjäger, clad in battle armor. Gefreiter Fritz Braun walked among them, proudly wearing his uniform. A skull helmet hid his face, but Stowy knew it was him. He was short for a spacer; not even six feet tall. The shortest in his platoon. Almost too short to be considered a pure Aryan. Sometimes, back at the Munich townhouse, Stowy had heard him weeping at night, praying to Hitler to grow taller, begging to be spared euthanasia. Well, they had spared him. Short he might be, but he was still good cannon fodder. Perhaps the machine guns of the enemy would do what Aktion T4 had not.

The Wolfjäger had landed inside a hangar. The place was massive—the size of the Frauenkirche in Munich, a cathedral Uncle Baer took his impure children to every Christmas. From inside her rucksack, Stowy could only catch glimpses through her "peephole." She saw towering airlocks. Viewports that showed the stars. Dozens of Wolfjäger transporters, Rattenjäger starfighters, and other small vessels. Was all this truly inside a starship? How could any ship be so large?

Boots thumped. Boots with little steel skulls on the tips. From inside the fallen rucksack, Stowy could see those gleaming boots, though not the rest of the soldier. She cowered and pulled the sack tightly shut, closing the makeshift peephole. Like a smaller version of her, Algernon cowered in her pocket.

A spacer's voice rang out. "Welcome to the *Barbarossa*, boys! The Führer's Fist!"

The troops cried out, including little Fritz Braun.

"Hail Hitler!"

Stowy had always thought it silly. How they still saluted Hitler all these years later. She had refused to hail him once at school. Her hand still bore the slender scars from the teacher's ruler.

So Stowy was aboard the *Barbarossa.* Yes, she knew of this ship, a terror from the twisted mind of Dr. Anneliese. The *Barbarossa* was the flagship of the Weltraumwaffe. The largest ship ever built. The ship that would lead the fleet into the new universe.

It was time.

The *Barbarossa*'s engines rumbled.

Stowy shivered inside her sack, clutching Luna, as the starship roared and blasted into the distance.

CHAPTER SIX
Little Ketya's Little Cars

The Boreal Forest
Earth
September 3, 2207

James King stood in the sunset, his smoking pistol in hand. Beside him lay the corpse of the Nazi pilot. Two or three miles away, the wreckage of the Golden Eagle smoldered on a snowy mountainside.

Where the hell am I? King wondered.

He took a step, winced, and rubbed the small of his back. Damned sciatica acting up again. He popped an aspirin, swallowed it without water, and stared around, wincing in the cold wind.

Where on Earth was he? In the chaos of battle, King had not seen where he crashed. Somewhere mountainous and icy, that was all he knew. Conifers grew across the mountainsides and valleys, and frozen rivers gleamed between them. He was somewhere in the boreal forest.

King tapped his temple, and his MindLink came to life. He tried to log into MindWeb. The telepathic network had worked up in space, probably thanks to servers aboard Freedom Fleet warships. But down here on Earth, King couldn't get a connection. No way of knowing where he was, then.

He spat. "Goddammit. What a day."

He needed to be back up there. In space. In the battle. He

glanced up, and in the darkening sky, he saw what looked like a meteor shower. Thousands of slender lights streaked, and tiny explosions popped like sparkles. It was odd how, from down here, the battle in space seemed so beautiful. Fireworks. Like the Fourth of July fireworks his father would take him to see in Nebraska.

The war spread across the surface of Earth too. Before crashing down, King had seen that much from space. Battles blazed in Earth's oceans and across all her continents. Maybe Nebraska too. Had the war reached home?

His son must be fighting too. Bastian was a marine brigadier, commander of the Freedom Brigade, which had once served aboard the starship *Freedom*. King's stepson must be fighting too; Lieutenant Evan Fletcher (who had lost his uncle aboard the *Patton*) served under Bastian's command. King's wife, the beautiful Kim, mother to Evan—had she joined the fighting? His best friend, Larry Jordan—was he still flying his commandeered Wolfjäger, or had *Patton*'s explosion washed over him? What about Rowan and Oli, King's grandkids, and Alice, his daughter-in-law? All his family was beyond his reach. Dammit, King hated not knowing. Hated worrying. For his loved ones. For all the soldiers fighting. For all humanity.

For a moment, a wave of grief hit him.

Ben. Ben Fletcher was gone.

Countless more lives—lost. Officers he had known. Spacers he had mentored. Countless other souls. Wiped out.

For that moment, the weight of grief nearly crushed him. He took deep breaths, forcing himself to lock the grief in a box. He would open that box later, unchain the grief, and wrestle that demon. Right now he still had a war to win.

He took a deep breath, considering. His top priority was getting back to civilization. And then back into the fight. When he flew in deep space, Earth seemed very small, a blue speck nearly lost in the vastness. Down here, without a working ship, it was King who was tiny and lost, the wilderness vast.

Embedded into her dashboard, the Golden Eagle had an emergency broadcaster. The antique that she was, Goldie still used radio signals. Radio was outdated tech, but a few of the older logistics starships—good old barges full of food, water, and ammo for the troops—could still receive it. King might—*might*—just be able to call for help. Assuming the radio was still in one piece. Assuming any part of Goldie was in one piece.

The smoking wreckage lay quite a ways off. King stared at the distant pillar of smoke. His poor old starfighter.

Well, looks like I'm up for a hike, he thought. Leaving the dead Nazi to the scavengers, King began to walk.

Normally two or three miles wasn't a long walk for him. But the terrain was rough. Snow piled up, hiding boulders and logs, and the ground sloped steeply at spots. The cold wind howled, stinging King's face with sleet. And he was old. Today he felt every one of his sixty-eight years. His bones creaked like the pine branches in the wind.

Maybe I should take this new antiaging drug, he thought as he walked. Pain stabbed his lower back, then spread across his hips and thighs. It had been a few years since the Spider War, since the rah torturer had stretched him on the rack. But his back still hurt. When he swallowed, his throat blazed. It had been decades since Katyusha had sliced his neck, and that wound still hurt too. Some wounds never fully healed. And aging made it all worse, tossing fuel onto the fires of his pain. King gritted his teeth, rubbed his scarred neck, and kept walking.

No. He didn't trust drugs. Especially not a drug that killed ten percent of those who took it. Well, okay—maybe he trusted *some* drugs. He fished through his pocket for his bottle of aspirin and popped another one. He used to drink booze all day to deal with the pain. Aspirin wasn't too bad.

The rough terrain battled him every step. It took King hours to cross those two or three miles. By the time he reached his shipwreck, he was covered in snow, shivering, yet somehow also sweating beneath his jumpsuit. He had been shot down once before. It had been during the Third World War against the Red Dawn. Back then, a young and brass pilot in his twenties, Lieutenant James King had shrugged it off. That young, angry bulldog was back on his feet and fighting within hours. But that was forty-five years ago. Tonight, a man pushing seventy, King just wanted to crawl somewhere warm and sleep for days.

But he didn't have that luxury. The war still raged above. This time not against Katyusha and her empire. Not against the Russians, Chinese, and North Koreans, united around the ideology of equalism, the space-age successor to communism. No. This time he was fighting a new empire. A new ideology. Or rather—a very old empire, following a very old ideology, which had seemingly crawled out of history, armed with modern tech. The whole thing still felt like a bizarre nightmare.

Maybe I did take that antiaging drug and it fried my brain, he thought with a snort.

Then again, just a decade ago, nobody had believed aliens were real. Until massive alien spiders attacked Earth. Kim had taught him about parallel dimensions. Was that where the Space Reich had come from?

He stared at his shipwreck. Not much was left of his beloved Golden Eagle. The starfighter's fuselage smoldered on the mountainside. Pieces of Goldie had scattered far and wide. All that work, meticulously restoring her—gone. King felt a pang of grief. He loved his ships. Almost as much as he loved people. Three years ago, he had lost the greatest ship of all time. The flagship of the Freedom Fleet. The Grand Dame of the Stars. The starship *Freedom.* He had never stopped grieving for that loss. Perhaps he never would. Losing the Golden Eagle reopened those old wounds.

A blast sounded above. King looked up to see fire in the night sky. Chunks of another starship burned up in the atmosphere, etching red lines through the darkness. A reminder that the battle still raged. The Nazi menace was still bombarding the Freedom Fleet.

They caught us by surprise, King thought, staring at the fire in the sky. *They hit us hard. They wiped out cities. Destroyed capital ships. God help us.*

How long was it since the war began? King wasn't sure. At least a day and night. Two days? Three? It all blended together. In all that time, King had not slept, eaten, or drunk anything. He didn't care about his own discomfort. He just wanted to get in touch with those he loved.

He returned his attention to his shipwreck. With a branch, he nudged charred chunks of metal away from the cockpit. Surprisingly, most of the controls were still in one piece, even if the starfighter had collapsed around them. While the engine ran on fuel, the dashboard sucked power from a battery. And amazingly, that battery was still working. Kim had truly done a good job restoring the Golden Eagle's innards. Thank God for small miracles and smart engineers.

They're both still up there looking after me, King thought. *God and my wife.*

He tapped the radio controls. Still working. He sent out an emergency broadcast into the ether, requesting aid. He used an older Alliance encryption key (he didn't know the current ones), but if anyone up there could still read radio, they were old enough to know the old keys. King could imagine the radio waves rising through the air, then dispersing in the storm of battle. Probably useless. King might have to survive out here until MindWeb returned to the surface. And who knew how long that might take?

He sat down in the shattered cockpit. Amazingly, his

cowboy hat had survived under his seat with only light charring. King removed his helmet, placed the hat on his head, and felt a little better. A little sense of home.

A gust of wind blew, scattering snow, and there went the happy feeling. It was cold here. Damn cold. King hugged himself, breath frosting. The broken fuselage was still hot, and fire still burned in the engine. That helped, but his old bones still ached; they yearned for the comforts of home. King melted snow on a hot piece of fuselage and drank. His stomach growled. It wanted more than water. War was like that. War wasn't just about fighting an enemy. It was also about finding food, water, shelter, seeking the basic needs of life while the world crumbled around you.

Once he felt a bit warmer, King unzipped his spacesuit. He was still wearing his ranch clothes underneath—jeans and a flannel shirt. He pulled a pack of gum from his pocket and chewed.

As he waited, hoping somebody (ideally friendly) picked up his signal, King fired up MindPlay. The hallucinatory interface hovered before him in the night. It looked like a hologram, one he could reach out and manipulate, but it was all in his mind, an image generated by his neural implant and painted directly onto his brain. The interface of windows, buttons, and icons offered an array of applications he could hallucinate. Most MindPlay apps required a MindWeb connection, but not all.

Seeking comfort in the frigid, miserable night, King loaded up some memories. Core memories. Saved in high fidelity in his MindPlay chip. MindLink memories, stored digitally in the neural implant, were more immersive than normal "wet" memories, stored in the brain tissue. MindLink memories (or MindMems, as some called them) were like reliving the memory in a hyperrealistic dream, complete with all the sounds, sights, and smells. It was Earth's closest thing to a time machine.

In one memory, Bastian was only a toddler. Two years

old, maybe three. King was holding him overhead, running through a park, as Bastian pretended to fly. Ah, running! King remembered being able to do that without pain. In another memory, King was older, marrying Kim Fletcher, his second wife and love of his life. In a third memory, King was twenty years old, dressed in fineries, graduating from military academy. His father was there—the famous commander, tall and strong. King had loved that man. Loved him with all his heart. Katyusha had slain that proud commander. She had murdered noble Ulysses King with his own knife. King shoved that painful memory aside for now. In this cold night, lost in the boreal forest, he immersed himself in the good memories of those he loved. Those who had fallen, and those he still fought for.

The sound of a roaring engine interrupted his memories. He shut off his MindLink and blinked, returning himself to the present. The warmth of sunlight barely touched him, like the mere hint of an embrace from an estranged lover, while the cold wind bit King with a fury, an arctic wolf gnawing on his bones. The images of his loved ones, smiling in summer, faded into the winter night like spirits returning to their tombs. The engine roared louder in the sky. King stared upward, squinting. A ship was descending, beaming a spotlight. King couldn't see much from down here. A dropship of some kind.

Well, it seemed like somebody had heard his broadcast. But who? Was this an Alliance dropship, ready to take him back to his fleet? Or a Wolfjäger, here to capture, torture, and finally kill him? His message had been encrypted; had the enemy cracked it? Standing on the hilltop, King's hand strayed toward his pistol. He still had a few shots left.

A voice sounded from above, thrumming through a speaker. "Remove your hand from your weapon, Admiral King! You are among . . . friends, dare I say? Well, we shall see."

The voice had a foreign accent. But with the crackling

speaker, roaring engine, and wind in his ears, King could not identify *which* accent.

The dropship thumped down onto the snow beside the shipwreck. The spotlight turned away. King blinked away the glowing afterimages. His vision slowly cleared.

The dropship was red. Red! The Space Reich! The—

But no. That was no swastika symbol on the hull. That was a golden equal sign.

Symbol of equalism. The ideology of the Red Dawn.

A hatch opened in the shuttle. A squad of burly Russians emerged, wearing fur hats, aiming assault rifles at him.

"Well, well, look who we have here!" said the tallest Russian, a burly NCO with a thick white mustache. "Admiral James King. The bulldog himself. Come with us. Katyusha would like to speak with you."

*****

King stood, staring.

Russians.

Just great.

Yeah, yeah, he knew the Russians were allies now. The Red Dawn—the whole horrible lot of them—had fought alongside the Alliance against the rahs. But King could never trust them. Never trust Katyusha.

I can forgive the knife to my throat, he thought. *But I can never forgive her killing my father.*

He raised his chin, not budging from his shipwreck. "If Katyusha wants to talk, she's gonna have to come down here."

The Russian soldiers glanced at one another, then burst out laughing. The towering NCO with the white mustache took a step closer. King read the name stitched onto the brute's uniform. *Starshiná* Peter Zhukov.

"Now, now, Bulldog!" Zhukov said. "You know that Premier Katyusha, most courageous of revolutionaries, is a busy woman. For the glory of Red Dawn, she is slaying fascists in the Great Patriotic War!"

King crossed his arms. "Well, maybe you should go join her."

"Believe me, King, we are no cowards. We have no wish to be hiding here on this mountain with you. Not while the fascist scum attack our world. We desire to return to glorious battle. Come with us. Between her victories in space, Katyusha will spare you a few moments. Why she bothers with an old American cowboy, I don't know. I do not question my Great Leader."

King rolled his eyes.

This old American cowboy beat Katyusha in the Third World War, he thought. But if King had learned anything in the wars, it was this: There was no point arguing with a Russian. And during the Spider War, when they had united against a common foe, Katyusha had, well . . . sort of . . . saved his life. Multiple times. King didn't like admitting that.

Could he trust her now? Should he resist these men? Even if it came to violence? Eyes narrowed, he sized them up. Fifteen burly Russians, most of them half his age, all of them armed to the teeth. In his state—alone, exhausted, with only three bullets left—he wasn't winning this battle. Hell, not even at his prime could he defeat fifteen burly Russians. Not like this.

"So, cowboy," Zhukov said. The mustached Russian raised a pair of electric manacles, the kind designed to shock you if you tried to break free. "Will you come the nice way? Or must I use the shackles?"

"Put those damn things away," King grumbled. He trudged across the snow, shoving his way between the Russians toward their dropship. "Get me back up into space."

As he approached the dropship, he recognized the design.

A Medved armored troop transporter. Mark III? No, it had four cannons on the prow. A Medved IV then. The latest and greatest. It looked similar to the Rhino dropships the Alliance used. With one important difference. Rhinos had a cannon on the stern. Red Dawn ships never had weapons on the stern. Or armor, for that matter. Because Red Dawn ships never turned to flee. And if they did—well, they deserved to be shot down.

It was damn foolishness, of course. To leave your rear unarmored—on purpose? But, well, a good equalist soldier was meant to always charge headfirst at the enemy. Of course, in the heat of battle, that didn't always work. Soldiers—even radical equalists—sometimes lost their cool. Sometimes found an enemy on their tail. During the Third World War, countless Russians, Chinese, and North Korean equalists had died because of their lack of stern armor. Millions maybe. King had challenged Katyusha about that once.

The premier had shrugged. "Good riddance. Katyusha needs no cowards in her army!"

God, he hated that woman.

King stomped into the shuttle, hoping no lucky Germans sneaked up behind their stern.

The Russian troops entered with him. There were no seats. They strapped themselves against the bulkheads, and the Medved soared into space. The g-force punched King in the gut. He squared his jaw and raised his chin as they roared skyward. The Russian troops stood around him, tall and dour. They weren't wearing spacesuits or helmets. In the Alliance, space marines always wore them. What if an enemy shot through your hull, exposing you to vacuum? But, well, spacesuits and helmets weren't cheap. And the Red Dawn, for all its might, seemed perpetually strapped for cash. What they lacked in funds they made up for in sheer population. With over two billion people under her rule, Katyusha had many troops to spare. To her, they weren't people. Just cannon fodder.

A Russian private offered King a box of cigarettes.

"A smoke, Admiral?" the kid asked. By God, the soldiers these days looked barely old enough to shave.

King shook his head. "I'm more of a cigar man."

The kid shook his canteen. Liquid swished inside. "Some vodka, maybe?"

"I quit drinking."

"Good." The private slapped him on the shoulder. "It is why you live so long, old man. But in this war? Ah, in this war we all die. So might as well die drunk." He took a sip from his canteen.

King looked away. The Russian kid was like a walking stereotype. Then again, there he was—an American wearing blue jeans and a cowboy hat, a six-shooter at his hip.

As they flew higher, King glanced out the porthole. The clouds had cleared, revealing the lay of the land. He had crash-landed in Siberia, it seemed. No wonder the Russians had gotten to him first. The landscape dropped down below. The Medved breached the atmosphere and soared into space. At once, the battle was blazing all around them.

Far in the distance, King could make out small blue lights. Alliance ships, he thought. But that might as well be another universe. Right now King found himself within the Red Dawn fleet. And it was fighting for its life.

Thousands of Red Dawn ships flew here. Most were Chinese. Many were Russian. Some were North Korean or South American. But in the chaos of battle, they all looked similar. Their red hulls sported golden filigree, and ornamental balustrades lined their dorsal hulls. Their cannons were shaped like dragons (on the Chinese ships) or bears (the Russians). The designer, King thought, meant to evoke grand carracks from the Age of Sail. To King, the red warships looked like flying opera houses, just with more cannons.

The Weltraumwaffe found itself fighting several battles at once. While some German warships fought the Red Dawn, others were battling the Alliance and the Desert Thorns. The Weltraumwaffe seemed up to the task. It was unleashing furious bombardments, devastating multiple foes at once. And the Nazi numbers seemed to be growing. King wasn't sure where they were coming from, but there were definitely more Nazi ships in space now than before his crash.

Nearby, a German dreadnought fired its cannons at a Russian destroyer. The Red Dawn ship cracked open, spilling molten fire and dying spacers. The wreckage of many Red Dawn ships floated all around.

Even after all this destruction, three thousand Red Dawn ships still flew—a grand armada. They vastly outnumbered the German starships. Yet despite massive numerical advantage, the equalists were struggling. The Weltraumwaffe ships were newer, deadlier, better armored, better armed, superior in every way. It was quality vs. quantity. Neither side had yet emerged the victor. From what King saw, it could still go either way. Relying on their superior technology, the Germans might hope to knock down the Red Dawn capital ships, then break the remaining fleet. Yet the equalists, with their vast numerical superiority (coupled with undeniable courage), could still overwhelm the fascists with sheer numbers. At this point, King thought it a coin toss.

How well was the Alliance doing? He peered through the little window, trying to see his beloved Freedom Fleet. But the blue lights had vanished behind the fire and steel of the German-Russian front.

The Medved rose toward a formation of heavy Russian warships. Within the Red Dawn, individual nations still maintained some autonomy and operated their own fleets. What united them was equalism (which King sometimes called "communism for the space age"). That and a healthy fear of Katyusha. While China formed the largest and mightiest force in the Red Dawn, it was Katyusha, a Russian, who ruled them. Long ago, she had exploited the weakness of China's frail emperor to seize power over the union. Since then, Ketya "Katyusha" Petrova had ruled over the Red Dawn with an iron fist.

King gazed at the Russian capital ships. Truly, they were machines of macabre beauty, masterworks of engineering in red and gold. Some even sprouted towers with striped teardrop domes. King had likened them to opera houses. But up close, they looked more like chunks of the Kremlin given engines and flown into space. Upon each Russian prow rose a figurehead, forged of silver and gold, depicting the Bolshoi Premier—Katyusha herself, fist raised, leading the way to battle. You gotta hand it to Katyusha. She never let war interfere with her sense of style.

No wonder she's always broke, King thought.

*****

The Medved flew toward the largest of these Russian monstrosities—a full dreadnought. The starship was a good mile long, lined with brass cannons and stone balustrades. Her exhaust ports were the size of Ferris wheels. Her prow guns could blow up small moons. A figurehead the size of the Statue of Liberty rose upon her prow, adorned with wings the size of sails. It depicted Katyusha (of course), holding aloft a sword. The name of the starship appeared below the figurehead. The RDS *Gagarin.*

King snorted. So Katyusha had named her ship after Yuri Gagarin, the first man in space, then commissioned a gilded figurehead of herself. Typical. The *Gagarin* truly was an eyesore. King had heard of Katyusha constructing this new affront to space, humanity, and good taste. The woman went through flagships faster than King went through socks. How many flagships of hers had King seen destroyed already? There was the *Lenin*, the *Baba Yaga*, the *Tolstoy* . . . Judging by the ferocity of the German blitz, and Katyusha's penchant for charging blindly into enemy gunfire, he doubted *Gagarin* would last any longer than the others.

Indeed, as King watched, the Russians were trying to break through a German line of frigates. The *Gagarin* had her energy shields down. She was firing torpedoes, relying on her armor to protect her. A German broadside pummeled the charging reds. A missile slammed into *Gagarin*'s prow and exploded, scattering black smoke. The filigreed plates of red armor cracked but held. Katyusha's gilded figurehead pointed the way onward through the flames.

As the Medved approached, a hatch opened in *Gagarin*'s scarred hull. The dropship entered the mothership, and the hatch slammed shut. With a thump and clatter that rattled King's bones, the Medved slammed down onto the hangar deck. Katyusha's fleet didn't bother with landing skids. Too expensive. A useless frill for capitalists. Why pay for *landing* when slamming down was free? (Of course, Katyusha always had money for her grand figureheads and gilded equal signs. The woman certainly knew her priorities.)

The Medved popped her hatch. The Russians grabbed King's arms, ready to drag him out. King shook himself free.

"Get your dirty paws off me."

He shoved past them, stepped out the dropship, and marched across the hangar. He headed toward a corridor hatch. A blast hit the dreadnought, shaking the deck. Another torpedo, by the sounds of it. King swayed on his feet and kept walking. He knew his way around a starship and would find the bridge. (Hopefully, the bridge would still be there by then.)

Speakers were thrumming through the starship. "*Triumf Revolyutsii*," the anthem of the Red Dawn, was playing on a loop.

This rendition included the bombastic orchestra, the male choir, the whole shebang. The Red Dawn ships always played their anthem in battle. Partly it was to inspire the troops. Partly to cover up the noise of enemy torpedoes slamming into you. The anthem's drums boomed almost as loudly. King's MindLink translated the lyrics from the Russian.

The Red Dawn rises
Glorious and mighty
To light all the world
And cast back the dark!
Katyusha our leader
Forever triumphant
Will smite the Alliance
For the glory of—

King tuned out the rest of it. He hated that goddamn song. He had heard it enough as a young man, battling the Red Dawn in space and on the sands of Mars. The bastards still hadn't changed the lyrics. Even now, fighting this new enemy, they bragged about "smiting the Alliance."

Across the hangar bay, deckhands looked up at him, confused. If you were a Russian deckhand, it was confusing enough to suddenly find yourself in a war against Nazis. Toss in a grizzled old American cowboy, complete with the hat and revolver, stomping across your deck, and, well . . . was it any wonder the deckhands were rubbing their eyes?

Peter Zhukov, the Russian *starshiná* who had seized King in the Siberian wilderness, walked a step behind. Frost still coated the big NCO's white mustache. His squad of goons stomped along with him.

"Slow down, John Wayne!" Zhukov said, laughing. "You are our prisoner. Yet you lead us through our ship?"

"Prisoner, huh?" King grunted. "I thought I was your honored guest."

Zhukov shrugged. "In the Red Dawn, is there any difference?"

The young private, the one with vodka in his canteen, slapped King on the back. "We are all prisoners here, American friend. Welcome to the Red Dawn."

He found the ship's central corridor. All the Russian warships had similar designs. He marched down the hall, boots tracking mud across the red carpets. His back still hurt, but the fury burned away the pain for now. How dare Katyusha send her goons to kidnap him?

He marched for a long time. This was a large ship. Murals spread across the walls, depicting the story of the Red Dawn and its glorious victories. The first fresco showed Lenin on a hilltop, delivering a sermon to the masses. The next mural depicted Stalin, fist raised, leading his troops into Berlin. Hitler was painted cowering at Stalin's boots, fruitlessly begging for mercy (King didn't remember that particular moment from the history books). He marched onward down the hallway. Next the murals showed the Soviet Union racing into space. Yuri Gagarin, namesake of this dreadnought, floated on the ceiling among the stars.

Then the story reached more modern times. The Russians, Chinese, and North Koreans founded the Red Dawn, an axis to fight the western hegemony. They were no longer communists, they insisted, but equalists, dedicated to fighting the inequality and decadence of capitalist democracy. A grand mural depicted the Third World War, which King himself had fought as a young man. He remembered winning that war. But in *Gagarin*'s murals, it was the Red Dawn that emerged victorious. Katyusha herself was depicted triumphant, echoing Stalin's pose from the earlier mural. This time it was not a painting of Hitler cowering at her feet—but him, James King!

Fury blazed across King. He increased his pace, barely even seeing the next murals, which depicted Katyusha smiting the rahs and winning the Spider War. (King remembered that victory being more of a collaborative effort. But in these murals, there was no mention of the Alliance having any role. Just Red Dawn warriors defeating the spiders on their own.)

At the end of the corridor loomed double doors, highly ornate and adorned with golden equal signs. Seeing red, King shoved the doors open and marched onto *Gagarin*'s bridge.

* * * * *

"Katyusha!" King roared. His voice echoed across *Gagarin*'s bridge. "What is the meaning of this? Why have you brought me here?"

The bridge of the RDS *Gagarin* looked like a grand opera house. Ornate balconies thrust out from the bulkheads, reminiscent of opera boxes. They contained the stations of science and navigation officers. A military band—an actual band with all the tassels and trimmings—stood in an orchestra pit, playing the national anthem over and over. Red curtains, elegantly tied with golden ropes, framed a towering viewport. The screen showed the enemy ahead—a wing of German warships, their guns blazing.

In the middle of the bridge rose a dais. Upon the dais stood a throne of gold and red velvet. Katyusha was not sitting on her throne today. She was on her feet, pointing her saber ahead. She didn't even notice King. She was too busy shouting.

"Onward, brave warriors of the Red Dawn! Onward and smite the fascists! For the glory of Katyusha, onward to victory!"

Her back was turned to King. She did not see him.

"Katyusha!" he cried.

She didn't hear him either. Hell, with that military band

blasting in his ears, King could barely hear himself. The drums beat so loudly the workstations were rattling. The trumpets blared like klaxons.

Katyusha tossed back her head and laughed as the cannons boomed. Exploding ships lit up the viewport, bathing her with light. She was a striking woman with a black bob cut and proud shoulders. Her red uniform sported tassels, gilded buttons, and a dozen medals. A naval cap topped her head, and golden equal signs glinted on her armbands.

"Yes, cower before us, fascists!" She thrust her sword toward the German warships on the viewport. "You thought you would only be fighting weak American capitalists? Ha! Behold the might of Katyusha! The Great Stalin crushed you in 1944, and glorious Katyusha will crush you in—"

King grabbed her shoulder. "Katyusha!"

She spun toward him, chest rising and falling. Her skin was pale, her features sharp. She might have seemed carved from marble but for her eyes. Those eyes were molten flame. The premier seemed ready to slice King's head off, but then recognition filled her eyes, and she lowered her saber.

"Oh, *privet*, Jamechka. Nice of you to come." Her arched eyebrows rose. "Look at you. You got *old*."

"We're the same age, dammit," he growled.

She laughed—a trilling sound. "Only our brains, Jamechka. You like Katyusha's new body, huh?" She wriggled, running her hands over her curves. "Only twenty-one years old! Fresh from the factory."

"Yes, I know all about how you get your new, young bodies." King snorted. "You clone yourself. Grow your replacements in labs. Then scoop out their brains and plant your own inside."

"And it feels great!" Katyusha stretched and pirouetted. "Show Katyusha another woman her age who can pirouette like this." She winked. "Seven years at Vaganova Ballet Academy. You should try it, Jamechka!"

"Ballet?"

She laughed that trilling laughter of hers. "A clone, Jamechka! Russian scientists can grow one for you, if you like. Best scientists in galaxy are Russian, you know. They grow you a nice, young, sexy body. Then you and Katyusha can rule together, young and virulent!" She shook her fist at the deckhead.

"To grow a living human—a clone of yourself—and then butcher it?" King shook his head in disgust. "What kind of a monster does that?"

She shrugged. "You disapprove, Jamechka? Well, don't worry. From the looks of it, you'll be dead before Katyusha's next clone." She laughed again and patted his cheek. "Katyusha only kids, Jamechka! You will live to be a hundred, *da*? So another ten years or so." She winked, turned back toward the towering viewport, and pointed her blade at the enemy. "Onward, Red Dawn! Onward to victory! For the glory of the motherland! For Katyusha!"

The *Gagarin*'s cannons boomed. The bridge vibrated, and torpedoes raced out to pound the German lines. A chunk blasted open in a Weltraumwaffe frigate, and Katyusha laughed. She kept laughing as four Red Dawn corvettes—her own ships!—shattered in the German meat grinder.

"Katyusha, dammit! Don't just rush at them in a mad banzai charge. You're losing too many ships. Haven't you ever heard of strategy?" He shook his head wildly. "Why am I here anyway? Give me a shuttle. Send me back to my fleet."

She glanced at him. "Oh, but Jamechka! It is far more fun here with the Red Dawn. And with beautiful Katyusha to inspire you to glory. Because Katyusha could, uh . . ." She chewed her lip. "Could use some, er . . ."

"Advice?" King asked.

She flushed and clenched her fists. "Not advice! Katyusha already knows how to crush her enemies. But, well, you see, the fascists and the capitalists think so much alike! If you could give Katyusha some insight into the mind of an evil Western imperialist, perhaps she could find some use for you here." She nodded. "That is all."

King sighed. "In other words, the Germans are winning, and you need help."

She glared at him. "Nobody can win against Katyusha! The glorious Katyusha wins every battle!" She laughed maniacally. "Katyusha will crush the fascist enemy under her bootheels, invade their universe, and overwhelm their feeble defenses. Katyusha will kill their men, enslave their women, indoctrinate their children, and then *she* will be the one who—"

"Watch out!" King said, pointing at the viewport.

Katyusha spun toward the screen. A volley of German torpedoes was flying in fast. Twenty torpedoes or more, each the size of a starfighter.

Katyusha winced. *"Pizdets."*

When the curse word was too strong for MindLink to translate, you knew things were serious.

"Those are big enough to shatter our armor and destroy the *Gagarin*!" King said. "Raise your shields!"

"Never!" she cried. "Katyusha does not defend, only attacks! Mashinkis—launch! Launch for Katyusha!"

The deck rattled as the hangar bays opened underfoot. Out flew Russian shuttles. Not big, armored Medved dropships this time. These were smaller shuttles, which the Russians nicknamed "Mashinkis"—little cars. They were roughly analogous to the Sparrow shuttles the Alliance used—large enough for a pilot and a handful of passengers, only lightly armored, and normally used for quick, easy missions. If a Medved was a tank, the Mashinki was a light jeep.

As King watched from *Gagarin*'s bridge, the Mashinkis raced toward the incoming torpedoes . . . and flew right into their warheads.

On the viewport, the light flared. All twenty torpedoes exploded. Along with twenty Mashinkis. King winced and turned his head aside. Finally the light faded. The dust settled. The Red Fleet charged onward, barreling through the debris.

"Katyusha," King said slowly, "tell me those were unmanned shuttles."

"What?" She snorted. "And spend money on AI? No, no, Jamechka. Patriots flew those shuttles. Proud sons of Russia who willingly gave their lives for the motherland! And for Katyusha." She placed a hand on her heart. "We shall forever honor our comrades' sacrifice. It is such a heavy burden. Katyusha's heart shall never heal from—" She gasped. "More torpedoes incoming! Launch more Mashinkis! Fly, sons of Russia, fly for your motherland!"

More suicide shuttles flew out. King looked aside in disgust. Yes, Katyusha was fighting Nazis, the very definition of evil. But that didn't make her methods any more palatable. Not to King. He felt sick. They said the enemy of your enemy was your friend. Katyusha made that very difficult.

Another Mashinki exploded outside. And another. They kept flying kamikaze-style into the incoming torpedoes. None of the Mashinki pilots were actually *fighting*. None were firing missiles of their own. From what King could tell, the Mashinkis didn't even have guns. The pilots were acting like living interceptor missiles. Another Mashinki flew into a German torpedo. The blast flared, filling *Gagarin*'s bridge with red light. Katyusha stared at the destruction, teeth bared.

"Dammit, Katyusha, are those shuttles even armed?" King cried.

She raised an arched eyebrow. "Why bother? Ammo is

expensive. Pilots are cheap." She sliced the air and pointed her saber ahead. "Onward, comrades! To victory!"

A growl rose in King. He couldn't hold back. "Katyusha, you are evil!"

She spun toward him, face flushed. "Evil, Admiral King? Did you never send soldiers to their death, O holy one? You speak of evil. There is no evil in history greater than Nazism. There is no ideology more repugnant, more vile, more monstrous. Is it evil to sacrifice lives to defeat them? Katyusha will sacrifice soldiers, yes. Same as all generals! Same as you. For victory against the darkness of Nazism, there is no cost too high. You can cower and pontificate all you like, American. You can feel superior to us Russians. But we won the Second World War. We Russians defeated Nazism last time. And with blood, sacrifice, and love of the motherland, we will do it again!"

King gritted his teeth. Maybe Katyusha wouldn't be broke if she stopped sacrificing shuttles. Maybe she wouldn't be morally bankrupt if she stopped sacrificing lives. She was using the same methods she had used against the Alliance and the rahs: overwhelm the enemy with numerical superiority. And damn how many of her troops died in the process. It was brutal, heartless, and—King had to admit—effective. To Katyusha, the ends justified the means. King would prefer to die with honor than live in disgrace. The two would never see eye to eye.

"I've wasted enough time here," King said. "I'm ge—"

"*What?*" Katyusha shouted.

The band stopped playing. Even with the blasts hitting the hull, it suddenly seemed silent aboard the bridge of the *Gagarin.*

"I said I . . ."

King's voice trailed off. Katyusha wasn't looking at him. She was staring out the viewport at the battle, face white, lips tight. Fury danced in her eyes, and her fist trembled around her saber's hilt.

Three of the Mashinkis, launched on kamikaze missions, were turning to flee.

The dinky little shuttles came flying back toward *Gagarin.* The German torpedoes (which the Mashinki pilots *should* have flown right into) were following like hungry barracudas.

Now there is courage, King thought, inwardly saluting those defiant Russian pilots.

Katyusha grabbed a gilded transmitter, which hung from her throne. It looked like an antique phone receiver.

"Cowards!" she screamed at the Mashinki pilots. "How dare you flee from battle, dogs! Charge at those torpedoes like men! Katyusha herself orders you!"

But the Mashinkis kept retreating back toward the mothership.

A trembling voice came through the speaker. "Please, *Gagarin*, let us back in!"

Katyusha glanced toward her artillery officer. "Why aren't you firing?"

The man blinked. "Does Katyusha wish us to fire at the torpedoes, or . . ." He gulped.

Katyusha leaped off her dais, shoved the officer aside, and grabbed his cannon controls. She pulled a yoke, aiming *Gagarin*'s prow cannon, then shoved down two levers.

A beam shot out, slamming into one of the fleeing Mashinkis.

King's eyes widened.

Dear God. She's murdering her own men.

"Katyusha, stop this madness!" King cried.

She didn't seem to hear him. Head tossed back, laughing manically, she fired again. A second Mashinki exploded.

"Death to traitors!" she cried. "Do you see this, American? This is how Katyusha deals with weaklings."

She fired again, but this time she missed. The third

Mashinki made it back into *Gagarin*. Katyusha spat and cursed in Russian.

"Katyusha will deal with him later."

King pointed. "The torpedoes, dammit!"

Katyusha waved dismissively. "Don't worry, Jamechka. Katyusha will take care of those." She fired a laser beam, destroying one torpedo only a megameter away. The light bathed the bridge. She fired again. This time the torpedo exploded right off *Gagarin*'s prow. Debris pattered the Russian dreadnought. The third torpedo came racing in. Katyusha fired—and again she missed! Snarling, she fired again and—

A blast shook the bridge.

Control panels exploded, blasting out sparks and smoke. A balustrade shattered, and its stone pillars flew across the bridge. Light flared, blinding King.

His knee gave out. He knelt, covering his eyes with his arm.

Katyusha's laughter rolled through the bridge. "You see that, comrades? Katyusha hit it! Katyusha hit the fascist torpedo!"

"What, a meter away?" King said, coughing and waving aside smoke.

Katyusha shrugged. "Only a little dent to our prow. Barely a scratch. Katyusha's beloved flagship is not damaged, and . . ."

Her voice trailed off.

She stared through the viewport. All the blood drained from her face.

King stared. He saw it too.

The German torpedo had indeed only scratched the prow. The same prow upon which stood the golden Katyusha figurehead, a statue the size of Lady Liberty. The blast had ripped the statue's head clean off. The rest was fine—the raised blade, the angel wings, the squared shoulders, the straight spine. But the head—blown off! (Adding insult to injury, the beheading revealed that the figurehead was not, in fact, solid gold, merely gilded. On the inside it was cheap steel.)

"Those . . . dogs!" Katyusha hissed. "Those . . . evil . . . fascist . . . dogs!" She tossed back her head and howled. "Katyusha will behead the Nazi admiral for this! Katyusha will cut off *all* their heads, and then cut their severed heads to smaller pieces! Onward, comrades! For revenge! No mercy! No fear! Onward to vengeance!"

The band burst back into a lively rendition of "Triumf Revolyutsii," the Red Dawn's anthem.

King seized his chance. In the confusion, he vanished into the smoke and stepped off *Gagarin*'s bridge. The guards were cowering from the rage of their premier. Nobody noticed King slip out.

He marched down the grand hallway with the murals. Medics ran by him, carrying a wounded spacer on a stretcher. Another blast shook the Russian flagship. *Gagarin* was still in the fight, but with Katyusha's reckless strategies, this ship wouldn't last long. Well, what did Katyusha care? She probably had a dozen clones in storage down on Earth. Probably with her brain backed onto a hard drive. After so many brain transplants, was it a wonder she had gone insane? Other Red Dawn leaders had begun to clone themselves too, to scoop the brains out of old bodies, plant them into younger ones. Every time, it was said, you lost something of yourself. Something of your sanity. Did anything of the original Katyusha still remain? Or was there only this caricature, stretched from surgery to surgery, a parody of who she had been?

They told King to treat his aging. In the Alliance, you didn't use clones. That was for equalists. But they had this new drug. It hardened your telomeres, they said. Went over every strand of your DNA and shaved off a decade of wear and tear. Well, King had been to more than one funeral of those who had taken the drug. A drug that killed ten percent of patients? All for the chance to be a little younger? Hell, if you asked King, it was just as barbaric as Katyusha's clones. Even if his legs and back did hurt. He had lived with the pain this long.

And he would die with it.

CHAPTER SEVEN
In the Spider's Web

RDS *Gagarin*
Flagship of the Red Fleet
Earth Orbit
September 4, 2207

King stomped into *Gagarin*'s hangar bay. He was ready to get the hell off this monstrosity Katyusha called her flagship.

A sudden pain stabbed his knee. His back throbbed, and his head spun. God, how long since he had slept? Was this the second day of the war now? The third? The *fourth*? King hadn't shut his eyes, eaten, or showered in all that time. Worse—he still had no news from his family. Since the Nazis had knocked down MindWeb—silence from his son and grandkids. That was infinitely worse than any physical pain.

The Medved dropship, which had picked King up from Siberia, was still in the hangar, along with several other armored troop transporters. The Red Dawn flew starfighters too, and undoubtedly the *Gagarin* had some in her bays. But those must be in another hangar, waiting for Katyusha to sacrifice them in some future "glorious" kamikaze mission. Here in the transport hangar, King looked around for a ride. He preferred a Mashinki. The big Medveds, with their cannons and heavy armor, were attractive targets for the German gunners—even German gunners on a budget whose torpedoes cost a fortune. But a Mashinki, cheap and dinky and nonthreatening, might just slip away without drawing fire. Unless Katyusha thought you were fleeing from battle, that was, in which case she would chase you into hell and back.

Still, King preferred the smaller vessel. He didn't feel like fighting Germans from a Russian dropship. Right now his primary objective was to return to his fleet. To the Freedom Fleet. To his fellow Americans. Once he was there, he could put on a proper uniform, get into a good all-American warship, and give the enemy some proper hell.

King was in luck. There was one Mashinki in the hangar. When he approached the shuttle, he noticed it was in bad shape. Burn marks scarred its dented hull. The exhaust ports were hot and smoking. The stench of space clung to the Mashinki. King understood. This was one of the Mashinkis that had retreated from the torpedoes. The one Katyusha had missed. A shuttle that could dodge a laser beam was a shuttle King wanted to fly.

That's my ride outta here, he thought.

He stomped toward the Mashinki. A few armored guards approached to block him. King shoved the younger men aside.

"Get out of my way," he grumbled, elbowing past them. "If you were going to shoot me, you'd have done it already. So back off."

He reached the Mashinki. Dents, scratches, and burn marks covered the hull. Smoke and grime hid the portholes. This shuttle had flown into hell and back. King tried the hatch. Locked.

The pilot is still inside, he realized. *Cowering.*

Katyusha had sent the pilot on a kamikaze mission. Sent him to fly into the German torpedoes. The pilot had fled. In the Red Dawn, that was a capital offense.

"The coward is still inside," said one of the hulking soldiers. King recognized him. It was Peter Zhukov—the mustached man who had grabbed King from Siberia.

"Let him be," King said.

Zhukov shoved him. "Step aside, old man."

The big Russian drew his sidearm, and for a second, King thought he had a fight on his hands. His hand shot toward his revolver with its last three bullets. But Zhukov wasn't interested in shooting him. The big Russian shot the lock off the Mashinki's hatch. Then, with a grunt, the burly NCO pulled the hatch open.

A young pilot was inside. He cowered, covering his head.

"*Pozhaluysta*, don't. Don't shoot. I . . . I just want to go home." A sob racked him. "I miss my mother. I just want to go home."

King frowned. He recognized the soldier. Young Anton. The corporal with vodka in his canteen. Just a kid. A scared, homesick kid trapped between the German meat grinder and Katyusha's wrath.

Zhukov aimed his gun at the corporal. "The punishment for treason is death."

King shoved the NCO's gun away.

Zhukov's plasma bolt hit the deck and skittered across the hangar, knocking over toolboxes. Curses, shouts, and "what the hells?" rose from the deckhands.

Zhukov wheeled toward King, eyes narrowing dangerously. "How dare you interfere with Russian justice?"

"Look at him!" King said, gesturing at Anton. "Look. Is that your enemy? That boy cowering in the shuttle, crying, missing his mother? Is that who you're here to kill? He's just a kid."

"He is a traitor," said Zhukov.

"Why?" King snapped. "Because he fled from certain death? I'd have done the same."

"He disobeyed orders!" Zhukov insisted.

"No officer may order a soldier to commit suicide."

Zhukov raised his chin. "Is that so, King? Really? You have never sent soldiers to death? Oh, you call it battle, yes. But you knew your soldiers would die nonetheless. Here in the Red Dawn, we are a little cruder, maybe. We don't hide behind false morality. We are here for one reason, King. To defeat Nazi Germany."

"Then go fight," King said. "Get back into your Medved, fly out, and face them head-on. Otherwise, get the hell out of my way." He shoved Zhukov aside and stepped into the shuttle. "I'm leaving. With this shuttle. And I'm taking the kid with me."

He sat in the cockpit and fired up the engine. The shuttle rattled and hummed. The kid curled up in the passenger seat, peering with bloodshot eyes. He had emptied his canteen.

"They never even gave me a gun," he said softly.

King shoved down the throttle. The shuttle skidded across the deck. They screeched and sparked toward the airlock.

"Well, if those guards are gonna shoot us, they'll have to do it now," King said.

But as the shuttle skidded by, Zhukov took a step back. It was hard to see through the dusty portholes. But it seemed like Zhukov was giving him a salute. Gripping the yoke with one hand, King returned the gesture.

The airlock opened. The shuttle flew out into space, King and the kid inside.

The battle still raged all around. German and Russian warships kept charging and firing their guns. Explosions blazed everywhere like miniature nebulae. In the distance, King could just make out the Freedom Fleet. The blue warships of the Alliance were busy fighting their own battles. While war filled space, it did not spare Earth below. Blazing missiles, flashing laser beams, and the blooming red flowers of explosions kept lighting the planet's dark surface.

A great war was lighting up heaven and earth, yet everything was so silent out here in space. Out here, he could not hear the blasts, not hear the screams of the dying, only the hum of the Mashinki engines. From space, war was a silent film of stirring gold and yellow and blue. It was almost beautiful. You could not see the mangled, burned bodies. You could not smell death. It was the great tragedy of war perhaps. That tapestry of beauty that revealed itself from afar. That stirring aura of glory and victory. War—that epic art form painted with violence. One did not see, at first, what lurked below. One did not see the mutilations. The soldiers with missing faces. With their skin burned off. With their guts on the ground. Yes, from the right angle, from here in space, looking at a painting of lights—you could make war look so beautiful. How many young men, lured by this beauty and promise of glory, had stepped through the light and found themselves in hell?

As the Mashinki flew through the battle, King turned to look at the FAS *Gagarin*. The dreadnought loomed behind. Zhukov and his guards stood in the airlock, watching the Mashinki fly off. Not firing. Letting them go. Zhukov seemed to wave, and then the dreadnought blazed onward, charging toward the German lines. King wished those soldiers luck. Wished they could get to go home someday. To see their families again.

Yes, there was some humanity to those equalists after all. King had been born and bred to hate equalists. The bastards had bombed America, had killed his friends, his father. King would never forgive them for that. But Zhukov, the kid, the other Russians he met aboard *Gagarin* . . . hell, most of them hadn't even *been born* during the Third World War. It was not those soldiers who had bombed Alliance lands. Not those soldiers who had raped and pillaged. *Gagarin*'s soldiers were victims of Katyusha, forced to follow her whims, forced to endure her insanity, forced to die when she ordered it.

But not this time. Not this one trembling private King had saved.

Deep in his gut, King knew the truth. During the Spider

War, he had needed Katyusha. Without her, he would have failed, and the rahs would have swarmed across the world. Once more, he needed her. Because she was a weapon. Maybe the best weapon Earth had. He must keep this weapon pointed against the Nazi menace—and hope it never spun around to stab him.

King flew through the battle, zipping under frigates, over destroyers, and through clouds of fighting starfighters. Thousands of starships flew all around. Starships of all sizes. Some were merely starfighters. Others were the length of city blocks. Some were dreadnoughts the size of skyscrapers. Torpedoes, lasers, missiles, bolts—they flew everywhere.

"We won't make it through!" the kid said, speaking in English with a thick Russian accent. "The battle is too thick here."

"We'll make it through," King said, tugging the yoke. The shuttle dodged a missile and flew around a German corvette.

"Where you learn how to fly?" said the kid. "You're good. For an old man."

"Old men are the best soldiers," King said. "Why do you think we lived so long?"

He shoved down a lever. A burst of afterburner shoved him over a cluster of Rattenjägers, and then they were racing between Russian destroyers, a whole fleet of them.

"Where you from, kid?" King said.

"From Liubinskii," the kid said. "Omsk Oblast. You know of Omsk?"

"It's in Russia. The Motherland."

The kid nodded. "*Da.* The Motherland." He scoffed and wiped his eyes. "As if I give a damn. I just want to go back. To my real mother. To our cows. To my home."

"I'll get you back there, kid. But not tonight. Tonight we got a war on our hands. And we need all hands on deck. You're gonna fight for *me* now. And we're gonna win this thing."

The kid nodded, dried his tears, and saluted King. "Let's

win this thing."

*****

The Mashinki raced through the battle. The dinky little shuttle was barely more than a tin can. Didn't even have armaments. A tin can for German target practice. Inside the death trap, King and the kid rattled in their seats.

"Haven't you Russians ever heard of seat belts?" King growled, trying to steer while the cockpit kept jolting. A piece of debris grazed the hull. The Mashinki jerked through space. King flew into the air, hit the bulkhead, then thumped back into his seat.

"Haven't you Americans ever heard of not flying into space junk?" the kid shouted.

You had to shout. The shuttle's alarm had begun to wail. Red lights flashed through the cockpit. King grunted, pulled the yoke, and swerved around a Wolfjäger. The Germans were everywhere! As he flew, that damn klaxon kept blaring. King looked at the array of buttons and levers across the cockpit. Which one turned the alarm off? The labels were all in Russian, and his MindLink was on the fritz, not translating the Cyrillic letters.

"Will you turn this damn alarm off?" King shouted. "Kid, make yourself useful."

"I can't turn it off, Admiral!" the kid cried. "It is automatic. When the emergency is over, the emergency alarm will stop sounding. Oh, and—it's Anton."

"What?" King snapped.

"You keep calling me kid. I'm eighteen. My name is Anton." He blushed. "Sometimes they call me Ant."

"Good for you, kid, now find a way to shut off the alarm. Before I shoot the damn speakers."

Gritting his teeth, King focused on flying. He was in the thick of the Russian-German front now. In the distance, he could see his beloved Freedom Fleet. The fleet he had served for half a century. The fleet he had once commanded. A fleet that was his home. Like the Red Dawn, the brave Alliance ships were engaging the Nazi menace. That was where King was needed. Where he could be most useful.

Once he reached the Freedom Fleet, he could obtain information. About where the Nazis had come from. About the situation on the ground. And about his family. Regardless of his family's fate, he would keep fighting. But he needed to know—was he fighting to keep his family safe? Or to avenge their deaths?

The Alliance starships had MindWeb servers. Sitting in the Russian shuttle, King tried to reach them. To connect from here. Didn't work. He was still too far. Once he was closer to the Alliance flagships, he could connect to their MindWeb cloud, then maybe—just maybe—learn about his family. Maybe even telepathize with them. Just hearing the voices of his son and grandchildren would mean the world.

To reach the Freedom Fleet, he must pass through the gauntlet. For that, King needed to muster all his flying skills. As a young man (back in the Bronze Age), King had been known as a great pilot. One of the best. Well, tonight he wasn't at his best. He was exhausted. Hungry. Thirsty. Achy. He was old, dammit. But tonight King flew like never before.

He zipped up and down, left and right, dodging missiles, plasma bolts, and buckshot, rolling around warships, racing through clouds of starfighters. All around the Mashinki sprawled the grand, abstract painting of light. The art of war. It was a strange thing—how death became beauty in the blackness of space. A nebula was the graveyard of collapsed stars and extinct civilizations, yet to the human eye, it was beautiful. So was war in space. Up here, death shone in purple, red, and golden hues.

The marines always told us pilots that we didn't understand death, King thought. *Maybe they were right. We don't see or smell the bodies. Up here, it's all fireworks.*

He flew under a Russian hulk, its engines blown out and its teardrop domes cracked. He raced onward, dodging debris: floating stone balustrades, brass cannons engraved like bears, and a tumbling figurehead forged of bronze, depicting Lenin, hero of the Red Dawn. As he hurtled by, Comrade Vlad nearly hit King's Mashinki.

King flew onward. Within moments, he found himself flying through the Chinese fleet. At a glance, the Chinese ships looked similar to the Russian ones. All starships in the Red Dawn had some similarities. The red paint. The golden equal signs. The elaborate brass cannons. But the Chinese ships (the most plentiful in the Red Dawn) had some differences too. Golden scales coiled across their hulls, giving the impression of a dragon's undulating body. Dragon heads rose atop each ship's prow, bearded and proud, staring with crystal eyes. The Chinese starships reminded King of antique dragon boats.

A few of these "dragon boats" were massive frigates. One was even a dreadnought—a dragon the size of a city neighborhood. But most of the Chinese ships were small. Thousands of their starfighters—little dragons with snarling mouths—swarmed across space. King recognized the model. They were called Xianglongs. Star-dragons. The newest generation of Chinese starfighter. By a wide margin, Xianglongs were the most widely produced starfighter in the world. The equalists pumped them out by the hundreds of thousands.

The Weltraumwaffe was attacking here too. Three German starfighter carriers loomed above like storm clouds over hell. They were gargantuan machines, sporting black hulls and blazing red swastikas, terrors woven from a madman's nightmares. Like reanimated corpses spewing swarms of flies, the ghostly carriers discharged clouds of Rattenjägers from their airlocks. The dark starfighters of Nazi Germany swarmed to meet their Chinese foes.

From a distance, the dark Rattenjägers looked like ravens—terrible undead ravens with burning red eyes, their beaks ravenous for flesh. The rising Xianglong fighters looked like tiny dragons, each sporting a dazzling coat of iridescent scales. Ravens and dragons flashed through space, thousands of them mingling together, rolling, firing, lighting up space. Into this electric storm did the little Mashinki fly.

"Why are you flying through the cloud of starfighters?" Anton shouted. The young Russian was as pale as a skull.

"Quiet, kid, I'm trying to concentrate," King muttered. He leaned sideways, pulling the yoke with both hands, dodging a dragon ship. He shoved the yoke, jolting forward, and then slipped under a charging Rattenjäger. Instantly more starfighters were all around, German and Chinese alike. Missiles streaked back and forth. King kept handling the yoke, jaw tight, eyes flicking, aware of everything, zipping his way through.

Anton turned green. "Go *around* the dogfights, around—"

"Shut up, kid! If we fly around the dogfights, those German carriers will use us for target practice. It's safer in the herd."

"A herd? This is a bloodbath!"

"Good, lots of places to hide then."

The kid pointed. "Admiral!"

"I see it," King said, swerving around the incoming torpedo. The missile slammed into a Xianglong behind the Mashinki. The dragon starfighter exploded. Firelight washed the Mashinki's cabin, and clouds of scales fluttered through space, each catching the light and blazing like sparks from a campfire.

Just light. Just fireworks. King never even saw the Chinese pilot who had just died. Never heard his last scream. Or his last prayer. Who was that pilot? Before his death, was he too confused? Tired? Hungry? Starved of information in this surreal nightmare of a war? King would never know. Up here—a flash of light and then silence.

He was almost at the Freedom Fleet now. Almost there. Almost with his people.

How long had it been since that morning? Since King stepped out of his cabin, went for a ride, and got swept up into hell? How long since he had kissed Kim goodbye, then flew off to war?

He wondered if Kim still waited back on the ranch. Most likely not. Most likely, Colonel Kim Fletcher would have donned her uniform and reported to duty.

In King's mind, she was waiting on one of those Alliance starships. Bastian would be there too, maybe with the little ones in tow. It was strange. Millions were dying down on Earth. King could see the bombardments. But he just kept thinking about his family. King had always told himself that he fought for humanity, and now guilt filled him. With humanity in peril, was he revealing the true man inside—a selfish man who cared only for himself and his own?

No. He refused to feel guilty. His duty was to his world. To his beloved fleet. Every soldier, no matter his vows, no matter his dedication, thought of family first. Some soldiers had large families, others were lonely orphans, but everyone still remembered a home, remembered a mother's embrace. No matter how big, tough, and mean the soldier was, no matter how patriotic and eager for victory, this remained true. King must remember he was just a man. Not a machine. He would recognize his selfishness, a selfishness perhaps inherent to every man. And he would work around it.

He flew toward a cluster of Xianglongs. Hundreds of the little dragon starfighters schooled ahead, moving as one great, fluid beast. The Chinese pilots would recognize the Russian Mashinki as a fellow vessel of the Red Dawn. King would be safe among them. And right beyond the swarm of dragons—the Freedom Fleet.

King flew toward safety.

A shadow rose behind the dragons.

A terrible machine blocked the sun. Eight black limbs spread out, each as long as a city block. A red engine swirled in the center of this mechanical monstrosity. What the hell was that? Was that a ship?

The black limbs swung, plowing into Xianglongs.

The dragon starfighters tumbled every which way, rolling into the distance, crashing into one another. Suddenly they seemed less like dragons, more like dragonflies.

King stared, barely believing what he saw. A chill ran through his bones.

Behind the dragons rose a great black spider, hungry for flesh.

* * * * *

"It's a rah!" Ant cried. "The rahs are here!"

"No!" King growled. "Calm down, kid. That's not a spider. Not an alien. It's a ship. Look! A Nazi ship."

"Oh, is that all?" Ant said. "Just a giant Nazi ship shaped like a spider? Wow, don't I feel better!"

The old American and young Russian stared at the monstrosity. Swastikas adorned the spider's metal legs. Yes, it was definitely a machine. A huge machine. King had called it a *ship,* but that seemed somehow wrong. Ships had prows, sterns, some semblance of sanity. This was more like some strange, mechanical monster from the mind of a madman.

The mechanical spider swung its limbs again. More

Xianglongs tumbled into the distance like dragonflies in a summer storm. Some Xianglongs rallied and fired plasma bolts at the approaching spider. The barrage bombarded the bizarre machine's armor. The metal arachnid brushed it off. Like a starving man at a Chinese buffet, the spider advanced through the swarm of dragons, devouring all in its path.

"We have to take out that ship," King said.

Ant looked ready to faint. *"What?"*

"The Nazi spider. It's too dangerous. We must crush it." He shoved the throttle, racing closer toward the mechanized monster.

"Admiral, are you insane?" the Russian private cried. "We don't have any weapons! How are we going to defeat that monster?"

"I don't know," King muttered, flying closer. "I'll think of something."

The alarm kept blaring.

King slammed his metal fist into the speaker, crushing it. The alarm died with a pathetic mewl. Better.

He flew around a few cracked, floating Xianglongs. As he raced by, he could see the dead Chinese pilots inside. One man's cockpit had shattered, and the spider's legs had crushed his torso. Loose organs floated through space, still attached to the corpse by strings of flesh like macabre balloons. King flew onward. Even as a pilot, he finally got close enough to see death. The marines were right; up close, war was ugly business.

The spider loomed ahead. King had underestimated its size. In his Mashinki, he was like an ant approaching a tarantula. Upon the spider's torso blazed a red sphere, crackling, swirling like the red storm of Jupiter. The eight limbs were spinning, swinging, and firing dark strands like gossamer woven of night itself. The dark web hit Red Dawn ships, wrapped around them like midnight serpents, and began eating through their hulls.

"What the hell is that stuff?" King muttered. "I saw SS grunts on the ground firing it from their rifles."

"Umbrions," said Ant.

"Umbrions?" King said. "Particles of living darkness taken from the space between universes? I don't think so, kid. Those are only hypothetical."

Ant shrugged. "That's what Katyusha told us. Looks like the Nazi scum discovered umbrions. In addition to discovering how to portal between parallel universes. They seem to be ahead of us technologically."

"Yeah, well, I'm used to it," King muttered. "I still wear a wristwatch."

Ant raised his eyebrow. "When MindLink can show you the time?"

"I don't like MindLinks!" he snapped.

He focused on flying. He was getting closer to the strange, galactic spider. The Nazi monstrosity wasn't a spaceship, he saw. It was a *mecha.*

A cockpit bulged from the metal abdomen like a boil. A pilot stood inside, surrounded by joysticks. A female pilot. From this distance, King could not see her face, not even at maximum magnification. But her body was unmistakably feminine.

And . . . she had six arms.

King blinked. What? But yes, when he zoomed in, he saw it clearly. The pilot had six arms! They stretched out around her. With each hand, she held a joystick. Her two feet, meanwhile, seemed strapped onto pedals. Like that, she was operating all eight spider legs. Had the Nazis genetically engineered a human with eight limbs to pilot an eight-legged ship?

Kill the pilot and you kill the spider, King thought. Normally he was loath to kill women, even enemy combatants. Even deranged enemies like Katyusha. He had been raised that way on the farms of Nebraska. A man never hurt a woman.

But when it came to Nazis, King was willing to make an exception. That woman had swastikas all over her ship. And given half a chance, she would ravage American ships as readily as Chinese ones. She was going down.

The little Mashinki raced toward the towering mecha. The eight-limbed Nazi woman finally noticed the dinky little Russian shuttle. The colossal spider turned toward King. But then a charge of Xianglongs drew her attention, and the woman pulled her joysticks. The spider turned to battle the Chinese starfighters, knocking them aside with long metal legs. The tableau reminded King of some arachnid version of King Kong swatting aside biplanes.

"Hey, kid," King said. "I don't suppose you got spacesuits in this shuttle of yours."

"There should be emergency suits under the seats," Ant said. "For breaches."

"Miracle of miracles," King said. "Katyusha actually gave you some supplies. How generous of her."

"Well, she saved rubles by not giving me any weapons."

"Put your spacesuit on," King said, an idea forming in his mind.

The kid frowned. "What are you—"

"Put your suit on, soldier!" King growled.

"All right, all right," the kid muttered. "You do realize I'm not your soldier, Admiral?"

"You are now. You became one the instant you defected from the Red Dawn. Now put on your spacesuit."

King zipped up his own spacesuit. It was his spacesuit from home, the one he had pulled on in his barn before flying off to war. God, it seemed like a lifetime ago. He put on his helmet, found a spare oxygen tank under the seat, and slung it across his back. Soon the kid was wearing a Red Dawn spacesuit. A yellow equal sign adorned his red helmet, symbol of his union and ideology. To Katyusha, that was all young Anton was—a pawn of equalism. A pawn sent off to die. Well, not on King's watch.

"Here," King said. "Grab the wheel."

He stomped out of the cockpit, leaving the kid at the yoke. He needed to fight that creature ahead. And he couldn't do it from a Mashinki.

He needed a starfighter.

He stepped toward the shuttle's hatch. Yes, Mashinkis just had crude hatches. Not even airlocks.

"Kid, you got your visor down?" King shouted.

"*Da, da*! What are you doing, you crazy American?"

King lowered his visor.

"Killing Nazis," he muttered and pulled the shuttle hatch open.

* * * * *

Space sucked the air from the shuttle, inhaling paper cups, cigarette butts, and scraps of paper. King clung onto the hatchway, beholding the battle. The dogfights stormed all around. Missiles flew everywhere, etching white and gold lines across space. Ahead rose the mechanical spider.

I should have taken a goddamn Medved, King thought.

He stood in the shuttle's open hatch, gazing out at space. It was ridiculous. He should be flying to the Freedom Fleet! Not getting bogged down in battle here on the German-Chinese front. But something about that woman in the spider . . . The way her body moved. The way her hands reached from joystick to joystick. Something about her drew him. She was dangerous. She was poison. She was the venom in the spider, a temptress, a black widow who devoured her mates. And King knew he must face her.

"Kid!" King said. "Can you hear me?" He tapped his

helmet. Sometimes Alliance MindLinks had trouble interfacing with the Red Dawn's neural implants.

"*Da, da*," the kid said, speaking in King's mind.

"Yaw left fourteen degrees, then pitch downward five. See that Chinese starfighter?"

"The one with the dead pilot inside? And no wing?"

The Xianglong was careening nearby. Like the others, this little ship resembled a Chinese dragon boat, complete with golden scales and a dragon's head. If you asked King, it was a ridiculous design. It looked like it belonged on a carousel, not a battle. But the Red Dawn was all about appearances. To Katyusha, war was a masquerade, and she wanted all her guests dressed in fineries.

"Fly me closer, kid. Trust me."

"Crazy American," the kid muttered. The Mashinki swerved through space.

Standing in the open hatchway, King took a quick snapshot of the battle. The dinky shuttlecraft flew among swarming starfighters. All around, countless Xianglongs (small and slender dragons) battled Rattenjägers (big, dark ravens). To King's left rose the surface of Earth, a curving blue wall, flashing every second with another blast. The war still raged across the surface. To his right, far beyond the zipping starfighters, the Freedom Fleet flew in higher orbit. From here in low orbit, even those mighty starships were just little blue streaks. Ahead, and closer to King, rose the mechanical spider. The arachnid mecha was still smashing its way through clouds of Chinese starfighters.

"A bit to the left," King telepathized to the kid. "Pitch just another degree down and . . ."

There.

There it was!

The Xianglong with the dead pilot inside.

King leaped from the Mashinki.

"Crazy American!" the kid cried from the cockpit.

King flew through space, eyes narrowed, lunging toward the Chinese starfighter.

The kid was right. This was insanity. The physics involved! King must account for the moving Mashinki. The moving Xianglong. The gravity of Earth. The human brain couldn't intuit physics in space. He needed a computer or—

He slammed into the dragon-shaped starfighter.

Hard.

King groaned. He had hit the Xianglong's fuselage. He slid across the scaly hull and nearly tumbled off into space. At the last second, he caught the tail fin. Starfighters mostly fought in space, but they had folding wings and tail fins. Just in case they needed to fly in the air. Or in case retired admirals needed a handhold.

When impacting with the fuselage, King knocked the starfighter into a spin. A *wild* spin. He clung onto the rotating starfighter like some beaver clutching a spinning log. Everything spun around him—the thousands of starfighters, the larger capital ships, the giant spider. Even planet Earth itself seemed to swing around King like a tetherball. He felt like a cat trapped inside a dryer. Trying to ignore the dizzying array, King crawled up the fuselage.

The Xianglong was damaged. The German spider must have kicked the Chinese starfighter with one of those long, metallic legs. The fuselage was dented, and the canopy had shattered. Glass shards perforated the broken corpse inside. The bloody face stared with cold, dead eyes. Ah, there it was again. There was the death at the heart of this luminous painting of glorious battle. It was an empty note in a symphony. A black hole in the center of a glittering galaxy. A dead wasp inside a ripe fig. Something buried. Something tragic. Like a blooming garden, bursting with colors and birdsong, that hid the gravestone of a dead child. King grabbed the poor pilot by the shoulders; he looked barely older than twenty. King heaved the corpse out of its seat. The young pilot tumbled into the distance, then Earth's gravity grabbed the body and began pulling it downward.

Make your way back to Earth, friend, King thought. *Let your atoms disperse across the sky, sea, and soil. You came from the earth. Now you return to the earth.*

He strapped himself into the pilot seat.

"You crazy American!" rose Ant's voice in his mind. "You did it, you crazy bastard!"

King glanced up. Anton was flying the Mashinki not far above. Close enough for peer-to-peer MindLink range. At this distance from the Freedom Fleet and its MindWeb servers, this was about as much telepathy as King would get.

Focus, Jim, he told himself.

He stared at the control panel. A foreign array of buttons, toggles, and screens spread around him. He had never flown a Chinese starfighter.

But hey, since leaving his cabin door with a cup of coffee, he had fought the Waffen-SS from horseback, flown an antique Eagle against German warships, crashed into Siberia, got kidnapped by burly Russians, and escaped the Red Dawn flagship (and its deranged clone commander) in a dinky little shuttle without guns. So why not fly a Chinese dragon-shaped starfighter against a German spider mecha? Might as well, if you asked King.

He grabbed the yoke and got to it.

* * * * *

Say what you liked about Xianglong starfighters. And King liked to say a lot. That they looked ridiculous, what with those dragon motifs—more like toys than actual starfighters. That they were mass-produced with every corner cut. That they were unsafe; they barely had armor, their canopies were fragile, and the pilot seats couldn't even eject. Say all that. But you couldn't deny one thing.

These babies could fly.

Flying the Xianglong, King was in his element. He zipped among a thousand other starfighters—other nimble Xianglongs and angry German Rattenjägers. Missiles and bullets flew his way, and King dodged them all. In this ship, he could fly like a butterfly.

He had always loved flight. He came from a long line of pilots. As a kid, he would take the family cropduster and fly for hours over fields, farms, and forests, just wanting to feel the air beneath his wings. Then, when he was a youth, he would fly space-racers. The kind that were basically just starfighters with their weapons removed. For hours, young Jimmy King would fly along the asteroid belt, explore the rings of Saturn, and glide over the silver craters of the moon.

My father was a pilot. And his father before him. Going back generations. But not my son.

No. Bastian had never taken to flight. Flight was not in his gut or his heart. The boy had tried. Even applied to flight school. Couldn't do it. Couldn't get it. Until he had chosen a different path—the life of the marines.

You carried that burden for a long time, King thought. *You thought you shamed me. Our family. But you make me so proud.*

As King flew toward the mechanical spider, he didn't know if he'd survive this battle. Or the battle after this one. Or the one after that. This would be a long war. If he died, King just hoped it was after he got to see Bastian. At least one more time.

The spider saw him approach. The mechanical arachnid turned to face him, exposing her underbelly. In any other animal, that would be a sign of submission. But not here. Not with this black widow. Upon her underbelly blazed that churning red cauldron, a heart of fury—the core that powered this beastly machine. The eight legs extended, as long as city streets, tipped with shining, crackling blades like lightning bolts.

Now that he was closer, King saw letters engraved onto the spider mecha. So this terror of the Reich had a name. Whether it was the name of the ship, the model, or the manufacturer, King did not know. But he understood what it meant. *Spinnenmutter.* Spider mother.

In the spinnenmutter's cockpit stood the woman. The woman with six arms. Each of her hands gripped a joystick, and her feet controlled pedals. Like that, she was manipulating the spider's eight limbs. She seemed like some Hindu goddess with many arms. A spider goddess. Her visor was faceless, featureless. Not a skull visor like the other Nazis had. Her entire helmet was smooth and polished like a black pearl or the heart of some deep-sea creature, reflecting the stars.

The spider mecha pounced toward King.

He pulled the joystick. The scaly little dragon reared. Again King had the impression of a delicate dragonfly facing a hungry tarantula. The mechanical limbs swung toward him. Each of those limbs was wider than King's entire starfighter. The remains of other Xianglongs, crushed and bloodied, clung to the spider's legs like bugs on the soles of well-worn boots. The sunlight caught scraps of golden scales like discarded snakeskins.

King dodged one spider limb. Another. A third. But the mecha operator was too quick. The spinnenmutter pounced, and one of her legs slammed into King's starfighter.

He tumbled through space. Once more, he felt like a sock in a dryer. His head rattled inside his helmet. His neck ached. His orthopedist was going to hate him. King managed to wrestle control of the yoke, steady his flight, and aim his starfighter's scaly head at the spider. As the towering arachnid lunged, King fired two missiles.

They were *long-ya* missiles. Dragon-teeth. The Chinese

mass-produced them by the billions. Back during the Third World War, King had lost friends to these sleek white missiles.

The long-yas slammed into the mechanical spider. Long-yas could rip through starfighters like they were paper planes. But they barely dented the spinnenmutter's thick armor. The huge spider shrugged off the missiles as if they were spitballs. The eight-limbed woman pulled the controls, and all eight spider legs pointed at King. Bores dilated on the limbs' tips. The spider opened fire.

More of those smoky black bolts flew toward King. Umbrions, huh? Whatever they were, King had seen them carve through metal and flesh with equal ease. He flew up and down, side to side, dodging the assault. He leaped like a fish cresting a wave, then opened fire with his Gatling guns, destroying a swarming volley of black bolts.

He must get closer to that spider. At a distance, she had the advantage. But if King could get closer, he could buzz around her like a wasp flying too close to your head to smack. And then—then he could sting!

*****

King whipped around one spider limb, then another. He kept flying his starfighter, moving closer, closer to that strange woman in the cockpit. She turned her head toward him, and though she wore a mask, he could feel her eyes piercing the distance, boring into him.

He fired more long-yas.

This time King fired at the joints of a spider leg. Right where the limb connected to the metal body.

He hit!

The missiles exploded.

The joints twisted, and that terrible limb tore free!

The leg tumbled into the distance, carving through Chinese starfighters like a boomerang slicing through a swarm of dragonflies.

Heartened, the surviving Xianglongs charged to battle. A thousand glittering dragons, scales gleaming in the sunlight, raced toward the spider that plagued them. As the spider swung her remaining seven limbs, swatting them aside, King flew in closer. And stung again.

He aimed at another joint, which connected a spider leg to the abdomen. His missiles hit again! Explosions twisted the joints. This spider leg too detached. As large as a skyscraper, the mechanical limb crashed down to earth, crumpling in the atmosphere and racing toward the Pacific in a blaze of fire.

Rattenjägers, seeing the spider in trouble, came racing to assist. The Nazi starfighters engaged the swarm of Chinese dragon ships, giving the spinnenmutter some much-needed respite. Most of the Xianglongs turned to battle the ravenlike starfighters of the Third Reich. But not King. He was still focused on that spider mecha. On the woman in the cockpit. The woman with eight arms. The woman who kept staring at him. Who felt so familiar. Her shape, the way she moved . . .

Firing his Gatling guns, King flew closer toward the spinnenmutter's cockpit. She stared at him from inside, that smooth, polished helmet still hiding her face. Her head looked like an egg carved from obsidian. King noticed that she didn't actually have six arms. Not really. Two of the arms were real. But the other four were prosthetics strapped onto her torso. Earlier, from a distance, he had thought the Nazis had genetically engineered a woman with six arms—the perfect pilot for a spider mecha. But of course not. Of course the Nazis, obsessed with the purity of their Aryan race, would not genetically modify what they perceived as Darwinian perfection. Theirs was a twisted, malevolent version of Darwinism, one that would have horrified the famed biologist. Everything that Nazism touched it infected, like a spider spreading its venom through the corpse of a captured fly.

King flew closer, determined to fire on the cockpit.

With two spider legs missing, the woman found herself with two free hands. Releasing the joysticks that had once controlled the severed limbs, she reached for control panels. She tapped buttons, and hatches opened across the spider's armored abdomen. Machine guns emerged and opened fire.

Bullets slammed into King's starfighter.

The canopy was missing (it had shattered when flown by the previous pilot, the poor kid). There was nothing between King and the gunfire. He ducked. Bullets pinged against the starfighter's hull, missing King's head by inches. At least they were just regular bullets, not umbrion rounds; that was something. King flew lower, flipped upside down, and tried to aim his missiles.

Bullets slammed into his prow, ripping through the thin, scaly hull. The dragon's head split open. One wing ripped free and hurtled into the distance. Damn cheap Red Dawn starfighters!

King tried to control his flight. But he was spinning madly. The spider's machine guns roared again and—

White light.

A *ping.*

A bolt of fear.

A realization. A bullet had pinged off his helmet! His head rang like a bell. For a second, he wondered if he was still alive.

Yes. Thanks to the wonders of modern helmet engineering, he was still breathing. He was still flying. Racing to collision. Racing right toward the swirling, molten core of the spinnenmutter!

King grabbed the yoke. He tried to turn away. The controls were dead.

An ejection seat would sure come in handy right about now, he thought.

Instead, he did things manually. He unbuckled his seat belt. He lifted his old bones from the chair. Coiling madly, the starfighter raced toward the inferno.

King leaped out into space.

The Xianglong slammed into the spinnenmutter's engine. The starfighter ripped apart like a chipmunk sucked into a lawnmower. The spider jolted, and her remaining legs curled inward. Was the machine dead? King dared to hope.

No such luck. The mecha coughed and sputtered, but the machine still moved. Still hunted. And the woman in the cockpit was still alive.

King was flying through space. Just a lone cowboy in a spacesuit, armadas clashing all around.

* * * * *

King floated through space.

He had no jetpack. No way to direct his flight. But he still had his two handguns. One was the antique revolver from the ranch, a collector's piece, a weapon that had already shed much blood this war. The other was his Trogdor, a modern plasma gun. King drew the latter, aimed away from the mechanical spider, and fired.

The recoil shoved King backward. For a moment, he glided through space. The arachnid mecha loomed behind him, casting a deep shadow. King winced, bracing for impac—

He slammed into the spider.

His spine hit the metal hull.

King roared in agony. It felt like he was back on the rack again. Once more—tortured by spiders. Back then, an alien spider had stretched him. Today it was a mechanical spider the size of a warship. As the pain leaped through him, it was suddenly too much. He was too injured. Too old. These stunts had been crazy even for a young, healthy man. He would die tonight. He—

Control yourself, he thought. *Shove down the pain. Plow through it.*

He regained his composure, then flipped himself over and pressed his belly against the hull. With his fingertips, he clung to the mechanical spider. It was difficult with his right hand, the real hand. But his left hand was a prosthetic built like a medieval gauntlet. The metal fingers gripped the mecha's craggy hull with the strength of pliers.

Like a spider himself, King began to climb the hull. The surface was pocked and scratched from the bombardment. He found many handholds. Did the woman in the cockpit notice him climbing? Had she seen him eject? Or did she think he'd been pulverized inside his Xianglong?

As he climbed the hull, King glanced over his shoulder. The battle raged. He beheld the surface of Earth far, far below, still blazing with explosions. Still the streaks of ballistic missiles scratched the sky, and the cities burned.

Closer to King, the various fleets battled in low orbit. The space forces of a hundred nations were fighting this war. Roughly, they organized themselves into four great powers. The Freedom Fleet comprised several subfleets: the American Eagle Fleet, the Royal British Fleet, the Indian Tiger Fleet, and the fleets of twenty other Alliance nations. The Red Dawn fleet, meanwhile, included the Dragon Fleet of China, the Russian Bear Fleet, and others. In the Desert Thorns flew the nations of North Africa and the Middle East (other than Israel, whose fleet flew for the Alliance). The fourth great power was their common foe—the Weltraumwaffe, the space force of the Nazi Fatherworld.

For decades, the Alliance and Red Dawn had fought each other. Briefly they had united to fight the rahs, but then again fell into enmity. Could they align once more to defeat a new common foe?

Of all the fleets King saw, the Dragon Fleet was the largest. Right now the Chinese juggernaut was slamming into the Weltraumwaffe, overwhelming the Nazi fleet with sheer numbers. While fewer than the Chinese, the Germans were better fighters, and they were giving a good account of themselves. Hundreds, maybe thousands of ruined starships floated in orbit. Every second, another hurled into deep space or tumbled toward Earth. As Earth exerted its gravity, the fleets kept spinning around the planet like bugs in water swirling around a drain.

King returned his focus to his task. Disabling this spider!

He crawled along the spider's underbelly, making his way around the swirling round engine. The same engine that had sucked up his Xianglong (no sign remained of the slender starfighter). From afar, the spinnenmutter's engine had seemed like a cauldron. Up close, King saw that blades spun inside, stirring a heart of fire. Pipes ran from the inner core into each arachnid limb, powering the cannon on the tip. Two of the metal legs were missing. The stumps sparked and pulsed with gleaming dark energy. Clouds of that strange, shadowy ash (could they really be umbrions?) curled into the distance.

King climbed onward along the spider's underbelly. In space, there was no up and down. Perspective was arbitrary. He could have imagined himself crawling on a horizontal surface. Or even imagined himself crawling downward headfirst. But he chose to imagine himself climbing *upward*. As if the spider was rearing and he was ascending its belly. It was funny. Even after countless hours in space, King still clung to notions like up and down, still chose a perspective to anchor himself. That was how deeply ingrained life on the surface was in the human mind.

We're not evolved for space travel, he thought. *Our brains can't handle it. But some of us are like the first fish to leave the ocean. Just able to take a quick gulp of air. That's me. I'm that fish. I'm that crazy sonuvabitch who keeps crawling where nature says you don't belong.*

Above King, a machine gun jutted from the spider's hull. With rumbling gears, the gun turned toward him. The woman in the cockpit had seen him.

The machine gun opened fire.

Already, King was leaping off the hull.

The machine gun missed! The spider's bullets sparked against her own craggy abdomen. Floating backward in space, King fired his Trogdor. A plasma bolt shot out. He hit! Right in the machine gun gears. The gears melted and jammed. The machine gun kept firing but could no longer swivel or aim. The bullets just flew harmlessly into the distance.

King fired his Trogdor into open space, using the recoil like a jetpack. He flew toward the arachnid mecha. Right toward its cockpit.

A canopy bulged from the metal spider like a giant eye. The woman stood within the steelglass bulb. Her feet operated pedals. Her two real hands grabbed joysticks overhead. Her prosthetic arms (two on each side) were strapped onto her torso. They moved with the organic fluidity of real limbs. Altogether, the woman gave the impression of a spider. A queen spider in the center of her nest. She stared at King. Her visor gleamed, reflecting the battle.

King saw himself reflected in the polished surface. With his spacesuit, his helmet, and his drawn gun, he struck an imposing figure. You could not see his aching bones, the weariness in his heart, the white hair, and the worries of the world in his eyes. All that woman saw, no doubt, was an assassin coming to kill her. And she was right. Maybe that was all that remained of King. Just a killer. Death in a spacesuit.

The woman in the mecha was struggling with a joystick. She was, he thought, trying to aim the machine gun King had disabled. Well, not gonna happen. Not with those gears melted.

And if she was hoping any Rattenjägers would save her, she would be very disappointed. The Chinese Xianglongs, while not particularly powerful, did a fantastic job overwhelming the German Rattenjägers with sheer numbers. A thousand dragonflies could overwhelm even the hungriest raven.

"You're mine," King growled.

He aimed his Trogdor at the canopy's hinges. He fired.

A blast of energy melted the hinges. King grabbed the entire bubble canopy—a hemisphere eight feet in diameter—and ripped it off the mecha. He hurled the steelglass dome aside. The canopy floated into the distance like the world's largest contact lens.

The woman in the cockpit released her joysticks. She drew a sidearm.

King reached out with his metal hand—a hand like a gauntlet. He grabbed her wrist and twisted. The woman cried out. The gun fell from her hand.

The woman stared at him. She was wearing a spacesuit and helmet. The vacuum should not have harmed her. Yet she froze as if turned to ice. This close to her, her gleaming visor lost some of its reflectivity. He could just make out her eyes now. One eye was blue. The other was red and glowing, though King couldn't tell whether it was a bionic eye or some high-tech contact lens.

Whatever the case, he knew those eyes. He had gazed into them countless times.

Their MindLinks connected.

He heard her voice.

"You!" she whispered.

He growled and aimed his gun at her head. His plasma would shut her up.

But he hesitated, finger on the trigger. Those eyes! Those eyes he knew so well!

A distant, lumbering dreadnought cast a shadow across the battle. In the shadow, the woman's visor lost all reflectivity. It was no longer a mirror, just simple glass. And King could finally see more than just her eyes. He saw her full face.

It was her.

It was Kim. His wife.

She drew a knife from her belt and thrust. The blade sank into his thigh. Right where the femoral artery was.

King gasped and released his wife.

"Kim!" he whispered.

She kicked him hard in the belly.

He flew backward through space, the knife embedded in his thigh, his blood floating in the vacuum. As he tumbled away, he could not stop seeing those beautiful eyes. Eyes that had shone with delight as she stabbed him.

CHAPTER EIGHT
Crows in the Sky

Earth's Orbit
5,000 miles over Papa New Guinea
September 4, 2207

King tumbled through space, a knife in his thigh, his spacesuit breached. The air was fleeing around the blade. He was getting cold. The battle spun all around him with a million streaking lights and explosions. But he saw her face.

The face of his wife.

Kim Fletcher-King. Operator of the mecha spider.

Kim—working for the Nazis. Kim—swastikas on her arms. Kim—a heartless killer.

Impossible. Yet it had to be her. He knew that face. And she had recognized him!

"You!" she had whispered.

Kim. Kim, why?

He would not live much longer. The tear in his spacesuit was small, and the blade blocked most of it. But air was still seeping out. Space was slithering in like a venomous serpent. Soon his heart would stop, and he would float forever, cold and dead, around the planet. To any casual observer, he would be just one more corpse among countless. Just an old warrior who had died doing what he loved.

But I never loved war, he thought. *I love Earth. I love the rustle of golden fields, the sound of flowing streams through the meadows, and the warm smile of Kim Fletcher. I never loved fighting. I just have the misfortune of being very, very good at it.*

He looked at Earth. Let the beauty of his world be the last thing he saw.

A voice filled his head, speaking with a Russian accent.

"You crazy American!"

It was Anton. The kid. Wherever he was, their MindLinks were close enough for telepathy.

"Shut the hell up, kid," King growled. "I'm dying. I don't want your voice to be the last thing I hear."

"You're not dying on my watch, you crazy cowboy bastard!"

And there came the Mashinki. The Russian shuttle was dented, scratched, and charred, but she was still spaceworthy. Ant sat at the helm. The kid wasn't a great pilot, but he was getting some great flying experience tonight. He flew closer to King, lining up the shuttle hatch with this tumbling, dying old man.

King reached out.

His metal hand grabbed the hatch.

He yanked it open, then pulled himself into the shuttle. He stumbled into the cockpit and slumped into the passenger seat.

The kid still held the yoke. His skin was pale, his eyes bugging out with fear. He stared at King.

"You look like shit, American."

King closed his eyes. "I feel worse."

The shuttle had lost its air. The knife in King's thigh was the only thing keeping the hole in his suit plugged. But not fully. Air was still bubbling out, pink and misty with blood. It was hard to think.

"Hey, hey! American!" The kid shook him. "You not going to die, are you? I need you to vouch for me. In the Alliance Fleet." He gulped. "I'm defecting. You need to tell your crazy

American friends not to shoot me."

King forced his eyes open.

Home stretch. Stay strong. Stay alive. For your family.

In his mind, he saw Kim's beautiful eyes. He saw the madness in them as she thrust the knife.

No. It couldn't be her. Couldn't be his Kim. Yet her voice echoed in his mind.

You!

And then something happened which King could only describe as a miracle. Through the haze of battle, he spotted her. A familiar starship.

The *Lioness*. Flagship of the Freedom Fleet.

Once, years ago, King had commanded a flagship. From aboard the legendary starship *Freedom*, he had led the Freedom Fleet, the mighty space force of the Alliance. Some had called the *Freedom* crude, even ugly, a machine of pure brutality and no grace, a relic from a barbarous era best forgotten. Nonsense. If you asked King, the *Freedom* had been the finest ship ever flown. A grand old lady of the stars.

But the *Freedom* was gone, making room for modern, more graceful ships. Ships with all the bells and whistles of innovative technology, the work of engineers who considered aesthetics, not just functionality. King knew the *Lioness* well enough. He had flown inside her before. She could not be more different from the *Freedom*, yet even King, a crotchety old technophobe, had to admit: the *Lioness* was a fine ship in her own right. She was a deserving flagship and a worthy successor to *Freedom.*

And he knew *Lioness*'s commander well. Gal "Spitfire" Levy. She was like a daughter to him.

King pointed a metal finger. It was hard to keep his arm up. "See that big American ship over there? The *Lioness*?"

The kid nodded. "*Da*. Your American starships are hard to miss. You build them big and ugly. Like your heads. Ha!" He took a swig of vodka from his canteen.

"Fly to the *Lioness.*" King slapped the kid's canteen away. "And stop drinking and flying."

With one eye, Anton peered into the canteen. "Your fellow cowboys will shoot us out of the sky, American." He shook the canteen, then sighed and capped it. "They will only see a Russian shuttle. With a Russian pilot who is far too sober for this shit."

King shook his head. "No. They'll detect my MindLink. Fly to the hangar. Go on. Hurry. *Faster.*"

His head spun. He could barely focus, barely see. He floated in a dream. Everything hurt but the pain was starting to fade, and that terrified him.

The kid wasn't a bad pilot. Not a great pilot, but not bad. What he lacked in experience he made up for with quick reflexes (particularly impressive given the amount of vodka in his system). Ant weaved through the battle, skirting German missiles and starfighters, and nearly crashing into several Alliance corvettes.

King smiled thinly. "Might . . . might wanna . . . apply to flight school. Someday."

His head was spinning. He needed a doctor. Needed air.

Where was he again? Ah, right, a Chinese starfighter. No. No! He was in the Mashinki now. With the kid. And the shuttle had lost its air. And he had a hole in his suit. Where was he now? In the back cabin? No. No, here in the cockpit.

He couldn't *think*, dammit. Scraps of thoughts kept rising, only to flutter away like dollar bills in the wind, and no matter how hard he chased them, they slipped from his grasp.

The breach in his suit. It was losing air. He had an oxygen tank, but something wasn't working. His brain wasn't getting the oxygen it needed. Why? Where was he?

Struggling to focus his eyes, King stared through the . . . porthole? No, a viewport. A gargantuan capital ship rose ahead.

The hull was blue and white. An Alliance ship. The *Lioness*. Right.

"Jim?" came a voice over MindWeb. "Jim, is that you?"

A familiar voice. Was he back on MindWeb now? Ah, yes, they must be detecting his implant from the ship.

"Jim, your oxygen levels are low!"

Who was saying that?

A hatch opened aboard the *Lioness*. The kid flew the Mashinki inside. The Red Dawn shuttle slammed down into the hangar. It screeched across the deck, raising showers of sparks. Damn, cheap Russian-made shuttles without landing skids. Katyusha's little machine was scratching up a beautiful Alliance deck.

Guards in blue ran up, aiming their pulse rifles at the skittering Russian shuttle. Alliance men. Good, all-American boys. They didn't fire, but they kept their fingers on the triggers. Supposedly, the Russians were allies now. And the guards could detect King's MindLink inside the shuttle. But those boys still weren't taking any chances. King didn't blame them. He had never learned to trust the Red Dawn either, even after joining forces against the spiders. Katyusha was like an untamed pit bull. One moment she was your fiercest defender. The next—she could bite your face off.

Finally the shuttle screeched to a halt. The kid popped the hatch, and air—sweet, real air!—flowed into the cabin.

King also found himself staring down the muzzles of the guards. He sighed. Nothing was ever easy.

* * * *

For a moment, King just sat in the shuttle, breathing. Ah, breathing! King had always taken it for granted. Never again. Truly a wonderful thing!

As he breathed, his mind cleared. He blinked, coughed,

and rose from his seat. His molars slammed together. Ah, there was the goddamn sciatica! A knife in his thigh, King limped out of the shuttle. The American guards stared at him, rifles raised, not sure what to make of this strange old spacer.

"Lower your guns!" rose a voice from the distance. The voice was feminine, soprano yet commanding. "That's an admiral you're looking at."

The guards lowered their guns at once.

"Ten'shun!" shouted one of the guards. "Admiral on deck!"

Cheeks flushed, the guard snapped King a salute.

King returned the salute, cracked his neck, and took a few steps between the guards. The hilt still stuck out from his thigh.

A tall woman marched across the deck toward him, chin held high, boots clattering. Everyone on the deck, from pilots to mechanics, stood at crisp attention. Not for King, the famous admiral, but for her. There she was—Gal "Spitfire" Levy herself. Commander of the flagship. The pride of the Freedom Fleet (at least if you asked James King).

Spitfire wore a perfect service uniform. The navy-blue trousers, blazer, and cap gleamed with brass buckles, and a ceremonial saber hung at her side. Her hair was a rich mahogany, aside from a single white stripe, and she wore it in a thick braid that hung across her shoulder. Two golden stars gleamed on each of her shoulders, denoting her a commander.

In the Freedom Fleet, commanders were senior officers. A young ensign or lieutenant could fly a starfighter or dropship. A captain commanded a small warship, usually a corvette. A major or colonel could command a frigate or destroyer. But the rank of *commander* was higher still. It was just one rank below the admiralty. There were only a handful of commanders in the entire Freedom Fleet. Theirs were the great capital ships, vessels like flying cities.

Hailing from Israel, Spitfire was the first Middle Eastern officer to command an Alliance flagship. Until now, the job had always gone to Americans and Brits. She was also the first woman at the job. And to complete the hat trick—she was the youngest flagship commander in Alliance history.

At forty-two years of age, Spitfire was staggeringly young to command the *Lioness*. Most commanders were in their sixties; the command of a flagship was the final triumph of their careers before retirement. But King had raised, trained, and molded Spitfire. Ever since her father had died, King had raised little Gal to fly. For years aboard the starship *Freedom*, he had groomed her for command. He knew Gal "Spitfire" Levy was a damn fine officer. Just like her father.

Yehuda Levy had been like a brother to King. And yes, Spitfire was like a daughter.

She stepped closer. Her features were sharp, her jawline merciless. She raised her chin and crossed her arms. She was a slender woman, some might say willowy, not big and bulky like King, but her height, her square shoulders, and her confident dark eyes gave her an aura of command. She was every inch the starship commander. And King still remembered the girl who ran barefoot down the corridors of the *Freedom*, waving a wooden sword.

"Well, well," Spitfire said, examining King. "Look what the cat dragged in."

"Cats don't drag bulldogs," King growled. "I go where I please. You got a problem with that, punk?"

She glared at him a moment longer, then burst into laughter. Tears filled her eyes. She embraced King, kissed his stubbly cheek, and stroked his hair.

"I worried we lost you, old man. I'm so glad you're here."

King snorted. "It would take a silver bullet to kill me. You know that, Spitfire."

She took a step back and looked him over, head to toe. She winced. "You look like shit."

"So I've been told," King muttered. "Gal, have you heard from Bastian?"

She pursed her lips. "Not yet. I was hoping you had. We still can't get MindWeb to connect to Earth."

King nodded. Bastian, his beloved son, was a big, strong marine. He could protect himself. But King couldn't help but worry. He remembered Bastian and Spitfire as children. They had been raised as siblings, would spend so many hours running around the *Freedom*, playing Captains & Aliens. They were in their forties now, both senior officers, but King couldn't stop worrying about them. To him, they would always be his children.

Speaking of children . . .

King gestured toward the dented Mashinki. "Spitfire, there's a Russian kid in there. He saved my life. Treat him well."

Spitfire cocked an eyebrow. "Why is he hiding? Is he shy?"

"Scared half to death. And possibly hungover. Now come on, Spitfire. Walk with me to the bridge of this ship. I want some answers."

Spitfire blinked. "Your leg, old man—"

But King was already marching down the corridor, knife in his thigh and everything. As he walked, spacers stared at him, aghast. His civilian spacesuit was charred and tattered. His leg bled. A sudden *boom* rocked the ship. King swayed, placed a hand on the bulkhead, then kept walking.

Spitfire followed close behind. She gave him that honor—walking one step behind. She was commander of this ship, a great leader, the scion of a military dynasty. Yet a part of Spitfire would, perhaps, always be that little orphan girl. The scared child whose father had died fighting the Red Dawn. To her, King would always be the man who took her in. Who taught her to fly. Who raised her to command. This was her ship, but even here, she showed him deference.

As he walked, King checked his neural operating system. Good. From here aboard the flagship, he could finally access MindWeb. But only within the Freedom Fleet. He couldn't connect to any servers or people on Earth. Or even contact Katyusha to organize some kind of collaboration (if such a thing were possible with the crazed premier).

King scanned again and again for Kim. She wasn't showing up.

She must be out of range, he thought. *Down on Earth or . . .*

He thought of that mechanical spider. Those eyes he knew so well.

You!

"Ridiculous," he muttered. It was the lack of oxygen to his brain. He was remembering things wrong. Maybe this whole horrible war was a dream.

* * * * *

King stepped onto *Lioness*'s bridge. For a moment, he stood frozen, staring, taking it in.

"I know," Spitfire said, entering behind him. "It's beautiful, isn't it? The view always takes my breath away. Even now, three years into my command." She smiled crookedly. "Why didn't the *Freedom* ever have a view like this?"

Stepping onto *Lioness*'s bridge was like floating into open space. The bridge was located deep inside the starship, engulfed within layers of armor and force fields. But you wouldn't know it. As soon as you walked in, the bulkheads, the deckhead, the floor itself—they disappeared. Became entirely transparent. And you could see space all around you. It was an optical illusion. In reality, cameras covered the starship's external hulls. They streamed the videos into the local MindWeb server. In turn, the server pumped the video feeds into every MindLink that stepped onto the bridge. The result? When you entered this chamber deep inside the starship, it felt like you had just walked out an airlock. A hallucination, crafted by feedback from the hull cameras.

King found the whole design unnecessarily complex. Overwhelming. What was wrong with some old black-and-green screens? But modern officers wanted to see the battle all around them. To get a sense of it. Of course, what they saw wasn't what a man would see with his naked eyes in space. King had just come back from a long space walk, and he could tell the difference. On the bridge, the hallucination helped you, augmenting reality, molding it to fit the human mind. It zoomed in on distant starships. It outlined the constellations with silvery threads, giving you intuitive navigational references. And the software displayed strings of data everywhere across the vista, naming ships and detailing their stats. King didn't like this new style of bridge. This felt more like some showy planetarium, built to entertain and dazzle, not the bridge of a warship. He had always preferred the shadowy, cramped bridge of old dreadnoughts like the starship *Freedom*. But, well, the *Freedom* was gone now. And that old tech had faded from the world.

The ways of old warriors like me are fading away, he thought. *The kids like Spitfire love their shiny new toys.*

Yes, King felt particularly old today. His back still ached. His leg was losing feeling. But he forced his spine straight and squared his shoulders. Like everyone else, he was afraid, and he was worried about his family. But he was also an admiral. A retired admiral in a civilian spacesuit, yes. But right now, civilian or not, he was fighting this war. A war he didn't understand. A war against a shadow from the past. A war King had been fighting from the trenches, blinded by smoke and shadows, cut off from the view of the high command.

"So!" King said. "Will somebody finally tell me where the hell these Nazi bastards came from?"

The guard at the door stiffened. He stared at King—a grimy old man, his spacesuit tattered, a knife in his leg, a cowboy hat on his head. Undoubtedly, King was a bizarre sight. But thanks to the magic of MindWeb, the guard would be seeing King's admiral rank floating above him.

"Admiral on deck!" the guard cried and snapped a salute. His eyes dropped to King's leg. "Sir? You're hurt!"

No shit, King thought, limping to the center of the bridge. Officers turned to look at him, eyes wide. Then they hurriedly returned to their tasks. The *Lioness* was engaged in battle. At the moment, her prow cannons were firing at a line of German destroyers. But the battle was everywhere, extending for many megameters around Earth.

King surveyed the war in space. Thousands of warships were battling all around. And countless starfighters. The Alliance formations were still holding, though they had lost many ships. The Red Dawn had suffered even heavier losses. Much heavier. Katyusha was still leading her armada in reckless charges into the German lines. When first rising into space (by God, it must have been four or five days ago now), King had seen only a few hundred Nazi warships. Their numbers had swelled. Wherever they were coming from—they were still coming.

"Well?" King said. "Will somebody tell the ignorant, retired admiral? Where did these bastards spring from?"

A gruff, deep voice, speaking with an English accent, sounded ahead.

"From a parallel universe, old friend. A universe of infamy where evil reigns. A universe where the scourge of Nazism has spread like a tumor. And now that cancer spreads here. That is where they come from, old boy. And to that hell we shall send them back!"

*****

King inhaled sharply. He knew that voice.

A chair swiveled toward him, revealing an elderly man. Instead of a military uniform, the elder wore an old-fashioned, three-piece suit. The suit stretched across the rounded belly. A top hat hung askew atop the man's big, round head. He had a face like a bloodhound, jowly and garrulous, with a prominent underbite. But unlike a bloodhound, his eyes were not sad or droopy. Those eyes stared with fierce intelligence. The man was well into his eighties and still sharp as a rah claw. He walked confidently toward King, his cane swinging—an accessory more than an aid.

King knew him well. Here was George Balthazar Godwin himself. War hero. Statesman. Legend. High Commander of the Alliance. And King's mentor.

"James, my dear boy," Godwin said, "you look like shit."

"They keep telling me," King muttered.

The elderly man barely stood taller than King's shoulders, and he was a good fifteen years older. Yet there was deep strength to Godwin, a vitality that belied his years. He patted King on the shoulder.

"Get to the infirmary, old friend," Godwin said, his normally rumbling voice suddenly soft. He looked at the knife in King's thigh, then back into King's eyes. "Get yourself patched up. Get that thorn pulled out of your paw. Eat a good meal and take a long nap. Rest. Then put on a uniform. We're back in the wars, old friend. I'm going to need you."

Rest? Why rest when there were enemies to kill? King wanted to keep fighting right now. To ask for another starfighter. To go out again and battle the invaders. Just slap a Band-Aid on him, then send him back into the action. Forty years ago, that was exactly what he would have done. But he wasn't that young man anymore. No longer was Bulldog a brass young pilot who could fight for days on end. His head was spinning again, so he nodded. This might be a long, long war. He would need to pace himself.

Soon enough, King found himself in the infirmary. They pulled the knife from his thigh. It had just missed the femoral artery, and the skin around the wound had frozen and died in the vacuum. A dozen cuts across his body needed stitches, one of his ribs had cracked, and they said he was dehydrated. Oh, and his back was sprained. What else was new?

I've had worse, he thought. *And many others are having worse right now.*

It seemed unfair to King that so many young soldiers should be dying. Many of them were just kids. Just damn kids like Anton. Teenagers. Dying out there in space, blown apart, ripped open. While old men like him lingered on.

Lying in the infirmary bed, he tried to reach Earth's MindWeb. He tried to contact his son. His granddaughter. And his wife.

Her blue eyes stared in his memory. Eyes full of love, gazing at him in their home. Then flashing eyes full of rage, one red and blazing, boring into him like her blade.

Earth was still offline. His family wasn't answering.

"Kim," he whispered.

He tried to rise from bed. To get back into the fight. But something heavy flowed over him, knocking him back onto the bed, then pinning him down. It was exhaustion—a force as real as any foe. He tried to rise again but it consumed him, and he plunged into dreams in which he tumbled through space, lost in an endless battle.

Part II
Space and Land

CHAPTER NINE
Don't Talk to Strangers

The *Barbarossa*
14 megameters over the South Pacific
September 4, 2207

Stowy cowered in a dark, shaking place. As the torpedoes boomed and the klaxons wailed, she thought back to her grandmother.

As a little girl, Stowy had been frightened of thunderbolts and lightning. When she saw lightning outside her window, when she heard thunderclaps, she would run to her mother. But Mother was always so weary. She worked in the factories all day and sang for the troops all night, and Father was off to war. Back then, the great Spider War had still been raging. All the Fatherworld had mustered to destroy the spiders, those alien arachnids who called themselves "rahs."

(Since discovering that parallel universes existed, Stowy had wondered if the Fatherworld on the other side had also fought the spiders. So she crawled through the ducts of the *Barbarossa*, placed her ears against vents, and listened to spacers talk. And she learned it was true. In this parallel universe where *Barbarossa* flew, the Fatherworld had fought the very same aliens. At the very same time. But here, the planet wasn't called the Fatherworld. They called it Earth. In Stowy's universe, they had called the planet Earth long, long ago. But the Eternal Führer had rechristened humanity's planet. She had learned this at school, and the pupils had all hailed him, thanking the Eternal Führer for giving their planet its true name.)

"It's only thunder, Samantha," her mother would say, rubbing weary eyes. "Go back to bed."

Stowy didn't like being called Samantha. She liked being called Stowy. What her father called her. Because she always stowed away in his shuttles. She wanted to tell Mother that. But back then, she had not yet learned how to talk. So she only stood there stubbornly, too scared to return to her bedroom. The terrible thunder still sounded outside. Monsters! Roaring spiders in the sky!

"Samantha, please, I need to sleep," Mother said. "I only have an hour before work."

So Stowy would run to her grandmother instead. Granny lived with them in the townhouse. At the time, Stowy had believed her the wisest, kindest, and *oldest* woman in the universe (though in reality, Grandma was only in her seventies).

Another thunderclap rattled the windows. Stowy ran into the old woman's arms. Grandma rocked her gently.

"Oh, sweetheart, do you know what that sound is? Not bombs. Not monsters either. There is a castle on the clouds. A wonderful, magical castle where little girls are free to play the day away. At night, when it's time for these little princesses to sleep, they jump on their beds, driving their mothers crazy. The beds shake the castle floor, which shakes the clouds that hold up the castle. That's what causes thunder and lighting. Little girls who don't want to go to sleep."

Stowy would always giggle. Grandma was so silly. How Stowy wished she could speak to the woman! Yet it would be years before she learned that skill.

Well, now Stowy was older. Thirteen-and-a-half. And she could talk a little, and not only to her blanket. As Stowy cowered in the ductwork, as bombs exploded and war raged all around, she remembered her grandmother. As she curled up in Luna, her favorite blanket, Stowy pretended she was in the woman's warm arms. She pretended the explosions were only little girls jumping on their beds, and that her castle on the clouds was closer than ever.

She was no longer a little girl. No longer so naive. During the Great Struggle for Freedom (or World War Two, as Father had called it), children as young as her had fought. Countless thirteen-year-olds had swarmed into the American and Russian lines, sacrificing themselves to the Fatherland. They soaked up bullets, paving the way to freedom. With their lives, they had bought Hitler's victory. So no, Stowy was no longer a child. She was old enough to know that castles on the clouds were not real. And that the sounds outside were bombs hitting the hull. And that she might not survive the night.

Barbarossa was a starship the size of a city. Its HVAC ducts and service shafts spread like the tunnels of an ant colony. Stowy had sneaked aboard a week ago. Since then, she had crawled through miles of ducts, exploring this vast labyrinth. And she had seen only a small part of this sprawling realm. Sometimes she reached vents, and she could peer down into a mess hall, an armory, a Rattenjäger hangar, or an SS bunk. (Most of the spacers here served in the Wehrmacht, and they gave the SS—an elite unit of torturers—a wide berth.) Like this, Stowy could eavesdrop on officers, troopers, and pilots. Like at school, everyone here spoke German, which Stowy could understand fluently (though only speak with effort). By eavesdropping through the vents, Stowy learned where she was, how the war was going.

We're in the other universe, she knew. *We're fighting against the subhumans. In space. Above a world still called Earth.*

A blast hit *Barbarossa* again. The ductwork rattled. The little treasures in Stowy's pockets spilled out. She had been wearing the same dress for years now, patching each hole and tear with a new pocket. By now, her dress was mostly just pockets, each of different fabric. Inside each pocket—a treasure. A steel skull-shaped pin, which an SS officer had lost (Stowy worried it was imbued with dark magic, so she kept a close eye on it). A sour candy in a faded wrapper. A silver Reichsmark worth a fortune, found in an ancient shipwreck (or so she liked to imagine). A postcard from Propa, a resort town for Nazi officers, folded over several times. Her pet mouse. A large snail shell, which Stowy had filled with smaller snail shells, forming a rattle. And of course—plastic dinosaurs, her favorite childhood toys. Often, to calm herself, she would line up these treasures again and again. Few things soothed her as much as lining things up. She knelt in the duct, collected her fallen treasures, and stuffed them back into her pockets.

In this universe, we never won the Second World War, Stowy thought, reaching for a few crystals that had rolled into the shadows. *In this universe, Hitler died. In this universe, our glorious Third Reich fell centuries ago.*

It was strange. Stowy came from Canada—a vast, cold province of Germany. She was a proud Aryan daughter of the Reich. But in this universe, Canada had never become a province of Germany. No country had. Everything was different on this side of the portal. Would she be cured here? Would her autism, the impurity that doomed her to death, fade away? Would, in this universe, Stowy be able to speak to strangers? Would she stop lining up dinosaurs? Would bright lights and loud sounds no longer scare her?

"Am I cured here?" she whispered to Luna.

Yes, she could speak to her blanket (so long as nobody was watching her). And she could speak to Algernon, the mouse who slept in one of her pockets (so long as nobody else heard). But strangers were different. You shouldn't talk to strangers. Grandmother had told her so.

Grandmother had talked to strangers once. She spoke to

the people down the road. The ones folk whispered were part of the Resistance. And after that, Grandma disappeared. Stowy never saw the dear old woman again. Not unless you counted that body hanging in the distance from the crane. Yes, Grandma was gone now. But her words of wisdom remained. Thunder was the sound of princesses jumping on their beds, and you must never, ever talk to strangers.

Another blast rattled the ductwork. Another torpedo hitting the *Barbarossa.* Stowy clung to her blanket. Her treasures jangled in her pockets.

Boots thudded below the duct. Shouts echoed through the ship.

"The Amis' shields are strong."

"We're gonna board the bastards. The *Lioness* will be ours!"

"To the airlocks, men! Move!"

"Let's give those subhumans hell."

Stowy crawled through the rattling ducts. Another blast lifted her into the air. Thankfully the duct was narrow, so she only flew a few inches upward. But then the *Barbarossa* tilted, and she was sliding down the duct. She scrabbled for purchase, finally grabbing onto a vent. Steadying herself, she peered through the vent to the corridor below.

The Waffen-SS, the elite combat unit of the Schutzstaffel, ran below. They wore full battlesuits. The black plates of armor gleamed. Red swastikas adorned their arms, while the lightning bolts of the SS crackled with real electricity on their breastplates. Their visors were down, shaped as skulls. Stowy imagined these warriors of the Fatherworld as mechanical skeletons. She had heard that Dr. Anneliese was inventing actual skeleton robots, machines that were stronger and faster than men. But even the men below seemed like machines to Stowy, covered in metal, no mercy in their clockwork hearts.

Mercy? No, that did not exist in the Fatherworld. Only in the old forbidden books from Father's library. Only in the heart of a little impure girl who tended to her mouse and her blanket. Mercy was a thing for the weak and the broken. In this world, only the cruel prevailed.

But then again . . . this was a new universe. Maybe things were different here. Maybe she could be cured. Maybe, if she stayed here long enough, she would be able to talk properly, not just whisper while looking at her toes. Maybe she would become strong and cruel like Eva König, the Bitch from Berlin, or like Dr. Anneliese, whose twisted mind invented twisted machines. But so far, even after several days in this universe, she seemed like the same old Stowy. Still afraid of lights and noises. Still lining up her dinosaurs. Maybe, to be healed, she must get off this starship. And she must live among the subhumans.

In the Fatherworld, she had learned, there were three types of humans. There were the Aryans, the only real humans. There were the untermenschen—the inferior races. The Eternal Führer had wiped most of them out, but a few still lived in zoos so that children could learn about them. They had hexagrams tattooed onto their wrists, a mark of Cain; they were the lowest of the low in the hierarchy of pestilence. And then there were the impure. People like Stowy. They were born to Aryan parents, but something about them was broken. They were sick. Or deformed. Or, like her, broken in the head. Stowy had a black triangle tattooed onto her wrist—symbol of impurity. In the eternal struggle for purity, cripples like her were euthanized.

And now Stowy wondered. Were there other impures here in this universe? Oh, she knew there were millions, maybe *billions* of subhumans here. The soldiers kept talking about it. That was the main reason they were here, after all. They had come to this universe to exterminate its infestation of lower races. But what of those like Stowy? Aryans who were somehow less than human? Who were broken? Might they be cured here like in Stowy's dreams? Or would this universe too seek to exterminate her?

Panic swelled in her. But she wrapped herself in Luna, and she lined up her plastic dinosaurs along the duct, trying to calm down.

Remember Father's books, she told herself.

In those old books, the impure lived among the pure. They were treated, healed, cured. Not burned. Even the Elephant Man, Stowy's hero, had ultimately found love and shelter on Earth. She would find help here in this universe. She would not find a literal castle on the clouds, perhaps. She was too old for such fantasies. But she might find a place where she could be free, where doctors healed you rather than experimented on you, where maybe you could even talk to strangers.

A voice pierced the starship, high-pitched and grating, so loud that Stowy jumped.

"Move it, soldiers! We got a subhuman ship to purify. With me, Aryan soldiers! To victory!"

Stowy peeked between the vents. Her eyes widened, her heart pounded, and a gasp fled her lips.

A woman stood below, wearing a Waffen-SS uniform. The insignia on her shoulders denoted her *gruppenführer.* A general! Yet she seemed so young. Only a teenage girl. The *kindergeneral* removed her helmet, revealing rosy cheeks, blond hair, and two blazing eyes—one blue, the other red and bionic. Her lips stretched into a toothy grin. A predator's grin.

Stowy gasped.

She recognized that girl. Right there below the vent, leading the Waffen-SS, stood Eva König. The Bitch from Berlin. Granddaughter of Führer Helmut König.

Stowy had grown up hearing about Eva, the little heroine of the Fatherworld. All good Aryan children knew of *der goldene engel*, as Der Stürmer dubbed her. The Golden Angel. Eva König killed her first man at eight years old. At twelve, she fought in space, slaying the nefarious rahs. She slew a hundred alien spiders, they claimed. If anything eclipsed her prowess in battle it was her cruelty. Eva was known not only as a warrior but as a torturer. Every Monday morning, broadcast live across the Fatherworld, she tortured a convict to death, showing off her blades, pincers, and pliers. Children across the Fatherworld would gather every week to watch. If Stowy tried to look away, her teacher would smack her. And so she would watch. And she knew the perverse pleasure Eva König took in inflicting agony.

There, right below Stowy, not a meter away—that infamous torturer from the holofeeds. The scion of the König family. The future führer. Eva König herself! So close Stowy could reach through the vent and touch her.

Suddenly Eva froze. The young woman inhaled sharply, then raised her head.

Stowy scrambled away from the vent, heart pounding. She cowered in the duct above the corridor. Had Eva seen her? A beam of red light pierced the vent only a few inches away from Stowy. That was the light of Eva's bionic eye. She was staring from below! Stowy's heart beat so loudly she feared Eva would hear it.

Then the red beam of light turned away.

"Onward, Aryan soldiers!" Eva cried. "For the Fatherworld!"

Boots thumped. Stowy peered through the vent again. Eva and the other SS soldiers were running down the corridor, heading to the hangar bay.

Eva's voice echoed through the starship. "Let's kill some subhumans!"

"Hail Eva!" cried her troops.

Their voices were moving farther away. Stowy's heart kept

hammering. She clutched Luna close to her body.

"Did you hear, Luna?" she whispered to the blanket. "They're going to get into dropships. They're going to fly out of the *Barbarossa.* And fly into the *Lioness,* an Ami starship." A shudder ran through her. "Amis. You know, Luna. *Americans.* Like in Father's library."

Stowy knew her history. How America was a country full of subhumans and subhuman-lovers. How they had tried to develop nuclear weapons first, but Hitler beat them to it. How New York burned in the atomic blaze. What year had it been? 1946, Stowy thought. Yes, in 1946 Hitler had nuked New York City. The famous photo had hung in Stowy's classroom, depicting Hitler standing atop the Statue of Liberty's head, hand in the air. The massive copper head still lay among the rubble of Manhattan, a swastika etched onto her forehead, a memento of victory. Hitler had decreed that it should never be moved, and still it corroded in the ruins, centuries later. But in this universe . . . that had never happened. In this universe, the Amis and their allies had won. And they were still here, centuries later. Still fighting!

In the stories, the Allies were brutal. Stalin, they said, was the greatest butcher in history. And America was a cesspool of lower races, beasts not even human—more like wild beasts. Well, so they said. So what? Stowy was done believing the stories. Too many stories! Fake. Fairy tales. Lies. The Fatherworld considered slavs and Amis to be subhuman. And it considered Stowy impure.

The enemy of my enemy is my friend, she thought.

And so she made the choice. It shot terror through her. Her head spun and she could barely breathe. But she knew it was the right choice.

She had always been good at stowing away. So she would stow away in Eva's dropship, make her way onto the American ship, and hope to find new life.

* * * * *

Stowy crawled through the ducts, as fast as a mouse fleeing a snake. After escaping Uncle Baer's hospital, she had spent years hiding in the streets of Munich. Often she would slink along rooftops and through pipes. She could crawl faster than she walked. Stowy did not know all the ducts inside the *Barbarossa.* Learning this labyrinth would take years. But from in here, she could hear the cries of the soldiers, their thumping boots, and the shrieks of Eva König. As they raced below in the corridor, she crawled above through the ducts.

Am I jumping from the frying pan to the fire? Stowy wondered. *Am I escaping one group of monsters into another?*

The Germans were cruel, yes. But would the Amis be any better? In the Fatherworld, history books accused the Amis of enslaving Africans and killing Native Americans. They were a cruel, genocidal race of slavers—not like the noble Aryan race. (Stowy had always thought that silly. The Fatherworld bragged of purifying the world of subhumans. Then, in the same breath, chastised the Amis for genocide. What the Nazis admired in themselves they loathed in others. Stowy's father had once called that *cognitive dissonance.*)

All those stories of Ami cruelty returned to Stowy now. Would the Amis capture her, experiment on her, even euthanize her? Were the stories true? Were the Amis wild animals, monsters, creatures more like zombies than men?

No. Of course not! That was just Luna talking.

"No more second thoughts, Luna!" she whispered. Her blanket was always whispering in her mind, trying to talk her out of trouble. Usually that was wise, but tonight Luna was just trying to scare her. Stowy ignored her blanket's little voice.

Soon enough, the ducts reached one of *Barbarossa*'s hangar bays. Peeking through a vent, Stowy saw a vast chamber. It must have been the size of two football fields. It was hard to believe such a chamber could exist inside a starship. And indeed, this hangar was only a small part of the starship. The full size of *Barbarossa*, the largest ship ever built, defied Stowy's comprehension.

Through the vents, Stowy examined the hangar. The airlocks were closed, sealing out the vacuum of space. Red banners hung from the deckhead far above, emblazoned with swastikas. Most of this cavernous hangar was empty. The starfighters had all launched to fight. But a handful of dropships still stood here. The Wolfjägers were big, bulky ships covered in armor. They were named after wolves, but they reminded Stowy of ankylosaurs. Like the little plastic one she had, all covered in armor. When she lined up dinosaurs, she usually placed the ankylosaurus last. So it could defend the rear with its armored tail.

The SS troops were racing toward the Wolfjäger dropships. Eva ran among them, her hair streaming like a golden banner. They all held heavy Lugerheulens, the new guns from the nightmares of Dr. Anneliese. Unlike earlier and simpler guns, like those that had killed Stowy's parents, Lugerheulens shot umbrion rounds. Stowy shuddered. Umbrions. Particles of darkness. Usually, darkness simply meant the absence of light. Until Dr. Anneliese discovered a new kind of darkness. An uber-darkness. Umbrions, particles captured between dimensions, were the antimatter to protons. They could swarm like living shadows, devouring light and life.

Stowy knew how devastating umbrion rounds could be. A few years ago, back when she had still gone to school, her teacher had once taught her something wrong. The subhumans from history, the teacher had claimed, had DNA that was 98% human. Like a gorilla. The next day, the Gestapo arrived at the school. They took everyone out to the yard. As the students watched, the Gestapo lined the principal and teachers up on a stage. As if they were dinosaur toys. And the Gestapo mowed them down with their Lugerheulens (a brand-new gun at the time). Stowy never forgot how that black smoke got inside them. How it seemed almost to consume the teachers from the inside out.

Subhumans, the Gestapo later explained, had no human DNA at all. Not 98%, not 97%, not 1%. That was the meaning of the word subhuman. They were not human. They were *below* humans. In the mud and filth under the Aryan heel. The new teaching staff should know that. And if any good student wished to report more heresy against the Eternal Führer's teachings, well, the Gestapo was always there, happy to help.

Since that day, Stowy had always feared those guns. And feared subhumans more than ever. Now she was racing *toward* soldiers with Lugerheulens, heading *toward* a ship of subhumans!

Among others, Stowy became meek. Timid. Shy. No, not shy, perhaps. *Anxious* was more accurate, Stowy thought. She feared other people, and among them, she always lowered her eyes. She trembled. She mumbled and whispered if she could speak at all (usually she could not). Yet when alone, something happened to Stowy. She became . . . well, not brave. She didn't think herself brave. But she could speak to Luna and Algernon and her dinosaurs. She got angry sometimes too, punched the walls, and screamed. And she became headstrong. Impulsive. It was why she would sneak into Father's shuttle. Why she had escaped the hospital. Why she had claimed the Braun family's attic and stole their food. And why she was here, aboard the *Barbarossa.* Despite her autism, despite her timidity around others, in the shadows she became an impulsive, daring little thing, a mouse that could show its teeth.

Eva and her soldiers were entering the Wolfjägers now. Stowy would have to make her move. But how? She was here in the ducts. And deckhands were everywhere below, racing across the hangar, busy at their tasks. This was a ship at war, and the hangar crew had their hands full. They were waving batons, opening and closing airlocks, directing the traffic of big Wolfjägers and small Rattenjägers alike. The hangar was a place of movement, bright lights, loud noises, and many staring eyes. Not quite the paradise for an autistic girl with sensory sensitivities and a healthy fear of people. And not exactly heaven for sneaking around, either. If Stowy simply dropped from the vent, and if she survived all that stimulus, somebody in the hangar would see her. To make things more complicated and crowded, even *more soldiers* were rushing into the hangar now, ready to deploy in their Wolfjägers. How would Stowy ever sneak from the duct, across this busy hangar, and into a Wolfjäger? A tall order. Even for her, the mistress of sneaking.

Just then a klaxon wailed.

Red lights flashed overhead.

"Incoming!" cried the foreman, and the soldiers dropped to the deck and covered their heads. Inside the duct, Stowy did the same.

The *boom* was deafening. The blast rattled Stowy around the duct like a marble inside a pipe. A few of her plastic dinosaurs fell from her pockets. She stuffed them back in, coughed, and peered down the vent.

A torpedo had hit *Barbarossa*! A dent appeared in the hull by an airlock. Soldiers were running and shouting everywhere, the red lights kept flashing, and the alarms kept wailing.

"Incoming!" rose the foreman's voice again.

It was Stowy's chance. As the next blast hit, she ripped off the vent, then leaped downward from the duct.

It was a long drop.

As she fell, another *boom* thudded all around her. The hangar shook.

It was a *really* long drop. Longer than Stowy had estimated.

She fell a terrifying distance, but *Barbarossa* jolted under the bombardment. As if through magical intervention, the g-force slowed Stowy's fall, and she landed like a cat. A clumsy cat. A clumsy cat that never landed on its feet. Yet one that, thankfully, had nine lives.

"Meow," she whispered.

Already she was scampering again, leaping from shadow to shadow. Ammo crates had fallen over. Some had spilled their dangerous loads onto the deck. Spacers ran around, shouting, trying not to slip over the rolling bullets. Stowy sneaked between the deckhands, racing toward one of the Wolfjägers. The very one Eva was now entering.

A way to reach the Amis, Stowy thought. *My fellow affronts to purity.*

Stowy shoved the crate she was hiding behind. The big wooden box overturned, spilling grenades. The little bombs rolled across the deck like the devil's marbles. Soldiers shouted and pointed. During the distraction, Stowy bolted forward. Like a falcon's shadow in a storm, she darted right into the Wolfjäger.

Success!

Well, almost. She had made it into the Wolfjäger. But she still had to hide. The Waffen-SS filled the dropship. Thankfully the shadows were thick, and the soldiers were distracted by the rolling grenades, the smoke, and the enemy blasts that kept hitting *Barbarossa.* There were no ducts inside the Wolfjäger, but Stowy found a hatch into the crawlspace. She scampered between soldiers' boots, opened the hatch, and crawled under the deck. All without anyone seeing. Yes, there was a reason they called her Stowy.

Now *this* was success! She was inside the dropship. Inside the crawlspace. Right under their steel-tipped boots. And they didn't suspect a thing. Stowy covered her mouth to stifle her giggle. Next stop—the Ami ship!

"All right, soldiers!" Eva screamed above. Her boots thumped atop the crawlspace, only inches from Stowy's head. "Strap in. We're flying to *Lioness* to show the Amis hell!"

"Hail Eva!" the troops cried.

"Remember, soldiers, for the Glory of the Reich, we shall—"

Eva suddenly fell silent.

Stowy crouched in the crawlspace below Eva's feet. Her heart froze. She peered through a tiny crack in the hatch.

"What is this?" Eva said. The young SS officer knelt. "A dinosaur?"

Oh no.

Stowy patted her pocket. The one where she normally kept her plastic ankylosaurus.

The pocket was empty.

A few soldiers above snickered. Not Eva though. The Golden Angel wasn't laughing.

"Why is there a plastic dinosaur in my dropship?" the *kindergeneral* cried.

"Maybe he wants to come along for the battle," said one soldier. The others laughed. Eva silenced them with a snarl.

Stowy's heart stopped beating.

No. Führer, no.

"Look at this!" Eva said. "Handprints on the deck. A child's handprints."

The deranged young general grabbed the hatch.

Stowy began scampering away down the crawlspace.

Hands grabbed her ankles.

Stowy screamed, and Eva pulled her, and all her little dinosaurs, and all her little treasures, spilled from her pockets. Stowy scrabbled for purchase but caught only her dice, her snail shell, and her T-rex without a tail. And then Eva was yanking her out from the hatch.

Right into the cabin of the dropship.

Stowy's hope crashed. Her success had become a failure. There would be no castle on the clouds, no new life. Only a torturous death.

*****

Stowy struggled like a fish on a line. Eva held her up by her ankles. The *kindergeneral* was not a large woman (she was barely a woman at all, and more of a sadistic child), but her battlesuit augmented her strength. Modern battlesuits were marvels of German engineering; more treats from Dr. Anneliese's cupboard of forbidden toys. With this extra electric strength, Eva König held out Stowy with one hand. She displayed Stowy to the troops, then shook the girl so that more treasures spilled from her many pockets. Out tumbled rare coins, a plastic worm, two pieces of chalk, a folded drawing of John Carter and Dejah Thoris (Stowy had drawn them herself), a small Elephant Man skull (which she had made from clay), and another dinosaur (her beloved parasaur). Thankfully Algernon clung on, hiding inside one pocket. As the trinkets rained, Eva laughed. Her laughter was a cold, cruel thing, a sound like falling icicles or clashing blades.

"Look at this, soldiers!" Eva said. "I caught a little stowaway."

The soldiers laughed.

Stowy tried to scream. Tried to beg. But she could not make a sound.

"We should keep her as our mascot," said one soldier, an *oberjunker* (a common rank of enlisted killers and torturers—the little devils of the SS). He lifted his skull helmet, revealing a gaunt face with a huge, toothy grin and bulging eyes. One was a bloodshot yellow eye, the other an adlerauge. Scar tissue surrounded the bionic eye.

"Commander, can we keep her?" asked an o*bersturmführer,* a junior officer, just young, self-important, and stupid enough to risk speaking so casually to the granddaughter of the führer. "Good for morale!"

"She might be a subhuman," warned another soldier, an *oberscharführer.* The hulking NCO kept his face hidden behind his skull visor, but judging by his rank, he was an older, more experienced soldier. "She might have sneaked aboard from an Ami or communist ship."

The *oberscharführer* stepped forward. With thick, gloved fingers, he grabbed Stowy's cheeks. He squeezed them so tightly her teeth ached.

"This one is Aryan!" the *oberscharführer* said. "Look. Good stock. Light eyes. Ears a bit too big, but she'll grow into them. Definitely a human. One of ours."

Eva tilted her head, squinted, and scrutinized Stowy. Her eyes burned. The real blue one burned just as brightly as the red bionic one. Stowy had to look away. She was still hanging upside down like the catch of the day. All the blood was rushing into Stowy's head.

"No," Eva said softly, her voice like a slithering serpent. "No, this one is impure. Look."

Holding Stowy's ankles with one hand, Eva reached out her other hand. She grabbed Stowy's sleeve and ripped it clean off, revealing a slender, pale arm.

And on that arm—a tattoo. The *schwarzes dreieck*. An inverted black triangle. The mark of shame. The Third Reich's symbol for the disabled.

Soldiers gasped.

"She's diseased!" said one soldier.

"Toss the rat into the incinerator," said another.

Stowy squirmed. Perhaps, if she could talk, she would have begged. But once more, in her terror, she had become mute.

If she could not plead for her life, she must fight for it.

She clawed at Eva, but her fingernails only scraped across the young woman's armor. She kicked, trying to free her ankles, but Eva's grip was iron. Hanging upside down, Stowy flailed around like a newborn baby. Finally Eva gave her a sharp, ringing slap across the cheek. Stowy's head spun.

"No," Eva hissed. "No, we won't kill this one. The tattoo. This one must be an escapee. One of Dr. Baer's little nieces has run away, it seems."

Stowy froze.

Her insides turned to ice.

Dr. Rudolph Baer. The Madman from Munich. Or Uncle Baer, as he liked his little patients to call him. Was he here? Here on this ship?

For a long time, Stowy had suppressed the memories. That terrible year, that agony in the laboratory, vanished into the shadows of subconscious trauma, only rising to clatter and claw in her nightmares. But now the horrors reemerged into waking hours. Snippets of memories floated through her mind. Uncle Baer, a man with the face a vulture, flaying a child alive. Then giving a boy a candy and a kiss. The vulture cutting children apart, then stitching them together, creating little Frankenstein monsters. Then volunteering at the local orphanage, reading stories to children. Uncle Baer, inviting children into his office for chocolates and movies, then showing them his lampshades made of human skin. Some lampshades still displayed triangle tattoos. All those memories kept flooding Stowy, coming faster and faster now. The gas chamber in his lab. A place for children he was done experimenting on. The pile of gray corpses. The smoke rising from the chimney like ghosts.

No, she thought. *No, I can't go back. Not to him. Not to that nightmare.*

She had escaped that lab. That monster. Was he really

here? Here aboard the *Barbarossa*?

Oh, she should have stayed in the attic! Even the gutters and slums of Munich were safer. Why had she sneaked into *Barbarossa*? She had stepped right into a trap. Foolish mouse!

As Stowy panicked, dangling by her ankles, Eva scrutinized her. Slowly, *der goldene engel*'s lips stretched into a crooked smile. Her eyes narrowed with wicked delight.

"You're trembling, little one," Eva said. "You're one of Uncle Baer's lab mice, aren't you? I've heard talk of one who escaped. A naughty little mouse who didn't like being experimented on." Eva pouted, and then her grin returned, wider than before, a deranged grin that showed too many teeth. "It's time to return to your loving uncle's care."

A tear flowed from Stowy's eye.

"No," she whispered.

Eva frowned. "What's that?"

"No," Stowy whispered. A whisper? Barely even that.

Eva shook her madly. "I can't hear your squeaks, little mouse."

But Stowy couldn't speak any louder. She tried. Oh, how she tried! She strained, forcing air through her throat, forcing herself to speak louder. But she could only emit the faintest of whispers. It was so soft Stowy couldn't even hear herself. Perhaps she was only mouthing the words.

"No. Please."

Eva laughed. She looked at her troops. "Aryan soldiers! Keep your guns warm and your fury hot. We'll invade the Ami ship soon. First I have a special delivery for our dear Uncle Baer."

Eva marched across the hangar, grinning, holding Stowy by the ankles like a huntress carrying a captured grouse. Stowy flailed and lashed her fingernails, desperate to free herself. It was hopeless. Eva was older and larger, and her battlesuit gave her unnatural strength.

"Oh, Uncle Baer!" Eva called out in a singsong voice. "I caught a little mouseling by the tail!"

As Stowy hung there, feeling like a mouse, she realized how catlike Eva was. Even covered with battle armor, the young sadist moved with a feline grace. Her smile reminded Stowy of the Cheshire cat, whom she had seen in Father's forbidden library.

"Oh, Uncle Baer!" Eva sang, stepping into the corridor.

Her bionic eye shone. Undoubtedly, she was summoning the doctor telepathically. Stowy knew all about those eyes. To climb the ranks, officers of the Third Reich must duel one another with rapiers. They lost fingers sometimes. Or their lives. To lose an eye was the true mark of pride. That was when you could install your adlerauge, an initiation to a club. The bionic eye connected directly to the brain, allowing telepathic communication. Eva's singsong cries were for Stowy's benefit. To mock her. To terrify her. And it was working.

A shadow appeared down the corridor, lengthening and growing across the wall like oozing oil. A tall shadow with a slight hunch. With hands like claws. With a nose like a vulture's beak. A shadow from her nightmares.

"Uncle Baer!" Eva sang, then cackled, her blue eye shining with delight. She loved war. She loved killing. But more than anything, Eva König loved tormenting her prey. She was more than willing to postpone killing for some good old torture. She was a cat playing with a mouse, not intending to devour the prey, merely torment.

The shadow grew larger still, claws the length of swords stretching across the wall. And then he emerged in the flesh from the darkness. A tall, bony doctor in a lab coat. A doctor with a beaked nose. With a nervous tongue that often licked thin lips. With hungry eyes. Even his bionic eye somehow seemed hungry. His skin was gray and liver-spotted, his bald head framed with gray hair, his neck long and gangly. A man? No. A huge vulture was approaching, a carrion bird, beak ready to peck, to rip through flesh, to pull out innards.

"My my, tut tut," he said. He was always so soft-spoken. "If it isn't one of my little mice! A poor little mouse who got lost in the cold. Little Stowy, you poor soul! Come, sweetheart. Come to your uncle."

His talons clutched her.

His lips peeled back, revealing tiny sharp teeth.

And then Stowy no longer whispered. She screamed.

The scream welled up from deep inside her. It was the scream of the children in the gas chamber. The wail of specimens as the experiments commenced. The roar of her parents dying in the gunfire. The snap of her grandmother's neck. The cry of a world fallen—a lost world of forbidden books, crushed under the scourge of Nazism. It was the scream of a little girl, but it was also the scream of a world.

The cat released the mouse. And the vulture began carrying her away.

"Oh wait!" Eva said.

And oddly, pathetically, Stowy dared to hope that Eva would save her.

"You forgot something." Eva strolled closer, then handed Stowy her plastic dinosaur. "Your toy."

Laughing, Eva strutted back to the hangar, ready to fly toward the Ami ship. Ready to invade that castle on the clouds. The vulture carried Stowy away, pulling her into the darkness until the castle vanished behind the storm.

CHAPTER TEN
Ready or Not

The FAS *Lioness*
High Earth Orbit
September 5, 2207

In his dreams, King was back aboard the starship *Freedom*. Not yet an admiral. Not yet quite so old. A commander aboard a dreadnought at war.

This was long before the Fatherworld had invaded. Back in those days, King and his spacers were fighting the rahs. Alien spiders. Nasty creatures hellbent on conquering Earth. The *Freedom* led the Alliance, smote the spiders, and saved Earth from their webs.

But not everyone was saved.

King remembered a girl. A little magical girl said to live in the HVAC ducts of the starship *Freedom*. Some called her a fairy. A magical being. She seemed barely real at all.

Her name was Samantha Perry.

Nobody aboard the *Freedom* knew how the little girl had ended up inside their ductwork. An orphan fleeing a dark past, she had smuggled herself aboard as a stowaway. Like a mouse, she scurried through the ducts. They would hear her crawling and giggling in the night.

They named her Stowy. At first she had been shy, hiding from others. Some said she was only a legend. But as she grew older, she emerged from the vents sometimes. The crew left her plates of food, blankets, dolls and toys (she especially loved dinosaurs). Spacers caught glimpses of her sometimes. A girl with messy light brown hair, an impish smile, and big ears. She wore a tattered dress covered with pockets and only one stocking. Their little Stowy—sooty, scrawny, but always laughing. She was orphaned, autistic, and eternally cheery. Stowy had become the mascot of their ship. Soon enough, she was joining them in the officers' lounge—playing cards, throwing darts, and choosing songs in the jukebox.

In his dreams, King was playing with her. Laughing with her. Sometimes she would sneak into his quarters at night, take books off his shelf, and read for all hours of the night in the recliner. King would find her in the morning, sound asleep with books on her lap. She had become like a granddaughter to him.

And when she reached eighteen, she joined the Alliance. She became a soldier.

A soldier King sent to war.

A soldier who gave her life to save his.

His dreams changed. He was there again. In his quarters as the spider queen invaded. He saw again the stinger enter Stowy's chest. And again, like he did most nights, King held young Stowy in his arms. She smiled at him as the venom spread, as her life flowed away. And again he wept.

Most nights King dreamed of those he had lost. He dreamed of Oliver Darjeeling, the steadfast boatswain of the *Freedom.* Of Yehuda "Lion" Levy, his fellow fighter pilot. Of many others. His brothers-in-arms. Yet as time went by, he dreamed about his brothers less and less. And it was Stowy, little Stowy, who haunted him more and more. Most nights he still held her lifeless body, weeping over the girl he had sacrificed to a spider goddess.

* * * * *

The alarm blared.

King jerked awake. A gasp fled his lips, and the dying wisps of dreams still floated around him. Monstrous spiders haunted those dreams, clawing at his neck, breaking his back.

An elfin face floated up from his memory. Stowy. Yes, he had dreamed *that* dream again. The dream where he held her, unable to revive the orphan.

I'm awake now, he thought. *Just a memory. From a long time ago.*

For a moment, King was confused. Where was he? He lay on a thin mattress, staring around at a small, shadowy room. A bunk. A military bunk on a starship.

It all flooded back. The battle in space. Fighting a doppelgänger of his wife (surely, it couldn't actually be Kim herself, could it?) in a mechanical spider. Making his way into the FAS *Lioness*, flagship of the Freedom Fleet. And finally, after several days of nonstop battle, crashing into bed and plunging into the pit of slumber.

Yes. That was where he was. Aboard the *Lioness.*

Dammit. As a young man, he could always come to his senses so quickly. During World War III, he would sleep with his gun under his pillow. Wake him up, and within a second, he had his finger on the trigger, ready to fight. But that was half a century ago. These days, it took him longer to remember where he was after a dream.

As he rose from bed, his back creaked. That never used to happen either. His leg gave a jolt of pain too. Ah yes, the fresh injury from the knife. An addition to his roster of aches and pains.

Welcome to the club, new friend, King thought.

Another memory hit him like a sledgehammer. A new memory. Ben Fletcher's death. The grief physically ached—a sickness in his stomach, a tightness in his chest.

And what about Larry Jordan? Last King had seen, his

best friend was flying inside a commandeered Wolfjäger by the exploding *Patton.* Had that blast taken the Phantom too?

I can't lose both Larry and Ben, King thought, the waves of grief hitting him. *I can't lose more people I love.*

With a deep breath, he took control of his emotions. After the war, there would be time to grieve. Right now he must fight.

He glanced at the clock. 4:15 in the morning. He had slept for a good six hours. (Of course, mornings and nights didn't have much meaning in space. But to simplify logistics, all starships of the Freedom Fleet observed EST, the time zone of their headquarters in Washington DC.)

"Six hours," King muttered. How much of this war had he missed? Anything might have happened in six hours! It wasn't long for a night's sleep. But in a war like this, six hours was an eternity.

Even in retirement, his MindLink gave him security clearance. King connected to *Lioness*'s central computer and downloaded her latest status logs. He reviewed the past few hours, quickly catching up. (Not quite as relaxing as mornings back on the ranch, leafing through the newspaper while sipping coffee.)

Lioness had taken multiple torpedoes on the hull. For now, the flagship was recovering on the sidelines, hovering in high orbit on the outskirts of the battle. She was halfway to the moon. Mechanics were crawling over her hull, patching her up, while ammunition ships restocked her. In an hour or two, she would return to the front line, joining her fellow warships in battle against the Weltraumwaffe.

As King was studying the logs, his MindLink chimed. A gruff, deep voice filled his brain, speaking with a British accent.

"King! You awake, old boy?"

The call was audio only. No visual hallucination. But there was no mistaking Godwin's voice.

"Yes, sir," King rasped, then coughed. The old neck injury always seemed worse when he first woke up. He was communicating telepathically, but like many of his generation, he voiced the words while thinking them. Old guys like him never quite took as naturally to telepathy as the younger spacers.

"Good, good!" Godwin telepathized. "Join us in the war room in ten minutes. The top brass is meeting, old boy. And I want you with us. We'll figure out a way to win this thing. We'll bring you up to speed—no need to pore over hundreds of log files. See you soon."

The call disconnected. King was grateful. Even after decades of using the implant, it still creeped him out. Letting others into your brain like that . . . Goddammit, he should have removed the thing when he had the chance.

He reached for his jeans, flannel shirt, and cowboy hat, then noticed it, and his hand froze.

A uniform was hanging on the wall. A navy-blue Free Alliance uniform with the insignia of an admiral on the shoulders. If there was any doubt this was for him, they had even sewn on a fabric name tape. ADMIRAL JAMES T. KING.

Well, King guessed it was official now. He was no longer just a cranky old man who found Nazis at his doorstep, then got swept up into an adventure. He was a soldier again. An officer. A leader. He was sixty-eight. He thought his days of war were long, long behind him.

But they wanted him back. They needed him. And dammit, he needed this too. Evil was sweeping across the world. King would not simply sit on his rocking chair, whittling away as the world burned. For his grandkids. For his own sense of duty. He would wear this uniform again.

After dressing, he stared at himself in the mirror. Yes, he was an old man, and war was a young man's game. But his back was still straight, his shoulders squared, his jaw strong. He wasn't just any old man. He was the man who had stormed the deserts of Mars, charging into the Red Dawn lines, to battle Katyusha herself. The man who had faced the rahs and flown a dreadnought into their star. The man who had lost a wife and found new love. Who had raised a son. Who loved his grandchildren—and who earned their reciprocal love. Neither age, injury, nor illness could tarnish the legacy of a man, nor could it douse his strength. All those men were the parts of his sum, and he carried their strength and honor still.

He strapped a sidearm onto his belt and left his bunk. As he marched down the narrow starship corridor, a thought rose in his mind.

I was never meant to die on the farm. I was always meant to die in battle.

He pushed the thought aside, reached the war room, and stepped inside.

* * * * *

The war room was full of gray-haired, steely-eyed admirals and commanders. They rose as King entered, their uniforms jangling with buckles and pins. A few stood here in the flesh. Most were here as hallucinations (a little icon over their heads identified them as such). In reality, they were back aboard their own starships. MindWeb projected their forms here in *Lioness*'s war room.

King surveyed the attendees. Spitfire was here, of course. Even admirals showed deference to Gal "Spitfire" Levy, commander of the flagship. The tall, dark-eyed woman saw King enter and gave him a little wink.

I was hoping you could command my starship someday, King thought. For decades, he had groomed Spitfire to inherit the *Freedom*. He was proud beyond words that Spitfire thrived even without that grand old dame of the stars.

King studied the other officers in the room. He knew them all. King had served for decades in the Freedom Fleet. Every man and woman here was a comrade. Every one—a fine officer.

And then King's eyes widened.

He spotted an old officer in the back. A tall man with dark skin, white hair, and a bright smile. Larry "Phantom" Jordan was here!

"Larry!" King blurted out, unable to control himself.

The old commander stepped around the table toward King. After several days of war, Jordan looked no worse for wear. He wore a full uniform, complete with all his service ribbons. His smile was still bright.

"Goddamn you, Larry," King growled. "I thought you were dead."

Jordan slapped him on the shoulder. "Sorry to disappoint you, old man. I'm staying around to torment you for a while longer."

Throwing propriety to the wind, the two old friends embraced. They had been fighting side by side since they were teenagers. They had flown starfighters together against the Red Dawn. Commanded the *Freedom* together against the rah menace. And now, in this war too, they were reunited. Finally they collected themselves, took a step back, and snapped crisp salutes.

King looked around the room. The war room was the most secure part of a warship, complementing the bridge. The bridge controlled navigation, flight, battle, and a thousand other tasks that kept a warship fighting. The war room was where long-term decisions were made. The bridge was for tactics. The war room for strategy. The bridge was instinct. The war room was deep thought. On the bridge, you determined the fate of ships. In the war room—the fate of humanity. Back when he had commanded the *Freedom*, King had made his hardest decisions in the war room. It was there he had etched the path of his life—and the lives of those who followed him.

But that was the *Freedom.* And that grand old ship was gone. He was aboard the *Lioness* now and no longer in control. He was back in uniform, but he still wasn't sure what task Godwin would assign him. A battle group to command? A subfleet perhaps? Or maybe he was just here as an adviser, an elder warrior to coach the younger officers? In the past few years of his service, he had become accustomed to being the ranking officer in every room he entered. But even admirals had bosses. Including Admiral James King.

Speak of the devil. Just then the door opened, and the boss himself entered the war room.

"Good morning, everyone!" boomed George Godwin. "Thank you for coming so early."

As always, Godwin wore his old-fashioned three-piece suit and top hat. The Alliance High Commander usually came from military stock, but once he took the job, he became a civilian. Short, rotund, and genteel, George Godwin reminded King of Mr. Peanut. But his avuncular exterior belied his strength. One could see that strength in the old man's eyes. They were shrewd eyes, full of iron will. Good old George Godwin. During the Third World War, King had served under him. Back then, Godwin was one of the youngest officers to ever make admiral, a wunderkid forged in the fires of war. Today, half a century later, he had not slowed down. It was hard to believe this energetic, forceful man with the booming voice was an octogenarian.

He took the drug, King suddenly realized. Rejuvenex. The drug that made you ten years younger. It was also likely to kill you. One out of ten Rejuvenex users—dead.

The crazy bastard rolled the dice, King thought, looking at his high commander. *And won.*

Maybe King himself should get over his fear, roll those dice himself. This was war. And during war, he was used to risking his life. So why not try it? He was sixty-eight. If he could return his body to fifty-eight, gain some lost vitality, speed of thought, strength, if he could turn his newfound strength against the enemy . . .

But it wasn't just about the risk of dying. It was something deeper. A fear of admitting he was old. Admitting he was slowing down, both in body and mind. Once he admitted that, he would be admitting weakness. And how could Admiral James "Bulldog" King, renowned for his strength and leadership, a war hero—how could he confess weakness? How could he, the famous soldier, admit his back ached most days, that he woke up several times a night to pee, that he sometimes spent long moments lost after waking, wondering where he was? If he went to a doctor, asked for the drug, he would be admitting what he had lost. He wasn't ready to do that yet.

Maybe someday. For now he had a war to win.

"Is everyone here?" Godwin rumbled. His voice always sounded like tumbling boulders. "Good. Good. We have much to discuss. But before we begin, I must—must!—show you who we're dealing with. If you'll turn toward the screen on that bulkhead. But brace yourselves. This won't be easy viewing."

Godwin tapped a button on his cane. A hallucinatory screen materialized on the bulkhead. It began to play a reel of videos from Earth.

Gasps sounded across the war room.

Officers cursed. Some shouted. Others swore revenge. Several broke down and wept.

King stood still, simply staring.

"Yes, it's disturbing, isn't it?" Godwin said. "These are the images coming in from Earth. What the Nazis are doing down on our planet. Such cruelty. Such evil." The old man's eyes dampened. "It's hard to comprehend."

The videos were short. Only a few seconds each. They kept coming, more and more of them. King watched them all, refusing to look away. He saw the Nazis throw babies into the air and use them for target practice. He saw them heat up metal rods until they glowed, then ram them into little girls. He saw them burning people alive. Skinning. Deforming. Cutting babies out from wombs, then beheading the newborns. They mutilated children while making their mothers watch. They raped mothers while making their husbands watch. They castrated husbands but refused to give them the mercy of death. To the Nazis, this was not just about killing. Any fool with a gun could kill. They made art of atrocity. And as they practiced their dark art, they laughed. The Nazis *laughed* as they mangled, defiled, and butchered the people of Earth.

The others turned away, sick. One woman ran off, covering her mouth, her skin green. But King just stood there. Staring.

He had seen evil before. He had seen the forces of the Red Dawn bomb cities. He had seen the rahs tear men and women apart. But he had never seen anything like this. No, the Nazis weren't just brutal enemies. They were sadists. Perverted lovers of torture and mutilating. And they were gleefully living out their perverse fantasies on Earth. This wasn't an army of soldiers. It was an army of Jack the Rippers.

"Turn it off, man!" an officer finally cried. "Dammit, we'll never sleep again."

Godwin finally, blessedly turned the video off. He was pale, but his eyes quickly dried. He stared at everyone in the room. He was short, in his eighties, and not physically imposing, but that glare was pure iron.

"I'm sorry I had to show you that. But you must know who our foe is. What he's doing. Why we're fighting."

The reels had ended. But King still saw the horrific images dancing before his eyes. He would see them in his dreams. He would never stop seeing those horrors.

"We must destroy this enemy," King said, echoing everyone's thoughts.

Godwin nodded. "We must indeed. That's why we're here. To figure out how we defeat this evil. There's no use mincing words. We were all caught with our trousers down. Time to pull them back up, regroup, and strike back hard."

Godwin tapped his cane against the tabletop. A shared hallucination materialized above the table, courtesy of MindWeb. The software was painting the same hallucination inside every brain, crafting a star map. Earth shone in the center, roughly the size of a melon. Upon the war room's deckhead shone three lights, clustered close together, representing Alpha Centauri. The Milky Way shone across the bulkhead, while the sun blazed behind Godwin's head.

Throughout the war room shone thousands of luminous icons, representing starships and their positions. Red Dawn starships appeared as glowing little equal signs—the symbol of equalism, the ideology that united Katyusha and her ilk. Freedom Fleet starships appeared as winged stars, a symbol of freedom—it was the love of freedom that united all Alliance nations. The Desert Thorns, a union of Middle Eastern starships, appeared as little thorny roses. They were the smallest of the unions, though they still fielded hundreds of starships. Those were the three great unions of humanity, together representing over two hundred nations. Bitter old foes, they now fought united.

The enemy warships appeared on the hallucinatory map too. Floating swastikas represented the locations of Weltraumwaffe ships. Over the past few days, the Nazis' numbers had grown and grown. Thousands of swastikas hovered throughout the war room. The fleet of the Third Reich outnumbered all three Earth fleets combined. The Germans were carving through the defensive lines, and their ground forces were advancing across Earth. For a long moment, everyone in the room just stared at the unfolding brutality.

"Yes, they came in hard, all guns blazing," Godwin said. "A true blitzkrieg. And they're winning. But we free folk are not out of the fight yet. We can still show Fritz we've got some spunk."

"Have we figured out where they're from?" King said. "Last I heard, the leading theory was parallel universes. But I'm out of the loop. Fill me in."

"We're all confused, old boy," Godwin said. "This attack bamboozled us, I dare say. But we've captured some Jerry officers. And interrogated them. We've been piecing things together. In short—yes, old boy. A parallel universe. The science confirms it."

King shook his head in wonder. "Damn. Kim always talked to me about parallel universes. Apparently, designing a portal to a parallel universe has been all the rage in engineering circles lately. But Kim always thought it was only theoretical. A good field of study, perhaps, but not something you could actually build."

A high voice came from the doorway. "Well, I was wrong. It *is* possible. And the Nazis built it."

King spun toward the door.

The pain flared where she had stabbed him.

There in the doorway, she stood. The woman from the mechanical spider. The woman he loved. His wife, Kim.

* * * * *

She stepped into the war room. Like King and Jordan, Kim had donned a military uniform. Brass buckles adorned the navy-blue fabric, and a steel gear glinted on her lapel, denoting her a member of the Engineering Corps. Her blond hair was pulled into a sensible ponytail, streaked with silver. She stared at King. Their eyes snapped together.

The images flashed before his eyes. Kim inside the mechanical spider. Swinging huge metal limbs. Slaying countless spacers. Kim—stabbing him in the leg.

Then she was running across the war room, and she leaped into his arms.

"Oh, Jim," she whispered onto his chest. "Thank God you're okay. I was so worried. For a few days, I didn't know if . . ." She wiped her eyes, smiled, and kissed his lips.

He stood stiffly for a moment, not sure what to do. Then he snapped out of his paralysis. He embraced her, and he held his beloved wife in his arms.

It was real. She was real. The real Kim.

The woman in the mecha had a bionic eye, King thought. *She was not my wife. A doppelgänger. A mimic from a parallel universe.*

"I'm here, Kim. I'm here." He caressed her cheek. "Have you heard from the kids?"

She nodded. "Yes. Bastian and Evan are both alive and well. They're fighting in Europe. Pushing back against the ground invasion. Alice is with them. They're in good spirits." She couldn't help but laugh. "Those three always are. No matter what hell we find ourselves in."

"And the grandkids?" King said.

"With my sister. Safe and sound."

King let out a breath of relief. He had been carrying that anxiety for days now. Not knowing the fate of his family had gnawed him hollow. They were alive. All of them were alive. The relief flowed over him, a physical sensation of warmth, and King felt ten years younger. Didn't even need a drug.

Then came the guilt. And the grief. How dared he feel relief when Kim had lost her brother?

"Kim, you've heard about Ben?" he whispered.

She nodded. Her eyes dampened.

"Oh, Kim, I'm sorry." He held her close.

For a long moment, he simply embraced her, comforting her as best he could.

Finally King remembered he stood in a war room with the Alliance High Command. He turned toward the others. Kim collected herself too. She tugged her uniform straighter and raised her chin. For a moment, King felt embarrassed at having revealed such emotion among his peers. But Godwin had a twinkle in his eye.

"I'm happy for you, old boy," Godwin said. "And I'm proud of Bastian and Evan who are fighting bravely in the thick of things. My own grandchildren are fighting in this war. All seventeen of them." The rotund old man turned toward Kim. "Now, Colonel Fletcher! You are an expert on parallel universe portals. Please explain to us—how is this possible?"

Kim bit her lip. "Sir, I'm far from an expert. And I'm not a physicist, merely an engineer."

"Merely an engineer!" King said. "Kim, you're a miracle worker. You saved the starship *Freedom* more times than I can count."

"Yes, well, I never had to fly her into another universe," Kim said. "But I'll try to explain what little I know."

"She's being humble," King said.

Kim stepped to the front of the war room. All the admirals and commanders stared at her. She remained composed, though King knew she was uncomfortable. Kim hated being the center of attention. Like him, she was an introvert. She thrived in shadowy engine rooms, tinkering with machines, not in conference rooms. King could sympathize. He had climbed the ranks in his long career, but in his heart, he was still just a pilot, and he felt more comfortable in a cockpit than in the war room of a dreadnought.

"Parallel universes," Kim said. "For a long time, they were only hypothetical. Then, over time, more concrete theories began to emerge. We studied them at NovaTech Industry. Nobody could quite agree on the physics involved. Not even the brightest scientists. Historically, some scientists believed that every single choice splits the universe in two. I debate between coffee and tea this morning? Boom, I just split the universe in two. One in which I drink coffee, the other in which I drink tea. You get out of the left side of your bed instead of the right? Two new universes. You get the idea."

King frowned. "But that would create billions of universes. Can you imagine it?"

"Far more than billions," Kim said. "We don't have numbers large enough to calculate how many universes that would create. Every human, every animal, every alien making a choice—the universe splits again. And in each of those universes—countless more splits occur every second, fractaling again and again."

"We'd get an infinite number of universes," King said. "Nearly so, at least."

"Well, technically, the largest number we can imagine is still nowhere near infinity, but . . ." Kim nodded. "Yes, for all intents and purposes, infinite universes. For a long time, that was the dominant theory. But some scientists and engineers held a different view. This is the view of NovaTech Industries. And mine as well. In this theory, only huge, monumental events split universes apart. Choosing between coffee or tea? No big deal. Not nearly momentous enough to split the universe."

"But big events can," King said.

Kim nodded. "Yes. Consider the asteroid that wiped out the dinosaurs. Something that Earth-shattering (and I mean literally Earth-shattering) can actually split the timeline apart. In one timeline, the dinosaurs went extinct. That's the timeline we live in. In another timeline? The asteroid just missed. And the dinosaurs reigned on. And humans never evolved."

Might have been for the best, King thought.

"What about big events on other planets?" King said. "There might be an infinite number of planets out there. If each planet splits the universe only once, we're back to infinite universes."

"We believe that universal splits can be local," Kim said. "Pockets in spacetime where timelines shift, but outside the affected zone, there's no change. According to this interpretation, there's only one parent universe, and within it are pockets of altered timelines. Like bubbles rising on a giant pizza dough, each with mini-universes inside. But we're not entirely sure. It's a lot to figure out." She smiled wryly. "That's why I've been so busy at work."

"Understood," King said. "That might explain why the Nazis had to appear at Alpha Centauri instead of here at Sol. Because they had to fly outside the affected zone. Outside the bubble on our pizza dough."

Kim nodded. "Yes, that was my conclusion as well. Scientists have begun to develop experiments to detect some universe-splitting moments in history. I myself worked on the detectors. Universe splits leave little ripples in spacetime, which we can detect and date. The dinosaur extinction left those signatures. Since then, there were a handful of other events that split the universe in two. One was humans discovering fire. In another universe, we think that humans remained mere apes. A third event was the fall of Rome."

"So there's a universe where the Roman empire still exists?" King said.

"We think so," Kim said. "It's possible one of these Earth-shattering events was the Second World War."

"Literally Earth-shattering again," King said.

Kim nodded. "Yes. But I must clarify. This is all still hypothetical. Another possibility—a very real one—is that the universe did *not* split naturally because of World War II. But that Nazi scientists split it."

King frowned. "Why would they do that?"

"I don't know," Kim said. "It might have been unintentional. The Nazis were dealing with some scary science, Jim. Really creepy stuff. Everyone knows the Nazis were looking into atomic energy. But they also dabbled with the occult, mixing dark magic with their science."

King raised his eyebrows. "Surely you, a woman of science, don't believe in dark magic?"

She sighed. "I don't know what I believe anymore. It's possible the Nazis were dealing with powers they couldn't control. Maybe a secret Nazi experiment cracked the universe in two. Entirely by accident. Like I said, this is all still hypothetical. We don't know yet. At NovaTech, we were never able to do it ourselves. Clearly Nazi science is more advanced than ours."

King scratched his cheek. "Whatever caused the split, it happened in 1944, yes?"

Kim nodded. "We think so, yes. We can see the evidence for that by studying the right patterns in the spacetime fabric. The split occurred sometime around 1944, give or take a year. Back then, both the United States and Nazi Germany were racing toward the bomb. In our universe, we Americans developed the bomb first. We won World War II. In a parallel universe, the Nazis developed the bomb first. And destroyed the United States. And conquered the world. And then spread across the stars."

King suppressed a shudder. "Imagine it. Life in their universe. A world where Hitler won. Entire races—exterminated. Freedom—crushed. Humanity falling to evil. The end of human civilization."

Godwin raised an eyebrow and stepped back into the conversation. "The end of civilization, old boy?"

King nodded. "Yes, sir. They have starships. They have armies. Presumably they have cities, an economy, a society. But civilization? No. To me, civilization means more than being able to govern a bunch of people. It means being *civilized.* Being decent. Having a society worth living in. What the Nazis created in their universe ended human civilization. And now they want to end it here." He clenched his fists, both the real and metal one. "And we won't let them."

"That's the spirit!" Godwin said. The old man raised his fist in the air. "We'll give the Jerries hell. Just like we did back in the 1940s. By Job, we'll do it again."

Cheers filled the war room. Part of King felt that spirit of battle. He raised his fist too. He felt the excitement pound through him. Yes, war was terrible. War was brutal and tragic. But war could also be glorious. War could show the savagery of man but also his courage, nobility, and honor. All his life, King had been a warrior. And all his life, he had been torn between the glory of battle and its horror. Even now, in this room of fierce leaders, his fist in the air, a chill filled King.

He would fight, yes. With all the honor and courage he could muster. But he would also grieve for the dying. And he would fear the loss of all he held dear—not just his family but his world. His civilization. It was because of that fear that he must fight. Because of those people and values he loved. He would defend them. With all the strength left in his old, tired body. With all the courage still in his soul.

For his family. For the woman he loved. For Earth and for freedom.

*****

But there was still one thing that niggled at King.

"I have a question," he said. "Before joining you aboard the *Lioness*, I fought in my old Eagle starfighter, but I was shot down onto Siberia. After a brush with Katyusha, I commandeered a Chinese starfighter, continued fighting behind enemy lines, and . . ."

Mumbles rose among the admirals and commanders, and King lost his train of thought. Everyone was staring at him. Their eyes shone in admiration. One young officer raised his fist. King hadn't meant to brag about his exploits. He had simply been stating a fact. But he must remember who he was. A war hero. A famous admiral. Something of a legend maybe. Especially to the younger officers. They were now witnessing the famous James "Bulldog" King perform more deeds of valor. At least, that was how they saw it. They didn't know how much King hurt, both his body and soul. Didn't know how much he was afraid.

Well, two in the room knew. Jordan, his best friend, and Kim, his wife. As the others mumbled in awe, Jordan actually rolled his eyes.

"Oh, he's just bragging," the white-haired commander said. "He was probably taking a nap in the cockpit when all hell broke loose."

"Very funny," King said. "Now let me continue my story. I was fighting in a Chinese starfighter. And I faced a . . . I was going to say ship. But it wasn't a ship. It was a mecha. Like the kind we use in our docking and armory bays to lift heavy munitions. But this mecha was the size of a starship. And shaped like a spider."

"Ah, yes," said Godwin. "One of the dangerous toys from the twisted mind of Dr. Anneliese. *Ingenieur des Schmerzes*, they call her. The Engineer of Pain."

King felt that knife again. The sting of the blade digging into his thigh. The eyes of its wielder, one eye of ice, one of fire.

"There was a woman in the cockpit," King said softly, remembering. "Operating the spider mecha."

Godwin nodded. "A woman who looks remarkably like our very own Kim Fletcher-King, your beloved wife?"

King glanced at Kim, who stood behind the table, then at Godwin again.

"Will somebody tell me what the hell is going on here?" King said. "Why the hell is there a version of Kim out there, one of her eyes bionic, flying a giant spider?"

Godwin tapped a button on his cane. Everyone in the room suddenly hallucinated a woman floating above the tabletop. She spun around lazily, letting everyone see her. The woman was about fifty years old, her blond hair pulled into a tight braid. She looked remarkably like Kim, but she wore the black uniform of a Nazi officer, and LED swastikas glowed red on her arms. One of her eyes shone red too, scanning the room.

Godwin pointed his cane at the hallucination.

"Dr. Anneliese Heisenberg-König!" Godwin said. "The most powerful woman on the Fatherworld. Wife of the führer himself. *And* top engineer of the Nazi regime. Among her many achievements? Discovering, isolating, and harvesting the umbrion particle. Designing the Überlichtantrieb warp drive, which all Weltraumwaffe ships use. And finally—building a portal between parallel universes. But she also has hobbies. Such as building giant spider mechas."

"Yes, I get it, she's an evil genius," King said. "Why the hell does she look like my wife?"

"Because she *is* me," Kim said softly. "Me in another universe."

King spun toward his wife. Kim gazed at him, eyes soft, and gave him a sad smile.

"Kim, she's nothing like you!" King said. "Oh, she *looks* like you. But she's a Nazi! She's—"

"A product of her environment," Kim said. "Are we really so different? Both engineers. Both developed new military technologies. Both soldiers married to powerful men."

King stared at his wife. Over the past few years, he had gotten to know the soft, loving Kim. The wife. The companion. But now he saw the soldier again. Kim was the veteran of many battles, a senior officer, a confident leader. And in her own way, Colonel Kim Fletcher-King was as powerful and imposing as Dr. Anneliese Heisenberg-König.

"So let me get this straight, Kim," King said. "You're telling me that a version of you exists in that parallel universe? A universe where the Nazis won the war? That we all have some . . . some shadow versions of ourselves? Evil twins?"

"Not exactly. It's more like . . ." Kim cleared her throat. "Before we continue, can somebody please get rid of that floating hallucination of my lookalike in a Nazi uniform?"

"Pardon, Colonel." Godwin tapped his cane again, and the hallucination of Dr. Anneliese vanished.

"Thank you." Kim tugged at her navy-blue uniform. "As you all can see, I wear the uniform of the Alliance, not the black uniform of the Space Reich. I have an American name, not a German one. And I have both my eyes. Anneliese and I are not twins. Not even sisters. We're more like . . . cousins."

"Cousins," King said.

"Back in 1944, our universe split in two," Kim said. "So did the fate of the Fletcher family. In our universe, the Fletchers remained the Fletchers. My ancestors continued to live in a free America, and eventually I was born, a little prairie girl. But in the shadow universe, the Nazis conquered the United States. I suspect that my family changed its name to a German name. Or married into a prominent German family, maybe. It might have saved their lives. And those lives were very different. At first, maybe, my ancestors struggled to survive under German occupation. Then they joined the Germans and rose high in the ranks. And finally a girl was born. Anneliese. She's not quite me. She might be a little older or younger. If you ran a DNA test on her, I bet we'd have different DNA. She's probably mixed with more German. So no, she's not me, and she's not my twin. Maybe not like a cousin either. She's more like . . . who I might have been. Who I became in that shadowy universe."

King tried hard not to shudder. He wanted to show strength here. But this chilled him to the bone.

"A doppelgänger," King said. "The doppelgänger is a creature from German mythology. The name means double-walker. The doppelgänger is a version of you from the night world."

Kim grimaced. "Yes. Doppelgänger. That works."

"Do we all have these doppelgängers from the Fatherworld?" King said.

"I don't," came a somber baritone from down the table.

King turned to look at his old friend, a man with dark skin.

"Nor do I," said Spitfire.

King looked at the *Lioness*'s commander. Her Star of David pendant gleamed.

Other voices came from across the table.

"Me neither."

"Same here."

King looked at them. He understood. They did not match the Aryan ideal. When King looked at Jordan and Spitfire, he saw dear friends. To the Nazis, they were subhumans. In the shadow universe, their families would have been exterminated long ago.

"But *I* might exist in the Fatherworld," King said. "So far, several Nazis seemed to recognize me. Or at least they thought they did."

Godwin nodded. "Of course they did, old friend." The old

man stepped closer, cane tapping. He reached up and placed a hand on King's shoulder. "King, old boy, in the Fatherworld, your doppelgänger is—"

An alarm blared, interrupting Godwin's words.

Red lights flashed, filling the war room.

The map was changing.

They all stared. Godwin clutched his cane, eyes narrowing shrewdly. The admirals leaned forward. King stepped closer to Kim. Close enough for their elbows to brush. They dared not hold hands in such a formal setting, but both wanted to feel each other's warmth. They watched the map together.

The Weltraumwaffe was changing formation.

The Nazi fleet was forming a huge spear in space. Thousands of warships formed that spear. At their lead, forming the tip of the spear, flew the *Barbarossa.*

King stared, a chill in his bones. The *Barbarossa.* Terror of the stars. Flagship of the Third Reich. A super-dreadnought. A nightmare that dwarfed any ship built in this universe.

And then the Weltraumwaffe charged. The Germans drove into the Alliance lines, carving into the Freedom Fleet like a true spear through flesh.

"They're coming for us," King said. "For our flagship. They know we're here. They're coming for the Alliance High Command."

Godwin nodded. "Everyone—to the bridge!"

*****

They ran down the corridor. The *Lioness* was a massive ship, spanning a kilometer from stern to stem. She was smaller than the true behemoths of old, such as the *Freedom.* But not by much. And she was the largest ship in the modern Freedom Fleet. The bridge wasn't far from the war room, but today the run seemed miles long. And no, not because King's back was hurting again. His own personal pain was at the back of his mind. Let him break every bone in his body! Right now, only saving others mattered. His family. His fleet. His very civilization.

The Weltraumwaffe was charging. The Fatherworld's fleet was making a great push to win the war quickly. Could they do it? Conquer Earth within a week? Would the Nazi blitzkrieg overwhelm the Alliance, and in this universe too would civilization fall?

Dammit. King needed to be on the bridge *now*. Would be nice if he could portal there instantly. The Russians had begun to use portals within their starships, letting them hop from deck to deck. That would certainly come in handy here aboard the *Lioness*. But portals were alien technology. During the Spider Wars, the Russians had stolen the tech from the rahs. The Alliance didn't trust aliens, and it certainly didn't trust wobbly portals designed for scuttling spiders. It was just good old American ingenuity here aboard the Freedom Fleet's flagship, thank you very much. Which, today, meant some good old running.

RIP my back, King thought.

Finally they reached the bridge. Once more, MindWeb made King hallucinate that the bridge deck, bulkheads, and deckheads disappeared, revealing a view of space all around. The workstations, monitors, and deck officers seemed to float in open space. The kids like Spitfire loved this technology. (Yes, Spitfire was in her forties, but to King, anyone younger than fifty was a "kid.") To these "kids," the so-called neural revolution was an adventure. But King found the hallucination disorienting. What was wrong with good old viewports? He summoned MindPlay, the operating system of his MindLink implant, and tried to shut off the hallucination, to make the bulkheads visible again. The option wasn't available. This hallucination was hardcoded into the bridge. Damn modern starships with their ridiculous telepathic tech! And to hell with the neural revolution.

At times like these, King missed the *Freedom*. He really did. Ah, that had been a starship! His beloved. His grand dame of the stars. King still thought about her every day. You didn't have to hallucinate any features there. What you wanted, the *Freedom* offered for real.

Well, no use pining for the past. His son always told King he was too nostalgic. That there was no reason to fear modern technology. That was the curse of being old; you always looked to the past, because deep down inside, you worried you didn't have much of a future left. So like a good modern officer, King stared through the invisible walls at the battle.

The *Lioness* was in high orbit now. Earth shone in the distance, no larger than a basketball held at arm's length. Myriads of starships separated *Lioness* from the planet. The battle flared in some areas, waned in others. The largest front was being fought in low orbit over Siberia. That was where Katyusha was battling thousands of Weltraumwaffe warships. So far, the Germans seemed to be gaining the upper hand, but Katyusha was fighting fiercely, not shy about sending entire warships on kamikaze attacks. The Germans down there had their hands full. King, who had fought Katyusha before, knew her ferocity well. He still felt the pain of her knife on his neck. Every damn day.

A smaller portion of the Weltraumwaffe was charging into the Alliance lines. Only a few hundred starships. But they were the larger, more powerful ships of the German war machine. And leading them was *Barbarossa* herself, and truly she was a monster. No not she. *Barbarossa* was male, King remembered. Since time immemorial, men had considered their ships female. First ships that sailed the sea, then starships that sailed the cosmic ocean. This was true in both universes. But the Germans thought *Barbarossa* was too powerful, too dominant to be a female. (Clearly they had never met strong, fierce females like Kim and Spitfire,

King thought.)

Male or not, *Barbarossa* was plowing through the Alliance formations, leading the Nazi assault. The German guns were blazing hot, leaving a trail of Alliance hulks. The Alliance comprised many democratic nations around the world. The United States, India, Great Britain, Japan, Canada, Israel, Australia, and many others contributed warships to the fleet. Germany too—this universe's Germany, a democratic nation whose Nazi past remained in the past. United, these nations' ships formed the Freedom Fleet. United, they fought against this scourge from beyond. United, they were strong. But was their enemy stronger? The *Barbarossa* seemed unstoppable, smashing his way forth. He was flying toward the *Lioness*.

Right now the *Lioness* flew among many other American ships. Her hull was still gaping open at spots. Mechanics in spacesuits were clinging to the scaffolds. Her armories were still being restocked. A logistics freighter was attached to *Lioness*'s airlock with a tubular space bridge. Ammunitions were flowing down the tube like nutrients down an umbilical cord. *Lioness* was on the ropes, her breath knocked out of her. And the enemy was charging ever nearer.

Ready or not, fight they must.

And fight they shall.

CHAPTER ELEVEN
Why We Fight

Nebraska
Earth
August 29, 2207
Three days before the Nazi Invasion

It was Saturday morning, and the grandkids came to visit. King had been keeping himself busy in retirement. He rode his horses, collected his coins, and whittled wooden figurines. He was even learning guitar, and his old fingers were beginning to master those Johnny Cash songs.

He was alone a lot.

His wife, an engineer at NovaTech, worked long hours. His son, an infantry officer, spent most of his time at his base. Most days, King had lots of time to think. To remember. He thought of friends he had lost. He thought of Stowy, mascot of his ship, a fairy princess slain by the spiders. He thought of Mimori, the soul of *Freedom*. And sometimes the grief made it hard to breathe. Even when he kept busy, the memories were never far.

They said you should never leave an old veteran alone with his memories. But he was Admiral James "Bulldog" King. The war hero. The tough guy. The grumpy old farmer with all the cool scars and cooler war stories. He was strong. A leader. A pillar for them to lean on. Nobody knew how broken he was. That he needed help. Nobody knew he still saw the faces of the fallen.

But his family could banish the grief. His family always brought him joy. It was Saturday, and they were here.

Bastian rolled up in his truck, raising clouds of dust across the Nebraska landscape. He was a big man, and he drove a big truck, a heavy American machine with tires that could crush boulders. Shuttles were cheaper, flying was faster, but that was Bastian. He was a man of the ground. The first King in generations to become an infantryman rather than a pilot.

"You reach for the stars," Bastian had once told King. "But I'm the salt of the Earth."

The truck rolled to a stop by King's log cabin. Out came Bastian, a giant of a man. His arms were like tree trunks, his chest like a starship's prow. Even now, a man of forty, Bastian still shaved the sides of his head, leaving a mohawk like a skunk's tail. If you asked King, it was ridiculous. But that too was Bastian. He didn't care what others thought. (Especially not what his father thought.)

Bastian pulled him into a crushing embrace. "Dad!"

His wife hopped from the truck next, carrying a basket of oranges. Alice was nearly as tall and strong as her husband. A Nebraska farm girl, she was bright as a summer day over fields of rustling wheat. Blue ribbons adorned her two blond braids.

"Hi, Pops." She hugged King, her grip nearly as crushing as Bastian's.

The grandkids emerged from the truck next. Rowan was thirteen, a somber girl with brooding eyes. She too carried memories of the Spider War. Her half-brother, Oli, was only three, still innocent. He had been born after the terrible spiders.

"Pop-Pop!" Rowan cried and ran toward him. She was serious at school, they said. She didn't often play with other children, preferring to read books or write poems. Yet when she saw King, she would always smile. And King always smiled back.

"Hey, kiddo."

She jumped onto him and hugged him. King twirled her around.

"Pop-Pop!" cried Oli, running toward him. The toddler leaped onto them, and King laughed, holding both grandkids in his arms.

"Kids!" Bastian boomed. "What did I tell you? No jumping on Pop-Pop."

King laughed. "You can jump on me all you like, kiddos. I'm the strongest man in the world, you know."

Oli's eyes widened. "Really?"

"Really!" Rowan said. "He is."

"He is not!" Bastian said. "He's sixty-eight and has a bad back." He glared at King. "And he needs to take it easy."

King snorted. "Your dad is just sour because he's only the second strongest man in the world."

Rowan blew Bastian a raspberry. "Yeah, Dad. Stop being jealous."

They all sat for lunch (roast beef sandwiches), then played poker (not with real money, so the kids could play too). Alice had baked apple pie, and everyone tried Bastian's homemade beer (even Rowan was allowed a single sip, which she promptly spat out). Kim showed everyone the blueprints of the new machines she was working on. Everyone smiled and talked and laughed a lot.

I wish you were here with us, Stowy, King thought.

He thought about the girl often, that lost little orphan, a stowaway on his ship. The King family had unofficially adopted her. She had been like an older sister to Rowan. Like a daughter to Bastian.

Like a granddaughter to me, he thought.

But he still had a living granddaughter. He had his beloved Rowan. And his heart overflowed with love.

That afternoon, King took her out riding. It was just him

and Rowan. A Saturday ritual. They had not missed a Saturday in three years.

For hours, they rode along the fields of Nebraska. Rowan told him stories from school, from her adventures chasing frogs and dragonflies, and some stories that she just made up whole cloth. King told her tales of the old wars on Mars.

They did not often speak about the Spider War. That war still lurked in Rowan's memory. The fear of spiders still haunted her.

That Saturday, on that ride among the fields, she saw a spider in a tree, and she shouted, wept, and trembled. King remembered that terrible night years ago when a rah had crept into her room, had trapped her in its web.

Two granddaughters. One lost to the spiders. One freed from the web. Or perhaps not entirely free. Perhaps Rowan never would be. Some cobwebs would forever cling to her.

King sat her on his horse (good old Buck), leaving her own horse to walk unburdened. They shared a saddle as they rode home. The girl trembled as Buck walked between the fields of wheat.

After a long time of silence, Rowan said, "Pop-Pop, do you ever have bad memories?"

"Yes," King said. "I have bad memories too. Of the wars."

"Really?" She turned her head, looking at him. "But you're the strongest man in the world."

He nodded. "Even the strongest cowboys are sometimes scared. We just keep on riding our horses."

Rowan nodded and wiped her eyes. "Just keep on riding."

King mussed her hair, then placed his cowboy hat on her head. It dipped down to cover her eyes, and she giggled.

He prayed that Rowan never knew war again. That Oli never knew war at all.

The rest of the day, the family relaxed in the cabin. The

fireplace crackled, Alice dozed on the couch, and King spent a while building a new ship in a bottle. Rowan kept busy for a long time in the workshop, privately working on a "secret project." King wasn't allowed inside. Finally Rowan approached him.

"Pop-Pop, I made you this. My dad helped a little. It's made of real metal."

She held out a medal that hung from a ribbon.

Bastian looked over from the recliner where he sat, bouncing Oli on his knee.

"She used the welding tools herself. I only supervised."

King took the medal. On its surface, Rowan had engraved: #1 GRAMPA.

"Thank you," King said softly.

She blushed. "It's a bit silly, I know. But I wanted to make it for you."

His eyes stung. "I'll treasure it."

"Will you add it to your box of medals?" Rowan said. She pointed to a shadowbox that hung over the fireplace. Inside, King kept and displayed his war medals. Eleven of them shone inside. For valor. For leadership. For his wounds.

"No," King said softly. "No, not this one."

Rowan lowered her eyes. "I guess it's silly. Just something I made."

"Rowan, this medal means more to me than anything in that box." King slipped the medal into the pocket of his flannel shirt. "I'll keep yours right here. Over my heart."

Alice walked into the room. "Who wants strawberry pie?"

Bastian frowned. "We just ate your apple pie."

"And now it's time for strawberry!"

They all laughed and sat around the kitchen table again. They ate pie and played another round of poker. That evening, Bastian and his family drove back home. King returned to his detective novels, his ships in bottles, his train set, his coin collection, and all the other hobbies he used to keep himself busy, to forget the pain. And in his shirt pocket, he kept Rowan's medal. And he treasured it.

He kept that medal in his pocket. Even now. Even here in this new war. Rowan was down on Earth somewhere. Beyond his reach. Beyond telepathy. King was here in space, but he carried her medal against his heart, and he never forgot why he was fighting.

*****

The *Barbarossa*
High Earth Orbit
September 5, 2207
Five days into the Blitzkrieg

Wolfgang König, Grand Admiral of the Weltraumwaffe, stood on the deck of his flagship, his hands clasped behind his back. A thin smile spread across his lips. It was time to kill some Americans.

Hopefully more than just *some*.

Wolfgang had not slept or eaten in five days. Not since passing through the portal into Unreineland, the impure universe. It was hard to believe this place was real. For a long time, Wolfgang had thought it only a myth. A parallel universe? A reality in which Hitler had lost? In which the Third Reich was a distant memory, and the subhuman slavs and Amis ruled the world?

But it *was* real. He was flying through it. And it sickened him.

The subhumans were everywhere. Billions of them.

The slavs were flying those big red ships of theirs. Slavs! Their name literally meant "slaves," yet here they were, flying starships. And the Americans! A bunch of subhuman mongrels. If any Amis still had any pure Nordic blood in their veins, it was polluted from the darkest swamps. Amis didn't have a gene pool; they had a cesspool. And the planet below! Swarming with parasites. Semites and gypsies clutched this version of Earth with their tentacles.

Wolfgang stared through the viewports on the bridge. He saw the Russian warships below and the American Fleet ahead. He saw the planet overflowing with rot. It was a nightmare world. A vision of hell. A reality where humanity had been perverted, infected, mutated into monstrous forms. It sickened Wolfgang.

"We will purify this universe," he said. "We're not only here as soldiers. We're here as exterminators." He raised his voice to a shout. "Glory to the Fatherworld!"

His bridge crew repeated the battle cry. Their voices echoed across the bridge. "Glory to the Fatherworld!"

Barbarossa flew at the lead. Behind him charged three hundred warships—the capital ships, the best in the fleet. By now, the fifth day of the war, the entire Weltraumwaffe had emerged from the portals. They were not all big capital ships, but each one was a terror. Ten thousand German warships, superior to the enemy in every way, surrounded Earth in a noose. Slowly, hour by hour, Wolfgang was tightening that noose.

Right now Wolfgang was charging into the American Fleet, shattering their front line. With only three hundred warships, he was breaking them.

He had ordered the bulk of the Weltraumwaffe to battle the other subhuman nations. His fellow Aryans were in lower orbit now, fighting the Russians, Chinese, British, and various other riffraff. There was even an independent Israel in this universe. And it had starships! Ha! Wolfgang could not wait to share that tidbit with his father, Führer Helmut König. The old man would enjoy a hearty laugh.

And, perhaps most sickening of all, there was a German fleet here. A fleet of a diseased, weakened Deutschland that had surrendered to the communists and capitalists in disgrace. Shame of shames—Unreineland's Germany had a smaller fleet than Israel's. Wolfgang would destroy them both with equal malice.

But that was later. Right now Wolfgang must focus on the main enemy.

The American Fleet.

Wolfgang had recognized them early on as his most dangerous foe. The Chinese fleet was larger. The Russian fleet was more ostentatious. But the American Fleet was the superior dog in that kennel of mongrels. The Freedom Fleet, they called it. Ha! A ridiculous name. Wolfgang would break them.

The mighty guns of *Barbarossa* boomed again. Torpedoes slammed into the FAS *George Washington*, an American frigate. The warheads exploded with umbrionic fury. The dark particles scattered, sucking up light and energy. Ah, umbrions! The great weapon of the Fatherworld. When an umbrionic weapon impacted—whether bullet or bomb—it hurt the enemy twice. First came the kinetic energy, ripping through the target. Then out spread the umbrions, the antiphotons. You could not see them, not even with a microscope. Wolfgang imagined them as greedy little blobs of darkness, gobbling up light, heat, and energy.

Unreineland didn't know about these particles. Same as they had not known about parallel universes. What more can you expect from subhumans? Of course their knowledge was inferior. To them, umbrionic weapons must seem like magic. When Dr. Anneliese had discovered umbrions, she had changed the face of warfare forever.

That still didn't make Wolfgang like her any better. In fact, her ingenuity, her genius, her indispensability to the Fatherworld's war machine—they made her all the more intolerable. Wolfgang's upper lip twitched. Just the thought of that woman on his starship soured the glory of this battle.

Yes, she invented good weapons. Wolfgang would have sacrificed those weapons, would have tossed her into the fire. Her and her cursed creations. Oh, if only he could challenge her to a duel! If she wasn't his stepmother . . .

Ahead, a fresh volley of torpedoes hit the FAS *George Washington.* The American ship was named after a historic figure Wolfgang recognized. A pre-1944 figure. Before that monumental year, the Fatherworld and Unreineland had been the same—just Earth. It tickled Wolfgang that the two universes, so different, shared so much history.

Dark explosions rocked the American ship. The *Washington* tore in half, spilling out spacers. The Amis kicked in space like frightened little ants. *Barbarossa* gained speed and plowed through them. Corpses shattered against the flagship's prow.

Wolfgang smiled. "Just like driving a BMW through a cloud of mosquitoes."

His bridge officers laughed. Of course they did. They always laughed at his jokes. The curse of being a feared Nazi admiral; you never heard genuine laughter.

They stormed onward. Ahead flew another American ship. The FAS *Truman.* A starfighter carrier this time. Ah, even larger prey! Excellent. Of course, compared to *Barbarossa*, even this pride of America (no doubt a juggernaut in their unimaginative minds) was small.

There had never been a ship like *Barbarossa.* Not in either universe. Two miles long he was, stern to stem. Thousands of cannons thrust from his hull, and a million ammunitions filled his warehouses. Fifty thousand spacers flew aboard him. Five full divisions. He was the greatest weapon of the Fatherworld. The greatest weapon ever built. *Barbarossa* was more than a starship; he was an army unto himself. Even the mightiest American warship seemed like a sparrow compared to this dark eagle of the stars.

The *Truman* opened fire. The American torpedoes shattered against the German shields and armor. Onward *Barbarossa* charged, cannons booming, plowing through her enemies, carving a way forth for the Weltraumwaffe. The *Truman* shattered, and *Barbarossa* charged through her ruin and flew onward, forever advancing, always killing, piercing deeper and deeper into the enemy fleet. Songs would be written about *Barbarossa*'s glorious charge.

About my glory! Wolfgang thought.

At a mere forty years of age, he commanded the Weltraumwaffe, the Fatherworld's space force. He was young for the job, but his father trusted him with it. And Wolfgang's ambitions did not end here. He dreamed of being more than an admiral. He craved command of the entire Wehrmacht—the full armed forces of the Fatherworld. As Reichsmarschall of the Wehrmacht, Wolfgang König would command not only the fleet, but also the infantry. The armored divisions and artillery. The navy, including its deadly submarines. The marines. It would all be his.

He must only get rid of the current Wehrmacht commander. His dear old uncle Dieter König. Curse the man!

The führer's words returned to Wolfgang.

"Prove yourself worthy in space, son," Father had said. "And I'll let you duel my brother." He raised his fist in the air. "The winner will command the Wehrmacht."

Wolfgang bared his teeth. "Let me duel him now, Father! I'm ready."

"No." The führer shook his head. "Prove yourself in the impure universe. Only then will you be worthy to face my brother with the blade."

Well, here Wolfgang was. In Unreineland, the impure universe. Proving himself.

The torpedoes slammed into another American ship. Another frigate—gone! Cheers rose across *Barbarossa*'s bridge. Onward the German flagship charged through the American forces.

Now if only Father would let me duel that mad wife of his . . .

"Well, well!" came a voice from behind, high and feminine. "Don't you look pleased with yourself. You'll be dueling old *Onkel* Dieter in no time."

Even as the battle blazed, Wolfgang spun away from the main viewport. His upper lip peeled back in a snarl.

It was *her*!

A woman came swaying across the bridge, a crooked smile on her lips. At fifty years of age, she was still in the full bloom of her beauty, but hers was a savage beauty. The beauty of a snake before it spat its venom. The beauty of a thunderbolt before it struck. The beauty of a spider's web before it trapped the fly. She wore a tight black outfit covered with cables, motors, and rods, giving her inhuman strength. It was one of many machines her mad mind invented. Dr. Anneliese Heisenberg-König. Top engineer of the Fatherworld. Inventor of the Überlichtantrieb warp drive. Discoverer of the umbrion particle. A thorn in Wolfgang's side.

My hideous stepmother, he thought.

"Get off my bridge," he said.

Anneliese's smile widened into a grin, showing too many teeth. A predatory grin.

"What's wrong, son? Aren't you happy to see your mother?" She pouted. "Come give Mommy a kiss."

Wolfgang forced his anger down. She was goading him. He mustn't step into her trap.

"What's the matter, Anneliese? Lost your battle with the Chinese fleet, so now you're bored?" Wolfgang turned back to the viewport. "While you sulk, grieving the loss of your spider toy, I have a war to win."

She pounced across the bridge, grabbed his arm, and sneered. Wolfgang was a giant of a man. He stood nearly seven feet tall, and his fists could shatter trees. Yet Anneliese, a woman half his size, grabbed him with strength superior to his own. The motors hummed across her black suit, and the cables thrummed.

"Naughty boy." She licked her teeth. "This enemy is not so easy to beat. You underestimate the Freedom Fleet. That will be your downfall." She leaned close and whispered into his ear, her tongue flicking against his earlobe. "Don't worry, my precious boy. Thanks to modern medicine, I'm still young enough to give your father another son. You can be replaced."

The crew was trying very hard not to listen. Officers kept staring at their control panels, focusing on the battle.

Rage blazed through Wolfgang. How dare this impudent woman invade his bridge, taunt him, and humiliate him in front of his men? She had been a curse on his family for decades. She was a curse on the Fatherworld.

Wolfgang grabbed her—hard—intending to rip the cables off her suit. To crush the motors that gave her this strength. But as he gripped her, those motors crackled to life. A force field blazed across her body, shimmering like eel skin. Electricity flowed into Wolfgang's fingers. The blast slammed against him, rattling his bones. The blow would have knocked a lesser man down—even killed him. Wolfgang merely grunted and shoved her aside.

Anneliese laughed. "Did you burn your fingers, little boy? Should I kiss them better?" Her laughter filled the bridge.

She had laughed that day too. That horrible day almost twenty-three years ago. But Wolfgang still remembered. He still dreamed about it most nights.

He had been seventeen, a man already, a cadet who fought against the enemies of the Fatherworld. But even at seventeen, he had depended on his mother. He had lived for her, done everything for her. He was an only child. Perhaps that was why. During the days, he dueled, he fought, he invaded enemy worlds. Sometimes he killed dogs for fun. But at night, he always came home to his mother, and he always sought comfort in her embraces.

Then *she* came into their lives.

A young, brilliant engineer. A savant, some called her. A cocky young woman named Anneliese. Discoverer of the umbrion particle.

With this foul weapon, she slew the Reichskanzlei guards. She invaded the residence of the König dynasty. The family that ruled the Fatherworld with an iron fist. The family that, for two hundred years now, oversaw the empire Hitler had founded. Her umbrionic decay spread through the Reichskanzlei like the Angel of Death, wilting all in its path. Elite guards withered before her, frozen black to the bone. Finally, wreathed by these demons of dark anti-light, Anneliese sauntered toward Helmut König himself. Führer of the Fatherworld.

Wolfgang had been there, a gangling youth. He raced toward the murderous young woman, struck her, tried to slay her. With the strength of her mechanical suit, she had tossed him back with a laugh. Young Wolfgang had fallen onto his backside, cracking his tailbone. The ultimate humiliation.

Then young Anneliese, all of twenty-seven years old, raised her Lugerheulen. The first ever made. A piece now displayed in a museum.

Young Wolfgang, lying on the floor, writhing in pain, was sure that Anneliese had come to murder his father.

But no. She pointed that rifle at Magda. Wife of the führer. Wolfgang's mother.

Wolfgang still remembered how Mother's flesh had darkened. How her skin had withered, bunched up, then slipped off like the skin of chicken boiled too long in the broth. Wolfgang had held dear Mutter Magda in his arms, begging her to live. To breathe. He got some of the umbrions on his own flesh. He still carried the scars. Whenever he looked at the dead patches on his hands, he remembered holding his mother's corpse.

Young Anneliese had laughed that day. Her laughter echoed through the Reichskanzlei.

"I've slain your wife, Führer König!" the young engineer cried. Her chest rose and fell, her cheeks flushed, and her eyes sparkled.

There were no guards left to seize her. Every guard in the palace lay as a withered, blackened corpse.

Anneliese stepped toward the führer. She clutched him and whispered into his ear, "Now you're mine. By the ancient customs, I demand it."

"Kill her!" Wolfgang screamed, eyes damp, all of seventeen. He still held his dead mother in his arms.

But Father only stared at Anneliese with lust. His eyes moved up and down her body. His gaze caressed her curves, and he licked his lips.

"No," Helmut König said. "She broke no laws. She has followed the old ways. She'll take your mother's place."

Twenty-three years.

Twenty-three years with this murderess in their house.

Since then, she had tormented Wolfgang. Mocking him. Tempting him. Laughing at the lust she saw in his eyes. Wolfgang would go out, find children on the street, and shatter their skulls against the walls. Aryan kids, yes, but who cared! Father had made him stop (something about a waste of good future soldiers). So Wolfgang would send his servants to bring him cats, simply so he could crush their heads in his fists. You could not crush a human skull in your hands—God, Wolfgang had tried!—but he could easily crush cat skulls. Sometimes even the skulls of little dogs.

Yet nothing soothed him. Nothing took the anger away.

"Let me duel her!" young Wolfgang cried a thousand times.

Father always refused.

Well, Father wouldn't be alive forever. Someday Wolfgang would sit on the man's throne. And let Anneliese pull her little stunts then!

All those thoughts, those memories, that rage—they flowed through him within moments. As they had so many times. Wolfgang shoved them aside for now.

She's trying to distract me, he thought. *To taunt me into making a mistake.*

He would contain his anger, remain in control, and break the American Fleet. And would gain power. And then he would break *her.*

Onward the *Barbarossa* charged. Onward through the American lines! The cannons boomed, the enemy ships shattered, and Wolfgang realized he was clutching his fists so tightly the palms bled. Blood speckled the floor.

Anneliese only laughed.

CHAPTER TWELVE
When a Lioness Roars

The FAS *Lioness*
High Earth Orbit
September 5, 2207

The enemy kept charging.

The Weltraumwaffe plowed through the Alliance lines. The German cannons boomed. The umbrion torpedoes tore ships apart, scattering clouds of dark, smoky death across space. The Nazi ships became like a ghost fleet riding on a storm. And at their lead, a demon risen from hell, flew *Barbarossa.* He was something beyond a dreadnought. A machine like a city. A mechanical god. In the storm of war, his prow appeared like a face, the bores of cannons forming two gaping black eyes.

With a storm of swastikas, the Weltraumwaffe drove like a blade into the Alliance. Explosions lit space. Casualty counters skyrocketed. Across High Earth Orbit, space lit up with myriads of battling warships.

The Freedom Fleet, the space force of the Alliance, was not one single, homogeneous fleet. It was a union of national subfleets, each hailing from an Alliance nation. The Tiger Fleet of India was the largest of these subfleets. Right now the Tigers were storming against the Weltraumwaffe's starboard flank. The Sun Fleet of Japan hit the Weltraumwaffe on their port side. The Caracal Fleet of Israel savaged the Weltraumwaffe from above. The tiny country's armored, diamond-shaped starships fought with fury, spinning like tops, firing cannons from every facade. The Royal British Fleet, serving Her Majesty Queen Elizabeth III, soared toward the Weltraumwaffe from below, all cannons blazing.

Meanwhile, the Eagle Fleet—the American ships—charged toward the Weltraumwaffe head-on. Within the larger Freedom Fleet, the Eagle Fleet subunit was mightiest. The Americans had fewer ships than their Indian allies. But the American ships were larger and (if you asked King—not that he was biased) deadlier. And mightiest among them was the *Lioness.* She was not only flagship of the Eagle Fleet—but of the entire Freedom Fleet. The *Lioness*—leader of freedom! The ship to inspire the hearts of warriors!

And she was . . . not at her best.

The grand flagship was stuck at the back of the fleet. She was undergoing repairs and restocking. Scaffolds covered her cracked hull like scabs. This lioness was hurt, but she slowly rose from the reeds, ready to fight again.

Gal "Spitfire" Levy stood on a floating dais in the center of the bridge. Everyone must see the commander, must obey her orders. In her navy uniform, her saber at her side, she struck a confident, even heroic figure. Maybe King was hallucinating, maybe just remembering, but where this proud commander stood King saw a little girl, barefoot, holding a toy starship in her hand.

Spitfire did not glance at him. The commander kept her gaze at the oncoming enemy, projecting strength and confidence to her officers. But telepathically, she reached out to King.

"I'm scared, Bulldog."

"I am too," he telepathized back. "Courage, Spitfire."

"Charge at them, sir?"

"What does your gut tell you?" he asked.

"Charge at them."

King smiled thinly. "Charge at them, kiddo."

Spitfire drew her saber. She pointed ahead at the oncoming German war machine. Right at the *Barbarossa.*

"*Lioness*—charge at them! Damn the umbrions, full speed ahead!"

And the *Lioness* charged to battle. As she raced through the darkness, she shed her scaffolds. Her tubular bridge dangled from her airlock like some clinging serpent; then it tore off and tumbled into the distance. Onward the *Lioness* flew. Her prow shields flared to life, forming a hemisphere of light. Explosions blazed around her, washing over the shield. From a distance, the starship must look like a charging comet awash with fire. Her engines rumbled and glowed blinding blue. Perhaps it was MindWeb. Perhaps it was just King's imagination. But standing here on the bridge, in his mind, he saw the *Lioness* fly, and she was glorious.

He also saw the enemy ahead. And the sight chilled his bones.

The *Barbarossa* was plowing through the American vanguard. The dreadnought's cannons blazed. Torpedoes streaked forth, slammed into American warships, and their warheads detonated, scattering umbrion clouds. The dark particles sucked up all light, all heat, all hope. American hulls shattered. The darkness swarmed into the ships like smoke, devouring life, consuming light itself. The dark clouds rolled over starships, an oncoming storm. The lights of ships went out. The starlight vanished. Desolation swept across the Freedom Fleet like the Angel of Death over Egypt.

Toward this dark cloud the *Lioness* flew, and the light of her engines and her blazing prow bought hope to all who saw her. She gained speed, flying among the frigates, carriers, and destroyers of her fleet, passing by these grand warships and charging onward toward the vanguard. Toward the front line. Toward the great battle ahead. The *Lioness* roared to battle.

Aboard her stood warriors of legend. George Godwin, who had commanded fleets against the Red Dawn in the Third World War. Larry Jordan, the phantom pilot, an ace killer who swept through battlefields like a ghost. Gal "Spitfire" Levy, rising star of the Alliance, baptized in the flames of the Spider War. Kim Fletcher-King, inventor of interstellar portals, worker of miracles.

And him. James King. A living legend, some called him. He had thought he could be just an old man on the range. Just another golden-ager puttering about his farm. Not somebody tormented by war. Not somebody who sent soldiers to their deaths. Just a retiree playing at being a cowboy.

That was not him. It never was.

Because fifty years in space forged a man. Fifty years aboard a warship crafted a man who would not break. A leader who would not turn away. An officer who would not shirk his duty or abandon those who needed him. And so here he stood. With his old friends. Flying toward death incarnate. And should this battle finally break him, should the umbrion clouds snuff out his light, he would die as he lived. Fighting for his world. And for his family. His back straight. His chin raised. Defiant. He would die as the man he was.

Onward, onward the *Lioness* flew. Closer, closer charged the *Barbarossa.* The Nazi juggernaut dwarfed the American flagship. Neither ship fired yet. In space, modern deflector technology made firing from a distance impractical. If you could see the incoming torpedo, you could shoot it down. There were exceptions. There were laser weapons that fired at the speed of light (though modern shields often handled those). There were even torpedoes that could create hyperspace portals and tunnel through them (they cost too much to be used that often). But in most modern space battles, you wanted to get close. Close enough to overwhelm your foe's shields and deflectors. Close enough to grab 'em by the belt buckle. It was the great irony of space warfare. They had all the space in the world, yet they fought like the navy fleets of old, storming toward each other on the waves.

Closer, closer they charged. The *Lioness* took lead position in the Freedom Fleet. The *Barbarossa* led the Weltraumwaffe spearhead. The *Lioness* fought for freedom and civilization. The *Barbarossa* fought for murder and domination. One ship painted white and gold. The other—a dark behemoth, unholy sigils burning with red flame upon her prow.

Few wars are fought between good and evil, King thought. *But this is one.*

"Ma'am, we're all ready to fire!" said the gunnery officer, a youthful-looking major with a Tennessee accent. He sounded confident. But King heard the subtext. *Can we please fire already?*

"Hold," said Spitfire.

They flew closer. Both flagships were gaining speed. They were only a minute or two away from crashing together.

"Ma'am?" said the gunnery officer.

"Hold," Spitfire whispered.

King understood what she was doing.

Grab 'em by the belt buckle, he thought.

Barbarossa's prow rose from the umbrionic storm right ahead, rearing and blazing with red cannon bores like eyes. A double-headed eagle, blacker than nightmares, spread her demonic wings upon the leviathan's hull. It was an apparition from hell, lunging toward its prey. The bridge hallucination made King feel like he was out there, floating in space, facing the tidal wave.

"Fire!" Spitfire cried.

Her voice stormed across the bridge, and *Lioness* jolted as her cannons boomed. Shock rings of energy blazed out in blue coronas, and streaks of light stretched across the distance as the torpedoes flew.

Light flashed—the *Barbarossa* firing interceptor lasers!

A split second later—detonation!

The torpedoes had hit something. Warheads blazed with light.

"We hit!" cried the gunnery major. "We broke through their shields and hit!"

King stared, eyes narrowed. "They're not stopping."

That dark behemoth kept charging—right at them.

"Fire, fire again!" Spitfire cried.

The cannons of the *Lioness* boomed. Torpedoes streaked. The enemy lasers took out many in space. Other torpedoes shattered against *Barbarossa*'s force field. One hit the juggernaut's bow, clipping the wing of that dark eagle, and another warhead blazed into the keel, ripping out chunks of shielding. But *Barbarossa* was still not stopping.

She was seconds away now.

Seconds away from ramming into the *Lioness*.

"Pitch low!" Spitfire shouted. "Under them!"

The helmsman shoved the yoke down with both hands. The mighty flagship plunged. Everyone swayed on their feet. *Barbarossa* roared closer. The two ships were seconds from impact. They weren't going to make it.

As *Lioness* plunged, officers clung to their workstations. King stood still, hands at his sides, staring at the incoming monstrosity. He did not know who *Barbarossa*'s commander was. But he made a vow then.

I will kill you.

Lioness's helmsman leaned down on his yoke. The flagship plunged deeper, faster. The *Barbarossa* reared and then—

The two great starships were passing by one another!

Barbarossa rumbled overhead, several times larger. The *Lioness* streaked below the behemoth's underbelly like a beluga swimming under a blue whale. They were so close King thought he could reach out and touch *Barbarossa*. Spitting distance. Reach out and grab 'em by the belt buckle.

At this speed, it was only for a heartbeat that the two ships flew hull to hull. And during that heartbeat . . . hangers opened on *Barbarossa*'s underbelly.

And like a mother reptile dispersing her eggs, the *Barbarossa* spewed out dropships.

Wolfjägers. Dozens of them.

"Fire on those ships!" King cried.

The gunner was already firing the dorsal hull cannons. Rounds pounded into one or two Wolfjägers. But at this distance, everything happened so fast. Within seconds, the Wolfjägers were thumping onto *Lioness*'s hull. Their drills spun. Their spikes drove in. They attached to the *Lioness* like remoras.

They got us by the belt buckle, King thought.

*****

The bridge of the *Lioness* rattled. Screeches and rumbles vibrated through the ship. The enemy dropships had latched on. And like parasites burrowing into a host, they were carving the hull open.

King spun toward a telemetry officer.

"Put the exterior hull on-screen," King said. "Live view."

The young officer gulped. "Sir, we can't."

King blinked. "The *Lioness* doesn't operate telemetry drones to film the exterior?"

The young officer paled. "I can get engineering to kludge something together if you—"

"Just pull up the schematics of the ship, dammit. Display them on . . ." King looked around at the panoply of screens that floated across the bridge. "Oh, I don't care. It's all hallucinatory anyway. Just show me the damn ship."

The young officer gulped. "Yes, Admiral. Right away, sir."

Spitfire spun toward King. She glared. Her voice sounded in his head. *Stop tormenting my bridge crew.*

King glowered back. *I wouldn't have to if these damn modern ships of yours had proper display screens.*

Oh, the invisible bulkheads were impressive. The hallucination of floating in deep space was beautiful. As they died in a fiery inferno, the view would be great!

King shoved his cynicism aside. No time for that now. Fifty-odd megameters behind them, the *Barbarossa* was beginning to turn.

"He's coming in for another round, spacers!" Spitfire cried. "Helm, turn our starboard beam toward him. We'll hit him with a broadside."

"Yawing to the starboard, aye," said the helmsman, comfortingly calm in the storm.

"All security teams—head to the upper deck!" Spitfire said as the *Lioness* turned.

Finally the tactical officer got a schematic up. A glowing hallucination of the ship materialized on the bridge, roughly the size of a bathtub. It floated in midair, showing the internal corridors, shafts, and layered decks. The schematic wasn't smart enough to show the Wolfjägers attached to the hull. But it *did* show pulsing, glowing areas where the hull was being drilled into. That was where they'd find the enemy dropships.

"Spitfire," King said. "I recommend sending a full company of the *Lioness*'s marines toward each breech. Ship security won't be enough."

Spitfire stared at him, eyes blank. "Sir, you didn't know? The *Lioness* doesn't carry a marine detachment."

"What?" King cried.

"This isn't the *Freedom*, sir. We do things differently here. Now let me command my ship!" She spun toward her gunners. "Ready, gunners! Fire!"

The starboard cannons boomed, unleashing a broadside of torpedoes.

King blinked. A warship this size—without marines! He had only been retired for three years. What had happened to his beloved Freedom Fleet?

The *Barbarossa* was charging back toward the *Lioness* at breakneck speed. As *Lioness*'s torpedoes streaked, the Nazi juggernaut unleashed umbrion clouds like an octopus spraying ink. *Lioness*'s torpedoes flew into the Stygian storm . . . and within those astral clouds, still a few megameters away from their target, the warheads detonated. White light flashed, blinding like exploding stars. But within seconds, the umbrions devoured the light like shadowy demons sucking up souls.

The *Barbarossa* stormed closer, roaring through the desolation, and opened fire.

Umbrion bolts slammed into the *Lioness*, ripping through the shields, and hitting the armored plates along the hull.

The hull *cracked.*

The ship jolted.

The alarms wailed.

Everyone swayed across the deck. While Spitfire was shouting orders, King studied the ship schematics. Hull breach on the starboard. Bad news. But King was more worried about the smaller breaches on the dorsal hull.

Those Wolfjägers had drilled holes across the flagship's top. The schematic displayed little swastikas, each representing another Nazi soldier, flowing into the *Lioness* like bacteria into a wound.

*****

The battle raged through the *Lioness.*

Standing on the bridge, King saw it on the schematics.

Saw the little swastika icons flowing through the hallucinatory ship. Saw the blue lights of spacers wink out.

The enemy was not trying to destroy the *Lioness*. Of course not. No more than they were trying to destroy Earth. They were not here to destroy wholesale. But to capture. To conquer. To purify.

King remembered the videos from Earth. The ones Godwin had shown him. The rape, torture, mutilation. That was what these heartless bastards wanted. They could have nuked Earth. But they wanted to crush this world one person at a time. To plunder. To terrorize. And finally implement their perverse notion of purification. Should the *Lioness* fall to the Reich, she would become a terrible weapon in the Nazi arsenal, and a ship forged for the good fight would become a blade of the devil. They must not let *Lioness* fall into enemy hands!

King drew his trusty Trogdor. The sidearm was small but mighty. He stepped toward the hatch, ready to leave the bridge, race toward the upper deck, and face the enemy head-on.

"Hold on, old boy!" boomed Godwin's rumbling voice.

Another blast hit the *Lioness*. The ship jolted. Sparks flew from the control panels.

King froze, halfway toward the doorway, and looked back at Godwin. The Alliance High Commander stood wreathed in smoke. Soot covered his three-piece suit.

"I'm going out to fight," King said.

Godwin lifted his fallen top hat, dusted it off, and placed it back atop his bald head. "You're an admiral, King. Not a marine. I need you by my side."

King gestured at the schematic. "The enemy is coming closer."

"And if you storm out there to meet them, not wearing any battle armor, just wielding a little sidearm, they'll shoot you down like a dog." Godwin stepped closer and grabbed King's wrist. "We might lose this battle, old boy. But I cannot lose *you*. I'll need you in the battles ahead. There's an escape pod on the bridge, hidden behind the hallucinatory view. It can travel down a tube to a secret airlock. Should we lose this ship, you and I can escape. There will be more ships to command. Fleets to lead in battle. I can't afford to lose you in a skirmish. You're too damn important, King."

King froze, torn between his honor and his commander. His honor demanded that he rush to battle. That he charged the enemy head-on, age be damned, bad back be damned—he must fight! But his sense of duty also demanded that he obey his commander in chief. Reluctantly King turned away from the hatch. He stood by his old mentor, his gun raised.

As he stood there, the Nazi forces swarmed through the ship.

Gunfire rattled. The screams of spacers echoed. Dying screams.

And then—laughter. Men chortling. Singing.

"Show me video streams from those corridors," King said to Tactical.

"But sir—"

"Now, soldier!" King barked.

The tactical officer nodded, tapped buttons, and screens materialized around King, showing the battle aboard the ship.

These were no normal German soldiers advancing through the *Lioness*. They were shock troops of the dreaded Waffen-SS. Between 1933 and 1945, a chunk of history both universes shared, the SS had exterminated millions of innocent people. It was the SS that had run the death camps. They were infamous for their brutality and sadism. To King, honor was life. But to the SS, life was cruelty. King became a soldier to defend the weak and helpless. The SS became soldiers to crush the weak, to exterminate the helpless.

King saw them in the video streams. They wore black battle armor and helmets with visors like skulls. Lightning bolts crackled on their chests, symbol of their order. They advanced mechanically, stomping like machines, firing their Lugerheulen rifles. The umbrion rounds tore into Alliance spacers. The antiphotons burrowed into flesh, sucking out all energy and life, leaving gray husks of men.

Across the schematics, dozens, then hundreds of blue lights were turning off. Each blue light—a MindLink. A living soul. A fallen hero. Someone's loved one. Husbands, wives, parents. Light by light—going out like the stars under a storm.

Meanwhile, Spitfire was busy commanding the *Lioness*, dueling the *Barbarossa* in space. But that was just a distraction, King knew. The true battle was here. Within.

Barbarossa could have blown *Lioness* out of the sky long ago, King thought. The German flagship was just keeping them busy, letting the SS parasites do their work.

The enemy advanced, taking deck after deck. Moving toward the bridge. Killing everyone in their path.

King looked at Godwin. "Sir. I must go fight. My honor demands it."

Godwin stared at him, eyes narrowed. "Your honor will get you killed someday, Admiral King."

"I don't doubt it. My goal has never been to live the longest I can, but to live the best I can. And the best life is a life of honor, of serving others, and fighting for those who cannot fight for themselves."

Godwin stared at him, eyes hard. Finally the gruff old man nodded. "Godspeed, James King."

King rushed toward the door.

Larry Jordan was already there, his own handgun drawn.

"Thought you could go to war without me, Bulldog?" the aging commander said.

King harrumphed. "Must you follow me everywhere?"

Jordan nodded. "Even to hell, old friend."

"Good. Because we've got devils to kill."

Both veterans were in their late sixties. And both stormed into the corridor with the courage of old soldiers who had cheated death many times. Guns raised, they charged to battle.

* * * * *

They did not have to run far.

The *Lioness* was a large ship, but the Waffen-SS had already taken most of her, and the Nazi troops were moving deeper and deeper. They were nearly at the bridge now. Hundreds of them were aboard, each a perfect war machine, bred from infanthood to kill. They drank hatred with their mother's milk. In kindergarten, they learned to kill animals with sticks and stones. As youths, they fought one another in gladiator battles, culling the weak. Bodies scarred, eyes gone, they became half men, half machines. Bionic eyes sent tentacles into their warped brains. Drugs coursed through their veins. Their battle armor was a masterwork of engineering, giving them inhuman strength.

They stood seven feet tall or close to it. Not because of genetic engineering. Their ideology forbade such tampering; how could one presume to alter Aryan DNA, which was already pure? Yet over the centuries, through culling the weak and kind, they had altered themselves. As man domesticated animals to suit his needs, so did the Nazis of the Fatherworld alter their gene pool with selective breeding. Anyone too small, anyone too weak, anyone infirm or disabled, anyone simply not cruel enough—it was to the incinerators with them. After centuries of such culling, here they stood. A race of supermen. Taller, stronger, crueler than the free people of this universe.

They thought themselves superior. And in battle, they

were.

The sounds of war rose ahead. Just down the corridor. Smoke filled the innards of the ship. The overhead lights had shattered, plunging the corridors into shadows. King couldn't see more than a few steps ahead. But he could hear the battle. The screams of the dying. The laughter of the killers. The splatter of flesh against the deck. The roar of bullets and the strange howling of umbrion rounds. He could smell the battle too. The stench of it! A smell like charred meat, gunpowder, and excrement. That was something else you never faced in a starfighter. The smell of it all.

Ahead, in the shadow, lay hell. And King and Jordan marched down the corridor, heading toward it. They wore no battle armor. They had no assault rifles, just plasma pistols. They were old men with achy knees, with stiff joints, with too much weariness blanketing their hearts.

But King had learned something in his long, long years of service. Fear the old soldier. Fear the old man in a game where men die young. Over the decades, war had slain millions around King. Yet he had marched through. His sword kept thrusting as so many other blades shattered. He was the sword that would not shatter, he was the light in the darkness of space, he was the man who bore the torch of Earth, and he would thrust that flame at the devil. The Nazis had culled the weak on their world, creating a race of the strong. But here, in this universe, war had done the same. And from the ashes of those old wars came marching James King.

He chambered a plasma round, raised his Trogdor, and marched through the smoke toward the fray. And with him marched a phantom. Larry "Phantom" Jones. They had met half a century ago, two young fighter pilots. With them had flown Yehuda "Lion" Levy. Together, the three aces had shaken the galaxy. They had smote the Red Dawn. They had conquered stars.

Then Yehuda had died, leaving his daughter, fiery little Spitfire. Then Jordan and King had grown old. Then the space between the universes had frayed, and in came spilling the shadows of their past. The Fatherworld was the shame of humanity, the festering wound beneath history's scab. Now all that rot came gushing forth, and King and Jordan met it with fire.

They raised their sidearms and pulled the triggers.

Their Trogdors roared out fire.

King and Jordan. The bulldog and the phantom. For decades, they had fought side by side. Their guns sang together again. One more time. Perhaps the last time.

The balls of plasma rolled through the umbrion clouds. For a second, before the umbrion could extinguish their light, the plasma revealed the scene ahead. Dozens of SS troops stood there, staring with bionic eyes. Their skull visors gleamed red. Their steel-tipped boots stomped upon the corpses of American spacers. Then the plasma hit their armor, and flames roared toward the deckhead.

The German armor stopped the bolts. And onward marched the skeletal soldiers. Their Lugerheulens howled. Dark, smoky rounds flew down the corridor.

King and Jordan pressed against the bulkheads, seeking cover behind pipes and control panels. The umbrion particles filled the corridor, dousing what little light remained. A chill filled the hall. King's joints ached like they always did in winter. Through the murky haze, the Waffen-SS marched onward, boots crushing bones, bionic eyes piercing the darkness.

"Their armor is weakest on the visors," King said. "Aim for the eyeholes."

"I know how to shoot, Jim," Jordan said.

They leaned from behind the pipes and control panels, firing plasma bolts. King hit one! He hit one in the head! The armored Nazi stumbled back, shook sparks off his helmet, and kept advancing. Dammit.

Jordan hit another trooper. The plasma entered his eyeholes, and the giant Aryan fell. His armored limbs twitched, then fell still.

"Aim for the eyeholes, Jim!" Jordan said.

"Smartass," King muttered.

Cries sounded from a nearby corridor.

"For freedom!"

A group of spacers, all clad in Alliance blue, raced toward battle. They had come from the ship's midsection. They were not combat soldiers. Not marines or even guards. They were warehouse workers, a cook or two, a janitor. But they lifted the guns of fallen warriors, and they fired them at the Nazi force.

"For freedom!" King cried, voice raspy.

"For freedom!" boomed Jordan in his thundering baritone.

The two old men joined their younger peers. Together they charged at the enemy. They ran through the umbrion clouds, through spurting plasma and crackling electricity, and over the dead, and they fired at the Nazi scourge.

Another SS trooper fell.

And a third!

King roared as he fought. An umbrion bolt grazed his ear. Blood splattered. He kept fighting. A bolt hit his left shoulder. He roared and fought onward.

Jordan cried out. An umbrion bolt hit his leg. His knee buckled, but he pulled himself up and kept shooting. More of the enemy fell.

"We will stop you with fire!" King cried. "We will stop you with our own flesh and blood. You will not take this ship!"

From down the corridor rose laughter.

A girl's tinkly laughter. Almost sweet. Yet in this corridor of butchery and death, the sound of a girl's innocent laughter became a disturbing sound, a *wrong* sound, like the sound of a baby giggling in a graveyard. King shuddered.

The girlish laughter sounded again, louder now. A voice followed, rising from the darkness. A high, feminine voice.

"The ship is already ours! This is only mopping up."

King squinted. Through the umbrion clouds and fire walked an SS officer. A female. Shorter than the others, slender and graceful. She wore body armor, but her skull visor was raised, revealing a young, almost cherubic face, the cheeks pink, the nose small, the lips plump. Her left eye was as blue as the sea after a storm. The right eye, her adlerauge, shone with red cunning. As she walked, a grin twisted across her face. A demonic grin that showed too many teeth, stretching to the last molars.

And something about her looked so familiar . . .

* * * * *

I've seen her before! King thought, staring at the girl. *But where?*

The taller, older Nazis stood back in deference. The young woman walked between them, a gun in each hand. She looked so young. Just a teenager. Yet the insignia of a *gruppenführer* topped her shoulders. This little girl was a general. Had she, like Katyusha, implanted her brain into a younger clone? Or was this general truly so young?

"Hail Eva!" cried a Nazi officer and snapped a salute.

"Hail Eva!" cried the other troops.

A trooper raised his fist, holding a spacer's severed arm. He brandished it like a trophy. "God bless Eva König, our future führer!"

So. Not only a general then. A scion of the führer himself. No wonder they had slapped those general ranks on her young, slender shoulders. Nepotism was the multiversal constant.

The girl's grin widened further. She sauntered between her soldiers, stepping over the corpses of Alliance spacers. One Alliance spacer stirred on the deck; the man was still alive, gasping for breath. Eva laughed and kicked his face, crushing the nose and scattering teeth. She walked onward, a spring to her step.

King, Jordan, and the other living soldiers of the Alliance roared and opened fire.

Eva's visor snapped shut, replacing her fair, pink-cheeked face with a metal skull. The other Nazis had visors shaped like somber skulls. Not Eva. Her skull visor was grinning.

The führer's granddaughter crouched, then leaped through the gunfire toward her enemies.

Like an acrobat, she spun through the air. Plasma bolts rolled past her. The Alliance kept firing. But Eva dodged every shot. She hit the deck, bounded upward, kicked off a wall, rose toward the deckhead, then lunged onward. King stood his ground, firing again and again. He hit her! But the plasma merely washed off her armored shoulder. She kept moving with inhuman speed. Perhaps her battlesuit gave her extra agility. Perhaps she was simply faster than any human on this side of the multiverse.

Laughing, Eva landed among Alliance spacers. She grabbed one. Just a cook still wearing his apron. Her gloved fingers tightened around the man's arm. Motors hummed inside her suit. And Eva ripped the man's arm off.

Blood spurted. Spacers cried out in horror, falling back.

Eva laughed and advanced. She grabbed another spacer, lifted him overhead, and ripped his body apart. She tossed down the corpse and kept moving.

Gunfire blazed against Eva, sparking against her armor. That maniacal skull visor of hers leered. She walked through the fire.

King kept shooting. A few spacers turned to flee, but he stood his ground. He hit her visor again and again. Why wasn't anything entering her eyeholes?

He fired another bolt, and then he noticed it. He *did* hit that eyehole! And a tiny force field shone, just large enough to cover Eva's eye. It looked like a ghostly contact lens, as airy as a soap bubble, but it was still powerful enough to block plasma. So. Her suit was more powerful than those of her underlings. Even her eyes were protected. Did her suit have any weak spots? If so, King wasn't finding any.

Jordan was firing too. He wasn't having much more success. As he fought, Jordan was leaning against the wall, and sweat beaded on his brow. Black scars were spreading across his leg. Umbrions! The particles were moving across Jordan like mold, sucking energy from his flesh.

King grunted. Dammit! Jordan was almost out of strength. So was King. Meanwhile, more spacers were falling dead. And Eva's troops were marching onward, heading closer and closer to the bridge.

Eva laughed, leaping around the Alliance gunfire. She fired her Lugerheulen, pulverizing a man's head, then bounded down the corridor. She was seconds away now. King fired a bolt right between the Sig runes on her breastplate. Eva stumbled back, snarled, and wiped off the plasma. Then she kept advancing. Would anything short of a nuclear bomb stop that damn girl?

"Fall back!" boomed a voice from behind. "King! Jordan! Fall back to the bridge!"

It was Godwin.

King snarled. Did his boss really want him to *run from battle*?

"Jim, they're breaking in!" rose another voice from the bridge. A higher voice. Kim!

His wife was there on that bridge. She needed him.

"Go, Jim!" Jordan said. "I'll cover you."

Eva leaped closer. Spacers ran toward her, guns blazing.

The *kindergeneral* took the fire on her breastplate, stumbled back a few steps, but then regained her balance. She grabbed men, snapped limbs, shattered necks. That was a machine! It had to be. How could that thing be human?

King cursed and began walking backward, firing his gun all the while. He kept having to load fresh plasma packs. He was running low. Each blast slammed into Eva, knocking her back a step but not knocking her down. He would need a goddamn bazooka to shatter that armor. Eva wasn't wearing a mech-suit. Her armor couldn't be more than an inch thick. Yet clearly it was made of advanced compounds and augmented with a force field. Right now King wondered if even a nuclear weapon would kill the girl. She brushed off more plasma and laughed.

"Is this all you got, Amis?" the girl said. "You just send old men who spit some fire?"

King kept stepping backward, heading toward the bridge. Jordan moved with him, limping. All the while, ahead of them, the enemy kept firing, Eva kept advancing, and spacers kept falling.

"We're getting our asses kicked," Jordan telepathized.

"She's toying with us like a cat with two old mice," King telepathized back.

They kept backing up toward the bridge. But the enemy kept advancing. Another bolt slammed into King. This one hit his metal fist, denting the prosthetic. One of the mechanical fingers cracked open. Then a blast slammed into King's leg. The same leg Dr. Anneliese had stabbed. King roared and fell to one knee. Eva licked her lips and advanced, catlike, toward him.

Just then the most bizarre thing happened. King must be hallucinating. George Godwin himself burst from the bridge, his coattails fluttering behind him like military banners. The old man tapped a button on his cane, and it transformed into a rifle.

"Get thee back to hell, spawn of Lucifer!" the octogenarian cried and opened fire.

His cane boomed. A blast of blue energy slammed into Eva. The blow cracked her armor, lifted her into the air, and hurled her into the distance. The girl slammed into her troops and slumped to the deck, dazed.

"Goddamn!" King said, eyes wide.

"Ah, there you are, old boy." Godwin brushed umbrion particles off his suit. "Good to see you."

"Sir!" King said. "What are you doing out here?"

"I caught a bad case of honor from you, King. And I intend to recover quickly. Come now! To the bridge!"

*****

Before the enemy could recover from the wrath of Godwin's cane, the three old men ran onto *Lioness*'s bridge. The hallucination of space still engulfed the bridge in a sphere, showing battling ships and distant stars. But chunks of the hallucination were missing now, revealed simple bulkheads. Some of the hull's exterior cameras, which fed the hallucinations with real-time data, had probably shattered. A few strobe lights flashed, bathing the bridge with eerie red light.

Spitfire still stood upon her dais, gazing out into space. The *Barbarossa* loomed ahead. Several chunks were missing from her armor, but the Nazi juggernaut was still very much in the fight. Spitfire simply stared for a long moment. She spoke softly, but standing at the doorway, King heard her clearly.

"Our shields are falling apart. We still have torpedoes, but no crew to load them into the cannons. Barely any crew left at all. And the enemy is within. We lost." Spitfire turned toward King, eyes haunted. "It's over."

Boots stomped behind King. Screams and laughter echoed from the halls. The enemy was getting closer. The last few Alliance spacers were dying. King checked the schematics of the ship.

Almost everyone—dead.

"Over here!" rose Kim's voice from across the bridge. "Hurry!"

King stared over smoldering workstations. A cloud of smoke obscured his wife. King took a few steps closer, wincing with each step. He could barely feel his wounded leg; that worried him, but at least the pain was fading. He waved aside smoke. Kim stood by a bulkhead, holding open a hatch.

It took King a moment to figure out what he was seeing. The hallucinations, which normally showed space outside, had shut down in this corner of the bridge. The hatch Kim held open? It led to a small chamber with seats. No, not a chamber. An escape pod! Yes, this was the escape pod Godwin had mentioned. The one hidden on the bridge. Located deep inside the ship, the pod would travel down a tube toward an airlock.

"Jim, come on!" Kim said. "Everyone, into the pod. They're coming. Hurry!"

Everyone hesitated. The bridge crew froze at their stations. They looked toward Spitfire, awaiting her orders. No one wanted to be seen fleeing from battle.

"Well, if no one else will go first, I will!" Godwin boomed. The elderly Englishman stomped across the deck, entered the escape pod, and sat down, coattails dangling between his feet.

Just then, the last Alliance guard fell. And the Waffen-SS burst onto the bridge of the *Lioness*.

* * * * *

The mechanized killers stormed onto the bridge, their dark armor shining in the red strobe lights. Their skull visors leered and their guns howled.

Lioness's navigator fell. A hole gaped in his head, and the umbrion particles spread through his skull, sucking up his brain like a tiny black hole. The comms officer rose to run. U-rounds hit his back. He collapsed, spine shriveling up like a salted slug.

King knelt behind a workstation. He only had three plasma rounds left. He fired all three at the advancing Nazis. One man fell back, screaming, clawing at his melting eyes. Jordan and a few surviving bridge crew opened fire too, bombarding the enemy. No hope for victory remained. But maybe King could buy time for a few last souls to escape.

King reached for another plasma pack. Damn! He was out. But the dead navigator had some ammo strapped to his belt. As the guns boomed all around, King rolled across the deck toward the corpse. His back creaked, and his leg screamed in protest, but King reached the nav station in one piece. He grabbed the dead officer's ammunition, reloaded, then rose from behind the workstations. His Trogdor bathed the enemy with fire. Another SS goon fell.

But more replaced them. Dozens crowded the corridor. Hundreds filled the ship.

"Everyone—into the escape pod!" Godwin called. "There's no shame in fleeing if we live to fight another day. Come on!"

So few bridge officers remained alive. Some raced toward the escape pod. They didn't even make it that far. The Nazi fire mowed them down.

Kim entered the pod next. The engineer took the seat beside Godwin and strapped herself in. Corpses lay strewn across the deck, some mere steps away from the pod.

"Jim!" she cried, her blue eyes damp.

Only three Alliance officers still lived on the bridge. James "Bulldog" King. Larry "Phantom" Jordan. And the daughter of their fallen friend, Gal "Spitfire" Levy. Three pilots. The heads of three military dynasties.

"Jim, come on!" Kim cried from the shuttle. "Get in!"

King kept firing. So did Jordan. Spitfire, meanwhile, completely abandoned battling *Barbarossa.* With her bridge crew dead, there was nothing the young commander could do. So she took cover behind a workstation, drew her firearm, and began shooting Nazis alongside the two old men. For all the damn good it did. They were hitting a few eyeholes but not nearly enough. For every trooper they slew, two more replaced him.

"Everyone into the shuttle!" Godwin boomed. "That is an order."

King glanced toward the ship blueprint. The schematic displayed icons of everyone aboard who still lived. Hundreds of swastikas were swarming through the ship. More and more were making their way toward the bridge. But some blue icons still shone! Some Alliance spacers were still alive! Maybe not warriors. Maybe not officers. They were the common workers of the lower decks. Warehouse laborers, mechanics, flight controllers, and all the other spacers who kept a ship running. Some were still alive!

"I'm staying," King said. "I'm the ranking officer on this bridge. And I will not abandon ship so long as a single spacer lives."

"And I'm the commander of this ship, and I'll go down with her," Spitfire said.

And that tore King's heart. Tore it right in half. He remembered the little girl running through the halls of the *Freedom*, making her toy spaceships fly. His little Spitfire. Yehuda's daughter. To King, she was family. Just as much as his son.

"Gal," he said softly. "Go. Leave. Live to fight another day."

Tears streamed down her cheeks. "I won't leave you."

More Nazi troops entered the bridge. They heard the emotional exchange. They laughed. They mimicked King and Spitfire.

"Aww, the *untermenschin* won't leave her daddy."

"Pathetic Amis!"

"What say we keep the woman alive, huh? She will entertain the troops, yes?"

Fury rose in King. He rose from cover and fired. An umbrion round slammed into his shoulder. He roared and fell back. Jordan cursed, ran toward him, but a round hit him in the chest, and the phantom fell.

"Larry!" King cried. He tried to rush toward his friend, but enemy fire drove him back behind a workstation.

"Damn you honorable fools!" Godwin cried. The octogenarian leaped from the shuttle, ran through the gunfire, and grabbed Jordan. The tall, aging commander was still alive. But barely. Godwin dragged him into the escape pod.

That left only two Alliance spacers on the bridge. King and Spitfire. They raised their guns, ready to die side by side. Two old companions. Two soldiers. King's heart broke that Spitfire should go down with him. She was so young. Far too young to die. But he could think of no better soldier to fight his final battle alongside.

And then the German troops parted, forming a path between them. And Eva König stepped onto the bridge.

The führer's granddaughter had lost the spring to her step. She no longer skipped with girlish abandon. As she shuffled forward, the *kindergeneral* cracked her neck and winced. A crack gaped open on her breastplate. Right between the lightning bolts. One of the Sig runes had stopped crackling with electricity, while the other just spurted sparks.

Again King was struck by how darn familiar Eva looked. He knew her! But from where?

"You really are a lot of trouble, Amis," Eva said. "But playtime is over."

"Jim, come on!" Kim cried from the shuttle.

King stood his ground. He would not leave. Not so long as anyone aboard was alive. Even if it meant his death.

Kim exited the pod. She made to run toward King. But umbrion rounds flew. A round hit Kim's arm, and she cried out, face twisting in anguish.

"Kim!" King cried, wanting to run to her. Yet even now, he did not abandon his post.

Thankfully, Godwin was there. The elderly leader grabbed Kim and pulled her back into the pod. Meanwhile, Spitfire was firing a pistol in each hand, knocking down enemy soldiers.

Her breastplate sparking like a welder's torch, Eva knelt for cover behind corpses. Her Lugerheulen rose over the fleshy barricade and howled like a wolf, spitting shadowy death. Plasma bolts and umbrion rounds stormed back and forth, a battle between light and darkness, fire and ice. The gunfire shattered what remained of *Lioness*'s bridge.

"King, damn it all!" Godwin roared. "We turned on the self-destruct sequence. This ship is gonna blow! With or without you. Hopefully without!"

Beside King, Spitfire gasped. She glanced toward the shuttle, eyes yearning. Then her face hardened and she kept firing at the enemy. She was determined to go down with this ship.

It was the honorable choice. She was commander of this ship. She would never abandon it. King had taught her this honor. He would expect no less from her.

And yet King could not let her die. Not Spitfire. Yes, she was an adult now. Forty-two years old. The commander of a starship. But to him, she was still that little girl.

I promised to take care of your girl, Yehuda, he thought. *And that's what I'll do.*

He ran through the fire and smoke. Umbrion rounds burst around him. Particles rained onto his skin, freezing him, sucking heat and energy away like tiny dark mosquitoes. King ran through the umbrionic haze, scooped Spitfire into his arms, and ran onward, carrying her toward the pod.

"Sir!" she cried. "No! Put me down!"

King ran onward through the storm, carrying Spitfire across his shoulder. The enemy raced all around. Plasma blasts streaked around King, momentarily blinding him. Nazis cursed and clattered down behind him. The gunfire came from inside the pod! Godwin, Jordan, and Kim—they were covering him.

As King ran, Spitfire struggled in his grip. "No! No, sir. Let me fight! I can't abandon my ship."

And as King carried her, he imagined not the tall, proud officer but the little girl. He knew she was a warrior now. A proud officer. A woman of honor. He knew she would never abandon her post. So let this be his choice, not hers. Let him tarnish her honor. Maybe she would forever hate him for this. So long as she lived. But she would *live*.

He tossed her into the pod.

Then he hesitated at the hatchway.

Kim stared from inside. She met his eyes.

"Jim?"

"I love you, Kim," he said. "Forever. I'm sorry. I love you."

"Wai—" she began.

He slammed the hatch door shut, sealing them inside.

"Jim!" his wife cried, voice muffled.

He shoved a lever. And the escape pod hurtled down a tube, racing toward the airlock. Toward space. Toward life.

Live, Spitfire. Live, Kim. Live, Jordan. Live. Live to fight another day.

Alone on the bridge, King spun to face his foes. He had taken a knife to the leg and several u-rounds to his body. Yet everything stopped hurting. Here, at the end, there was no pain.

This was right. This was honorable. This was how he must

die. He could not abandon a ship with living crew. He could not live with the shame. With his death, maybe he could give the others a chance.

He pointed his gun ahead, ready to die fighting.

* * * * *

Eva stood on the smoldering bridge of the *Lioness*, staring at the old bulldog. The young woman did not fire her gun. Nor did the soldiers around her. She merely stared at King, curious.

"You really do look like him, you know," she said. "They were right."

"Like who?" He should be firing his gun, fighting, not talking to her. But people had been mistaking him for somebody else all week. First the parachuting Rattenjäger pilot. Then Dr. Anneliese. He remembered their shocked eyes. Their voices. *You!*

"Who the hell do I look like?" he growled.

Eva shook her head in wonder. "You still don't know, do you?" She laughed. "You look just like my grandfather."

And then it clicked.

Why Eva looked so familiar.

She was three or four years older. Her hair was lighter. So was her remaining eye. But otherwise—she looked exactly like Rowan King. King's granddaughter.

Another doppelgänger, he thought. *A version of Rowan from a shadow universe.*

"Goodbye, Admiral King." Eva lowered her grinning skull visor, aimed her Lugerheulen at him, and fired.

At the same moment, King fired his Trogdor.

It was a one-in-a-million shot. The two rounds slammed into each other in midair. Plasma blazed. Then umbrion clouds filled the air, obscuring his vision. King stumbled backward, coughing. He glimpsed something. A figure running. Eva—

running toward him!

He fired again.

He hit her!

Then an umbrion round slammed into his chest. Right at the heart. And King fell.

He hit the deck, unable to breathe.

No worse for wear, Eva ran over him, her boots crushing his chest. She leaped into the air . . . and into the escape pod shoot.

She slid down the tunnel like a girl down a water slide, racing toward the escape pod.

King lay on the deck, groaning in pain. He was still alive. How the hell was he still alive? She had shot him in the heart!

His ears were ringing. Vaguely he heard voices shouting in German. His MindLink sputtered, crackled, then finally translated.

"The ship is about to blow!"

"The core is overheating."

"Run, soldiers! Back to the Wolfjägers. This ship is lost!"

King shoved himself onto his elbows, somehow still alive. The SS troops didn't notice the miracle. They were busy fleeing the bridge. Somewhere a computer voice was chanting a countdown. King could barely hear over the ringing in his ears.

I should be dead, he thought.

He looked at his chest. Eva's umbrion round had hit him. Right over his heart. He pulled from his shirt pocket the medal Rowan had made him. #1 GRAMPA. The umbrion round had cracked it in two.

Rowan saved my life from her own doppelgänger, he thought. *Incredible.*

He stared down the echoing escape tube. Three hundred yards away, the escape pod reached an airlock. The round vessel was ready to blast into open space. As King watched, Eva landed on the escape pod's exterior. She began clawing at the hatch, trying to rip it off. With her power gloves, it wouldn't take long. Then the airlock opened—and out shot the escape pod. The spherical vessel hurtled into space like a cannonball, Eva clinging to the exterior. They vanished into the battle in space.

Back on the bridge, King's hearing cleared enough for him to make out the computer's voice.

"Four minutes and four seconds to core meltdown."

Just over four minutes to escape the *Lioness*—a ticking time bomb the size of a town. It took King longer most mornings to get out of bed and pee. Sometimes, by the time he rolled out of bed, rubbed his aching back, and limped into the bathroom, he thought his bladder would explode.

Well, this starship was about to explode and scatter its atoms across space. Almost as alarming as a full bladder. Trying to ignore all the usual aches, as well as his new wounds, King limped across the deck, searching for the LOLS closet. Every bridge had one. Loss of Life Support closets contained everything you needed in case of a hull breach: oxygen tanks, spacesuits, helmets, even jetpacks.

On the exterior hull, more and more cameras were dying. The cameras normally fed the hallucination of open space here inside the bridge. As each camera died, another chunk of the hallucination faded. The view of space vanished, revealing the bridge's bulkheads. Another chunk of hallucination vanished, and—there! The LOLS closet. King yanked the door open, revealing a few spacesuits.

Moving faster than he had in years, King pulled on a spacesuit. Thankfully, modern spacesuits were nothing like the bulky old suits from the old days. King hated these new designs. The fabric was too thin and formfitting. What was wrong with the old bulky classics? Well, today, for the first time, he was thankful for modern technology. Instead of twenty minutes, the suit only took twenty seconds to pull on. Its buckles snapped together automatically. Its zippers moved of their own volition. He still had to struggle a bit with the pant legs and left sleeve. Every muscle in King's body cramped, and his back was about to hire a lawyer and send him a cease and desist letter, but within those twenty seconds, that suit was *on.*

"Sixty seconds to core meltdown," the computer intoned.

King glanced at the ship's schematics. A few blue lights still shone. Living Alliance spacers. Some were running to escape pods on their own decks. Others weren't moving. Maybe they were wounded. Maybe trapped. They were all, whether wounded or mobile, too far to reach a pod in time.

I'm the ranking officer aboard, King thought. *I vowed to go down with the ship.*

He glanced down the tube again. He could no longer see the escape pod. It had vanished into space.

Some of the people he loved were in that pod. His wife. His best friend. And his adopted daughter. Not to mention his mentor and commander in chief.

And Eva was trying to break in. Maybe she already had.

He would go down with the ship, gladly giving his own life for honor. But his honor also demanded that he protect his family. Right now he was torn between two duties. And he made his choice.

He limped toward the escape tube. It sloped downward like a water slide, leading to space and its myriads of battling ships.

"I hate war," King muttered and jumped into the tube.

CHAPTER THIRTEEN
Falling Down

The FAS *Lioness*
20 seconds before destruction
High Earth Orbit
September 5, 2207

King's bones rattled as he slid down the tube. He felt like a child who'd slipped and fallen down the world's longest water slide.

That or the world's largest kidney stone on its way to freedom, King thought. It certainly hurt as much. He hated war. He hated being old. He hated fighting a war while old. He should be whittling in his rocking chair now, his most pressing concern what to grill for dinner. Instead, he was racing at breakneck speed down the escape tube. Headfirst. The open airlock awaited.

The computer's voice rang through his MindLink.

"Ten seconds to detonation."

Like a Champagne cork, King flew into space.

"Nine seconds."

He shot into the distance, moving at incredible speed. His head rattled in his helmet. Even space wasn't a total vacuum, and scattered particles blazed against his visor, scraping the steelglass. The g-force flattened his skin against his skull.

"Eight seconds."

The battle raged all around him. The Weltraumwaffe and the Freedom Fleet were slamming together. Missiles and lasers streaked. Torpedoes slammed into hulls. Countless Eagle and

Rattenjäger starfighters blazed all around like sparks from a campfire. In the distance, other nations were fighting the Nazi scourge. But here, where King flew, his fellow Americans were battling the common enemy.

How long was left now? King wasn't sure. He could no longer hear that computer voice. He must be out of range. Five seconds maybe?

In the distance, he saw it.

The escape pod! And Eva was on the—

Light.

White light flooded the universe.

Out here in space, King couldn't hear the explosion. A good thing too. It would have shattered his eardrums. Through the light flew chunks of what had been the *Lioness*. Bits of armored hull, pieces of machinery, whatever had survived the explosion—it streaked into the distance and slammed into starships, carving into their hulls. Only by a miracle did nothing hit King. His suit was designed to withstand radiation. Otherwise, the immense heat and light from the blast would have cooked him alive. Once again he had escaped death by a thread's width. Bulldog? No. Tonight King felt like a battered old alley cat with nine lives, and by now he was running low.

He could see the escape pod in the distance. It was hurtling toward Earth. Eva clung to its exterior, pounding the hatch again and again. Sparks rose with every blow of her fists.

King's vector was off. He was shooting like a bullet into deep space. At this angle, he'd eventually shoot past the moon and onward to the stars.

Thankfully, even in his sorry state, he had remembered to slip on a jetpack from the LOLS closet. No handles or buttons. Neural interface only. Damn modern tech! As King hurtled through space, he must load MindPlay, scroll through options, telepathically tap the *Scan for Nearby Devices* option, insert his security code, and overall waste precious time before he could finally control the damn thing. Briefly, aboard the *Lioness*, King had almost come around to admiring modern technology. Or at least respecting it. Almost. Now, once more, he hated it with a passion.

Finally he wrestled mental control of the jetpack and activated the accursed thing. The motors thrummed. Without mechanical handles, he must control it telepathically. The younger soldiers (like his son) loved neural toys like these. Not King. Finally, by thinking about yawing (and cursing quite a bit), he managed to turn himself toward Earth.

By now the escape pod was halfway to Earth. Thankfully, while thousands of warships battled all around, nobody was firing on the small, spherical vessel. The Alliance, no doubt, recognized it as one of their own escape pods. The Nazis weren't shooting at the pod either. Maybe they recognized the infamous Eva König clinging to the exterior. Maybe they simply didn't bother wasting ammo on little pods, not when there were bigger, juicer targets to shoot. But once the pod entered low orbit, it would pass through the Russian formations on its way to Earth. And who knew what Katyusha might do?

If Katyusha recognized Eva, she'll open fire, King said. *And she won't care who's inside the pod!*

Great. As if things weren't bad enough, now he must worry about the deranged Russian despot too. Nothing was ever easy.

With a mental command, he gave the jetpack a burst of speed. He shot through the space like another torpedo, racing through the storm of swirling, battling starfighters. Dreadnoughts and frigates loomed all around like whales in the depths, casting deep shadows.

The escape pod was still flying toward Earth. On its way, it was nearing the Russian fleet. Most likely, the pod was flying on autopilot, and the software recognized Katyusha's fleet as allies. Technically, the software was right. Technically. They told King that the Alliance and Red Dawn were at peace. To him, it had always felt more like a ceasefire. An uneasy ceasefire. As uneasy as a long-tailed cat in a room full of rocking chairs. Normally, Katyusha was harmless. Normally. Until she was not. Playing with Katyusha was a game of Russian roulette.

Yes, yes, Katyusha had saved his life before. King remembered. He would never forget. In a rare show of honor, Katyusha had pulled him off the bridge of a starship hurtling into a star. Yes, there was some honor left in the madwoman. Even after all her brain transplants. But now, in her battle lust, inhabiting yet another clone, did any of her sanity remain? Or her mercy?

King was about to find out. The escape pod plunged into the Red Dawn fleet and hurtled between the gargantuan ships. It was like a goldfish swimming through a school of piranhas. With nothing but a spacesuit, jetpack, and scratched helmet, King followed.

As always, it struck him how flamboyant Russian starships were. Katyusha skimped on everything but appearances. Her shuttles lacked landing treads. Her troops often lacked weapons. And food. She cut corners everywhere. But in one area, she spared no expense—the art and elegance of her starship hulls. They looked like floating opera houses, cathedrals, and ballet halls lifted from Tolstoy's era and affixed with engines. Filigree adorned the crimson hulls, and golden equal signs gleamed on the prows. Brass cannons thrust out from those red ships, forged to look like roaring bears. They reminded King of the *Vasa*, among the grandest of sailing ships in history, a warship so bedecked in glory she sank on her maiden voyage, drowning under the weight of her gold and jewels. To Katyusha, war was not a painful necessity. To her, it was a thing of beauty. Of art. A grand masquerade. What was the point of fighting if you didn't look good? Millions were dying. And she was loving this.

King gritted his teeth, diving into the Russian lines.

He missed his retirement.

* * * * *

Below, the escape pod was tumbling between several Russian frigates, rolling toward Earth. The red warships were too busy bombarding a German destroyer. The pod raced by unharmed. King had to swerve several times, dodging flying missiles and umbrion torpedoes. One of those German torpedoes slammed into a nearby Russian warship, shattering her decorative balustrades and teardrop domes. Umbrion clouds formed dark nebulae in space, obscuring King's view. Telepathically controlling his jetpack, he flew above and around the clouds, seeking the pod.

Ah, there it was! The pod was in the thick of the Russian formations now. A few Sickle ships—Russian starfighters—were chasing the pod, probably just curious. King could imagine the Russian pilots' thoughts. *Was that really a woman clinging to the pod's hull? A Nazi woman! It looks like Eva König. Shoot her!*

"Katyusha!" King growled, sending his thoughts over MindWeb. "Katyusha, it's me. James King. Do not shoot that escape pod! Tell your goons!"

No answer.

Where the hell was the madwoman?

King saw the RDS *Gagarin*. The monstrous Russian flagship was battling several German frigates. Katyusha's dreadnought had taken heavy damage. Her hull was breached in multiple locations. A good chunk of the starboard was gone entirely. The gilded figurehead on the prow was still missing its head. But Premier Ketya "Katyusha" Petrova was still fighting, firing every cannon she had left.

The Sickle starfighters were getting closer to the escape pod. They were taking attack formation.

"Katyusha, dammit!" King said, directing his MindWeb signal to the *Gagarin*. "Listen to me! Don't shoot that escape pod!"

Suddenly her voice filled his mind. "Jamechka? Is that you? Katyusha cannot talk now. She is busy killing fascists."

"Katyusha, dammit, my family is inside that pod! Call your goons off."

She laughed maniacally. A blurry image of her appeared in his mind. She was standing on her bridge, a dripping gash on her cheek, pointing her blade forward. Her head was tossed back, her eyes alight. The firelight of burning control panels gleamed against her many medals.

"Haha, death to you, fascist scum!" she cried. "You cannot kill Katyusha. She will lead the Red Dawn to glorious victory against the invaders! Onward, equalist comrades! To glory!"

"Katyusha!" King said.

She looked at him. "Fine, fine." She waved dismissively. "Hear that, fleet? Everyone let the capitalist escape pod through."

King breathed in relief. "Thank you, Katyusha."

She blew him a kiss. "Anything for my darling cowboy. You owe Katyusha a kiss, yes?" Then she returned her attention to the enemy. "Onward, comrades! Death to fascists!"

The Russian starfighters pulled back, letting the escape pod fly onward. Eva was still clinging to the pod's rounded hull, struggling with the hatch.

Once Katyusha learns she let Eva König herself escape, she'll scream for my head, King thought. Well, he'd deal with that later. So long as his family was safe.

The pod was passing by the last few Russian ships now. From there, it was just a short flight to Earth.

With the Red Fleet thinning out, King shoved the pedal to the metal (telepathically, at least, which wasn't nearly as satisfying).

His jetpack thrummed. He roared forward, making a beeline toward the escape pod. The pod's autopilot was slowing it down, preparing for atmospheric entry. That let King, who was hurtling forth at breakneck speed, too quickly catch up.

Eva still clung to the round hull. She had managed to open the hatch! Kim, Jordan, and the others were inside the spherical pod, wearing spacesuits. They were shouting something, firing guns. Blasts hit Eva's armor, but the girl clung on.

King increased speed.

In the distance, Kim saw him. She looked at him and gasped.

Eva noticed. Clinging to the pod with one hand, the young sadist spun around. A wolfish grin twisted her face. When she saw King, that grin became a snarl.

She raised her Lugerheulen and fired.

King swerved, dodging an incoming umbrion bolt. He wanted to fire back but dared not. Too risky. His plasma might enter the pod and roast everyone inside. He kept chasing through space, swerving around Eva's barrage of u-bolts. The dark rounds were moving at breakneck speed, but King was studying Eva's movements, and he could anticipate where she would fire. An old soldier's instincts. One advantage he had over the youth.

Zigzagging through space, he flew closer, closer. Clinging to the hull, Eva stared at him, eyes ablaze, teeth bared. She fired from point-blank range. King held out his metal hand, blocking the blast on his prosthetic. The umbrions wormed through the gauntlet, reached his stump, and slithered up his forearm, freezing the flesh.

A split second later, King slammed into the escape pod.

He clung to the craggy exterior. The atmosphere of Earth roiled below, a vast ocean of blue and white gases, spreading to the horizons. They were seconds away from atmospheric entry now.

He glanced into the pod. The hatch was still open. Kim and the others were inside. His wife stared at him, love and awe in her eyes.

"Jim!"

With a snarl, Eva delivered a powerful kick to King's belly. He flew backward, nearly losing his grip on the pod.

"Watch your family die, Admiral King!" Eva cried, crawling through the hatch.

They were seconds away from the sky now.

King reached into the pod and grabbed Eva by the ankles. She yowled as King yanked her backward. It must have shocked her. She cried out. Thinking quickly, Kim reached out, grabbed Eva's wrist, and twisted. The girl's gun fell.

God, I love you, Kim, King thought.

For all her cruelty and technology, Eva was just a teenage girl, not much older or heavier than King's granddaughter. With ease, he pulled her out of the escape pod.

As the pod dived toward Earth, King clung onto the exterior with one hand. Meanwhile, with his other hand, he still held Eva by the ankles. She hung upside down, floundering madly like a fish, screaming imprecations.

"I will skin your wife!" she shrieked. "I will find your grandchildren, and I will sew their skin into lampshades! I will make you watch!"

Eva flailed in his grip, face red, eyes aflame.

"Leave my family alone, you Nazi piece of filth!" King said, then hurled her into the distance.

Eva tumbled through space, screaming, and slammed into the atmosphere of Earth. Within seconds, she was plunging through the sky in a fireball.

King slipped into the pod and pulled the hatch—

The pod slammed into the atmosphere.

King flew out the pod and nearly tumbled into the

distance.

A hand reached out.

Fingers curled around his wrist.

Kim pulled him into the pod, then slammed the hatch shut.

King tumbled onto the deck, banging his knees, as the pod plunged through the atmosphere like an asteroid. Fire blazed outside the portholes, and King grimaced. His damn knees! Add another ache to the list. God, he hated war.

Then Kim had her arms around him, holding him tightly as they fell from the sky.

* * * * *

The shuttle tumbled through the sky, wreathed in fire.

King worried that Eva had damaged the hull, that the pod would break apart. He wrapped his arms around Kim, trying to protect her from the mad rattling. If he must die, it would be while embracing his wife. Not a bad way to go.

But it was not his time. The pod survived entry, slowed down, and engaged its thruster engines. After surviving hellfire, the spherical shuttle glided above the blue, peaceful Atlantic Ocean.

Of Eva no sign remained. Last he had seen, Eva was plunging alongside the shuttle, a living fireball. Most likely, atmospheric entry had pulverized her, and her atoms were now scattered across sky and sea. Then again, Nazi battlesuits could take some serious punishment. Could Eva actually survive a fall from space? If so, she could be anywhere. Hopefully at the bottom of the ocean. Inside the belly of a shark.

King shifted in his seat. As the adrenaline wore off, his aches and pains returned to play. His joints creaked and he groaned.

"King, my boy!" Godwin boomed. "I say, what a spectacular performance. Good show, Admiral! Jolly good show." He slapped King on the shoulder. "How are you feeling?"

King grimaced. "Like I've been stabbed, shot twice, fired out an escape tube, and fallen from the sky."

"Ah, but still alive, yes?" Godwin winked and slapped him on the shoulder again. "Don't worry, old boy, we'll get you patched up and back to fighting Fritz again in no time."

"Wonderful," King muttered. "Can't wait."

"Stay still," Kim said. "I'm trying to patch you up." She splashed antiseptic into one of his many wounds.

King roared.

Nearby, Jordan raised his head and opened his eyes. "Oh, be quiet!" the old officer said. "I was trying to take a nap." His own leg was bandaged up.

"I hoped you were finally dead," King said.

"No such luck," Jordan said. "I ain't dying until you pay me back those twenty bucks you owe me."

"Hey, I won that poker round!" King growled, pointing at Jordan with his prosthetic. The gauntlet only had three fingers left. The index finger detached and clattered onto the deck.

Jordan raised his eyebrows. "You're falling apart, old man."

"So much for surviving this war in one piece," King muttered.

As they bantered, King noticed that Spitfire never cracked a smile. Never rolled her eyes. Never even looked at him. She sat in the pod, knees pulled to her chest, silent.

King sent her a quick telepathic message. "You all right, kiddo?"

She didn't even look at him. "I should have gone down with my ship. You had no right. No right to toss me into this pod."

She sent those thoughts on a private telepathic channel, but King felt as if everyone heard, as if everyone was judging him.

"You're right," he telepathized. "I had no right. And you should have gone down with that ship. I don't care. You're alive. You're angry, you feel guilt, you hate my guts, but you're alive. And I need you alive, Gal."

Finally she met his gaze. She glared at him, tears in her eyes. "Why?"

"Because I love you. Because you're family. Because I made your father a promise. Hate me all you like, but I'm not going to stop loving you. Or fighting for you."

All the fire left Spitfire's eyes, and only tears remained. She embraced him.

"I love you too, old man," she said, speaking loudly enough for everyone in the pod to hear.

* * * * *

The sun set. Dim lights came on inside the pod. As Kim worked at patching up his wounds, King studied the pod's control panel. They were still flying over the Atlantic, moving eastward. The autopilot was taking them to the closest Alliance nation. Which happened to be Great Britain.

King hadn't heard a news update all day. Was Britain fighting on the ground? What was the situation elsewhere on Earth? He tried to reach MindWeb. Offline again. Up in space, the Freedom Fleet was operating its own MindWeb servers (or at least had a few hours ago). Down here on Earth? Nada. King couldn't even call his son.

"This'll just hurt for a second," Kim said, then jabbed King with a needle.

He gritted his teeth. "Kim! What the . . ." He slumped in his chair. "What is that stuff? It feels . . ." He blinked. "Good."

Kim tucked away the needle. "Don't get too used to it, mister. This is a potent painkiller. Highly addictive. You get one shot of this. That's it."

King's head swam. The aches and pains flowed away. Potent? Understatement of the year. More like magical. He had forgotten what it was like. To be pain-free. It was almost like being young again.

Youth is wasted on the young, King thought. *When I was a young man, I never realized how fast, strong, and flexible I was. Until I had to fight a war as an old man.*

As they flew closer to Britain, King's heart sank. War was raging there too.

Before they even saw the coast, they saw the naval battles. Nazi warships, some a mile long, plowed across the ocean, swastika banners waving. Navy ships? How? Had the Nazis opened some aquatic portal too? King zoomed in, and he understood. Those were starships! Starships that could function in the ocean too.

The modern Kriegsmarine was bombarding Britain's coast. The Royal Navy was fighting back valiantly. But King spotted quite a few British battleships burning and listing. Fireballs flamed across the sky, reflecting in the water. Even in the era of space travel, the oceans were important to control. They gave you access to ports, rivers, and coastal cities. Not trains or cars or planes had made the simple boat obsolete. Spaceflight hadn't either.

As they flew over the naval battle, King tensed.

"How do you turn this damn autopilot off?" he said. "They'll see us. And shoot us from the sky."

"No need to worry," Godwin said. "The pod has advanced stealth technology. We're as invisible as a general when it's time to dig trenches, old boy."

King blinked. "You installed costly stealth technology on

escape pods? Where did you get the money?"

Godwin slapped him on the shoulder. "Debt, my boy! The golden goose that keeps laying eggs."

King muttered under his breath. Maybe Katyusha, a notorious spendthrift, had the right idea after all. She cut corners everywhere (other than cosmetics). The Alliance spent like a drunken sailor. Well, King would let the bean counters take care of that. He had a feeling that his son, granddaughter, and several more generations of Kings would be footing the bill for this war.

Under cover of night, they flew over Britain. Looking downward, King's heart sank. The Fatherworld had done what no enemy had accomplished since William the Conqueror. The Spanish Armada, Napoleon, Hitler—they all tried to invade Britain and failed. But now the Nazi troops, those horrors from the shadow world, rampaged across Albion. Their armored lines carved through the countryside. Their artillery bombarded cities. Their troops—it looked like a full division—marched in the night. Britain had not fallen yet. Even from up here, King could see the Tommies fighting back, giving the Jerries hell. It would be a long battle. Britain had been invaded—but Britain had not fallen.

"There's an Alliance base outside of London," King said. "I'll fly us there. We'll eat a good meal, sleep for a few hours, maybe get a doc to look over our wounds, then see about getting reassigned to another ship."

"Oh, that last part is taken care of, old boy," Godwin said.

King frowned. He looked at the jowly old man. "Sir? You have another assignment in mind?"

"You might say that, old boy. It's something you must see to believe."

King and the others prodded him for more information. But Godwin refused to say more. It was highly classified, he explained. He could not speak of it.

"Not out here," Godwin said. "Not until we're back in

Alliance hands. This is a secret I dare not speak of here. Just in case Fritz is listening."

King understood. There were protocols for revealing top secret information. It could not be done in a pod. Only in a room that's been secured against telepathic hacks and plain old bugs. It sounded like Godwin already had a brand-new assignment for King. Maybe for the others too. What was it? King couldn't guess.

The pod kept flying in silence for a while, gliding over England. The passengers stared down at the dark landscape. No battle raged here. They were miles from the front lines. Only a sea of blackness spread below the gliding pod, punctuated by the odd light of a farmhouse. Most of the towns had gone dark; they hid in the shadows, vague patches of darkness, barely distinguishable from the Stygian countryside. The farmhouses had their own generators; they shone the only lights King saw in Britain. In his weariness, he imagined the dark landscape as just more ocean, and the scattered lights of farmhouses seemed to him like paper lanterns floating on the waves.

"We're almost at London," King said. "We should be able to see the lights soon. If they still have lights."

They all stared in anticipation. Would they see the lights of battle? Or the lights of a free city, standing strong?

Spitfire pressed her face against a porthole. "I don't see explosions or fire."

"I don't see artillery flying," said Jordan.

Godwin remained silent and somber, his hands clutching his cane. "Only yesterday the cannons here were booming."

"Have we won?" Kim said, her blue eyes full of hope.

We. Kim was American. But tonight *we* was everyone in the Alliance. Hell, *we* was everyone from this universe. Even the Red Dawn and the Desert Thorns.

They flew over London and—lights! Lights shone below. Lights in windows. Streetlights. Car lights. London stood!

"London still has power!" Spitfire cried. "London Town stands tall!"

Cheers rose through the pod. King didn't join them.

He stared ahead. And he saw it. The Palace of Westminster. A swastika banner draped across Big Ben. The warships of the Fatherworld filled the Thames, and the Waffen-SS marched along London Bridge, carrying red-and-black banners.

London had fallen.

CHAPTER FOURTEEN
March of the Spiders

3,000 feet over London
Earth
September 5, 2207

Like a hot-air balloon made out of metal, the escape pod floated over London. A fallen city. A city in the clutch of the devil. And the Nazi claws were tightening. With five claws of war did the Fatherworld grip London Town. One claw—the Panzerwaffe. The lines of German armor rolled down the boulevards, crushing all in their path. Another claw—the Wehrmacht Heer. The German infantry marched across the rubble, eagle standards raised, boots thumping. A third claw—the Artillerietruppe. The great cannons of the Fatherworld still boomed, shattering city homes. A fourth claw—the Rattenjägers that flew above, starfighters of the Weltraumwaffe. The fifth claw—the breaking of the will. The swastika banners that hung everywhere were that fifth claw. As were the corpses of British officers that swayed from cranes. This last claw was called propaganda. A claw not to cut the flesh but the soul.

This devil had risen from Hell. Without warning. Without mercy. In his wrath, he grabbed cities. Crushed nations. This devil was called Nazism. Earth had defeated him long ago, banished him, buried him underground. Like a reanimated corpse, he rose again from the shadows.

From the escape pod, they watched in silent grief. King

lowered his head in honor of the fallen city. Kim leaned against him, her hair soft against his cheek. Godwin stared with cold eyes, clutching his cane. Jordan and Spitfire sat side by side, watching the city below, the fires reflecting in their eyes.

Yes. Fires. Grand fires that rose as tall as buildings. Not the fires of war. Not fires from bombs or missiles. Not here. Not this night. Here, tonight, the Nazis were burning books. They rampaged through libraries and homes, pulled out books, and raised great bonfires on the streets. The flames crackled and swirled skyward like fluted pillars.

"They could have nuked this city," King said. "They could have knocked down every building, killed every soul. That's not what they want." He gritted his fists—the real one and the broken metal one. "They want to turn us into them. Another Fatherworld. An abomination. A society where books are burned. Where other races and faiths are exterminated. Where the disabled are murdered. Where the only virtue is violence and all compassion is crushed. That is what they crave. Not to kill us. But to deform us into monsters."

Spitfire and Jordan looked up.

"Well, they want to exterminate me and Phantom here," Spitfire said. "According to the Nazis, we're subhumans. Wrong races. But you know, sir, what the Nazis have planned for their so-called fellow Aryans on our world . . . that sounds like a fate worse than death. I think I'd rather die than be brainwashed."

"Well, whether it's death or brainwashing, I'm not interested," King said. "London has fallen, but we have not. We still fight."

Kim bolted up. "And we're not alone." She grabbed his arm. "Look, Jim! There's still fighting in North London."

They all leaned toward the portholes. Artillery lights were streaking back and forth. Guns boomed. Indeed, in the northern city, the Alliance still fought! Stretching from Cockfosters all the way to Camden Town, the city still resisted! Lines of heavily armored British tanks rolled down the roads and blasted their cannons. Eagle starfighters fought over Broomfield Park. British and German infantry clashed along the streets. Far in the distance, in the northern shadows, King thought he caught glimpse of . . . could it be? *American* flags?

"I'll take us farther north," King said. "Then we can—"

Artillery fire rose from below.

King cursed and reached for a yoke, only to remember there was none. When not on autopilot, the pod only offered a telepathic operating system. Using his neural implant, King scanned for nearby devices, found the pod's software, and connected. His MindLink implant fired electric signals, causing King to hallucinate the pod's flight controls. Still no yoke. Just buttons, scroll bars, and toggle switches. Looked like something designed by a software engineer who had never flown a ship. Or spoken to anyone who had. King cursed, reached for the hallucinatory interface, hit the wrong button, and turned on the windshield wipers. He tapped another button, accidentally activating the entertainment system. Japanese pop music blared from the speakers. Spitfire bobbed her head. King cursed and shut it off.

"Need me to fetch you a manual?" Jordan said.

Spitfire bristled. "Hey, I was listening to that!"

"Dammit all!" King blurted out. "Where's that flight app again?"

"Jim, hurry!" Kim cried.

He growled. "Goddamn modern tech."

The enemy missiles streaked across the sky. Right at them. King finally found the navigation app, tapped the yaw button, and—

An explosion rocked the pod.

Everyone jostled inside the round cabin.

The portholes shattered, and cold air and smoke rushed into the cabin.

"We're hit!" Jordan cried.

"What gave it away?" King snapped, wrestling with the flight application (which mostly involved delicate taps on tiny buttons—not nearly as satisfying as literal wrestling).

"Damn, I was hoping it hit you in the face," Jordan said, clinging to his seat.

The pod was rattling. Fire raged outside. The motors howled in protest, and more artillery flew their way.

"I thought you said this thing has a stealth coat!" King snapped.

"It does!" Spitfire said. "That was just random crossfire. An unfortunate accident."

King managed to swerve around a rocket, but without a proper yoke or joystick, he felt so slow. "Well, there are more unfortunate accidents heading our—"

Another blast hit the pod.

The spherical vessel rolled through the air. The telepathic navigational system shut down entirely, leaving only hallucinatory wisps around King's fingers. (Briefly, King considered that the software developer had actually bothered coding in hallucinatory wisps in case of a system crash. The young programmer had probably wondered if anyone would ever notice his little morbid flair. King noticed.)

The pod tumbled through the sky, hull cracked. Air and smoke roiled inside. King held Kim with one arm, protecting her. With his metal hand's remaining fingers, he grabbed the porthole for purchase. The others rattled around. Spitfire slammed into him, wrapped her arms around him, and clung. More rockets flew all around.

Amazingly, the engine was still working, propelling the pod onward like a whirligig, until finally they rolled into the darkness north of the city. King leaned from side to side, trying to counteract the pod's spinning. The others saw what he was doing and joined him. It was like trying to balance a swaying boat.

Above shadowy farmland, the pod finally stopped spinning, but it was still hurtling downward at a steep angle. The little pod blazed through the night like a comet.

"Brace for a crash landing!" King said, trying to bring the hallucinatory controls back up. The interface began to reboot, displaying an animation of a dog running in circles. Someday King would find whoever had programmed this pod and murder them.

The interface finally came back online, and King regained some control of the thrusters, but not much. He did his best to slow down. But he couldn't do anything about the rapid descent. Right now it seemed they had two choices. A hard crash or a devastatingly hard crash.

"Dammit, gain altitude!" King said, tapping madly on a little Up button.

Defying him, the pod crashed through treetops. Branches snapped off and leaves filled the cabin. Every bone in King's body rattled. He banged against the bulkhead again and again.

The engine finally died. The pod plowed through a few more trees, tore off a barn roof, then slammed into a field.

The pod plowed through the field better than any tractor, leaving a deep, smoking groove for three hundred yards. King's teeth knocked together. His helmet banged against the bulkhead. His leg twisted. But he kept his arms around Kim and Spitfire, protecting them with his body. Before anything else, even his own life, he must protect his family.

A thought rose deep in his mind.

Does that include their doppelgängers?

Yes, it was his own family fighting him in this war. Dr. Anneliese, a version of his wife. Eva König, a version of his granddaughter. Was there a version of King's son out there too?

A version of James King himself?

He shoved those thoughts aside for another day. The pod plowed across the landscape, finally reaching the edge of Epping Forest, an ancient woodland north of London. The pod smashed through a few oaks, then came to a stop in the shadowy forest. There it sat among shattered wood, smoldering behind enemy lines.

* * * * *

For a long time, everyone just sat inside the pod, moaning.

"Is everyone all right?" King rasped.

Jordan winced. "I was shot in the leg, fell from space, and crash-landed onto a world overrun with Nazis. Other than that, just peachy."

"Well, you're alive, so shut up," King said. "Everyone else alive? And hopefully grateful for it?"

"Well, your big mouth certainly survived," Jordan said. "We know that much."

Spitfire and Kim both groaned and rubbed their bruised bodies. Aside from a few scrapes and bruises, both women seemed all right. All eyes turned toward Godwin, the oldest in the group. For many men, such a crash landing could be fatal. Especially for a man in his eighties. But Godwin had more energy than the rest of them combined. The octogenarian leaped to his feet and pointed his cane to the hatch.

"Come now! Tally ho! We're alive and well. Let us find our way back to the war." He pointed his cane into the darkness. "Onward, soldiers!"

King tried to rise, then fell back down. "Hang on."

Now all eyes turned toward him. He saw the concern in Kim's eyes, the fear in Spitfire's. Even Jordan's eyes softened.

"Jim, you all right?" the phantom said in his soothing

baritone.

Was he all right?

"No," King finally said. "No, I'm not all right. I was stabbed, shot twice, and banged all over. I've barely slept or eaten in a week. But it's more than that. You all saw her. Eva König. A girl who looks like . . ." His voice caught. "Like my granddaughter."

"Just a coincidence," Spitfire said.

"No." He shook his head. "A doppelgänger. And I'm worried that my doppelgänger is out there too. An enemy. A brutal enemy. A man without my injuries. Without my compunctions. A man who would stop at nothing to dominate or kill us. None of this is all right. I'm hurt and I'm afraid. But I will fight nonetheless." He stood up and groaned. "Just . . . give me a moment. To catch my breath."

He closed his eyes, just giving his battered body a few moments. Just a few breaths of air.

I'm too old for this, he thought. *I'm too tired. The memories are too painful. Too many good spacers died on that ship. Young men and women. While I, the old, linger on.*

He was an officer. A leader. A soldier. His job was to remain strong for his troops, for his family, for his world. Not to feel weak. Not to feel scared. Heroes were meant to be strong, courageous, invincible. King wanted to be a hero for his family. For the younger soldiers. But he feared letting them down. Feared they would see his pain. See his fear. See his failures.

Spacers died. A starship was lost. A world was falling. In the night, banged up in the pod, King felt like a man in the belly of a whale. The darkness felt vast, maybe insurmountable.

But he was still drawing breath.

His heart still beat.

His wife and adopted daughter were with him. And his son and grandchildren might still be out there, alive, needing him.

So long as they lived, so long as King could draw breath, he would summon what strength he had left.

And fight.

I still live, so I still fight. The motto of a soldier.

"All right." He stood up. "I'm ready." He limped toward the hatch, ready to march after Godwin.

"I'm not," Kim said.

King paused at the hatch. "Kim? Are you hurt?"

"No. But you are." The engineer placed her hands on her hips. "I bandaged your wounds. And then you went ahead and got a bunch of new ones. You need to rest." Her voice softened. "We all do. Maybe other than George Godwin, but that man is a miracle. The Alliance still fights, and the war will still be here tomorrow. We can take a few hours off. Or we'll end up killing ourselves."

King wanted to argue, to insist he was fine. But she was right. And it wasn't just him. Jordan was sixty-six and had two umbrion holes in him. Spitfire was younger, but an assortment of scrapes and burns covered her. King doubted anyone had slept or eaten much since the Nazis had invaded. What was it now? Five days? Six? By God, it couldn't be more than a week. And yet it also felt like years. Everything had changed. The world they had known. The people they had been. Only a week—but it was a new reality. As if this entire universe had flipped inside out. In a way, it had.

They set camp outside the escape pod among the hawthorns. In the shadowy distance, a few miles south of Epping Forest, the music of war rose in the night like the macabre song of crickets. Guns rattled. Every moment, another artillery shell shook the night. The gruesome lullaby pulled King into slumber. In his dreams, he was clinging to the pod exterior again, pulling Eva off the hull, then hurling her into the atmosphere. But in his dreams, before burning up, she raised her visor and looked at him, and it was not Eva at all but Rowan, his granddaughter. And when King turned toward the porthole, he saw his reflection staring back, and he was wearing a Nazi uniform.

*****

King wasn't sure how long he slept. When he woke up, daylight filled Epping Forest, though smoke and clouds hid the sky.

King walked toward the edge of the forest, then stepped out onto the farmlands. He now saw what he had missed last night. Artillery craters covered the farmlands, spreading for miles. A battle had raged here not long ago. Empty plasma batteries, burnt tanks, and mangled corpses lay strewn across the fields. Crows feasted. King returned to the forest and the crashed pod, a weight on his soul.

They set a rudimentary camp at the crash site, hidden among the trees. Here they changed their bandages, took medication, and ate a cold, dreary breakfast (the pod contained a small closet with battle rations). As they ate, King kept checking MindWeb. Amazingly, it was coming back online. Slowly. Bit by bit. He could read snippets of news reports. But long-range telepathy was still offline, so he still couldn't contact his son or grandchildren.

"Bastian, where are you?" he whispered into the smog.

"The news isn't good." Kim was pacing along the tree line, her arms crossed, her gold-and-silver hair pulled into a fraying ponytail. She was also downloading MindWeb updates. "The enemy took over half of Europe. Within only a week. The blitzkrieg devastated us. Half our fleet is destroyed. Now the Wehrmacht is pushing into Russia and China too."

"Lovely," King muttered.

Kim stopped pacing. She looked at him. "It gets worse."

"What could possibly be worse?" cried Spitfire. The young commander was kneeling nearby, tending to a campfire. Leaves lay strewn through her long brown hair.

In the firelight, she looks so much like Yehuda, King thought, missing his old friend. *She has his courage too.*

Kim stopped pacing. The engineer's face was pale. She looked at the young commander by the fire. "Some people—people from *our universe*—are joining them. Joining the Nazis."

Spitfire leaped to her feet. She was a tall woman, almost as tall as King, and as her eyes blazed with fury, she suddenly looked less like Yehuda in the firelight, more like a demon.

"*What?*" Spitfire cried.

"Yes, I saw that too," King grumbled. "Nazi sympathizers have always lurked on our world, even centuries after Hitler's death. Until now, they operated underground, weak and afraid. Now they're all coming out of their hidey holes, eager to serve the Wehrmacht."

"I'll kill them!" Spitfire said, face flushed. "I'll put them back into hidey holes—six feet under this time!" She panted with rage. "Traitors!"

King nodded. Leaving Spitfire to simmer and Kim to pace, he looked around for his commander. Where was Godwin?

Leaving the cover of the trees, King searched the scorched farmlands. The desolation spread to the southern horizon, where King could just make out pillars of smoke rising from London. It seemed like an alien landscape, dotted with smoldering craters like volcano vents or noxious bogs. Vultures circled under the ocher clouds, scanning for bodies below. The scavengers found many feasts in these burnt fields of England. Many more might soon join the dead. The fields had burned, and famine often crept in through the door war opened, slaying more than enemy bombs and bullets.

King had been to this country many times. He had friends

here, both living and fallen. Oliver Darjeeling, the former boatswain of the starship *Freedom*, had hailed from this fine land. So did Emily, one of King's officers, who had ascended to the throne of England, only to abdicate and return to her duties in space. George Godwin, his mentor. His own ancestors. All came from this land, and King grieved for its destruction.

Speaking of Godwin . . . where was the man? King walked over the charred crops. Finally he spotted a stocky figure upon a hilltop, gazing into the distance. The man's coattails fluttered in the wind, and he held a cane. King thought of Friedrich's *Wanderer above the Sea of Fog*. Godwin appeared to him like one of the artist's *Rückenfigur*, a rear-facing figure, brooding over an imposing landscape, contemplating the meaning of it all. It was ironic, perhaps, that the ruler of the Alliance, the force tasked with defeating Nazi Germany, should make King think of a German artist.

He walked uphill toward Godwin and stood beside the shorter man. They gazed together into the distance—not upon a sea of fog but of smoke. For long moments, they did not speak. The occasional blasts of artillery punctuated their silence. The crows were feasting below. Mostly on dead animals. Also on some dead men.

"It's quite a thing, isn't it?" Godwin said. "War. This is the third big one I've fought. You never do get used to it. The stench of it. You don't smell the death up in space."

"Sir, we're rested, fed, and ready to march," King said. "On your orders."

Godwin turned toward him. A small smile softened that jowly, garrulous face of his. "Ah, yes. There he is again. Admiral James "Bulldog" King. Hero of the red deserts of Mars. Smiter of the rahs. Scourge of the Fatherworld." He slapped King on the arm. "It's good to have you back. Remember, old boy, it's all right to be weak sometimes. It's all right to cower in the darkness some nights. So long as we get up with dawn and fight the beast another day."

King nodded. "Thank you, sir. For your wisdom."

Godwin heaved a sigh and looked over the landscape again. "My wisdom, you say? No, King, I've been foolish. Very foolish indeed. I should have foreseen this."

"No one could have."

"Oh, we couldn't know the Jerries would burst through a portal from another dimension, no," Godwin said. "I daresay not one of us imagined that scenario in our wildest nightmares. But we should have been on guard for *any* threat. For *any* attack. Whatever it may be. Especially after what the rahs did to us only eight years ago. We dropped our guard, King. Us old soldiers."

King lowered his head. He hadn't thought of it that way. But now guilt filled him. Maybe Godwin was right. King had fought wars. He knew of the dangers out there. He had suffered the rah invasion and fought the equalists on Mars. He should have remained on that guard wall. But he retreated to his ranch. He rode his horses, read his detective novels, listened to his Johnny Cash records, and whittled his little wooden figurines. Yes, he had let his guard down, and once more evil struck Earth.

"Someday we'll have to deal with our guilt," King said. "We'll have to contemplate our failures. Yes, we are responsible. I am responsible. I failed. But that doesn't mean we curl up and die. No. We get back up. And we fight back hard. Maybe we can never redeem ourselves. But we sure as hell can kill a lot of Nazis. Which is what I intend to do."

Godwin looked at him, eyebrow raised, then barked a laugh. "Yes, you are a savage, aren't you, Admiral King?"

"Only to my enemies."

"As every good savage should be."

King stared into the shorter man's eyes. "Sir, earlier, in the pod, you said you had a new assignment for us. That you couldn't reveal it inside the pod."

"Ah, yes!" Godwin said, his face brightening. "King, you're going to love this. See, there's something I haven't told you. Something I have, in fact, quite carefully been keeping secret from you. For three years now, I haven't said a word."

King frowned. "About what?"

Godwin patted him on the shoulder, and his eyes sparkled. "King, my boy, we've—"

Artillery whistled.

"Get down!" King cried, pulling Godwin to the ground.

An explosion rocked the land. A cloud of dust and smoke rose nearby. Hot sand and chunks of soil pattered against King. He spun around, staring toward camp. Kim, Jordan, and Spitfire were on the ground, covering their heads.

"What the hell was that?" Spitfire shouted.

Another whistle.

Another shell slammed into the landscape, and an explosion rocked the fields. This one got dangerously close to the pod. More and more shells whistled overhead, etching lines toward the north.

They're not aiming at us, King realized. *They're aiming at someone behind us.*

He stared south, seeking the enemy. And there they came, marching from the smoky horizon. The Wehrmacht was rumbling northward across the land. Heading right toward King and his companions.

* * * * *

The Wehrmacht moved with force and purpose. Hundreds of its tanks rumbled, crushing the English countryside. Crushing corpses. Thousands of armored vehicles rumbled. Countless infantrymen marched. A military band marched with them, barely overheard over the whistling artillery. They were playing *Ride of the Valkyries*. Hitler's favorite.

Aboard the *Lioness*, King had faced off against the Waffen-SS, an elite unit of torturers and murderers. The SS, which had begun as Hitler's personal bodyguard, took on multiple roles. Exterminating subhumans. Torturing dissidents. Operating death camps. Spreading terror and fear. The SS's combat unit, under the command of Eva König, undertook brutal commando missions—like invading the Alliance flagship. Thankfully, King saw none of those sadists here.

Here across the English countryside came the Wehrmacht, the main army of the Third Reich. They were larger than the SS. Less elite, perhaps, but their sheer size, weaponry, and savagery made them more powerful. They were trained for one purpose and one alone—killing. Like the SS, the Wehrmacht was fanatically devoted to the führer and to spreading Nazism across Earth. Together, the Wehrmacht and the SS were the führer's two fists. The Weltraumwaffe, the space force of the Fatherworld, was a branch of the Wehrmacht. This would be King's first time facing the Wehrmacht's ground corps.

Spitfire ran uphill to stand beside King. She placed a hand on his shoulder and gazed southward, eyes wide.

"A full German division is marching against us!" she said. "They must think we're serious badasses."

"They're not marching against us," King said. "We just happen to be standing in their way."

A wicked grin spread across Spitfire's face. She drew two handguns. "Good. Let these Nazis know this Jewish girl hits back."

Jordan joined her on the hilltop. The dark-skinned officer, a subhuman in the eyes of their foes, stared with defiance. He raised an assault rifle. "Let them come at us."

Kim stared at the pair with wide eyes. "You two are crazy!

Just us against an army?"

"That is the way of honor," Spitfire said. Her voice dropped. "My father ran once. He died running." A tear rolled down her cheek. "I won't run."

"So you'll die fighting?" Kim cried, running uphill to join the group.

Spitfire raised her chin. "I'll die on my feet."

"You'll die in the mud, screaming, like all the rest of them," Kim said. She grabbed Spitfire and Jordan. "Come, you two! Run for cover!"

Spitfire glanced at King, awaiting his decision.

King considered. If he were here alone, yes, perhaps King would stand and die for his damn honor. But could he let Spitfire die too?

Yes, honor was important. Honor was his life. But honor also had a tendency of getting good men and women killed. Right now, was it wiser to run? To live and fight another day? Katyusha would have remained to fight—and probably gotten herself and her entire crew killed.

"Run for cover, Spitfire," King said. "This is not the hill you die on."

He drew his firearm and aimed it at the advancing host.

"What?" Spitfire cried. "And you stay and have all the fun?"

"I'm not staying," he growled. "Not on this hilltop, at least. I'll just put down some suppressive fire. Back to the forest! We'll fight from cover. We'll fight from the shadows. We'll give them hell." He glanced at Godwin. "If you agree, sir?"

The old Englishman nodded. "Let's give the Jerries hell, by Jove! Today we fight from shadows."

As the artillery whistled overhead, as the band played, as the tanks rumbled, the companions retreated. They were a group of old veterans who found themselves in a new war. The youngest among them (Spitfire) was in her forties, the oldest (Godwin) in his eighties. They were bruised, battered, cut off from the Alliance. But they were still soldiers. And they would still fight.

"Did the enemy notice us?" Jordan asked as they ran downhill, moving northward toward their camp.

"Not sure," King said. "If so, they might just think we're farmers."

Just then, as they were racing across the desolation, an artillery shell slammed into the hilltop. Right where they had stood just a moment ago. The blast shook the land. Flames roared skyward. Chunks of soil and rock pattered across the ground.

"That was no random crossfire," Jordan said. "They saw us."

More shells whistled. The companions reached the cover of trees. They dispersed among the oaks, beeches, and hornbeams, hid behind the boles, and aimed their guns.

They waited.

The artillery shells whistled overhead. One burst not far behind, shattering trees. King stood behind a trunk, gun clutched in his hand. Waiting. Another shell burst. He stood his ground.

They don't know where we are, he thought. *We vanished into shadows.*

He sought his companions, but only Kim was close enough to see. The others were farther back among the oaks. He reached out to them telepathically. Good. His MindLink could still detect them peer-to-peer. MindPlay, his implant's hallucinatory operating system, hovered before King in the darkness like a ghost, visible to his eyes only. The screen showed him his companions' vitals. Their hearts were racing. His was too.

They waited, silent.

No more artillery fell.

And then the Nazi vanguard crested the hill.

First came the tanks, rumbling, roaring, crushing corpses

beneath them. They did not move on treads like old tanks. They walked on a hundred legs of metal, and each sprouted two cannons like stalks. They looked to King like mechanical bugs, armored spiders crawling across the land. They must be more toys from the twisted mind of Dr. Anneliese. Following them marched the troops, thousands organized into smaller units. Each unit carried a *Reichskriegsflagge*. The swastika banners fluttered in the smoky wind. Finally, in the rear, marched huge mechanical terrors. More arachnid mechas like the one King had battled in space. Spinnenmutters. Ten of the dreadful machines loomed over the German infantry.

Is she here? King thought. *Anneliese? My wife's doppelgänger?*

He didn't know. And if she was . . . would he have the heart to kill her?

* * * * *

The Wehrmacht kept marching northward, heading to further conquests. King couldn't stop them. But he could sure as hell make their job harder.

He didn't have many weapons. Just his old revolver (not of much use here) and his trusty Trogdor. He'd have to make them count. He remembered his battle with Anneliese.

"The spiders are weak at the joints," he telepathized to the others. "Let's try to crack some spider legs. Wait for my order."

Soon the Wehrmacht was marching right by. Their infantry fired rounds at the forest. U-bolts slammed into trunks. One whizzed right by King's ear, but he remained hidden. Kim pressed herself against a nearby hornbeam. U-bolts slammed into the tree's craggy bark. Her heart was galloping, each beat a bleep of light on her MindWeb stats.

"Don't worry," King telepathized to her. "They're not aiming at us. Not directly, at least. They're just laying down suppressive fire."

"Yes, well, that suppressive fire I shouldn't worry about very nearly took off my head," Kim said.

As it marched northward, one of the spider-tanks swiveled its hull toward Epping Forest. Its two cannons rose like curious insect eyes. Then those eyes blazed red and fired. Shells whistled overhead and exploded, shattering nearby birches. The world trembled and smoke filled the air. Chips of wood and shrapnel flew every which way. A shard of red-hot metal scraped King's calf. He winced, swallowing a shout. One more scar for the collection.

King hurriedly checked for nearby MindLinks. Everyone was still all right. But these were some close calls.

"Should I worry about that one?" Kim shouted telepathically. It shouldn't be possible to shout a thought, but somehow Kim managed it.

"Fire!" King said, sending the order to every nearby MindLink.

At once, all five companions reached around the trees and opened fire. Just five soldiers. Just five beat-up, scarred old dogs of war. Their average age was sixty-two. But they had been fighting together for decades, and they moved like one creature with five claws. Synchronizing telepathically, they concentrated their fire on one spider.

Not a small spider-tank either. One of the big mechas. A spinnenmutter.

Together, all six guns (Spitfire was firing two) hit the same spider leg. Right on the same joint. The joint connecting the mechanical leg to the armored torso.

The joint twisted and melted. The mechanical leg—it was several stories tall—buckled.

"Fire!" King cried, and again they fired in unison, aiming at a second leg.

That leg buckled too. And soon the entire spinnenmutter, a spider the size of an office building, was wobbling on its remaining legs like a baby deer. The pilot in the cockpit struggled with the joysticks, but he could not steady the unwieldy, wounded machine.

"Fire!" King cried a third time. And together, their guns took down a third leg. And then the entire mechanical spider was tumbling forward. Infantrymen shouted and ran. Many were not fast enough. The spinnenmutter crashed onto a Wehrmacht platoon, splattering its soldiers across the scarred soil of Britain.

Cheers rose among the trees. But the celebrations did not last long. At once the Wehrmacht turned its guns toward the forest. A fresh barrage of u-rounds slammed into boles, dispersing clouds of darkness. Light faded. The temperature plunged. And then the shells of the spider tanks whistled. One shell slammed into the empty escape pod, destroying whatever few supplies the companions had. Chunks of the hull flew through the air, slicing off branches.

The companions ran. They ran north through Epping Forest as shells burst all around, scattering toxic umbrion clouds. King did not suppose they struck a heroic sight—five wounded old soldiers, limping and groaning as they fled for their lives. But sometimes even heroes must live to fight another day. That was something Katyusha would never understand. Were she here, she would charge at the enemy, waving that skinny little sword of hers, leading herself and her troops into the crunching maws of the German guns. King tried to live an honorable life too, but unlike his old Russian foe, he knew where honor ended and stupidity began.

They ran north, fleeing the umbrion clouds and rumbling guns. The hosts of hell followed through the murk, uprooting trees and chewing up the soil with their motors and crushing mechanical mouths. Those meat grinders would not content themselves with soil and wood. They desired human flesh.

"You know what would really be nice around now?" Jordan telepathized to the group as they ran. "A nice, big dreadnought! Hell, I'd even settle for a starfighter carrier."

Another shell exploded nearby. The blast knocked King against an old oak. He grunted, pushed off the cracked bole, and kept running. His ears rang.

"Any brilliant plans?" Kim telepathized. "We can't run forever."

"I can," Spitfire said, racing ahead of the pack on her long, lithe legs.

"You're younger than us," Jordan said. "We're old and tired."

Godwin, who was twice Spitfire's age, was keeping up with the willowy commander. "Speak for yourselves! I'm as fast as ever."

Yes, Godwin must have taken that drug. For the first time, King regretted not undergoing the treatment too. In this era, everyone was trying to cheat death. Right now cheating death seemed like quite a feat. King had joked about being a cat with nine lives. How many did he have left?

Another shell exploded—this one just ahead. King knelt, covering his head with his arms, then ran onward. Up ahead, Spitfire cried out. Her icon flashed red on MindPlay. Her heart was racing.

"You're hurt!" King said.

"Just a scratch," she said. "Come on!"

They ran onward through the forest. The band played behind them as the shells burst all around.

"Is that the plan?" Kim cried. "Just run until they mow us down?"

But King remembered what he had seen when the pod was crashing down. That host in the northern shadows. That hint of red, white, and blue. American flags.

"There's hope ahead," he said. "Run!"

And then, suddenly, his MindPlay burst to life with thousands of icons. Thousands of MindLinks were coming into range. Thousands of Alliance soldiers.

As the shells boomed, as the Nazi war machine crawled, they emerged from the north, their flares casting back the umbrionic shadows. Marines. Thousands of American marines. Their guns boomed, lit the night, and tore into the Nazi hordes.

Hope was here.

CHAPTER FIFTEEN
The Shadow of Death

Epping Forest
England, Earth
September 6, 2207

The marines marched to battle.

Their guns boomed like drums. Their boots shook the forest. Their armored Rhino transporters rumbled, barely squeezing between the trees. Their cannons boomed, pounding the enemy.

King and his companions knelt among the trees, caught between two great armies. Shells, bullets, plasma, and u-bolts flew back and forth.

"Who are they?" Spitfire cried. "What brigade is this? Is this the Ninth Brigade from the Northern Sea?"

King stared between the trees. He could barely believe his eyes. The banners unfurled in the smoke, revealing a blue star with red stripes beaming from its sides like wings. He knew that symbol. He had spent his life under that banner.

"It's them," he whispered. "It's our boys and girls."

Jordan stared with him. He rubbed his eyes. "Impossible! They should be back in America."

"They're here," King said. "It's real. The Freedom Brigade."

Spitfire wheeled toward him. She gaped. "Bastian is here? How is this possible?"

King's eyes dampened. It was them. The brigade that had once served aboard the starship *Freedom*. The brigade that had lost its home among the stars. Fallen angels. Vagabond soldiers. The Freedom Brigade—the brigade King's son commanded. The Freedom Brigade—the proudest soldiers in the universe.

As the shells whistled above, as men fought and died, memories flooded King. That was the curse of age perhaps. The ever-present nostalgia. Those old images floated by. Holding his newborn son in his arms, cutting his cord, watching the baby learn to sit up, walk, talk. Bastian failing flight school, the first King in generations not to become a pilot. Bastian finding his mother dead in that hotel room, driven by loneliness into the arms of another man. A man who murdered her. Who shattered a family. Yes, Bastian broke that day. But from that pain a grieving son was reborn. He rose to become a marine. An officer. And finally the commander of a brigade.

And not just any brigade. The Freedom Brigade. The great force that had once flown aboard the starship *Freedom*. The might of humanity in space. Bastian had led his marines against enemies on other worlds. Now a new enemy was here.

And so was the Freedom Brigade. Because they had sworn an oath. Wherever the enemies of Earth crawled, flew, or festered, the Freedom Brigade would be there.

The marines charged to battle, and at the vanguard, as always, fought the most decorated platoon in the brigade. Bastian's Badgers. The legendary platoon where King's son had begun his career.

The troops charged onward, guns booming. King searched for his son in the smoke and chaos. But then a German shell slammed down nearby, scattering umbrions and plunging the world into darkness. King heard the troops run through the fog, charging to war.

A familiar baritone rose over the din of battle.

"Onward, marines! For freedom!"

"For freedom!" rose the voices of five thousand warriors.

"For freedom!" Spitfire shouted, running through the umbrion clouds to join the charge.

Oh, what the hell, King thought. He was achy, exhausted, ready to fall over and sleep for a month. But he shook off the weariness, raised his gun in the air, and charged with the marines.

"For freedom!" he cried out, voice raspy but loud enough to pierce the shadows. Sixty-eight? Who cared? He was an American. He was a soldier. He would fight. This old bulldog still had a few bites left in him.

He ran, and the other old folks joined him. War was a young man's game. But this wasn't just any regular war. This was an existential war. A war of humanity with its past. A war between the goodness and evil in mankind. Inside every soul lived an angel and a demon, and so did the soul of humanity forever find itself torn between good and evil. King had fought three great wars in his life. One war, against Katyusha, had been a war over economic ideology. The second, the Spider War, had been a war between humanity and aliens. But this war—this was a war against evil incarnate. A war where humanity must confront its past and decide its future. Would their future be one of freedom, hope, and compassion? Or a future of tyranny, despair, and malice?

Their voices rose in the darkness in a deafening battle cry: "For freedom!" They ran onward until they emerged from the fog. And there it loomed. The Wehrmacht, spreading to the southern horizon. The forces of evil.

Ten thousand German soldiers must have covered the scorched fields of England that day, and their mechanical spiders scuttled forth like creatures escaping a nightmare. Toward this swarming horde ran the heroes of Earth. They ran into the umbrion clouds. Into the flying shells. Into the booming gunfire. They ran into death's arms, shouting defiance. "We will live!"

King fired his gun. He hit an enemy soldier, one of the multitude. The man fell and thousands ran onward. King fired again and again, running alongside the marines, charging at the enemy head-on.

The u-rounds flew around him. Umbrions grazed his arm and thigh, sucking his heat away. King knelt by a fallen soldier—a young Tommy who must have died during the night. The body had not yet begun to rot. The British private looked barely twenty years old. So young to have given his life for his country. King whispered a prayer for the lad, then grabbed his body armor, his helmet, and his rifle.

"I'll carry on your battle, son of Earth," King whispered.

And he fought onward.

A baritone voice filled his mind.

"Dad? Is that really you?"

King couldn't help it. Even as he fought, tears filled his eyes. He couldn't see where Bastian was. He could barely see a damn thing in this umbrionic fog. He blinked the tears away and fought onward, shooting the enemy in the shadows.

"It's me, Bastian. I'm here."

"I can't see you, Dad."

"But we fight together!"

Onward they fought. In the shadows they killed. In the shadows American boys fell far from home. In the shadows they bled out, calling for their mothers. And in these shadows from the past, the living fought onward to avenge the dead. Because they all knew something. They knew that should they leave this shadow here, it would spread. It would consume the world like a cancer. And so here they were willing to kill, even to die, to protect what they loved most of all. That word that meant so much. That dream that could only be bought with blood. Freedom.

* * * * *

The battle seemed to last forever. Throughout the evening and night they fought. And when dawn rose, the sun barely pierced the clouds of smoke, and still the armies clashed. The Rhino transporters kept driving south, shoving back the enemy, like true rhinos shoving back a herd of giant spiders. King took rounds to his armor. He fell again and again, and each time, he got back up. He lifted plasma rifles from fallen men and fought onward.

The Alliance soldiers were outnumbered two to one. They fought with fire while the enemy shot ice. They fought for freedom while the enemy served a tyrant. Americans clashed with Germans. Rhinos grappled with spiders. Universes collided, and when the sun set, fire gripped Epping Forest, and the red light drenched the countryside of England.

In that night without darkness, the Freedom Brigade finally pinned the Wehrmacht against London, shattered their last spider, and drove the surviving infantrymen back into the city.

"We drove them back!" Bastian cried. "The countryside is ours. We halted the huns! Here we drew a line. Here we stand and will not fall!"

Bastian transmitted those words telepathically to all Alliance soldiers, but as he thought them, he bellowed them aloud as well. His baritone carried across the shadowy fields of England, and even within London, those crushed under the Nazi boot heard the cry, and perhaps they felt hope.

King still could not see his son. Two days had passed on the misty battlefield. Two days since the Freedom Brigade charged from the northern fog. Two days that King heard Bastian cry out in the darkness—and could not see him. The umbrion clouds were too thick. And both men were too busy killing. For two days and nights, neither James nor Bastian King ate or slept. They killed.

But throughout this battle, between slaying the Nazi invaders, King found stolen moments to check the MindLink map. And on the translucent map of the forest, he would see Bastian's icon, shining blue and bright, his warrior's heart still beating strong. And pride filled James King.

I'm a tough old bastard, King thought. *But I'm nothing compared to my son.*

Bastian was a natural leader. A charismatic officer who instilled lifelong loyalty in his men. It was the hallmark of his leadership that even in shadows, when they could not see him, his soldiers followed him without hesitation, charging blindly into the German lines. To them, Bastian was more than just any other officer. He was a leader they would follow into hell. And hell indeed they found here at Epping Forest.

Now, after two days in hell, as corpses from both sides littered the field, the battle eased. Both armies hunkered down to lick their wounds and regroup. Finally King had time to breathe, to treat his wounds, and to wander through the shadows, seeking his son.

* * * * *

Even during the lull in the battle, even so close, finding Bastian was no easy task.

An unnatural darkness clung to the land. Umbrions spread in a haze, freezing the tiny hairs on King's arms, cloaking the day in shadows. King could only see a few feet in any direction. With every step, he discovered a new corpse lying on the ground, frozen, crushed, lacerated. Rats were already scurrying, and the caws of ravens could be heard through the mist. Another step, another corpse. A step—a severed limb. A step—a lifeless face, screaming silently, eyes unblinking. Another step—an animal carrying a human hand. King walked through the mists of hell.

"Though I walk through the valley of the shadow of death, I will fear no evil, for you are with me," King whispered.

And he took another step. And another. Sometimes, instead of a corpse, he found a dying, writhing soldier on the ground. Some were weeping. Some were praying. Many begged to see their mothers. To go home. King treated whoever he could, giving them a hope for life. And when he must, he held a soldier in his arms, comforting the young warrior as he died. And he walked onward through the valley of the shadow of death, seeking his son.

This was a field of victory. But it was a cursed land. This was what victory looked like, King knew. What it had always looked like. Victory was a field of your broken, dying, or dead brothers-in-arms. Victory was a field of blood. Victory was grief and trauma that could never heal. But upon these foundations of flesh burned, shot at, torn apart, upon these bloodstained pillars of sacrifice did civilization rise. Far above this hell rose the kingdom of heaven. A kingdom for angels anointed with the blood of soldiers.

Through this field of gruesome victory he walked. Other men might have turned back, fleeing these horrors in the mist. Men fled in different ways. Some fled into the bottle. Others fled into insanity. Some fled themselves, while others fled into themselves. King had been in all those dark pits before, and the climb out had nearly ravaged him. But out from those pits he had climbed. Because his family always needed him. His world needed him. And now, across this field of new horrors, King kept walking. Never turning back. Never straying. Walking onward toward his son.

King could not see much in the umbrionic haze. But he could still see Bastian's MindLink hovering in his mind like a beacon in the mist, calling him. The little round MindLink icon was pulsing, monitoring the beat of Bastian's heart. A heartbeat.

Another heartbeat. King remembered that day forty years ago. Standing in the hospital room by Diane, his first wife. Thinking they might lose the baby. Watching little Bastian's heartbeat on the monitor. Beeping. Beeping. Strong. He had been born so small. King used to joke that he could fit Bastian into his shoe. And for hours and nights and weeks he had stood there, watching over his tiny son. Watching that heartbeat. Now again, an old man, lost in the shadows, James King followed the heartbeat of his son.

Upon a hilltop overlooking London he found him.

The tall man stood ahead, so large, towering over his troops. From such a small baby a giant had grown. King could see the big man only in silhouette against the smoldering city.

"Bastian!" King cried out, voice hoarse, eyes stinging.

The giant looked down from the hilltop.

"Dad!" he cried out, voice choked, and ran downhill.

The giant rumbled toward King, stepping into the light of a nearby flare. Brigadier Bastian "Badger" King was an imposing man. Tall and beefy, he had the physique, grace, and personality of a tank. His helmet had fallen off in the battle, revealing a mohawk hairdo. For this battle, Bastian had dyed his hair red, white, and blue. King had always told Bastian that damn haircut looked ridiculous, and now, with the dye, it looked more preposterous than ever. But right now, King was so relieved to see his son he would have overlooked a curly clown's wig.

The big man's eyes gleamed with tears.

"Dad!" he cried, crashed into King, and crushed him in his enormous arms.

It hurt. King was wounded all over, and now a human water buffalo was crushing him. But he barely acknowledged the pain. He squeezed his son in his own crushing grip.

"Bastian. Thank God you're okay."

Bastian kept hugging King for long moments. Finally he

stepped back, holding King at arm's length, and scrutinized him.

"Dad, you look like shit."

"So they keep telling me," King muttered.

Bastian pulled him back into an embrace. "It's good to see you, old man."

"Bastian, what about Alice? And the kids?" Sudden terror filled King that something had happened to them.

"The kids are fine!" Bastian laughed—that deep, rumbling, comforting laugh of his. "Staying with Kim's sister, safe as could be."

"And . . . Alice?" King said, nervousness leaping in him. "What about your wife, Bas?"

A voice rose from behind. "Alice is right here, Pops."

King spun around. Relief flowed over him.

Alice Allenby-King, his daughter-in-law, was walking toward him. Dust and blood stained her battle armor, and her two blond braids were singed at the tips. And yet a smile spread across her broad, honest face. She was a tall woman, as tall as Spitfire, but while Spitfire was willowy and graceful, Alice was nearly as burly and muscular as her husband. She had grown up baling hay, chopping wood, and chasing toads in the countryside of Nebraska, an all-American girl with golden pigtails, freckled cheeks, and a smile as bright as the sun. The farm girl became an Olympic wrestler (ending twelfth place at the 2198 Olympics), and then joined the Freedom Brigade, climbing the ranks to become its chief NCO. King knew Alice was a good soldier, but first and foremost, she was family. He pulled her into his arms.

"Alice! Good to see you, darling."

Her blue eyes, which could be so fierce in battle, softened. "We were worried about you, Pops. How are you? MindLink said you were stabbed. And shot twice. God, how do you feel?"

"I'm good!" King said. "Strong as ever."

"He looks like shit," Bastian said.

King laughed hoarsely. "I feel like it too." Then he pulled Bastian and Alice back into his arms. In this world of bloodshed and trauma, in this foundation of blood and sacrifice upon which civilization rose, it was his family that kept King fighting.

*****

They dug down outside London. The Rhinos rumbled across the landscape, digging trenches. Rhino dropships could fly in space, crawl over land, even survive underwater. Their horns were spinning drills. Normally used to drill into enemy hulls, those horns dug a line in the dirt today. South of that line—the Wehrmacht in London, spreading from the city to the southern coast of England. North of that line—the Alliance. And at its vanguard stood the Freedom Brigade. The homeless brigade. The shield of freedom.

King finally got a full night's sleep, his first in a week. The brigade's medics checked him over, patched him up, and did their magic. And indeed they were like magicians. Back in the Second World War, these injuries might have killed King. Today, in this *second* Second World War, modern medicine could regrow skin, heal punctured organs, hell, even do your taxes. (It was a joke King told the medics. They did not laugh.)

He even got to drink coffee that morning. After a week—beautiful, bitter coffee! What a luxury. Granted, King drank it while sitting on a burnt mecha leg, gazing upon a charred wasteland full of artillery craters and feasting crows. But *coffee*!

He raised a pair of binoculars. Past the wasteland rose London. The spinnenmutters were moving there, their spindly legs stirring the fog. From here, the starship-sized spiders seemed as small as mites. The arachnid mechas were building something outside the city. King watched them shove chunks of buildings and pieces of shattered starships. The spinnenmutters were raising huge barricades around London like a medieval wall. Above the barricades the Wehrmacht was installing artillery batteries.

"Taking the city won't be easy," King said.

Jordan sat beside him. The white-haired commander was nursing his own cup of coffee. Stubble silvered his dark, weary face. He took a sip. "Nothing ever is."

King heaved a sigh. "Look at us, Larry. We used to sit on a log by the creek like this, fishing and swapping fish tales. Now we're sitting on a giant spider leg, staring at a London covered in swastikas."

Jordan nodded. "Worst fishing trip ever."

King took another sip of coffee. He winced as the hot drink flowed down his throat. His neck was hurting more than usual today. The kiss of Katyusha's blade never truly healed. No, not Katyusha's blade. His father's blade, which she had stolen. King often missed his father. Even now, decades later, he missed the man's wisdom.

As he sat drinking his coffee, King watched a group of young marines clearing the rubble, searching for survivors. One of the marines, a young officer, was moving on prosthetic legs. Not ordinary prosthetics either. They were J-shaped beams of metal, flexible and strong, calibrated for speed. It was Kim's son. Evan. King still remembered the frightened private who had lost his legs years ago, fighting the spiders. That mortally wounded boy, lying on death's bed, had become a proud, strong officer. Every once in a while, Evan walked across the rubble on his J-shaped legs, found Bastian, and gave him a report. Outside the military, they were stepbrothers. Here at war, everyone in the brigade were brothers in blood.

Jordan noticed who King was watching.

"They're good boys," Jordan said in his soothing baritone. "They fought well. You must be proud."

King knew what his friend was thinking about. What

Jordan had not stopped thinking about since the war had begun.

King spoke softly. "Have you heard of Annie?"

"Not yet," Jordan said. "Not since this whole war began. I spoke to her a day before the enemy invaded. She was busy at work. In St Mary's Hospital, London."

Both men gazed south toward the city. The spider-mechas were still raising barricades. Behind the machines, swastika banners flapped from steeples. A chill ran through King's bones.

"Larry." He put a hand on his friend's shoulder. "I'm sure she's all right. The Germans need doctors too."

Jordan turned to look at him. "Even doctors with dark skin, Jim? Annie's mother was Irish, but they won't care. She looks like me. A subhuman." His mouth twisted bitterly around the word.

King hated to admit it. His friend was right. The Nazis wouldn't care that Dr. Annie Jones was an esteemed physician, that her honor would require her to heal even her enemies. She wasn't Aryan, and that would be enough to doom her.

King stared into Jordan's eyes. "Annie is a smart woman. And a tough veteran. We went through hard times together. She'll know how to disappear. To slink into alleyways. To survive."

"Jim." Pain filled Jordan's eyes. "You don't understand. She would never abandon her patients." He took a shaky breath. "I already lost a nephew and niece at Alpha Centauri. I can't lose a daughter too."

King's hand tightened around Jordan's shoulder. "We'll break into that city, Larry. I promise you. And we'll bring your daughter home. *Alive*."

*****

That evening, King trudged through the makeshift camp of the Freedom Brigade. The wind gusted, scented of distant fires and corpses. King raised his collar and lowered his head, keeping his face hidden from the sky. He wore a uniform, but no insignia topped his shoulders. There were eyes in the sky. There were eyes in space. There were eyes in the forests and fields. King—all the senior officers here—kept their insignia hidden in their pockets, and they kept their faces lowered. Just in case.

King kept imagining the Nazis up in space, peering through a telescope, seeing him shuffling along through the camp. And suddenly—a blast from above. A strike from orbit. And where an admiral had stood a crater would smolder. But no strike came. Katyusha was doing her job, battling the Weltraumwaffe in space, and keeping the Nazis' bionic eyes off Earth.

King trudged by a point-defense battery. The marines had scattered a few of those around the camp. They towered above King like the nephilim of old, their bores ten feet tall, aiming at the sky. Just in case any Nazis decided to attack from above. There were quite a few senior officers here after all. And George Godwin himself, leader of the Alliance. A juicy target indeed. Guards patrolled everywhere, nervously glancing at the shadowy horizons and the dark sky. Telepathy disrupters hummed, ready to jam any eavesdropping enemies. Security was high, but they all tried to appear casual, to project business as usual. Nobody must know that Godwin himself was here.

Leaving the artillery batteries behind, King approached a group of thirty Rhinos. The big, bulky transporters loomed in the night like slumbering dinosaurs in a primordial field of mist. Walking briskly through the fog, King approached one of the Rhinos, indistinguishable from the others. There were no guards outside, no sign that here would be meeting the Alliance High Command. Here the fate of the world would be determined.

King glanced around, then entered the Rhino.

The others were already there. They stared at him from the shadows, faces seeming pale like planets in a ghostly solar system. King took his seat among them.

Despite all the security and secrecy, everyone felt on edge. King saw it in their flicking eyes, their tense stance. They were on the front line, and violence might flare again any moment.

Rhinos were enormous machines. Years ago, they had served as the dropships of the starship Freedom. They dwarfed most modern dropships. They were antiques, relics of a past when the Alliance built things *big*. Rhinos were large enough to be considered warships in their own right.

And yet, on the inside, they were surprisingly cramped. Much of their size came from their thick, armored hulls and heavy engines. They were designed to carry fifty troops, but those troops stood crammed together, no room for a mouse to squeak between them. It was a tight spot to hold a meeting.

"Ready, everyone?" George Godwin rumbled.

One by one, they nodded.

"Good, good." Godwin nodded too, jowls quivering. "Thank you for joining me here."

The old man smoothed his three-piece suit, which had suffered a few burn marks in the battles. He was the highest-ranking man in the room. Indeed, in the entire Alliance. Godwin was a civilian, yet as Alliance High Commander, he commanded the full armed forces. The infantry, the fleet, all of it. This was Godwin's war to win or lose.

As admiral, King was the ranking officer in the room. Following him were Gal "Spitfire" Levy and Larry "Phantom" Jordan. Both had begun their careers as starfighter pilots. Both had climbed the rank to commander. In the Freedom Fleet, that rank normally gave you command of a major starship, likely a carrier or even a dreadnought. And indeed, both Spitfire and Phantom had once commanded Alliance flagships. Jordan had lost the *Freedom*, while Spitfire had lost the *Lioness*. The two orphaned commanders stood side by side, united in grief.

Brigadier Bastian King was here too. The big man, commander of the Freedom Brigade, crossed his massive arms over his barrel chest. Even inside the shadowy Rhino, aviator glasses hid his eyes. Luckily for King, the shadows hid that ridiculous mohawk of his. Someday King would sneak up while Bastian slept and shave the damn thing off.

Colonel Kim Fletcher was in attendance too. She was an engineer by trade, not a fighter, but King wanted his wife here. He valued her wisdom and insight, and while not a combat soldier, she had fought many battles. Sergeant Major Alice Allenby-King, the Chief NCO of the Freedom Brigade, completed the assemblage. The two women stood side by side, eyes gleaming in the shadows.

Here we are, King thought. *Us veterans of the starship* Freedom. *Still fighting as a group.*

Their starship had flown into a star. Its atoms had dispersed across the universe. Yet the bonds formed within that crucible lasted forever. Godwin was the odd man out—not wearing a uniform, not a veteran of the *Freedom.* But he was their commander, the leader of the free world, and they all turned to him for wisdom.

The short, stocky man stood before them, wearing his singed suit. He clutched his cane and stared at them one by one.

"Let us begin," Godwin said, "with a moment of silence for our fallen heroes."

Everyone lowered their eyes.

King looked at his wife. Her head was lowered. She was thinking of her brother, the courageous Commander Ben Fletcher, who had gone down with the *Patton.*

He looked at his best friend. Jordan too had his head lowered. He was thinking of his niece and nephew, missing at Toliman Station at Alpha Centauri. The Nazis had destroyed the station on the first day of the war. Most likely, Jordan's family there was dead.

King too grieved. For Ben. For thousands of other soldiers who had fallen in this war. And as he stood there inside the Rhino, honoring the fallen, he remembered those he had lost in earlier wars. Friends like Oliver Darjeeling and Yehuda Levy. And a little stowaway. A fairy girl named Stowy, an adopted granddaughter, taken so soon.

The weight of grief nearly crushed him.

Godwin raised his head and cleared his throat. The moment of silence was over. But King's grief would last forever.

* * * * *

Godwin spoke again, his voice rumbling like a starship engine.

"A miracle occurred in England! We were in the belly of the beast, facing the prospect of utter annihilation, when from the north swooped our dear friends from beyond the sea. The Freedom Brigade. With courage, determination, and an unrelenting desire to win, the American marines shoved back the lines of German troops and heavy armor. The enemy has been halted and now hunkers behind barricades, digging down, unable to proceed north. Few soldiers in history have achieved what the Freedom Brigade has achieved here on this land. For the first time in this war, after long days of despair and loss, we won a battle. This war has only begun. We may be fighting it for years. But we have halted the Nazi tide. Momentum is on our side—and we will keep striking!"

"Yes!" Spitfire cried, raising her fist in the air.

"Hell yeah!" boomed Bastian, leaping to his feet. The big marine looked strong enough to break down the barricades of London with his bare hands.

"Brigadier Bastian King!" Godwin said. He was a foot

shorter and twice as old, yet Godwin's voice rumbled as loudly as Bastian's. "You have a briefing for us, I believe? I shall give you the pulpit, sir."

Godwin sat down and held his cane between his legs. Moving clumsily in the tight quarters, Bastian stood at the "pulpit"—a little area between the table and bulkhead.

Bastian cleared his throat. "Hello, everyone. Thanks for coming. I, um . . . Hang on. Just need to find the right MindWeb files."

"Play *Freebird*!" Spitfire cried from the back of the room.

Bastian glared at her. Spitfire blushed and looked at her knees. She was trying not to laugh.

"Sorry," Spitfire whispered. "No humor allowed in the Alliance. Or music. Or fun. I know."

Bastian cleared his throat. "Will you please be quiet, Spitfire?"

She blinked at him innocently. "Sorry, sir. Shall I report to the principal's office?"

A few laughs sounded throughout the cabin. King sighed. Damn kids. Bastian was his son, Spitfire (almost like) his adopted daughter. They had grown up tormenting each other and never stopped.

"Will you kids knock it off?" King said. "This is a war, dammit."

Spitfire glanced at Jordan. "Was he this cranky during the Third World War too?"

"Just as bad at twenty as he is at seventy," Jordan said.

"I ain't seventy yet," King said.

"By temperament, you're way past it, old man," Jordan said.

"Will everyone stop bantering and get to the briefing?" King said.

It was over a week since the war began, and King was

starved for intelligence. He wasn't used to this. As commander of the *Freedom*, he had always been in the know. Entire teams of tactical, intelligence, and telemetry officers would always keep him updated around the clock. Stowy's mouse could cough somewhere in the ship, and King would know about it. This war? After being caught with his pants around his ankles, he had been rattled across land, sky, space, and everywhere but *in the loop*. He needed more information on the enemy. Desperately.

"Four days ago," Bastian said, "we captured several Nazi soldiers. We've been interrogating them."

"Thoroughly," added Alice. A wicked smile spread across her face, and she cracked her knuckles.

King frowned. "I don't condone torture. Not even of Nazis."

"I do," Spitfire said.

"Well, I don't," King snapped. "If we act like the Nazis, then how are we superior to them?"

Spitfire leaped to her feet. "Those bastards killed millions of people! *Billions* of people. They're evil." She flushed, remembering herself. "Sir."

"All right, all right, calm down everyone!" Bastian said, holding out his large hands. "We didn't torture anyone. We talked to them. We used some truth serum, some telepathic hacking, and that was the extent of it. Now can I talk about what we learned?"

Spitfire sat down, crossed her arms, and nodded sulkily.

King understood her. To the enemy, she was a subhuman to be exterminated. It was hard to show mercy to such an enemy. King held no pity for the foe they fought. No more than Spitfire did. But they were fighting for civilization. And so, despite the beast in every soldier's heart, despite the will for revenge, they must act civilized. This was not only a war of bullets, but a war of ideals. Against the most wretched evil, they must fight to maintain their honor. It was not an easy fight.

"First," Bastian said, "I want to tell you what we learned about our enemy. Who they are. Where they come from. Who they serve. Then we'll discuss the state of the war. Where we are, where they are, and what we do next."

Spitfire rolled her eyes. "I hate meetings. I want to go kill Nazis."

"Soon!" Bastian said. He looked back at the group. "First—a quick overview of our situation." He heaved a sigh. "I won't sugarcoat it. Things are ugly. The Nazis caught us with our pants down. And they hit us hard. Damn hard. They destroyed hundreds of our starships. They bombed entire cities into rubble. They even hit us with tactical nukes. Washington DC, Los Angeles, New York—they've been clobbered. In Europe, Asia, Africa—the situation is no better. Half of Russia and China are smoldering. The body count? We don't know. In the millions. Tens of millions, probably."

For a moment, everyone was silent, letting the horror sink in.

King had seen a lot of this from space. He had seen the mushroom clouds. The fires. But he hadn't known the true extent of the devastation.

Bastian continued speaking. "The Nazis hit us hard and fast. A blitzkrieg tactic. They wanted to shock us. To overwhelm us with massive firepower. To conquer Earth within a week. And they very nearly did. But we finally seem to be finding our bearings. We're digging down and fighting back. We stopped the enemy's assault here in Britain, and we're fighting back hard everywhere. The war is on every continent. In every country. It's in our cities. It's on the high seas. It's underwater. It's in the air. And it's in space."

King finally asked a question that had been niggling him. "Bastian, the Freedom Brigade is American. How did you end up here in Britain?"

"I believe I can answer that, old boy," Godwin said. "I deployed them here. We got word of the Nazi high command landing in Britain. Digging down in London. Our brave Tommies took out many Jerries, but we needed some help from our friends. At London, we have a chance to strike the Nazis hard and take out some of their most important leaders. I wanted the best men and women for the job. That meant the Freedom Brigade."

Bastian actually blushed. "Well, we're good. The best? I don't know."

"I do," King said. "The Freedom Brigade is the best damn marine force in the Alliance. I wager you're the best brigade in two universes. I saw you destroy armies of alien rahs, and you're excelling in this war too. You're the right soldiers for the job. Now tell me more about the Nazi high command. Who are we dealing with? And where the hell did they come from?"

Damn, King hated being out of the loop like this! He relished this chance to finally learn more.

Bastian nodded. "Right. Before I discuss our battle plans, I'll fill you in. Here's what we learned about our enemy . . ."

* * * * *

Bastian tapped his temple—a polite way of informing people he was using his MindLink. A shared hallucination appeared above the tabletop. It depicted Berlin. Modern, twenty-third-century Berlin. Yet not the one from this universe. In the hallucination, swastika banners draped Berlin, and statues of Hitler rose in city squares. The hallucination zoomed in and out, showing different parts of the city. Airships and starships floated above, swastikas upon their hulls. Countless troops marched along the streets. The modern Gestapo, their black battle armor adorned with crackling red skulls, swept from home to home, crushing the world in an iron grip.

"This is a neural composite from the memories of several soldiers we captured," Bastian said. "This is how they remember Berlin. Their Berlin."

"Another universe," King said. "A universe where Hitler won World War II, and the Nazi Empire is three hundred years old."

Kim stared at the hallucination in wonder. "Look at those airships. They're using graviton engines! I wish I could get my hand on those designs. And look, down in the city! More of those big metal spiders. Oh, what I wouldn't give for blueprints!" She looked at Bastian. "We need to find one of their engineers. I want to know how they built their universe portal."

"If I catch one, he's yours," Bastian said.

"Or *she*," said Kim. "According to our intel, the greatest Nazi engineer is Dr. Anneliese Heisenberg-König. My doppelgänger."

A collective shudder passed through the room.

"Yes, the doppelgängers," King said. "I saw two of them. One of my wife. One of my granddaughter. Both tried to kill me."

"You sure those were doppelgängers?" Jordan said.

"Very funny, smartass."

Bastian stared at King, a strange look in his eyes. Normally loud and bluff, Bastian spoke slowly now, his voice contemplative. "So you saw Dr. Anneliese, wife of the führer, inventor of the Spinnenmutter, the Lugerheulens, and other Nazi technology. And you saw Eva König, granddaughter of the führer, commander of the Waffen-SS."

King nodded. "I did. My shadow wife. And my shadow granddaughter." His gut twisted. "I did not see my doppelgänger. Or yours, Bastian. If they exist."

"They do," Bastian said, voice even lower. "That's what I wanted to show you."

Alice stood up, walked to her husband's side, and put a

hand on his shoulder. "Are you sure, Bastian?"

He nodded. "They need to see." The big marine cleared his throat. "I'm going to show you a hallucination now. It will depict Wolfgang König, Grand Admiral of the Weltraumwaffe, the space fleet of the Fatherworld. He's the highest-ranking Nazi to have crossed over to our universe. From aboard the *Barbarossa*, he oversees the invasion of our world."

A hallucination appeared above the tabletop, depicting a Nazi officer. He was a beast of a man, tall and muscular, built like a tank. He wore a black coat, heavy boots, and a cap adorned with steel skulls. His bionic eye seemed to scan the Rhino's cabin. At first King didn't see the resemblance to anyone. Was this truly a doppelgänger? But the closer he looked, the more King saw it. The jawline was the same. The fierce look in the eyes. The stance and poise.

"This Nazi general looks like my son," King said.

Bastian nodded. "My doppelgänger. Not my clone. Not my twin. Our family branched off generations ago. He's not me. He doesn't have my DNA, he doesn't have my name, and he doesn't have my life story. Certainly not my morals. He's me as I might have been. As I am in that other universe."

King grabbed his son's arm (which felt a little like grabbing a tree trunk). "You're not him in any universe." His voice shook with rage. "You're a good, honest man. And that . . ." He pointed at the hallucination of the Nazi general. "That is an abomination."

"A shadow," Bastian said. "We all have one. Dad, I need to show you another doppelgänger."

Bastian tapped his temple. The hallucination of Wolfgang König disappeared. A new hallucination replaced it, depicting another man.

This new man was older, gray-haired, and mustached. Like all high-ranking Nazis, he had one bionic eye. But his real eye, steely gray, seemed even less human than the adlerauge. He wore a black military uniform, red swastikas on the arms. Oddly he bore no insignia.

"This is Führer Helmut König," said Bastian. "Patriarch of the König family and leader of the Fatherworld."

King stared at the familiar face.

He knew, of course. Eva had all but told him. In the chaos of battle, King had managed to suppress that fear. But yes, he had known. For a long while now.

"My doppelgänger," King said.

Part III
The Battle of London

CHAPTER SIXTEEN
In the Blessed Mother's Arms

St Mary's Hospital
London, England
Earth
September 8, 2207

The skeleton stood on a framework of metal wires and rods, staring with four eye sockets. Most of the skeleton was normal. The skeleton of a child, probably younger than Stowy. Yet from the top of the skull grew . . . another skull. A second head, upside down, attached by the cranium. Both skulls were perfectly formed. Stowy could even see the adult teeth waiting to push out the baby teeth. One body. Two heads. Not even two heads side by side. But one head growing from the other! Those four eyes peered at her, entreating.

Bury us. Give us peace.

Stowy hugged her safety blanket close to her chest. Luna was scared too.

"I can't," she whispered to the dead girl. Or were they girl*s*? Two girls with one body?

An oily voice rose from behind.

"Ah! I see you've met little Ingrid and Greta. A marvelous specimen, isn't it? One of my favorites. I brought her all the way from the Fatherworld to keep me company."

Snakes of fear crawled through Stowy. Whenever she was afraid, she imagined fear as little blue serpents, no larger than her fingers, slithering through her, making her shiver. And that voice always awoke the snakes.

She turned to see him there, watching her. He smiled kindly. An avuncular smile. With his beak of a nose, stooped shoulders, bald head, and beady little eyes, he looked like a vulture. His smile was kindly. A genuine smile. A smile that tugged at the corners of his eyes. He was not a cruel man. He loved her, took care of her, gave her candy when she was good. How could she think him a monster?

Stowy lowered her eyes, saying nothing. She wanted to talk. To say, "Yes, sir, beautiful specimen." Or something else to please him. To stop him from punishing her. But she could only stare at her feet. The words lodged in her throat.

"Ah, poor little Stowy," the vulture said. He reached into his lab coat pocket with fingers like talons. "Here. Have a chocolate. Good German confectionery."

She reached for the chocolate. But he pulled his hand back.

"Uh-uh-uh, little Stowy," he said. "Little girls who did not wash their hands mustn't taint their candies. Eat it from my hand. There."

She ate the chocolate from his hand like an animal. She wondered how much candy he had offered Ingrid and Greta. Could both heads eat chocolate?

The vulture stroked Stowy's cheek. His fingernail scraped across her skin. A fingernail? No. This was a *talon.* A long, savage vulture talon, a claw designed to crack bones.

"Aren't you going to thank me?" the vulture said, leaning closer, his smile still so kindly. He smelled of chocolate and medicine and ashes.

"*Danke, Onkel Baer,*" Stowy whispered, staring at her toes.

She had managed to talk! Only whisper, yes, but that was something. Maybe this strange world was indeed curing her. Or maybe she simply feared his scalpels.

"Excellent enunciation!" The gaunt doctor mussed her hair. "That's my little Stowy. Retarded children can be helped. I always did believe it. Perhaps that's why I kept you alive for so long." He turned toward the strange skeleton, and a sigh rolled through his body. "These ones, you see . . . I tried to keep them alive. The way I keep you alive. What a marvel they were!"

They looked again at the skeleton of the little girl with two heads. Stowy peered into the top skull's eyes. That head had lived its life upside down. What must it have been like? Stowy wished she could speak to those girls.

"*Onkel* Baer," she whispered, "why did they die?"

"Their condition killed them," Dr. Baer said. "Craniopagus parasiticus. It's an extremely rare type of parasitic twinning occurring in about one of ten million births. What a treasure to have found her! What a crown jewel for my collection of unusual children! Ah, yes, these ones I did not incinerate with the others. When they died, I could not toss their bones into the furnace like common children. No. I embalmed my Ingrid and Greta. For months, I tried to preserve their purity. To keep their bodies from rotting with my special chemicals. Yet I could not resist opening their glass coffin, touching their skin, holding their little cold hands. Sometimes I slept with them in my bed. Until one morning, I awoke and discovered maggots eating the corpse. Still I tried to save their beautiful corpse, yet the rot spread. I knew they were lost." He shook his head sadly. "All that remains are the bones."

They stood silently, staring at the skeleton for a while longer. During her year in the Munich hospital, Stowy had seen him experiment on hundreds of children. Seen him kill them all, then toss their corpses into the furnace. Why did he save this one? Was it truly just their rarity, or could he feel actual compassion, even love? She dared not speak to ask again, merely stared at her toes.

He stroked her hair. "You see, little Stowy, Ingrid and Greta are like the multiverse. One universe. One reality. From which branched off a mirror image. An abhorrent monstrosity. A world in which everything is upside down. A universe like Greta, the deformed head growing from Ingrid's cranium. That is where we are now, Stowy. In the deformed head of a monstrous multiverse. That is why I brought the sisters with us. Because they remind me of where we are. An upside-down world."

He turned toward the window and gazed outside. Stowy joined him. They stood together, beholding a city beyond reality. London. London in the impure universe.

There was no London back in the Fatherworld. The Eternal Führer had destroyed it long ago with his terrible nuclear bombs. Even to this day, that London was a crater crackling with radiation. Stowy knew of Old London from her father's secret library. She had read *Oliver Twist*, *David Copperfield*, and other works of Charles Dickens set in this city. The Elephant Man, a hero of hers, had lived in this city. And there it was—London! A living, breathing city! Not in the pages of a book but right outside the window!

From here in St Mary's Hospital, Stowy had a southward view of Paddington, a district in central London. Steeples rose from the fog. Streets coiled into the distance like the tunnels of mice, lined with Victorian buildings. The characters in Dickens's novels must have lived in houses like those. Stowy could recognize a few locations from her books and maps. She had always been good at memorizing maps (a gift that had come in handy during her years in the slums of Munich). There was Hyde

Park, and she could just make out Kensington Palace among the trees. Farther back, she descried the dome of the Royal Albert Hall. And behind it—ah! The Natural History Museum!

Stowy yearned to visit that museum, to behold the dinosaur skeletons. And she would love to visit Crystal Palace Park, which featured Victoria-era statues of dinosaurs, dating to the earliest days of paleontology. She had a silver coin in one of her many pockets. Maybe she could even buy more dinosaur toys.

Ah, dinosaurs. Her great love. Even more than Dickens novels and the Elephant Man. Dinosaurs were her life.

As a young girl, she had found a book in the public library. Not a forbidden book to be kept secret. A book all Aryan children could read. *Das Zeitalter der Dinosaurier*. It featured wonderfully lifelike illustrations by Rudolph Zallinger, the famous artist. The same Rudolph Zallinger who had spent 1944 to 1948 painting the grand mural *The Age of Reptiles* at the University of Munich. A hundred feet wide, the mural portrayed dinosaurs from across the ages. Zallinger had begun painting that masterpiece the same year Hitler had won World War II. The same year the universe had split in two. Stowy wondered if Rudolph Zallinger had survived in *this* universe too, if he had gone on to paint dinosaurs for the subhumans too.

For hours, for days on end, Stowy would leaf through those pages, marveling at Zallinger's illustrations of ancient monsters. From a young age, even when Mother and Father still lived, Stowy had learned that other humans were cruel. That other humans would hurt her and her family. But nobody could hurt dinosaurs. Not the Gestapo. Not vultures with kindly smiles and claws that ripped out bones.

Stowy reached into her pockets and felt her remaining dinosaur toys. So had lost so many over the years. The few that remained were precious to her. A great desire, a need, filled her to line up those dinosaurs. To place the plastic toys on the floor and arrange them in a neat row, adjust them, align them tail to snout, to bring order from chaos. Why did she love lining them up? That Stowy did not know. That was a symptom of her condition perhaps. Autism. Her impurity. Her own abhorrent mutation.

Why am I still alive? she thought. She turned back toward the skeleton. *Why didn't he kill me and mount my bones too?*

She looked at him. She made eye contact with those terrible beady eyes, then quickly looked away, heart pounding. She clutched Luna more tightly to her chest.

"*Onkel* Baer," she whispered. "Please . . . please don't hurt Luna. And don't hurt my mouse Algernon. If you kill me, please don't hurt them."

His sharp, angular face softened. "Oh, Stowy, dear. You ran away from me. And you sneaked into Frau Eva's shuttle, causing so much trouble." He traced one of his clawlike fingernails down her cheek. "I will not grant you the mercy of death now. You and I will conduct many, many experiments together. Some useful for science. Others . . . well, for our own little pleasure, yes?" His eyes widened, and he raised his finger into the air. "I have an idea. Maybe we can try to attach a second head to yours? Create a little Ingrid and Greta?"

Stowy trembled. Tears filled her eyes. And Dr. Baer only laughed and gave her another chocolate.

*****

Freedom Brigade Camp
London, England
Earth
September 8, 2207

With a grand motion, Bastian swept everything off the tabletop, then unrolled a giant map of London. The big marine placed his hands on the tabletop, leaned over the map, and stared at his companions inside the Rhino.

"All right, here's the plan." He tapped the map. "Our positions are here, here, and—"

"Why aren't you using a telepathic map?" Spitfire said.

Bastian glowered at her. "What?"

"Just create a hallucinatory map with MindPlay, then share it with us telepathically," Spitfire said. "Like we always do."

Bastian raised his chin. "I didn't feel like it."

Spitfire leaned back in her seat and smirked. "You just wanted to dramatically sweep everything off a tabletop, then unfold a giant map to explain your plan, didn't you?"

King cleared his throat. "Spitfire, this is war. Try to treat it with a modicum of seriousness."

She crossed her arms. "Who uses a paper map these days?" she muttered.

"As I was saying," Bastian continued. "Our battalions encircle North London like a crown. Thunder Battalion and Lightning Battalion will enter the city here." He tapped the map. "Down the old M11 motorway. The Heer—the ground force of the Wehrmacht—is defending the road. Thunder and Lightning will have to fight their way through. Meanwhile, Hailstorm and Typhoon Battalions will enter from the northwest, down the old M1. We'll trap the Nazis in a pincer move."

"What about Nova?" King said.

Nova Battalion was legendary. Even the Red Dawn admired and feared them. Back in the old days of the starship *Freedom*, Nova Battalion had formed the vanguard. They were the elite troops of the Freedom Brigade, the deadliest marines the starship could deploy. If you saw Nova Battalion coming, you ran. Both Bastian and Alice had begun their careers there. And now Evan Fletcher served in Nova as a platoon commander. It was becoming a new King family tradition. For generations, they had been pilots. Now the King dynasty was serving with the brave marines, and James King, patriarch of his clan, couldn't be prouder.

I wish you were here to see our heroism, Dad, he thought. *To see your descendants. You'd be proud too.*

He missed the old man so much it hurt. No, King would never forgive Katyusha for taking Ulysses King from him.

"Nova will deploy in our Rhinos," Bastian said. "While the four other battalions hit the enemy on land, Nova will stage an aerial assault on the city."

Spitfire's eyes bugged out. "With those artillery batteries on the barricades? They'll shoot you down like ducks."

Bastian glared at her. "You're not a marine. Stay in your lane."

"And you're not a pilot! Stay on the ground." She leaped to her feet. "Seriously, Bastian. They have a lot of ground-to-air firepower. They'll gun you down."

"Every path we take, we'll meet their guns," Bastian said. "We'll hit them from three sides. Try to overwhelm them. The faster we act, the better. They're still digging down and raising defenses. In another day or two, it might be too late."

Spitfire chewed her lip. "Part of me wants to storm into the city now and start killing Nazis. The other part wants to wait for reinforcement."

They both turned toward King.

"What do you think, Dad?" Bastian said.

"Yeah, Dad?" said Spitfire (only half mockingly).

King frowned. "Bastian, you're commanding officer of the

Freedom Brigade. The decision is yours."

"Yes, but you're the . . ." Bastian said. "You know. The commander. Even here."

King heaved a long, weary breath. "Yes, this does remind me of the old days." He looked around the interior of the Rhino. "Metal bulkheads around us, monitors, cannon controls, the machinery of war all around . . . And us. Our little team. Discussing battle plans." He shook his head, scattering the nostalgia. "But the starship *Freedom* is gone, son. We're in a Rhino transporter parked on Earth, not on a dreadnought's bridge in deep space. This brigade is yours. Without a starship to command, I no longer have authority over your marines. The decision is yours."

For a long time, they were quiet. The group looked at one another. James King, once the commander of the starship *Freedom*. Larry Jordan, once his XO. Spitfire, once leader of Freedom's starfighter fleet, groomed to someday inherit the dreadnought. Kim Fletcher, ship engineer. Bastian and Alice, commanders of the ship's marines, ready to enforce *Freedom*'s will on the ground. The old gang.

Yes, this all felt so much like the old days. But so different. They had all changed so much. Moved on. Pursued new careers or (like King) retired on a farm. Yet this war had swept them up from across the globe, then tossed them together here on this field outside of London. Here inside the hull of this armored transporter—a family. Once again—planning battles to save humanity.

And King thought too of those he had lost. Of the fallen. Of Yehuda "Lion" Levy, father to Spitfire. Of his dear friend Oliver Darjeeling. Of Queen Emily, who still lived yet was beyond his reach. Of Mimori, his sweet Mimori, who was said to be just a machine yet had a soul. And of course, as always—Stowy. His precious little fairy girl, sacrificed to the spiders.

King thought of them all, dead or lost, who were not here with him today.

It's not the same, he thought. *Not without that big ole starship around us. We belonged up there. Without* Freedom, *we're lost.*

* * * * *

Bastian lifted a chunk of wood, which he had whittled into a castle and painted black. It looked like a rook from a giant's chessboard. Bastian thumped it down onto the map. "Here, according to our intelligence, is the headquarters of the Wehrmacht division in London."

"Did you actually spend all morning carving wooden pieces for your map?" Spitfire said. "MindWeb has free hallucinatory icons, you know."

"Gal!" King warned.

"Sorry, Dad." She winked at him.

Bastian tapped the black wooden castle. "This is St Mary's Hospital. Right in the heart of London. This is where the Nazis have set up their headquarters. From there, they oversee their British campaign."

King frowned at the map. "A hospital?"

But he understood. Of course.

Bastian nodded. "In a hospital. Embedded among the staff and patients."

Rage soared through King, burning him from the inside. The old wound on his neck tightened painfully. "The bastards are using human shields."

Bastian nodded. "Indeed. They're smart. They know we'd never bomb a hospital. They're using our compassion against us."

King's metal fist tightened. He had replaced the gauntlet's

broken fingers, but now they creaked and threatened to crack again. "Those sick bastards."

"Yep, they're Nazis, all right," Bastian said. "Who'd have thought Nazis could be evil, huh?"

"Damn it!" Spitfire leaped up and pounded the table. "Who says we have to play by their rules? Who says we must be noble all the time?" She panted, face flushed. Her fists clenched into tight little balls. "Katyusha would have bombed the hospital."

Bastian looked at her. "You're not Katyusha."

Spitfire loosened her fists. She slumped in her seat. "No. I'm not."

"I don't have the stomach for it either," King said. "We won't bomb the hospital from the air. We'll have to fight room by room, shooting Nazis while protecting the staff and patients. Until we capture the Nazi high command." He looked at Bastian. "Pull up the stats on the senior Nazi officers in St Mary's Hospital. I want everyone to memorize their faces."

Bastian nodded and tapped his temple, signaling that he was about to share another hallucination. (Tapping the temple was completely unnecessary. MindLinks operated by thought alone. But it was a habit most soldiers followed. By now it had become etiquette.)

The group hallucinated several Nazi officers hovering above the tabletop. To save space, Bastian was showing them only the heads. The disembodied heads floated, life-sized, staring at the companions.

"Bit gruesome, Bas," Spitfire said.

He rolled his eyes. "You're the one who told me to share hallucinations."

"Of maps, not severed heads!"

"They're not severed heads," Bastian said. "Not yet at

least. They're the commanders of the Seventh Wehrmacht Army, which is currently operating out of London, overseeing the assault on Britain. Look at their faces. Read their names. Memorize them. This is Britain's Most Wanted list, ladies and gentlemen. These are the men we must kill."

Little names floated above the heads. King studied them. All were middle-aged men with stern faces, wide jaws, and bionic eyes. Hard men. Men with the eyes of killers. King had known men like that in the wars. Men who lived for nothing but bloodshed. They would not be easy prey.

"This ugly son of a bitch here." Bastian pointed at one of the heads. "General Adolf von Schweppenburg. He commands the Seventh Army of the Wehrmacht, which is now occupying South England. He's known for his ruthlessness, fanaticism, and unyielding devotion to the König family."

"He's a dead man," Spitfire said.

Bastian nodded. "He's the guy we must take out. He's not the Big Kahuna of the entire Wehrmacht. It's Wolfgang König who's commanding the invasion of Earth. My doppelgänger. He's up there in the *Barbarossa*, beyond our reach for now. And even Wolfgang König isn't the top dog. It's his uncle, Dieter König, who commands the Wehrmacht from his bunker in Berlin. And higher still is Helmut König, Führer of the Third Reich. Both those men—the big cheeses—are back on the Fatherworld. Not even in our universe." Bastian cracked his knuckles. "We can't reach the real big names. Not yet. As much as I'd love to wring their necks, they're beyond our reach now. But General von Schweppenburg is down here on the ground. And killing him would deal the enemy a serious blow. To kill one of the enemy's generals! Ah, that would be something."

"I'll kill him myself," Spitfire said. "He's mine."

"This is a team effort, Spitfire," Bastian said.

She grinned and licked her teeth. "This is a competition.

And I intend to win."

While the two bickered (just like they would as children), King scrutinized the floating Nazi heads. One of the faces stood out. That one didn't have a wide jaw. His features were not the classic Aryan ideal. His face was long, gaunt, almost cadaverous, the nose like a vulture's beak. His eyes were the cruelest of them all. No name floated above him.

"Who's this one?" King rasped, pointing at the gruesome visage.

"—and just because I'm a pilot by trade"—Spitfire was saying—"that doesn't mean I can't fight in the vanguard with the marines, and it doesn't mean I can't be the one who kills General von Shitface, and—"

"Enough!" King said. "Spitfire, you can fight at the vanguard so long as you respect Bastian's command. It's his brigade. You join, you follow his orders."

Bastian gave her a smug look.

"Fine." Spitfire crossed her arms. "Even though I outrank him. I'm a commander, and he's a brigadier."

"Those are equivalent ranks, Spitfire," Bastian said. "A commander is just the fleet's version of a brigadier, so—"

"No, it's—" she began.

"Enough!" King said. "You both act like privates. And if you don't behave, I'll demote you both to that rank." King pointed again at the gaunt hallucination. "Bastian. Who's this? A name isn't appearing above him."

"Ah, yes." Bastian nodded. "That one. A real piece of work. We don't know his real name. The soldiers we interrogated called him *Onkel* Baer. Uncle Baer. One soldier called him the Angel in White. Maybe because he wears a white lab coat."

"Doesn't look like an angel to me," King said.

"He looks like Gargamel," Spitfire said.

King scratched his neck. It hurt again. "Bas, what do we know about him?"

"Not much," Bastian said. "But the German soldiers I talked to . . . they seemed scared of him."

King raised an eyebrow. "Scared of him? Of an old man in a lab coat?"

Bastian nodded and licked his lips nervously. "Yeah, it was real weird too. They would brag about their generals, but when it came to talking about *Onkel* Baer, they all got real quiet, as if he could hear them. As if he would hurt them. They all agreed he's in the Nazi high command. One of the top dogs. But nobody knew his rank or unit. Or even his full name. He's the personal doctor of the führer, they said."

"So why is this Angel in White here in our universe?" King said. "I thought the führer—my doppelgänger—is back at the Fatherworld."

Yes. My doppelgänger. Those words hurt to say. And not just because of his wounded neck. But the sooner they all accepted it the better.

"I don't know," Bastian said. "Given Baer's importance, he must be doing more than house visits. The soldiers we captured did mention something about . . ." He grimaced. "Experiments. Sick experiments he performs on children." A shudder ran through the beefy marine, clattering his body armor. "Whatever the case, he's a high-profile target. So I added him to our most-wanted list."

King nodded. "Understood. We'll get him too. Everyone—download these faces onto your MindLinks. Every man on this list is a dead man, and it's our job to kill them."

Spitfire cracked her knuckles and smiled wickedly. "I love my job."

Energy crackled through the room. Alice, who had

remained silent throughout the meeting, started going over battle plans with Bastian. They called in the battalion and company commanders and began ironing out fine details. Electric excitement filled the room. Eyes shone. Soldiers bounced on their heels. They were eager to smite their enemy.

But not King.

Spitfire might love her job, he thought. *But I don't.*

A great battle was coming. A battle more brutal than battles in space. A ground invasion. A battle in the crowded warren of a massive city. A battle among civilians.

King did not want to fight this battle. War was hell. And the deepest level of hell still lay ahead.

He looked across the room of officers toward Jordan. His old friend stared back, silent and solemn. Jordan understood.

"You can sit this one out, Jim," Jordan telepathized on a private channel. "You're not a marine."

"No, but I'm a soldier," King said. "We both are. Soldiers without a starship. Fallen angels. So we'll fight here in hell." He gave his friend a small, tight smile. "You *are* coming, aren't you?"

Jordan's eyes burned. "My daughter is in that hospital. In their headquarters. A hostage. There's no force in this universe that can keep me away."

CHAPTER SEVENTEEN
Angel of Death

The European Theater
Just outside London
Earth
September 10, 2207

They would not wait for reinforcements.

They would not let the enemy hunker down for long.

The Nazis wanted a blitzkrieg. A lightning war. So that was what they were going to get.

On a cold September night, the Freedom Brigade charged to war.

Lightning and Thunder, two legendary battalions, moved down the northeastern highway in the rain. Lightning's motto was *The Light of Victory.* Thunder's words were *The Sound of Freedom.* Once they had defended the prow and stern of the starship *Freedom.* Today they marched along cracked asphalt toward a bleak city in the shadows. They took some Rhinos and some mobile cannons, but most of them walked afoot. Two thousand men and women, all in battle armor. All carried Mordecai plasma rifles. They had lost brothers and sisters in Epping Forest, and they were raring for revenge.

Hailstorm and Typhoon, meanwhile, descended from the northwest like true calamities of nature. Hailstorm's motto? *With Furious Vengeance.* As for Typhoon? *We Are the Storm.* These two battalions used to board enemy starships and fight on alien worlds. Now they would bring their devastating firepower and merciless ambition to this evil from beyond the universe.

Finally there was Nova. The famous battalion. It was known by many other names. Katyusha's Bane. Spider Crushers. They were trained to leap from starships, jump through alien atmospheres, and deploy via dropship to the most dangerous locations in the universe. Their motto was *Death from Above*. And that was what King hoped to deliver to the Nazi scourge tonight.

He was an admiral, not a marine. But tonight he rode with Nova. Tonight James King was proud to fight alongside the homeless marines. The fallen angels of the starship *Freedom*. If you asked him, they were the finest warriors in two universes.

He stood in the Rhino's cabin as the machine rumbled forth. Standing room only tonight. Jordan and Spitfire stood at his sides. Like him, they were pilots by trade, but today they rode with the marines. Godwin had remained back at camp; a man in his eighties, he would not be fighting any ground wars. Kim remained behind with the high commander. She was an engineer, not a combat soldier. She would work on building energy shields for their makeshift camp.

Along with the three pilots stood fifty big, burly marines. At their lead stood Bastian and Alice. King swelled with pride to see his son and daughter-in-law standing tall, armed, and brave. He worried about them. He always worried about family at war. Whenever King would deploy Nova Battalion from the starship *Freedom*, whenever he sent his own son to war, the worry would eat him up. This time, at least, King stood here with his son. They would fight side by side.

The Rhinos rumbled across the charred landscape. They descended into artillery craters, rose again, and rumbled onward. Their engines roared. Clouds of dust, smoke, and disturbed umbrions rose behind them like a storm. Their treads crushed all in their path: boulders, abandoned guns, chunks of spider mechas, and skeletons picked clean by the crows.

Twenty of these metal monstrosities rumbled across the land. From stern to stem, each Rhino was a hundred feet long. They were the size of blue whales. Inside each awaited fifty marines in full battle armor, carrying plasma rifles, grenades, and the hopes of a world. They were dropships. Long ago, they had flown inside the starship *Freedom.* But like babies leaving their mother, they must learn to fend for themselves. And these were very large, very vicious babies.

Ahead rose the barricades the Wehrmacht had raised around London, forming some demonic doppelgänger of a defensive wall. Within only a week, the Nazis' arachnid mechas, the terrible spinnenmutters, had built this massive construction. The wall rose several stories tall, constructed from concrete chunks of buildings, crushed cars, and chunks of crashed starships. Corpses—thousands of corpses—lay mangled between these parts of metal and stone, rotting away, the mortar that held the wall together.

"Lucifer himself would be proud," King said, gazing upon the abomination.

Jordan sat beside him, face hard, eyes ablaze. His hands were tight around his rifle. "If Lucifer himself were here, I would consider him a saint compared to the monsters we face."

King knew what his friend was thinking. He knew the terror that lurked in the phantom's heart.

"We'll get Annie out," King told his friend. "You and I."

Jordan looked at him, but there was scant hope in his eyes. "She might be gone already."

"But she might still live!" King said. "For that hope I fight. To free Annie. To free millions of people in that city. To free billions of people on this world."

He realized his voice was unusually loud. Everyone in the Rhino cabin turned to look at him.

"Well?" Bastian said. "What else?"

"What do you mean?" King said.

"You always used to speak to us before battle," Bastian said. "Back on the *Freedom*. I thought this would be another inspiring speech. That was a bit short for a speech."

"I'm no longer your commander," King said.

"You are," Bastian said softly. "Always."

King looked at them. These brave soldiers who had once served under his command. Who still looked at him with loyalty.

A sudden passion seized King, and he spoke to them, the words just spilling out.

"Yes, we fight to save billions on this world. This is a world that has enjoyed freedom and prosperity for generations. A world that threw off the curse of Nazism over two centuries ago. Our enemy thinks us weak, decadent. And indeed, to them, coming from a brutal world, our Earth must seem soft. Like an overripe fruit that can be crushed in their fist. But there are hard men and women on this world. Warriors forged in the flames of war, hardened on the anvils of the rahs. Soldiers who fight to defend rather than exterminate the weak. Soldiers who fight to preserve freedom rather than crush it. Remember why we fight. Godspeed, soldiers of Earth."

Another speech before battle. To his soldiers. Just like old times.

As his last words still hung in the cabin, the Rhinos came within range of the barricades, and the enemy opened fire.

*****

Across the barricades of London, the Nazi guns boomed.

Machine guns rattled and cannons blazed. The barrage streaked toward the charging Rhinos. The firepower was mighty enough to destroy full warships.

Automatically, the Rhinos' point-defense systems kicked on. Laser beams blasted out, striking the incoming shells in midair. Warheads exploded a safe distance away, and explosions bloomed across the sky. But the lasers could not stop a hailstorm of bullets, and millions of rounds pounded the armored Rhinos, spilling umbrions. The tarry material splattered the Rhinos' hulls, dented and cracked the metal plates of armor, but could not break through. Even umbrions had their limits.

"Onward, soldiers!" Bastian cried, face flush with excitement. His smile was wide, savage, almost a snarl. "Onward to victory!"

"To victory!" cried the troops. Not only the fifty troops in this Rhino. But all five thousand across the brigade. With their MindLinks joined, they formed a hive intelligence, a single living organism that could break apart, crush its enemy between its pincers, and rejoin.

Nova Battalion, with her twenty Rhinos and a full thousand warriors, formed the central-assault force. But soon her sister battalions would join her from the flanks, and they would crush the Nazi menace between their claws.

Fearless, King thought. *We must be fearless.*

Yet still he felt that fear. He always did. He knew that men and women would die today. Soldiers he cared for. As if they were his own children. He knew that whether they won a victory or suffered a defeat, he would grieve. And like always, James King charged to battle nonetheless.

On the city barricades, the Wehrmacht artillery unleashed another barrage. Once more the Rhinos ignited their point-defense systems, and laser beams lit up the night, detonating shells in midair. But this time the enemy was wiser. While it bombarded the Rhinos, the Nazi war machine also fired shells toward the ground. Great craters bloomed open, scattering dirt, rocks, and umbrion clouds. One Rhino tilted into a crater and overturned. Another hit the brakes, etched lines across the ground, and tilted over. It teetered over a crater's ledge, then tumbled into the pit.

"Rhinos—rise!" Bastian cried.

Their engines roared.

Their exhaust ports blazed with fire.

The dropships rose from the ground, their treads dripping mud. And once more these big metal beasts took to the sky.

Each Rhino weighed hundreds of tons. Twenty of them soared, engines rumbling, thrusters blasting, flattening the ground below them. Dirt and rocks scattered, revealing buried roots, shrapnel, and corpses. The Rhinos charged across the sky, galloping over the clouds toward the city.

The artillery cannons rose. Booms shook the barricades as the great Nazi guns fired. One blast hit a Rhino in the underbelly. The hull broke open, and men burned inside. But the other Rhinos fired their lasers fast enough, and the shells exploded over the barricades, raining shrapnel down onto the gunners below. Hundreds of German riflemen raised their personal firearms, and they filled the sky with shrieking u-rounds, but they could not penetrate the armored hulls of *Freedom*'s orphaned dropships. Onward charged the nineteen Rhinos, entering the city, leaving a fallen brother behind.

"Make way to the hospital!" Bastian cried. "To St Mary's Hospital—charge!"

Onward they charged, onward over the barricades, onward over Buckhurst Hill down to the Woodford Green, onward into London, into the Nazis' nest of vipers. Onward to death or victory. To the Freedom Brigade, those were the only two options. Always had been. They would not flee. They would not surrender. They would win. Or they would die and with their corpses pave a path to victory for those who followed.

"To the hospital!" Bastian cried. "We're almost there. We're—"

His voice caught.

There from ahead, from the mists of Finsbury Park, they rose.

Spiders. Spiders the size of the London Eye. They were machines. Machines forged in the pits of the Fatherworld, born from the cauldrons of industry like true spiders hatching from underground eggs. Fifty or more rose from the city streets, unfurling their great metal legs. Their bodies hung above buildings, gazing with red eyes through the umbrionic clouds. Each of those spider legs was like a crane. Those slender, bladelike legs propelled the beasts over the city homes and streets. Then great engines erupted in their abdomens, and flames spurted from their underbellies, and up from London soared the mechanical spiders. The firelight glinted upon cockpits like bulbs of dew atop their abdomens. Inside each cockpit stood a pilot. A pilot with mechanical arms attached, turning them into tiny spiders controlling the huge metal suits.

Here were the spinnenmutters, nightmares from the mind of Dr. Anneliese. Like creatures from the closets of children, they emerged in the night to hunt. King had seen what these terrors could do. He had seen just one of these spinnenmutters destroy a hundred Chinese starfighters. Now fifty of those terrors flew in the night, red eyes blazing.

They were flying right at Nova Battalion.

"Take down those spiders!" Bastian shouted. "Rhinos—charge and fire!"

The Rhino cannons boomed.

The spiders answered with furious fire, their legs hurling umbrion spheres.

Shells slammed into arachnid exoskeletons. Swirling dark spheres slammed into Rhinos. The sky of London roiled.

Standing in the Rhino, King felt helpless. He was used to commanding starships in battle, to barking orders, to being in charge. Now all he could do was stand here in the Rhino's hold. One more marine. One more grunt. Over and over, blasts hit the Rhino, shaking everyone inside, rattling the bones within his old body. Fire blazed, and then the umbrionic darkness covered the world, and King saw only blackness.

* * * * *

Standing by the window in St Mary's Hospital, Stowy watched the strange battle in the sky of London.

The spinnenmutters had risen. She had seen such terrors during her years in Munich. At night, the mechanical spiders would crawl from underground, unfolding their long limbs, and walk across the city, their slender legs gracefully stepping over buildings, their motors like distant, rolling thunder. Stowy would hide as their red eyes scanned the alleyways, searching for thieves, homeless, and cripples like her. Now these arachnid machines were here. Here in London. Here in this strange dimension.

The Nazis called this world Unreineland. The impure land. A shadow of Earth in another universe.

And in the shadows, the monsters of the impure world rose to fight. Great, mechanical beasts rumbled across the sky, firing missiles at the spiders. Drills topped their prows like horns. To Stowy, they seemed like triceratops—a great herd of triceratops rumbling across the clouds. On their armored flanks, they wore stars and stripes—the symbol of the subhuman Amis.

I see spiders and dinosaurs in the clouds, but no castle, Stowy thought.

She had dreamed so often of another world. Of a glittering castle of marble on clouds of cotton candy. That dream had died. She had been transported to another world. Like she had always wanted. Yet she found bloodshed and monsters, and here again, she was trapped in a hospital. Trapped in a vulture's talons. Was there truly a world out here for her, a world beyond the battles? A world where she could speak freely, where she could be like other children? Or would the spinnenmutters weave their webs across the impure land, and Unreineland would be purified?

She blinked tears from her eyes, watching the battle. She had always loved dinosaurs. Whenever the anxiety pounded through her chest, whenever she trembled and hyperventilated, whenever she thought she would die from fear—she would pull her plastic dinosaurs from her pockets. She would line them up, snout to tail, and the anxiety would fade. She would bring order in a chaotic world, creating neat lines in a world that spun around her like webs. She would be with big, powerful creatures that no doctors could hurt.

And there, outside in the storm—dinosaurs.

Dinosaurs with drills on their snouts. Dinosaurs with Amis inside. Dinosaurs flying in a neat line, tail to snout.

Her tears fell. Of course there was hope here. Of course this was a good world. This was a world of dinosaurs. A world of impure little children like her. This was *her* world. She had, perhaps, not been born or raised here. But this was her home.

Dr. Baer's long, knobby fingers draped across her shoulder. He stood behind her, and his reflection materialized in the dark window. He loomed, towering and hunched over, his eyes like black holes sucking up all light and hope.

"Now, little Stowy, I have a surprise for you today. You are old enough now. I want you to meet your sisters."

She blinked up at him, then quickly looked at her toes again. "My sisters?"

"They're most eager to meet you. Their lives are sad, lonely affairs, though I do try to brighten their days with chocolates and marzipans. Meeting you will be the sweetest treat for them."

Stowy wanted to remain at the window, to watch the battle. How she yearned for those dinosaurs to crush the spiders, gallop down from the clouds, and save her from this vulture! Yet Baer had her in his talons. A vulture in a bear's fur. Gripping her shoulder, he led her out of his office.

They walked through the halls of St Mary's Hospital. For four days now, the hospital had been under the control of the Schutzstaffel.

The SS. Hitler's finest. The great institution that ran the Fatherworld. The Wehrmacht fought, died, and killed on the battlefield. Wehrmacht warriors flew starships, controlled giant spiders, and could destroy cities. But Stowy feared the SS more. The Wehrmacht was cruel, but the SS was sadistic. The Wehrmacht was coldly efficient, while the SS luxuriated in pain. The Wehrmacht had never hurt Stowy, while the SS had never stopped hurting her.

The Schutzstaffel had many branches. The Waffen-SS, under the command of Eva König, was the combat branch, enforcing the will of the organization with brute force and ruthlessness. The Gestapo hunted and tortured little children on the streets. Sometimes it killed their parents too. Or hung their grandmothers from a crane. And then there was the Totenkopfverbände. The Death's Head Unit. In this unit did Dr.

Rudolph Baer serve. It was this unit's symbol—a skull over two bones—that adorned his lapels.

Today, as they walked down the halls, Stowy saw many other officers with the steel skull and bones. Baer had chosen to wear his lab coat today, but the others wore long, dark coats and military caps, and guns hung at their sides. They were not doctors like him. These big, hulking men were just bodyguards. Brutes to enforce the good doctor's will. Back in Munich, there had been many doctors and nurses in the Totenkopfverbände. They had remained behind in the Fatherworld. Here, in this mirror world, in this new hospital, Baer reigned supreme.

As he led Stowy down the hall, she glanced into hospital rooms. And for the first time in her life, Stowy saw subhumans. Real subhumans. Like the ones she had learned about at school.

In her classroom, some subhumans were depicted as wild beasts, wearing furs, grooming one another in a forest. More like monkeys than humans. Others were depicted as greedy, nefarious bankers with long noses, rubbing their hands together as they connived. Those ones were more like goblins than humans. Yet when Stowy looked into the hospital rooms, the subhumans were nothing like that. Some had dark skin, yes. Most didn't have blue eyes or blond hair. But otherwise, well—what a disappointment! She had expected bizarre swamp creatures and ogres and goblins. Creatures who were frightening yet also fascinating, creatures who could take her back to their treetop realms or deep caves glittering with gold, where they would teach her spells and magical transformations. But Stowy found only . . . people. Just scared people. Doctors, nurses, patients. A little darker, a little smaller than Aryans. But just people.

"Please!" a patient said, rushing out into the hall. "Please, sir!"

Stowy looked at her. A woman with brown skin. With frightened eyes. She wore a hospital gown, and a tube ran from her wrist to an IV stick. She was speaking English, which Stowy spoke well. Her parents had taught her the old, forbidden language.

"Please, sir." The brown-skinned patient knelt before Dr. Baer. "Please let us go. Please don't experiment on me. I beg you."

Dr. Baer stood still, gazing down upon the begging woman. Stowy glanced into a nearby hospital room. Yesterday's "experiment" still lay on one of the beds. An SS guard stood in the room, making sure nobody tampered with the grotesque remains.

"Please, sir," the woman begged. "Please don't cut me open. Please don't—"

Dr. Baer drew his pistol. He put a bullet through her forehead.

Blood splattered the hallway. The woman collapsed.

Stowy started. She couldn't breathe. Couldn't look away. Her heart pounded against her ribs like a bird trying to escape a cage. Everything spun around her, and blackness floated like clouds of umbrions, leaving Stowy with tunnel vision. Her legs trembled so badly she could barely stand.

Dr. Baer leaned toward the corpse and spoke loudly in heavily accented English. "Wish granted, my dear!"

Then he grabbed Stowy, pulled her around the corpse, and dragged her down the corridor. And Stowy knew that the dead woman was lucky. And that in time, Stowy would envy her.

* * * * *

They walked onward through the hospital, heading by more doorways, more rooms with "experiments." Dr. Baer had only been here for a few days, but already the gangly doctor was giddy from all these new subhumans to torture. He was like a vulture who had found a pile of rotten carcasses ripe with maggots, a feast awaiting his ripping talons and ravenous gullet.

A few doors down, another woman stepped out from a room.

This woman was not a patient. She wore a white lab coat, and a stethoscope hung around her neck. A doctor? Could it be? Yet her skin was dark. Her hair was black and curly. She was what the Totenkopfverbände would deem a subhuman. A creature who should be living in the jungle, dancing naked with wild beasts.

But those stories were lies, Stowy thought. *This world isn't what they told us.*

She read the woman's name tag. DR. ANNIE JORDAN.

The woman walked confidently, chin raised, then halted in the middle of the hallway, blocking Baer's passage. Her eyes flicked toward the corpse in the hallway, the blood on the tiles. Fear filled those dark eyes, eyes that were so offensive to the Aryan ideal. But an instant later, strength drove back the fear, and the doctor's eyes shone with determination.

She's brave like a soldier, Stowy thought. *Maybe even like a dinosaur. I wish I could be that strong.*

"Excuse me, *Dr.* Baer," the woman said, draping the title with a good dose of cynicism. "But if you're done murdering patients for today, would you release my anesthesiologist from your little holding cell in the basement? I have surgeries to perform and they cannot wait."

No, Stowy realized. *No, she's not brave. She's terrified.*

The fear was still there in the woman's dark eyes. She was pretending to be strong. Putting on a show. Stowy saw her fingers trembling, saw Dr. Annie stuff them into her pockets.

Annie looked at her. And for a brief second, woman and girl made eye contact. Fresh fear filled Annie's eyes. Not for herself or for her patients. But for Stowy.

She's terrified that Baer is hurting me, Stowy realized. *She wants to help. But she can't.*

It was a funny thing. They said autistic children could not read body language, facial expressions, or emotions. They said these broken children were like robots. Yet Stowy could read all of that in just one glance.

Then Stowy lowered her gaze and stared at her feet. After all, she was still autistic, and eye contact hurt like raptor claws to your eyeballs. Even eye contact from a friend.

"Ah, here she is again," said Dr. Baer. "The famous American doctor Annie Jones." He stepped closer to her, sniffing like a predator debating whether to pounce, more curious now than hungry. His long, narrow nostrils flared. "You smell of blood, antibiotics, and fear."

She raised her chin and stared into his eyes. "Dr. Baer, I have a patient whose heart is about to stop. I need to perform surgery. Or he'll die. Send me back my anesthesiologist."

Dr. Baer narrowed his eyes and tilted his head. "Your patient, Dr. Jordan. Is he an Aryan?"

Dr. Annie's eyes flashed. She sucked in air between her teeth, forcefully composing herself.

"No. No, Doctor, I would not say he is."

Baer snorted and waved his hand dismissively. "Then skip the anesthesia. I always do with subhumans. Why waste it on animals?"

Annie seemed about to shout, maybe to weep, maybe to flee in terror. Great emotions strained her face, and her eyes dampened. But again she composed herself.

"I have Aryan patients too," she said. "This is a busy hospital. We need all our staff. Especially with all the wounded coming in. Some of those wounded will be German soldiers,

Doctor. *Your* soldiers."

Again he snorted. "Ah! The Wehrmacht. Boorish peasants who can barely tell the difference between a Lugerheulen trigger and a cow's udder. Cannon fodder is all they are. Let them suffer the sting of the scalpel's kiss. Your anesthesiologist dared criticize my medical practices."

"He heard the screams and was concerned!" Annie said.

"What sounds come from my surgical rooms are not his concern, nor yours," Baer said. "Do you have children, Dr. Jordan?"

She raised her chin. "That is none of *your* concern."

"Oh, I think it is, Dr. Jordan. Tell me, would you like to keep your womb? It is one of my favorite organs to collect. I have quite a few in jars. Trophies, if you will. Cross me, Doctor, and I will add yours to my collection."

She blinked. Her lips trembled. "You don't intimidate me."

"Your trembling would suggest otherwise. Your anesthesiologist is now undergoing some experimentation of his own. Tomorrow you may have what's left of him." He leaned toward the younger doctor, brought his lips close to her ear, and sneered. "You are only alive, Dr. Annie Jones, because I need doctors. But do not tempt me. Push me too far, and I would be happy to put a bullet in your head too."

With that, he walked by her, pulling Stowy along. As she stumbled by, Stowy glanced toward Dr. Annie. Again they made brief eye contact.

"Help me," Stowy mouthed silently. In English.

Then Dr. Baer yanked her along, moving quickly on his long birdlike legs. Stowy dragged behind him, his talons in her shoulder. If she resisted, if she threw a fit, if she tossed herself onto the floor and kicked and screamed, she knew what would happen. Bullet to the brain. Bang!

Maybe that was the easy way out. Maybe it was better to die quickly. Not to become an experiment. Some experiments could live for months, they said. Even for *years*. Wouldn't it be better to fight him? To scream, bite his arm, claw that long gray face of his, and end it all with a bullet?

But she could not. Because even here, even in this hospital of nightmares, even the pet of this monster, a light burned deep inside Stowy. A light that remembered the forbidden books in Father's library. A light that remembered a mother's embrace. A light that she saw reflected in Dr. Annie's eyes for just the briefest of moments. That light was hope. Hope that there was still goodness in humanity. That even in a world of utter darkness, hatred, and torture, there could someday be found love.

They descended to the ground floor. Things were far more chaotic here. Patients were flooding the emergency room. Thousands and thousands of them. Most were Wehrmacht soldiers, savaged by Unreineland's forces. But many were civilians of London too, coming to their neighborhood hospital for aid, risking the Nazi occupation for a chance at healing. Their skin was burned and hung in blistering sheets. Shrapnel had cut their flesh. Some were missing fingers or feet. Some were missing limbs. A few were missing faces. Battle raged outside, shells exploded, and gunfire rattled. The meat grinder of war was at work, and into the hospital poured the mangled mince.

The stench, the screams, the bright lights—it all spun Stowy's head. She clung to Uncle Baer. In her terror, she sought comfort even from him. All her life, Stowy had hated loud noises, crowds, and bright lights. Hated too much stimulus. It was a symptom of her autism, they had told her. Her brain enhanced every sound, sight, and smell. When too much stimulus hit her, it overwhelmed her brain. She was dizzy now. Not only because of all the stimulus. But because of all this suffering. They said autistics felt no empathy, yet Stowy wept for these wounded souls.

An SS officer rushed toward Dr. Baer and snapped a salute. The young officer sported a steel skull and bones on his military cap. Like Baer, this pale young man served in the Totenkopfverbände, the sadistic unit of SS torturers and hangmen. Every Nazi was a sadist, but only the most depraved joined the SS. And within the SS, the most sadistic—monsters among monsters—joined the Totenkopfverbände. The cannibals, the torturers, the mutilators, those who craved to inflict not only death but sublime suffering—this unit was their home.

"Hauptsturmführer Baer!" the young officer said. "The city people have been flooding the hospital along with our soldiers. We weren't sure what you wanted to do with them. Should we turn them away? Save them for you perhaps? Or . . ."

Dr. Baer looked across the room, taking in the crowds of wounded. He sucked his teeth, considering, then nodded.

"Get the local doctors to treat our soldiers," he said. "Shoot the subhuman patients."

"Yes, Hauptsturmführer." The young officer raised his open hand. "Hail Hitler!"

Baer returned the Nazi salute. "Hail Hitler."

SS officers began moving between the patients. They drew their pistols. As Baer pulled Stowy toward a corridor, gunshots rang out. Stowy screwed her eyes shut, trembling as she walked. Her head spun, and every *bang* of a pistol made her start.

Bang! Bullet to the brain. A mercy.

She did not look back. Did not want to see this. She had never forgotten the sight of Dr. Baer opening his gas chamber, of the little dead children spilling out, skin gray, eyes glassy. She did not need more haunting memories.

As he led her down a hallway, Stowy noticed something peculiar. SS officers were bustling about, concentrating around pillars and concrete walls. Stowy frowned and stared more closely.

A gasp fled her lips. Explosives! They were attaching explosives to the building's foundations! She recognized the bombs and the wires they ran across the walls.

Dr. Baer heard her little gasp. He looked down at her and smiled. "Yes, little mouse. They're wiring up the hospital with enough explosives to level the entire neighborhood. But don't worry. This is only a precaution. In case the enemy breaks in." He stroked her hair. "We won't let the Amis hurt you, little mouse. Of course not. If they take this city, if they break in . . . we will bring the building down atop them!"

Bang! A bomb. A building on your head. Quick too. Stowy wondered which would kill her. A bullet? A bomb? Anything seemed preferable to Baer's surgery room.

Suddenly tears were flowing down her cheeks. Deep down, she had dared to hope. That the American army would reach the hospital. That the triceratops ships would defeat the mechanical spiders. That the Amis would save her.

But now she knew that was impossible. Dr. Baer would never let it happen. If the Amis entered this hospital . . . Only death awaited. For them and for her.

* * * * *

Finally Baer took her into the basement of St Mary's Hospital. The lowest level of hell. It was underground that he kept his personal laboratory, the place where he performed his most gruesome experiments. It was strange. As if Dr. Baer wanted to keep his secrets hidden, buried. As if some part of him, despite all his atrocities, remained ashamed. Stowy believed in the light of the soul. And she knew Dr. Baer had none. There was nothing but malice inside that vulture. No compassion. No goodness. No soul at all. In his work, he obsessed over purity. Obsessed over creating the purest Aryan. And the only purity he achieved was the utter purity of his evil. There was no blemish to it, no crack in its facade, no path to redemption. Nothing but distilled wickedness, purer than the blackness between the stars.

And yet . . . Yes, a part of him must be ashamed, for he kept his deepest secrets, his foulest crimes, in the dark. Stowy did not have an intuitive understanding of human behavior. As an autistic girl, it all seemed alien to her. So she had spent her life analyzing others, learning how to interpret their glances, their movements, the words they didn't speak, and how to piece together these clues into a language. This man, eager as he was to deform and torture, was deeply, deeply ashamed.

That is what drives him, Stowy realized. His shame. On the surface, he must kill all those who knew his secret. Or he must convince them his little experiments were for science or the Aryan race. But here underground, in this strange shadow world, Stowy realized the truth. His crimes had become an obsession. A desire like lust. An addiction almost sexual in its depravity. Something that ate him up inside, and so he had built his hospitals around that throbbing black desire inside him, turning his shame into a temple. Purifying it.

Deeper they plunged. Down a dark staircase he took her. Stowy must walk in front. Baer loomed ever behind, his fingers gripping her shoulders. His shadow stretched across the staircase wall, seeming to swoop over Stowy like some vampire thirsty for blood. The stairs plunged into Stygian darkness. Rumbles, gurgles, and the laughter of little girls sounded below. Stowy froze. She wanted to turn away. To run back upstairs. Even the emergency room with all the corpses was preferable. Something lay down there in the pit. What devil lurked there she did not know. But she knew *something* was down there. Something wicked. The malevolence oozed.

He turned this hospital into his brain, Stowy thought. That was what St Mary's had become. The brain of a madman. In the upper floors, where his office nestled between the operating rooms—that was part of his brain. His cerebral cortex perhaps. The part that controlled logic, ambition, and knowledge of medicine. On the ground floor, the emergency room where his soldiers had shot patients—that too was his brain. An older, primordial brain. The reptilian brain. The part that controlled violence, fear, aggression. Bloodshed. Now they traveled deeper still. Traveled into the basement. The abyss. His subconscious. And in here . . . Oh, down here the demons came to play. This place defined him more than anything built atop it. Above? Oh, those were only sprinkles on the cake. Down here was the little, rotten corpse of a rat hidden within the layers of dough and icing.

They reached the basement door. A blast door. Like those in bomb shelters. It was built of green metal, crude like the hatch of a tank. Baer grabbed the winch and turned, and the door creaked open.

Darkness lurked beyond. A distant giggle sounded from the murk. Then a pattering of feet. Somebody was whispering in the basement. It sounded like a little girl, but then she fell silent. Nothing. Only silence.

Baer stuck his head into the basement.

"Oh little girls!" he said in a singsong voice.

Whispers sounded from the darkness, speaking in German.

"Is it you, *Onkel* Baer?"

"Did you bring us chocolate?"

"Did you bring us marzipan?"

"Did you bring *her*?"

Stowy trembled. She wanted to run, to flee this place and never return. Even if death awaited above, she must run! There were fates in this world worse than death, and there were worlds beyond this life. Yet his hands—his *talons*—gripped her more tightly.

"She's here," the vulture said. "I brought her to you. It's finally time that you meet her."

His talons released her, and he shoved her into the dark basement. She stumbled a few steps into the darkness. The floor was cold and sticky beneath her bare feet. Dr. Baer tapped a switch, and fluorescent lights flared to sudden, blinding life.

Stowy squinted and covered her eyes.

Voices screeched.

Between her fingers, Stowy glimpsed figures in the basement. Pale figures with sallow skin and red eyes. The size of humans. But not humans. They scattered like cockroaches, disappearing behind furniture, inside a closet, under a bed.

Stowy rubbed her eyes, trying to adjust to the brightness. She beheld a large, stark room. It seemed to serve multiple purposes. A crude, old kitchen lined one wall, covered with soap scum and mineral deposits, its green linoleum counters cracked. By another wall stood an operating table, and bloody tools hung above it from strings. Not just surgical tools but wrenches and hammers too. In the back of the room were several cages, stacked up, with bowls of food and water inside. The barred doors were open. The cages were empty. There was a bed too, neatly made, the sheets folded with military efficiency—the only neat part of the room.

"Come out, come out, little *kinder*!" Uncle Baer said in his singsong voice.

Silence.

Not even a breath.

Had Stowy imagined those creatures? Imagined those

voices?

Then she saw it. A thin, knobby finger with jaundiced skin and a broken fingernail. The digit was sticking out from a cabinet, securing the door shut.

There's a creature inside, Stowy thought, her heart stopping in her chest.

Finally a voice sounded, timid and girlish. It seemed to be coming from under the bed. "Is that her?"

Another voice spoke, this one from under the sink. "Is that our sister?"

A third voice—from the cabinet. "She's not like us."

"No," said Uncle Baer. "But she will be. Oh, she will be. Come out and meet her. After all, you are her clones."

Creaking and clattering, they emerged from hiding.

The kitchen cabinet opened. Out crawled the jaundiced girl. Yes, a girl, not a creature. A human! And yet . . . not quite a human. She had eight limbs like a spider. Two legs. Six arms with six slender hands, and the fingers were unusually long. Fingers almost like spider legs. Spinnenmutter operators had eight limbs, but four were prosthetic; this girl had eight actual limbs!

From under the bed clattered another girl. Stitches ran down her middle—from the skull all the way to the groin. As if somebody had cut her in two, then stitched her back together. One-half was facing forward, the other backward.

From behind rusty cages came a girl with organs that pulsed on the outside of her body. The heart beat, red and bright, enveloped only in a thin membrane of translucent skin.

Others came too, each more bizarre than the last, each mutated in a different way. But one thing they all had in common.

They each had Stowy's face.

And she could not help it.

She screamed.

CHAPTER EIGHTEEN
Angel of Life

London
Earth
September 11, 2207

Dawn rose, seeping through clouds with light like molten gold and the promise of a new day. For a brief moment, the sunrise reminded King of mornings on his patio back home. He would drag his old bones into the rocking chair, nurse a cup of black coffee, and read the newspaper. A real newspaper, with rustling papers and everything. Like they used to make 'em. He had to get it delivered from five states away, but it was worth it. He could almost hear the birds and the rustling fields.

But then reality came rushing back. This dawn did not illuminate the idyllic countryside of Nebraska. This morning dawned on war.

London lay in ruin. The war had begun only eleven days ago. Not even a fortnight. Hard to believe. It felt like years. Only eleven days of the blitzkrieg—and everything had changed. London might never be the same.

King was flying one of the Rhinos. During the night, an enemy shell had slammed into the transporter's prow, instantly killing both pilot and copilot. Miraculously, the controls still worked (sort of). And King, a seasoned pilot, was in the cockpit, flying the damaged machine. Jordan and Spitfire sat beside him (being fellow pilots, they did quite a bit of backseat driving). Bastian, meanwhile, was still standing in the hold with fifty other marines. The poor bastards had been standing all night, waiting for a chance to deploy.

King looked over the ruined landscapes below. It was a sorry sight. The blitz had devastated the city. For ten days, the Nazis had been bombarding London, desperate to overwhelm and crush the Alliance resistance. Holes peppered Big Ben, and an artillery shell was lodged halfway into the clock face. The tableau reminded King of 1902's *A Trip to the Moon.* The London Eye had fallen and lay across the city streets. London Bridge had fallen down as in the old nursery rhyme. Everywhere King looked, he saw the destruction. The bombed apartment blocks. The smoldering piles of rubble. The swastikas that still draped Buckingham Palace and the Tower of London. The despair.

But he was still fighting.

He was still inside a Rhino. Still flying with the Freedom Brigade. For hours, they brawled across the sky, fighting for every mile, beating back the spiders. Steadily, blast by blast, they moved toward the enemy stronghold. Not a fortress or castle. Not Parliament Hill or Buckingham or any palace. No. The Nazis had set up their command post in a hospital. These brave warriors from another universe—they hid behind women and children. St Mary's Hospital was the prize the Freedom Brigade must capture. That was the hill upon which they must plant the flag of freedom. Or the hill upon which they must die.

They were almost there.

Most of the spinnenmutters had fallen during the night. The spider mechas lay across the rubble. Curious Londoners, emboldened by dawn's early light, emerged from underground to climb atop these dead metal spiders the size of starships. Children played among broken metal legs, and some even climbed into the cockpits. A few intrepid teenagers were brave enough to pull out the dead German pilots, but when they tried to operate the mechas, only sparks emerged from the machinery.

A few Rhinos lay below too. In their fall from the sky, they had crushed buildings and shattered streets. The spiders had knocked them down in the night. Some of the marines inside had survived the fall. Armor battered, bodies bruised and aching, they had joined other infantry battalions and continued to fight on the ground. But only some. Many good marines had died. Too many. Both inside Rhinos and along the streets—they fell. Throughout the night, over three hundred warriors of the Freedom Brigade gave their lives.

The survivors fought onward through the morning.

The infantry brigades plowed along the streets. They took heavy sniper fire. They took assaults from cannons and machine guns. Their armor absorbed some of the barrage. But not all, and more fell for every block claimed. Onward they marched, fighting for every step. Shooting back with plasma, with grenades, with artillery shells. Where the Freedom Brigade marched, the streets crumbled. They left rubble in their wake.

King hoped there were no civilians in those buildings. From what he could tell, most Londoners had fled into the ancient tunnels of the Old Tube. They had sought shelter there during the Second World War centuries ago, and now they were sheltering there again. Yet whenever the shells flew, whenever buildings fell, King worried. He did not know if any civilians were buried beneath the rubble. He would gladly sacrifice his own life to win this war. Sacrificing other lives was a different matter. That had always been the great burden of command. As musicians played with notes, as artists played with hues and tones, as poets played with words, soldiers played with life and death. Their brushes were bombs and bullets. Their trumpets were the cannons that boomed. And this city had become a masterpiece of their deadly art.

As the infantry kept fighting on the streets, the surviving Rhinos kept flying. The rubble and clouds of dust parted below, and looking down from the Rhino, King saw London Zoo. In the chaos of crumbling towers, the zoo was among the safest spots in the city. He hoped the animals survived.

The hospital was close now. Just beyond Regent's Park, the Sherlock Holmes museum, and the cricket grounds. King could see the building in the distance.

A spinnenmutter was guarding it.

Only one spinnenmutter remained standing in London. A mother spider. She was the largest of her hideous family—a machine that could engulf Wembley Stadium within her legs. Blazing red swastikas adorned her black hull, and her engine churned within her abdomen, bathing the ruins with heat, melting metal and stone. In the mecha's cockpit stood a woman. She was a tiny figure within the gargantuan machine. Like an ant riding on a tarantula's head.

Standing in the Rhino cockpit, King raised his binoculars. He gazed across the park and rubble toward the spinnenmutter, zooming in on the cockpit.

He saw the face of his wife. The most beautiful face in the world. Yet this was not Kim. Here again rose Dr. Anneliese, and her evil had transformed her fair face into a demonic visage. Her eyes narrowed, both the bionic and real one, and her lips—so similar to those lips King would kiss!—parted in a wicked grin.

"Hello again, my shadow husband!" she cried, voice thundering over the ruins.

Jordan sat in the copilot's seat beside King. His eyes widened. "She does look like Kim."

King nodded. "A doppelgänger of my wife."

Again he felt Anneliese's knife sinking into his thigh. The

wound flared with icy pain.

Bastian peeked into the cockpit. "Dad! I recommend we deploy Star Vipers Company onto the street outside the hospital, then land with Wolverines Company onto the roof, and—" He frowned at the spinnenmutter ahead and raised his binoculars. "Is that Kim in there?"

"Her doppelgänger," Spitfire said. She sat in the gunner seat, feet up on the dashboard, arms crossed. "Try to keep up."

King looked at his son. "I suggest we deploy our Rhino marines in Regent's Park. It's two, maybe three klicks from the hospital. You can lead the marines down the streets. I'll stay in the Rhino. And fight that spider from the air."

Bastian glanced out the porthole. "Those streets aren't exactly safe. They're still crawling with Nazis between here and the hospital. Even a mile is a long way in a battle. We might be safer staying in the Rhinos while you fight the mecha."

"You won't be," King said, never removing his eyes from Dr. Anneliese. She stood across the park, staring from the distant haze, waiting inside her spinnenmutter. "I'm dropping you and the marines off in the park. You'll have to hoof it from here. Then we pilots—we'll take on the spider."

Reluctantly, the big brigadier agreed. In a way, it went against Freedom Brigade doctrine. Rhinos were designed to be the safest spots for a marine on the battlefield. The Rhinos carried the marines to their target, withstanding the enemy shelling. To drop off marines here into the viper's nest? To let them proceed afoot through the Nazi meat grinder? Yes, King understood Bastian's fear.

But King feared that spider more.

So, reluctantly, the Rhinos descended toward Regent's Park. They had softened the area with aerial and artillery bombardment, but many enemies still lurked within the ruins, and they had dug tranches across the park. King knew he was deploying his troops into danger. For a moment, he hesitated, wanted to keep flying with his men in the Rhino, to carry them while he battled Dr. Anneliese in the air. But he remembered the fire in her eyes. Remembered that wicked smile. She was the greater devil. The park was dangerous, yes, but the Rhinos would soon become deathtraps.

The bulky dropships landed in the scorched park. No trees or grass remained. All was charred black, strewn with mangled metal. Hundreds, maybe thousands of corpses covered the field—dead Tommies. Some had been lying here since the first day of the war. The stench of rot filled the air.

To intimidate the American brigade, the Nazi enemy had beheaded many of the British soldiers. The severed heads now leered atop spikes, swastikas carved into their foreheads. Graffiti marred a decapitated statue of Queen Emily: *WE KILLED THE TOMMIES, NOW WE KILL THE AMIS!* Barbed wire and caltrops covered the ground. Possibly mines too. Yes, it was with a heavy heart that King deployed his troops onto this field of death. It was with icy terror that he watched Bastian and his troops leap from the Rhino, let out battle cries, and charge.

That day, the Freedom Brigade charged courageously into the enemy fire. A thousand warriors of Nova Battalion ran, shouting for victory, as the enemy bullets bombarded them. As men fell, as limbs tore free, as blood drenched the field, they charged onward. And soon the other battalions joined them, racing into the fire, running over their dead. There in Regent's Park, over the corpses of heroes, the American and German infantries slammed together with flame and plasma and umbrionic darkness.

King wished none of his soldiers were down there. Let alone his son. If they must fight there, he wished he could be fighting at their side.

Yet James King was not a marine. He was a pilot. Always had been. Even now. His war was in the sky.

As the marines battled on the field, the Rhinos took flight again. They flew toward the last remaining spinnenmutter.

*****

With spinning drills and roaring engines, the Rhinos charged to war. Huffing and puffing smoke, grunting in mechanical rage, they indeed resembled rhinoceroses stampeding across the Serengeti. The Freedom Brigade had rolled into London with thirty of the cantankerous dropships. Half had fallen and lay shattered upon the rubble. The survivors flew onward toward St Mary's Hospital.

Guarding the hospital? The terrible spinnenmutter. A machine like a spider goddess, towering, waiting for them. Rhinos? They were mere horned beetles. And she was a venomous spider queen.

The mechanical spider began to move. Her legs thundered across the park, crushing soldiers, leaving deep pits. The terrible machine lunged into the air, roaring toward the approaching Rhino ships.

And the Rhinos flew to meet her.

Maybe we can't beat her, King thought. *But we can give the marines time. We can keep her off their backs.*

He gripped the Rhino's yoke. It rattled in his hands as the engines rumbled. Good. He liked to *feel* a ship he operated. To let a ship become a part of him. That was what modern AI navigational systems didn't understand. That flying wasn't just about coordinates and vectors and velocities. It was about expanding your consciousness throughout a machine, moving its parts like you moved your own limbs. In a way, it was almost like operating a mecha.

He was flying one of fifteen remaining Rhinos. Spitfire still shared the cockpit; she was manning the gunnery controls. Jordan, a seasoned pilot, had gone to fly another Rhino, relieving its wounded (and exhausted) pilot. The two old friends, two starfighter pilots by trade, flew side by side again. With them flew a few more Rhinos. A nice little herd of thick metal and fury.

King reached the spinnenmutter first.

Dr. Anneliese glared from the cockpit, eyes aglow. She swung three arms. And three spider legs the size of city blocks swung toward King.

He swerved. From the gunnery seat, Spitfire opened fire. A spider leg swung above. Another below. Then more legs were lashing, and King kept swerving around them, barely dodging them. It was much harder in a Rhino. In a starfighter? No problem. Give him an Eagle, and King would be flying rings around the spinnenmutter. But a Rhino was significantly larger and slower. It was the difference between driving a sports car and a semitrailer.

A spider leg slammed into the stern.

The Rhino rumbled through the air.

Spitfire fired again. The Rhino's machine guns spun and roared. Bullets pounded the spinnenmutter, for all the damn good it did. Might as well be shooting spitballs.

"Fire shells at it!" King said.

"We don't have many left," Spitfire said. "I need a good shot at a joint. To make it count."

King swerved around another swinging leg. "I'll try to get you a clear shot."

Meanwhile, the other Rhinos were attacking the spider too. Their bullets and shells pounded Anneliese's mecha. But this spinnenmutter was larger, more sophisticated than the others. This was an improved model. The mecha's hull shone with an iridescent glow whenever munitions hit. It seemed to be some kind of force field. It reminded King of a soap bubble, though it molded itself along the spider's form like gleaming skin.

Dr. Anneliese's voice boomed from speakers on the spider's hull. Her voice rolled across the sky.

"You cannot beat me, James King! You are only a doppelgänger. A weak, impure clone of a real man."

Spitfire glanced at him. "Ooh, she burned you!"

"Focus on shooting," King said. "There's your shot!"

He yawed and pitched his Rhino, bringing the cannons to bear on a joint in the spider's leg. From her cockpit, Anneliese stared across the distance. Her blue eye was wide and fierce and seemed to shine almost as brightly as her bionic eye. Even through the storm of battle, that distant blue eye caught the light, blazed like a neutron star, and pierced King. That eye knew him. Mocked him! She smiled crookedly and blew him a kiss.

Then Spitfire pulled her triggers, and two shells flew toward the spinnenmutter and detonated.

Again the force field flared, enveloping the spider like a second exoskeleton. The shells exploded, knocking the mecha back. But the translucent shield absorbed most of the blow. The spider wobbled but righted herself. Anneliese laughed in the cockpit.

"Pathetic weapons, you Unreinelanders built! And you are a pathetic man, James King."

She swung her arms, and spider legs the length of city streets lashed toward the Rhino. King swerved around most of them. But the armored dropship just wasn't fast enough. One leg slammed into the hull, and the Rhino spun through the air, rattling King and Spitfire in their seats. The seat belt dug into King's chest, bruising the skin.

He wrestled the yoke, managing to steady his flight. Just then, one of the spinnenmutter's legs fired a stream of umbrions. The dark torrent washed over the Rhino, sucking the heat from the cabin. The engines moaned and the Rhino dipped in the sky, losing heat, losing power. In the darkness, King could no longer see Anneliese, but he heard her voice tearing across the sky.

"My husband, the führer, is a strong man. A real man! An Übermensch. He conquers worlds. While you fly around in a tin can with a subhuman."

King growled, gave his Rhino a blast of afterburner, and the engines roared with new life. The dropship soared from the dark cloud, shedding its umbrion cloak. He faced Anneliese again. She gazed from her cockpit, eyes blazing with mockery.

"You are a mouse, and I'm the cat who will devour you. Soon I, a woman, will crush you. You're not even worthy of being killed by a man. You're a—"

Spitfire fired the Rhino's machine guns. Plasma bolts slammed into the spinnenmutter's speakers, silencing Dr. Anneliese.

"Thank you," King said.

"Couldn't stand her yammering anymore," Spitfire said. "Now let's go kill that bitch."

* * * * *

King regained control of the Rhino and charged toward the spider mecha. The other Rhinos were still bombarding the spinnenmutter, aiming at the leg joints. That method had worked against the other mechas over London. But this one had a force field, and nothing was getting through.

"Rhino pilots!" King said. "Fall back one klick and form

an assault formation around me."

With rumbling engines, the Rhinos pulled back to regroup. Below them, across the ruins of Regent's Park, the marines were still battling.

Jordan telepathized from the next Rhino over. "Jim, any bright ideas?"

"Yeah," King said. "We're gonna have to get close and use our drills."

"Past those swinging legs?" Jordan said. "Won't be easy."

"Nothing ever is," King muttered, then raised his voice. "Rhinos, charge!"

Their engines roared like thunderstorms. Their drills spun, shrieking like the wind. Their machine guns blazed, pounding the enemy like a hailstorm. Onward toward the spider they charged, and King imagined them like true rhinos racing across the dawn.

Dr. Anneliese worked her eight limbs madly. Spider legs rose and fell, casting not glimmering gossamer but umbrionic globs. This was a diseased spider that could only create dark, rotting things. The living webs of darkness grabbed several Rhinos, sucked out their energy, and slammed them onto the ground far below. One of the falling Rhinos crashed onto marines, crushing the brave soldiers. Every death stabbed through King's heart. Right now he must focus on the fight. Tonight he would grieve.

The surviving Rhinos charged onward. King, Jordan, and the other pilots swerved around the umbrionic torrents like fish darting around octopus ink. They flew closer. A dark blast hit a nearby Rhino. The armored machine crashed onto the city, plowing through Queen Mary's Rose Gardens. A swinging spider leg caught another Rhino, hurling it across the park. The dropship crashed into the London Zoo, raising a chorus of grunts, snorts, and howls. Zoo animals fled their enclosures and rampaged across the crumbling city.

In the chaos of falling Rhinos and spreading darkness, two Rhinos managed to reach the towering mecha. Their pilots? King and Jordan.

The Rhinos landed on the spinnenmutter. Their treads locked into the mecha's hull.

"We're like two mosquitoes who landed on a tarantula," Jordan telepathized.

"Mosquitoes are far deadlier than tarantulas," King said.

"Time to sting!" Spitfire said.

King stared at her.

"What, you two get to speak cheesy banter but I don't?" Spitfire said. "Is it because I'm not old like you, or because—"

"Spitfire, you're in control of the drill!" King said. "*Ram the drill into her!*"

Spitfire blinked, bolted up in her seat, and stared at the gunnery controls. Her hands danced over the various levers and joysticks. "Drill, drill . . . Ah! Drill!"

Grinning, Spitfire grabbed the right joystick and pulled the trigger. The enormous drill on the Rhino's head spun. Spitfire nudged the joystick, driving the drill toward the—

One of the mecha legs slammed into the Rhino. The spinnenmutter swatted off the multiton machine like a woman swatting a fly.

The Rhino spun through the air.

But Jordan, piloting the other Rhino, managed to stay attached. And his Rhino stung! His drill drove into the spinnenmutter's hull.

King watched, hopeful. But Jordan *just* missed the spinnenmutter's engine.

Dr. Anneliese screamed and swatted at him. Jordan's Rhino tumbled through the sky.

"Spitfire, get ready!" King cried, flying their Rhino back toward the mecha.

As Jordan still tumbled, King latched onto the spinnenmutter just below the cockpit. Spitfire drove the spinning, shrieking drill in.

The drill ripped through the force field like a knife through Saran wrap, then shattered the canopy that engulfed the mecha's cockpit. Inside, Dr. Anneliese screamed. Shards of steelglass flew everywhere. Inside the Rhino's cockpit, Spitfire leaned forward on her joystick, snarling. The drill thrust deeper into the mecha's cockpit, moving toward Dr. Anneliese. The Nazi engineer was strapped into a harness, trapped.

The drill reached the buckles of her harness, shattering them. The harness straps *snapped.*

Just then, with blinding speed, Dr. Anneliese leaped from the cockpit. She scurried through the shattered remains of the canopy and vanished from view. Meanwhile, the drill plowed deep into the cockpit where Anneliese had stood just seconds ago. Finally the drill jammed, impaling itself into a metal bulkhead.

"Where is she?" King shouted.

Then he saw her.

In the rearview monitor.

Dr. Anneliese was wearing a jetpack. The engines thrummed as she flew toward the Rhino's stern, stalking the dropship like a lioness, creeping up from behind.

The Rhino was attached to the spinnenmutter with powerful metal claws. King tried to detach. Then turn the Rhino around. To escape this demon. But the claws struggled to pull free from the spinnenmutter's hull. The controls were too slow. King was too slow. As he wrestled the joysticks, he watched the rearview monitor with mounting dread.

Hovering behind the dropship, The Nazi engineer drew two handguns and fired. Umbrion bolts flew into the Rhino's exhaust ports.

Anneliese tossed back her head and laughed.

The u-bolts burrowed into the Rhino like hungry worms through rotting flesh, seeking the heart. Seeking the Rhino's engine.

Deep inside the dropship, umbrions extinguished the burning fuel. The particles of darkness consumed the very photons, erasing them from reality. And the engines hummed down, dying not with a bang but a whimper.

For a second or two, the Rhino remained attached to the spinnenmutter. Then the multiton dropship finally ripped off the spinnenmutter's hull, flipped over, and plunged toward the distant ground.

* * * * *

Kim Fletcher-King. A colonel in the Alliance. Fifty years old. PhD in engineering. A mother. And a genius (if you asked her husband, at least, though King suspected almost everyone would agree). Throughout her illustrious career, Kim had invented many machines for the starship *Freedom.* Portal generators, allowing the ship to hop between stars. A rail system along the hull, allowing the Shield of David defensive batteries to quickly move into position. Force field windows, allowing the ship to fire torpedoes while her shields were up. Those inventions had saved the starship *Freedom* and her crew countless times.

One of her humbler, lesser-known inventions were gravity dampeners. Kim had spent her leave days designing the prototypes. King had asked her why she wasn't relaxing. Kim had replied this was how she relaxed.

The result of her relaxation? Gravity dampeners installed

along the inner hull of every Rhino. Should they detect a crash, the sensors activated fields of dense gravitons, reducing gravity around the passengers.

As the Rhino slammed onto a London street, the gravity dampeners wrapped around King and Spitfire, protecting them like invisible airbags. The Rhino hit the street hard, shattering concrete, and chunks of the armored hull warped, snapped, and flew across the road. But inside the cockpit, the two pilots survived.

"Once more, you saved my life, Kim," King whispered, wishing she were here. In his fight against her demonic doppelgänger, the real Kim was guarding him like an angel.

Spitfire cracked her neck. "Ow. I think Kim's grav-damps still need some work." She touched the back of her neck and winced. "This better just be a bruise and not whiplash. If it's whiplash, I'm putting it on your insurance."

"Deal," King said. He tapped his temple, sending out a telepathic call. "Phantom? Phantom, do you hear me?"

No answer. Was Larry "Phantom" Jordan still flying his Rhino in the sky? Had he crashed too?

"Larry!" King said.

Nothing.

King looked at Spitfire. "We better get out of this Rhino before—"

A figure swooped from above.

Dr. Anneliese slammed onto the Rhino's prow, grinning like a hungry panther landing on a safari jeep's hood. Her jetpack thrummed. The Rhino had no windshield, no large viewport, only monitors connected to exterior cameras. Anneliese's face appeared on the screens, as beautiful and cruel as the stars.

She wore a black catsuit. Cables and slender metal rods

ran along her limbs, down her spine, and across her chest. It looked like some strength-augmentation device, similar to the one Eva had worn when boarding *Lioness*. In addition, Dr. Anneliese still wore four prosthetic arms that sprouted from her torso. Normally, she used those extra arms for piloting her spider mecha. But even outside the spinnenmutter, those prosthetics seemed deadly. Claws sprouted from their metal fingertips like box cutters. Each claw gleamed in the firelight, reflecting the spinnenmutter, casting a panoply of red spiders.

With savage laughter, Dr. Anneliese clawed at the Rhino's mangled prow. Her six hands grabbed an armored plate and ripped it free. Cackling, the engineer hurled the gargantuan metal slab into the distance. It slammed into a few marines, crushing them.

Inside the Rhino's cockpit, the monitors shattered and collapsed. The control panel sparked. The bulkheads ripped free from the deck. King could barely believe what he was seeing. With strength the mightiest excavators could only envy, Anneliese was ripping out the Rhino's *entire prow*, exposing the cockpit.

Morning light and smoke filled the cabin where King and Spitfire still sat, coughing and bruised after the fall. The entire front of the cockpit—ripped away! Like ripping off a mountainside, revealing the chasm within. And there before them, right ahead, in the flesh—Dr. Anneliese.

The madwoman crouched atop the mangled hull, gracefully predatory, spiderlike and deadly. With a sudden, furious burst of speed, Anneliese lunged into the exposed cockpit. Her claws flashed toward King's neck, reflecting his face in thirty slender shards of death.

Before she could reach him, King already had his Trogdor drawn. He fired a plasma bolt into her chest.

A shimmering skin of energy materialized across Anneliese's catsuit. The cables and metal rods weren't only an exoskeleton, it seemed, but a force field generator. The plasma blast knocked Anneliese back, but it couldn't penetrate her iridescent armor.

At once, Spitfire was blasting her own plasma. More bolts slammed into Anneliese. Even one to the face. Her force field sparked, protecting her, but each blast knocked her back another step. The deranged engineer slid down the ravaged prow of the Rhino.

Spitfire ripped off her seat belt, leaped from her seat like a pouncing cat, jumped through the hole in the prow, and pursued her foe. The woman moved like liquid silver. Oh, to be that young and graceful again! King followed—more slowly, with more creaks, cracks, and groans. Spitfire was in her forties now, still strong and fast, yet perhaps a little slower than she had been. At her age, King remembered feeling a distinct sense of *slowing down.* But now, pushing seventy, being middle-aged seemed like the height of vitality. Joints aching, King limped across the charred prow of the Rhino, a dropship the size of a whale. Where was Anneliese? He looked around, seeking her. Where was Spitfire, for that matter? Both women had vanished into the fog.

The devastation spread all around. During the battle, they had crossed Regent's Park and flown over the crowded streets of Paddington. But it was hard to tell. There was almost no difference now between city parks and city streets. The rubble covered everything, and clouds of dust and umbrions obscured the distance. Smoke hid the sky, revealing only the silhouettes of circling ravens. Thousands of troops were fighting here, but the fog hid most of them. In the dust and smoke, the distant shouts and explosions sounded muffled. Like echoes of a dream.

Through the southern haze King could see it. St Mary's Hospital. It rose in the fog, gray and bleak, peppered with bullet holes. But golden lights shone in the windows. In this ashen wasteland, St Mary's was a beacon of light, warmth, and hope. And King knew, just by looking at it, just by feeling it, that the staff and patients of St Mary's were still alive. That Annie was still alive. That she, like every other alumnus of the starship *Freedom*, was doing her duty. Aboard the *Freedom*, serving as ship's chief medical officer, Annie had saved lives during battle. She would be doing the same thing here.

King must reach that building. Not only to kill the Nazi high commanders inside. But to rescue Annie—one of his own—and everyone else. To bring them back home.

Sudden pain stabbed him.

But Stowy won't come back. She's gone. Forever.

Yes, that grief still filled him. Her death, though years in the past, still haunted him.

He shoved the grief away for now. He would always mourn Stowy, the little stowaway of the starship *Freedom*. But Annie and the others were alive right now. He believed that with all his heart. And they needed him.

*****

"I can't see her!" rose Spitfire's voice from the shadows. "That crazy science bitch just disappeared."

The tall commander emerged from the fog. With a few graceful leaps, Spitfire joined King atop the battered Rhino. They stood in the open, gazing at the mist.

"She's out here somewhere," King said.

Spitfire spat. "Can't see a damn thing in this murk." She had removed her helmet, and the cold wind billowed her dark hair. Her sharp features seemed to sharpen even further as she scanned the desolation. In each hand, she held a loaded Trogdor.

"Where are you, Anneliese?" Spitfire muttered.

King and Spitfire scanned the battlefield. With the umbrion clouds, dust, and smoke everywhere, they couldn't see much. Every moment, German or American troops emerged from the smog, guns booming, killing or dying, then fading again into the mists.

A figure swooped from the fog.

King spun toward it, gun booming.

Damn! His shot went wide!

For a split second, he glimpsed Dr. Anneliese's face as she lunged toward him—her eyes bugging out, her grin showing sharp teeth. Her six arms spread out like a Hindu goddess, tipped with mirrorlike claws. Then she slammed into him, knocking King down onto the mangled prow.

She crouched above him, pinning him down, a hungry black widow who had caught a fat old fly. King tried to shove her off but could not. His back blazed with agony. Dammit, he was too injured, too tired, too *old*.

Atop him, Anneliese licked her teeth and drew an electric knife. The blade crackled like a little thunderbolt.

"You don't deserve that face of yours," Anneliese hissed. "It's *his* face. The face of the führer, not yours. I'll peel it off."

She lowered the crackling blade toward him.

Spitfire's Trogdor roared. Blasts slammed into the Nazi engineer, knocking her off King. The electric blade grazed his cheek, searing off stubble and some skin. A close shave indeed.

King shoved himself up. He knelt on the prow, blood dripping down his cheek. Anneliese had fallen several feet. She clung to the side of the Rhino with her eight limbs, a strange human spider.

For a moment, they stared at each other. King—from atop the Rhino. Anneliese—clinging to the side.

Then they leaped toward each other.

She lunged upward.

He leaped down toward her, roaring.

She slashed her claws, aiming for his neck, but King twisted in midair, and her claws sliced his shoulder. A split second later, he slammed his fist—the metal gauntlet—into her face.

King didn't like hitting women, but this wasn't a woman anymore. She had become something more like a spider. As his fist made impact, a force field shimmered around Anneliese's face. While the force field could stop plasma and bullets, it wasn't great with larger impacts. And King was a large, powerful man, even in his old age. He heard a satisfying *crunch* as his gauntlet hit. Anneliese fell backward, banged against the hull, then crashed onto the ground far below.

Odd. For a second or two, King almost pitied her. Almost thought of her as his wife. But that strange feeling quickly vanished.

He leaped off the dead dropship—the Rhino would never fly again—and swooped toward Anneliese. If plasma wouldn't work, his metal fist would finish the job.

King landed on the charred ground beside her. Anneliese tried to rise, and he kicked her down. Again she tried to stand up. Again he kicked her onto the dirt.

"It's over, you Nazi scum," he hissed.

He reached out with his gauntlet, grabbed her by the neck, and—

One of her mechanical arms slashed toward his belly, claws gleaming.

King leaped back, dodging the assault. Narrowly. Those claws still slashed open his uniform. Another inch and they would have disemboweled him.

Anneliese came at him, all six arms flashing, thrusting an array of thirty flashing claws, each one a blade. The many blades slashed up, down, left, right, flashing in the firelight. Anneliese had become a living garburator. She advanced step by step, grinning, her claws flashing at blinding speed.

"If I can't have your face, no one will!" Anneliese said, lunging toward him.

"He belongs to me!" rose a cry from above.

Spitfire! Spitfire came swooping from the shadows. Roaring in righteous fury, the Israeli pilot slammed into Anneliese, knocking the Nazi woman onto the ground.

One of Anneliese's claws slashed Spitfire's thigh. The tall commander cried out in pain, stumbled back, and clutched her wound. Yet even with her leg slashed open, Spitfire kept fighting, firing her plasma gun. Blast after blast hit Anneliese.

As the two women battled, King took a second to survey his surroundings. He realized that many soldiers were fighting around them in the fog. The Americans wore the blue uniforms of the Freedom Brigade, and many soldiers in olive drab—men of the Royal Infantry—had joined the fight. The brave Tommies fought as courageously as any American marine.

Facing them marched the German soldiers of the Wehrmacht, their black cloaks fluttering, their steel-tipped boots thudding. Swastikas blazed red on their arms. Their skull-shaped visors gleamed in the firelight, and their bionic eyes scanned the shadows. Their guns howled, unleashing umbrionic angels of death.

One force of freedom, one of tyranny. One army of life, another of death. In the fog and fire, the tableau resembled knights fighting a host of demons.

That's not too far off, King thought.

He stood in the heart of the battle. Thousands clashed in the streets outside St Mary's Hospital. Maybe tens of thousands.

King couldn't see far through the fog, but judging by the echoing screams and booms, the battle spread for miles around.

Spitfire let out a scream.

King whipped his head toward her, cursing himself for losing focus. Anneliese had cut Spitfire's other leg! The tall commander fell onto the dirt.

"Spitfire!" King said, meaning to leap toward her.

But Anneliese blocked his way, cackling. Lights shone across her catsuit, casting back the shadows, letting her see her prey. Anneliese suddenly seemed less like a spider, more like some strange angler fish from the deep sea, the kind that lured her victims with glowing bulbs. Indeed, there was no more humanity in her eyes than in the eyes of a predatory fish.

With Spitfire on the ground, Anneliese walked toward King, blades flashing, lights shining, a creature part woman, part monster. Her mind was as twisted as her body, a thing partly mechanical, the brain cells full of little gears, wires, and electrodes.

"Jordan?" King telepathized. "Jordan, you there?"

Anneliese kept advancing, savoring the moment. Her nostrils flared, and she smiled.

"Ah, the smell of war! The best smell in the world."

"I'd sooner smell your rotting corpse," King said.

With a snarl, she thrust one of her mechanical hands. The claws detached from her fingers. The little blades flew like ninja stars toward King.

He hissed, held out his metal hand, and caught one blade on the steel palm. Another scraped across his helmet. One sliced his thigh, while one sank into his shoulder.

Anneliese kept coming, grinning and licking her chops.

"What a weak, pathetic man you are," she said. "I would never be able to best my husband in battle. You, meanwhile, are barely a plaything for me."

King was going lightheaded. Losing blood. He didn't have

much fight left in him. With a howl, he shoved Anneliese with both his hands. She stumbled back into the fog, fell, and laughed. The fog seemed to carry her demonic laughter everywhere, to magnify and multiply it, until the entire mist seemed to be laughing.

"Phantom, you there?" King telepathized.

Finally Jordan's disembodied baritone spoke in his mind. "I'm here, Bulldog."

King could not see his friend through the fog. But he caught a brief telepathic vision of Jordan sitting in the cockpit of his Rhino. He was airborne.

"Lock onto my position," King said. "Bulldozer maneuver. Right over my head."

Jordan's eyes widened. "Bulldoze into *what*?"

"Get ready!" King cried.

Dr. Anneliese lunged from the fog. This time two of her hands held handguns. She fired. Umbrion bolts flew at King.

He charged toward her, fell to his knees, and slid across the mud. The u-bolts flew over his head. King pounced, grabbed Anneliese, and hurled her into the air.

It wasn't easy. Dr. Anneliese wasn't a large woman, but with all her equipment, she weighed a lot. But King summoned every ounce of his strength, and he hurled that woman into the sky.

His back gave a *crack*. He yowled.

Anneliese was airborne for just a second or two.

That was enough. The Rhino came roaring out from the fog—a huge, furious beast of metal and smoke, snorting and rumbling and very pissed off. The metal machine slammed into Dr. Anneliese with a thousand tons of pure kinetic energy and Rhino fury.

Dr. Anneliese flew through the air, a ball of cracking light and spinning blades. Her eight limbs curled inward like a wounded spider, and she slammed into a building across the street. Her force field flared. She hit that building with so much force that pillars cracked, walls shattered, and the entire building came crashing down atop her.

King and Spitfire ran for cover, shielding their heads under their arms. Jordan rumbled nearby in his Rhino, clearing a path through the rubble. Stones flew every which way and dust filled the air. King coughed and gasped for breath.

Finally the rumbles eased. King turned toward the building Anneliese had crashed into.

It had collapsed entirely, burying the mad engineer in rubble.

Spitfire brushed her hands one against the other. "That's that." Then she wobbled, caught her wounded legs, and sat down hard.

His own wounds ached, but King had no time to rest. Standing on the dusty London street, he stared at the fallen building. Was Anneliese dead? Had her force field protected her? Was she trapped under the rubble, still alive?

He had no way of knowing. He wanted to dig through the rubble. The Rhino could help. He wanted a body, dammit. Confirmation she was dead.

But that could take hours. He had no time.

He turned toward the hospital. It rose ahead from the fog. The first marines of the Freedom Brigade were already banging at the doors.

For now, Anneliese must remain under the rubble. With that much weight atop her, dead or alive, she wasn't going anywhere. King allowed himself just a moment to stand there. To breathe. Everything hurt, and he couldn't relax yet. But just for a moment—to breathe.

Then, in one of the most bizarre moments of his long, odd life, a group of arctic wolves emerged from the fog. They ran by King, silent as ghosts, and disappeared into the mist. Escaped animals from the London Zoo. Far in the distance, down the block, he could make out the silhouettes of giraffes in the mist, traveling southward to Hyde Park, perhaps seeking water and whatever trees they might still find.

CHAPTER NINETEEN
Sin Lieth at the Door

St Mary's Hospital
London
Earth
September 11, 2207

As bombs thundered above, as the hospital shook, as gunfire rattled aboveground, Stowy forgot about the war. She barely heard the rumble and roar of battle. All her attention was on those monsters in the room.

Her clones.

Each was more hideous than the last. One sprouted many limbs like a bug. One had been cut in two, then stitched back together, one-half facing the wrong way. One's organs pulsed outside her skin. Another didn't seem to have skin. One was only a head and a torso with little lobster claws. Soft claws. Like the meat after you cracked open and discarded the shell.

And each one had Stowy's face.

Monsters? Hideous? No. They were her.

Not her little sisters—but *her*. The same bedraggled, light brown hair. The same timid hazel eyes. The same elfin face. The same fear. Yes, that most of all. In their eyes, Stowy saw the same terror of the beast. And the same terror of the self.

The beast—the gangly doctor, the sadist, the mad scientist, Dr. Baer and his hideous little needles and melty chocolates.

The terror of the self—there they were before her. Nine clones. Nine paths she might have taken. Nine forms she might have become. Here were nine ways to feel pain, but there was only one way to die. And that was what Stowy yearned for now. Just death like a deep sleep—completely silent, completely still, like a dark room far from the noise of a city, a place to feel nothing. To forget. That was death to her. Not heaven with the angels, not hell with the sinners who burned, just a silent black room. A place as close to nothing as existed in the universe.

Her clones crawled and squirmed closer. They reached out and touched her. Some with fingers. Some with toes. One with soft lobster claws without shells.

"It's you," one whispered.

"The first."

"The original."

"The real Samantha."

Stowy spun toward Dr. Baer. Her throat burned. Her eyes stung. She couldn't speak. Couldn't! She tried to force words out. To ask him why. But her throat simply locked up. Her heart raced, her breath accelerated, and she must gaze again at her feet. Her hands reached into her pockets to clutch plastic dinosaurs. She tapped the stegosaurus's spikes one by one, over and over, a ritual, a way to calm her anxiety lest she fainted.

"You're trembling, little Stowy," Dr. Baer said softly. "Do they frighten you?"

Staring at her toes, she nodded. "*Ja, Onkel Baer,*" she whispered, finally able to emit the words. She hugged Luna close, but even her tattered old safety blanket failed to comfort her today. She wished her clones had blankets of their own.

"There is beauty to them," said Baer, his voice barely louder than hers. "I know they would frighten some souls. So I keep them hidden. They are my most magnificent creations. Up there"—he glanced at the ceiling—"I must perform experiments to save the lives of soldiers. So I shoot, burn, poison, asphyxiate, and torment my little patients with everything a brave Aryan soldier might face on the field of battle. And I study. Analyze. Seek ways to heal. To help the Aryan race. But down here . . ." A sigh rolled through him. "No, there is no scientific value to these little precious dolls. At least none that would benefit the war effort. But there is beauty. These dolls . . . they are my art." He smiled thinly, and his lips trembled with emotion. "The führer was an artist, do you know? Not the current one. Not König. The Eternal Führer. He was a painter before he became a god. I cannot paint, but"—he swept his hand across the room, gesturing at the deformed clones—"I can still create art."

Stowy wondered why he was telling her all this, why he was showing her these abominations.

"How?" she whispered.

He stroked her hair. "Before you escaped me in Munich, I took some of your DNA. You were lost to me, my precious little girl. So I recreated you. Many times over. I gave your clones accelerated growth hormones so they could reach your size within months. Oh, I must have made a hundred or more! Most I killed. I was angry, Stowy. Angry that you ran from me. So I killed you over and over. Scores of times. In many different ways. Then I made more copies and killed them too. But then I realized . . . No, that wasn't punishment enough. Death was a mercy for one who ran away. Life, ah! Life is the true curse. So I created these twisted copies of you. Creatures who live a life of pain and monstrosity. Finally, I thought, I should have my revenge!"

She looked at them. Those poor copies of herself. Yes, they were abominations, but she pitied them. They were whipping girls, punished for her sin, spending a life of pain to atone for her flight. They kept poking her, curious, batting their little eyelids, licking their lips (those who had lips). Like curious little magpies, they reached into her pockets and pulled out treasures. They found buttons, dice made from real human bones, a vintage franc coin from centuries ago, fallen insignia pins soldiers had lost (finders keepers, losers weepers), and various other treasures. One clone reached for Algernon, but the mouse bit her finger. The affronted rodent scurried around Stowy before finally settling into another pocket.

"But then, Stowy," Baer continued, "even after creating them, I realized that wasn't enough. Not enough to satiate my revenge. Because it was you—*you*—who escaped me. Not a clone—but *you*!" He clutched her cheeks between his fingers. "The original Samantha Perry. The girl with the memories of Canada. Of parents. Of home. Of what joy and love feel like. Those clones, oh . . . All they've ever known is pain. They're used to it. But you, Stowy, you . . . For a few years, you felt true joy. Only one who has felt true joy can experience utter anguish. And that is what I have planned for you, Stowy. Complete, utter anguish."

Algernon suddenly leaped out of her pocket, still agitated after his rough handling. As if he understood what was happening, the mouse leaped onto Dr. Baer and bit him on that gaunt, gray cheek.

Baer hissed and slapped at his cheek, trying to kill Algernon. The mouse leaped away, landed on the floor, and scurried away.

Stowy seized her chance.

As Baer clutched his wounded cheek and stamped his foot, trying to crush the fleeing mouse, Stowy made a break for it.

She darted around the doctor, heading to the door.

She heard his foot *thump*. Then a squeak cut short.

"Gotcha!" Baer said.

Tears in her eyes, Stowy fled up the staircase, leaving the ghastly pit below.

* * * * *

He gave his life for me, Stowy thought as she raced upstairs. *Algernon died so I can be free.*

Behind her rose a shriek. A terrible sound as from the gullet of an enraged bird. Not a graceful bird but a gangly, bald, patchy bird that ate carrion and guzzled down maggots. A vulture. She imagined that vulture beating its black wings, flying from the basement, chasing her, eyes bulging out, tongue wagging, beak eager to crush her bones. Uncle Baer was chasing, and Stowy fled upstairs toward the ground floor.

She burst into a hospital corridor. Just a regular, everyday hospital corridor. With nurses, doctors, guards, all the bustle of life. For a moment, it felt like waking up from a nightmare. Down in the basement lurked a dreamland, a hypnagogic land of aberration. And up here—the real world.

Or was it? This hospital was, in a way, a dream too. A parallel universe. A bizarre realm called Unreineland where subhumans and cripples like her lived alongside the pure. A nightmare below. An impure utopia above. Which reality would take over this strange fever dream?

Suddenly SS guards were racing down the corridor, shouting. Stowy cowered. But the SS didn't even acknowledge her. They ran right by Stowy, heading toward the emergency room.

A shriek sounded from the staircase. Baer's towering, gaunt figure burst from the basement like a vampire from a coffin, arms stretched out like wings.

Stowy fled down the corridor, following the SS soldiers. They still ignored her. They weren't after her. And then she heard it from ahead. From the emergency room.

Shouts! Shouts in English!

Stowy had grown up in Canada, where her family had secretly preserved the forbidden language. She understood the deep voices that cried out in the language of Father's books.

"These are the Alliance Marines!"

"Drop your weapons!"

"On the ground, everyone! On the ground!"

"Drop your weapons!"

Stowy gasped. Soldiers! Ami soldiers! And maybe some Tommies who still lived. Whatever the case—they were breaking in!

Sudden terror filled Stowy. Would the Amis kill her? Would they see her as just another Aryan, an enemy from an evil universe to exterminate? Was she trapped between two monsters?

The terror seized her. Once more, she froze. She could barely even breathe. The hallway was spinning.

Think of dinosaurs, she told herself. *Be strong like dinosaurs.*

She imagined them. Their muscles bulging and coiling beneath their scaly skin. Their horns and claws that could cut through wood and stone. Their grunts and bellows, deep cries to send enemies fleeing. She had dinosaurs in her pockets. Protectors.

Her mind cleared. Once more, she could think. Baer was right behind her. The Ami soldiers were ahead. Were the Amis her enemies? Would they gun her down?

Well, one thing Stowy knew. When Baer had promised her utter anguish, he had meant it. Stowy would rather run into Ami bullets than become a deformed monster like her clones. Fleeing the sadistic doctor, she raced into St Mary's emergency room.

A battle raged here. The Ami soldiers were breaking into

St Mary's.

Stowy clutched her blanket to her chest. She had seen murals of American soldiers back on the Fatherworld. They had been drawn across the walls of the Munich Veterans Infirmary. In those frescoes, the Amis had swarthy skin, hooked noses, goat horns, and bloodshot eyes. They rampaged across German villages, stepping on children, killing babies, and shooting mothers in their heads. Amis were not humans. They were subhumans. One of the evil, impure people the Eternal Führer had purified from the world. Yes, as she ran into the emergency room, Stowy was afraid. Her mind was full of visions from those murals. She could already imagine those bloodshot eyes, those drooling jaws full of vampire fangs. She could already feel their hooves step on her.

When she saw the Amis in the hospital, however, her perceptions shattered. What monsters? Again she saw only humans. No hooves. No claws. No fangs. Some had darker skin or eyes, but that was about the only difference. The Amis stormed through the hospital gates, shouting.

Chaos erupted throughout the emergency room. Countless patients crowded the room, a mix of London civilians and wounded Wehrmacht fighters. The SS, custodians of the hospital, had been hard at work, moving among the patients and shooting the so-called subhumans. While Stowy had been in the basement, the SS had killed dozens of patients, shooting them in the heads. But a hundred patients or more still lived. They cried out in relief as the Americans burst into the emergency room.

The SS was outnumbered. But they did not flee. SS officers were selected in childhood. The most vicious children on the playground were gleaned. Those who broke the noses and teeth of other children. Those who carved swastikas into the flesh of the weak. Those who caught and dissected frogs, squirrels, and cats. Especially those who collected the trophies. Those twisted little children were swept up from playgrounds and schoolyards—then broken. For years, their masters beat them, making sure no humanity remained, only jagged, broken shards in human form—like a statue of a human made entirely of knives.

Then, at eighteen, they were culled. Every SS cadet was given a simple order. Murder your own mother. Then desecrate the corpse. Those who followed this order became full-fledged members of the SS. They proudly wore the steel skull and bones on their caps. Those who couldn't do it? They were chopped up and served as dinner. Even Eva König, granddaughter of the führer, had been given that grim task. It was said that after killing her mother, Eva cut out the woman's heart and ate it.

That was how only the cruelest served in the SS. The masses? To the Wehrmacht! Those who saw pain as art? To the SS! Thus were men like Dr. Baer created. And those were the men in the emergency room. Their black military caps proudly displayed those steel skulls and bones.

The SS officers in the emergency room were already dripping in blood. They had killed many patients. Now they raised their guns from the patients to the Ami soldiers. These sadists would not run, would not surrender. Their only reason for life was to kill or die. Today they must do one, the other, or both.

And so must I, Stowy thought.

She knew this. She had escaped death too many times. Tonight she must kill or die. Tonight she must be a soldier.

Bullets whizzed back and forth. The Amis stood by the doorway, trying to shoot their way forward. Some living patients still lay across the emergency room floor. The SS crouched behind the sick, wounded Londoners, using them as human shields, firing over their weakened bodies toward the American troops.

Stowy expected the Amis to fall. After all, weren't they

soft, cowardly people? Surely they did not undergo the brutal psychological punishment all SS members endured. Surely their souls had not been shattered into shards of glass, then reforged as blades. Surely this battle would shatter them.

And yet the Amis did not flee.

They kept advancing.

Their battle armor was thick, protecting them from the Nazi u-bolts. Their weapons were powerful and accurate. A nearby SS trooper held a hostage—a young wounded woman, her arm blasted off. A big Ami soldier fired from across the room, shooting the Nazi right in the eye. The trooper collapsed, releasing the hostage. These were no ordinary Yankee soldiers, Stowy realized. They were an elite unit.

Stowy was crouching behind a waiting-room chair. Peeking like a soldier behind a barricade, she squinted, scrutinizing the nearby Ami. The one who had shot the Nazi between the eyes. The Yank's name appeared on his breastplate. BRIG. BASTIAN KING. Above his name appeared a symbol—a blue star with red stripes emerging from it like wings. Upon the star appeared letters in gold: THE FREEDOM BRIGADE.

As she watched, the big American—he was as big as a German!—fired his gun again. Another SS trooper fell, a bullet in his eye. The corpse slumped to the floor beside Stowy. A lifetime of sadism and torture—ended. In death, the trooper released the hostage he held. The hostage, a man with a bleeding head wound, fled and disappeared in the chaos.

Stowy stared at the dead Nazi beside her. His skull visor leered, grinning a rictus grin. His hand still gripped a gun. Stowy hesitated, then pursed her lips.

Kill or die.

A gun scared her too much. Guns were too loud. Too terrible. Guns had shot her parents in their faces.

Instead, Stowy took the dead Nazi's knife from his boot.

Chewing her lip, she tucked the knife into her belt. A tremble ran through her. She was scared of the knife too. Scared it would slip, would slice her. Oh, who was she kidding? She couldn't fight with a knife! She'd just end up stabbing herself.

No, she needed a real weapon. A *gun.*

Very well then. She tried to pry the dead Nazi's gun loose. But the corpse's fingers were tight, hard, unyielding like tree roots wrapped around a boulder. Touching them sickened Stowy. Finally, tugging with all her might, she *snapped* the dead man's index finger, then managed to pry the weapon loose. The sound of that finger bone snapping would forever haunt her.

The gun wasn't one of those big, powerful assault rifles the Wehrmacht or the Waffen-SS used. Not a Lugerheulen. This gun was small, the bore slender. After all, this SS trooper had served in the Totenkopfverbände-SS, a unit known more for sadism and torture than war on the battlefield. While cruelest of the Fatherworld's servants, the Totenkopfverbände were not the best armed. While they were excellent at terrorizing hospital staff and patients, they were a poor choice to hold back an armored infantry brigade with superior firepower.

And so the Americans, having dominated the Wehrmacht, were able to advance so successfully through the Totenkopfverbände lines. The Freedom Brigade was made for one thing and one thing only. Not to torture. Not to intimidate. Not to terrorize. Just to crush the enemy. And that they were doing well.

As Stowy held the gun, a realization struck her.

She stopped breathing.

Her heart nearly stopped pounding.

Of course.

Of course!

Dr. Baer had told her. It all made sense now. Baer *wanted* the Americans to enter! He *wanted* them to dominate the Totenkopfverbände! He *wanted* the Americans to take over the hospital!

Because it's loaded up with explosives, Stowy thought.

And she realized another thing. Dr. Baer was no longer chasing her. By now, his talons should be in her. When she looked behind her, Baer was heading the other way. Moving *away* from the emergency room. *Away* from her.

Oh God.

Her head spun.

Dr. Baer was going to bring the entire hospital down on their heads.

* * * * *

Stowy ran after him. Yes, for the first time in her life, *she* was chasing *him.* The mouse was hunting the vulture. This mouse, like Algernon, could bite.

Panic had seized the hospital, and crowds ran everywhere. Patients, staff, and soldiers mingled. Shouts rose from the eastern wing; Amis were breaking in there too. Gunfire rattled everywhere. Three SS troopers ran past Stowy, thundering toward the emergency room, guns drawn. Stowy scurried through this chaos, her feet—one bare, one clad in a striped stocking—squeaking against the tiles. She must find Baer. She must stop him before he detonated the bombs.

Ah! There! She glimpsed Baer's lab coat disappearing around a corner. Stowy followed, zipping her way around people. She must hop over a dead body, trying not to look, not to see those gazing dead eyes.

She chased him through the corridors and rooms of the hospital. She would only catch glimpses of his white lab coat—

quick flutters like ghosts that vanished around corners and through doorways. She followed doggedly, passing down corridors, through waiting rooms, even past operating rooms where hostage doctors still fought over the lives of German soldiers. Stowy was entering the southern wing of the hospital. This area was still under Nazi control. Though even here, Stowy could hear the sounds of battle. The Americans had surrounded the hospital. She heard their voices, their boots, their guns boom from the southern rooms.

He's waiting until more break in, Stowy thought.

Just then, a squad of American soldiers ran by her.

"Find the Wehrmacht high command!" their commander cried. "They're in here somewhere."

Stowy gasped. Bastian! Bastian King was the leader! The big Ami was leading a daring mission deeper into the hospital. The squad wore thick armor; they seemed to Stowy almost like clunking robots. Holograms hovered beside them, showing the faces of high-ranking Wehrmacht officers. Generals. Brigadiers. It was America's Most Wanted List, Stowy realized.

"Every man on this list is dead!" Bastian cried, running by. His soldiers followed, their body armor clattering.

Robots on a stampede, Stowy thought.

She must pin herself against the wall to avoid them trampling her. Each of those American soldiers was two, maybe three times her size, and they wore heavy armor to boot. They thundered by like buffaloes.

Big buffalo robots, Stowy thought.

What did they mean? Why were they seeking the Wehrmacht high command? This hospital was under SS control. The highest-ranking officer here was Hauptsturmführer Rudolph Baer, dear old Uncle Baer himself—an SS man. And the Amis were running the wrong way to catch him.

She wanted to call out. To shout: "You made a mistake! There's no Wehrmacht here. And the hospital is gonna blow up!"

She tried. Oh Lord, how she tried! She opened her mouth, and with all her willpower, she commanded her voice to emerge. But . . . not a peep. She had become mute. No matter what she did, no matter how hard she tried, when Stowy was nonverbal, she was not gonna talk. She had no more control over it than a girl without a tongue.

There was just so much stimulus in this hospital. The bright lights. The endless roar of battle. The *bangs* of gunfire. The movement of racing soldiers. Autistic people, Father had said, experienced the universe on overdrive. On some days, Stowy felt like a normal girl. And she wondered if she was even autistic after all. Then came times like this. Times with the lights, the sounds, the movements . . . and ah, there it was! There came the autism. The stimulus short-circuited her brain, leaving her mute and trembling. True, this was a battle, and battles terrified anyone. But to Stowy every day was a battle.

The American soldiers ran onward. Not knowing they had entered a trap. After wiring up the hospital, the SS had cleverly hidden the explosives behind vents and pipes.

And Uncle Baer was about to set off those bombs.

Stowy kept running. Finally, past a service door, she entered a shadowy chamber. The room towered. Machinery filled the place—furnaces, air filters, generators, and various other machinery that kept the building running. Gears the size of dinner tables spun on the floor and ceiling. Pipes rose along the walls like the organs of vampires and ghouls. The chamber seemed like the heart of some clockwork titan, a mecha from the haunted imagination of Dr. Anneliese.

She found the doctor there. Baer was walking along a mezzanine, approaching a huge metal lever. Gears turned below him, while pistons clanked all around. The lever connected to thick electric cables that ran down the wall, along the floor, and into pipes.

He's going to set off the bombs, Stowy thought.

She ran across the room.

Dr. Baer's hands closed around the lever. It reminded Stowy of vulture talons clutching bones. In the shadows, the vulture hadn't noticed her, this little girl scurrying like a mouse in the brush. The gangly doctor stood on the mezzanine, still and devious, like a buzzard upon a stony outcrop waiting for an animal to die. He held the lever, not yet pushing it, and gazed into the distance. He spoke softly, and his voice oozed like tar, filling the shadowy cavern.

"Now I am become Death, the destroyer of worlds."

He took a deep breath, prepared to push the lever.

Stowy found her voice.

"No!" she cried from below.

She had tried to scream. To let her voice echo with ferocity through the hospital. It came out as a mere peep. But it was enough to draw his attention.

He spun away from the lever. The vulture leaned over the mezzanine balcony, grin spreading, staring down at her.

"Ah, Stowy! So you've come to witness the end. You should have kept running, little mouse. You might have fled into the city. But you've come here. Good, good! We die together. May our souls spend eternity entwined."

Stowy drew her gun. The gun she had taken from the dead SS trooper. Standing on the floor among the machinery, she aimed the gun at Baer high above.

"Now, now, where did you find that little toy, mouse?" he said. "Throw it away, Stowy."

She cocked the gun. Tears flowed down her eyes.

"Do as I say!" he cried, voice echoing through the chamber like a vulture's shriek.

Memories of Munich flooded her. The year she had spent under his care. The images flashed before her eyes. Children he had burned with acid, removing their skin, then making them pose and smile for photos. Dwarfs he deformed. Women he raped and mutilated. Twins he performed rituals on. All the conjoined twins he created, cutting people apart, stitching them back together, trying to keep his Frankenstein creatures alive as long as possible. She had repressed memories from his house of torture, but they were still in her mind. They always had been. Now they flooded her.

He stared down at her, eyes hard. "Put the gun down, Stowy. Put it down or I will cut you open. I will tinker with your insides. I will—"

She fired the gun.

A u-bolt slammed into his shoulder, knocking him back from the railing.

The recoil knocked Stowy back too. She fell down hard and dropped her gun. It clattered away and fell between some gears, whose steel teeth promptly bit the weapon.

For a moment, lying there, she dared to hope. Was Baer dead?

No.

He came racing downstairs from the balcony, swooping like a carrion bird, face twisted in fury. Blood gushed from his shoulder. Umbrions were spreading from the wound, turning his lab coat black. The stains crept across him, the darkness swirling like fog. All pretenses of *Onkel* Baer—the avuncular doctor who gave chocolates and marzipan to his "nieces" and "nephews"—vanished. The umbrions stripped that mask away. All that remained was a figure in black, a malevolent spirit of sadism. A doctor? No, this was no doctor, no matter what degrees he had earned. He was a butcher. A perverted killer. The living personification of evil. He was coming right at her, and Stowy stood frozen with fear. She had no more gun. No more courage.

"You could have died in the explosion, buried with me under the rubble," he said. "It would have been painless. But now, well . . . I can spare a few minutes. To make sure you die deformed, broken, and screaming. A few minutes isn't much. But I'll make them feel like hours."

He opened his coat, revealing scalpels, saws, and pliers. And more than that. He had hung pieces from his victims inside his coat! Like a sleazy salesman with a coat full of counterfeit watches, Dr. Baer displayed ears, noses, scraps of skin with tattoos. Trophies of his kills. Back in Father's forbidden library, Stowy had read about Jack the Ripper. Stowy would stay up for hours, wrapped up in Luna, reading about the Ripper's horrifying deeds, scared but unable to stop reading. That was all Dr. Baer was. Jack the Ripper with power behind him. A depraved sadist the regime had elevated to doctor.

Gunfire rattled in the hospital. Shells exploded in the distance. But all that noise was outside. Muffled. Here in this chamber of machinery, it was just the two of them. The vulture and the mouse. He advanced toward her, lips parting in a Cheshire cat grin, revealing long, yellow teeth. His beady black eyes glittered. Suddenly, looking at this gaunt man, Stowy saw the boy he had been. A young boy collecting cats to dissect. Keeping the skulls of animals. Finding depraved lust in mutilation. Yes, that's all he was perhaps. Still that boy. They had draped him with a lab coat, given him the symbols and honor of the Fatherworld, called him a doctor, a scientist, an officer. But here, with all the masks peeling off—just a wanton boy with a broken mind. A mind like shards of metal, covered with sliced dead maggots. He drew his scalpels and advanced closer, and all Stowy could do was stare, paralyzed with fear.

A voice sounded from the shadows.

"*Onkel* Baer?"

Eyes shone in the darkness behind gears and pipes. A little girl crawled into the light. Her legs had been stitched together, forming a mermaid's tail. A Stowy clone.

"*Onkel* Baer?" came another voice.

Another clone crawled down the wall, moving confidently on eight limbs.

More voices filled the shadows, coming from behind the machinery, from between the gears, through the vents. "*Onkel* Baer? *Onkel* Baer?"

One by one, they emerged to surround the doctor. Experiments. Freaks, some might call them. The poor clones of Stowy, created to suffer punishment by proxy. Whipping girls. They had been raised in the shadows. They had never seen anyone but their dear "uncle" who gave them treats.

Until today. Until they had met Stowy. And now she remembered. When racing out the dungeon, Baer had left the blast door open. Out his little creations must have crawled. Through the battle. Maybe through the ducts. Finally coming here. Back to their uncle. Even now, even in their freedom, they had returned to him. They had never known love, only his perverse attention. Did they still crave it?

They tugged at his pants, at his lab coat.

"*Onkel* Baer, we want a chocolate."

"*Onkel* Baer, we want a marzipan."

"*Onkel* Baer, we want a bedtime story."

He tried to keep walking toward Stowy. But the clones were holding him back. Stowy gasped. No, they did not crave Baer's approval. They were helping her! Trying to protect her!

"Get away from me, you freaks!" Baer shouted, kicking.

He drove his boots into several clones. He crushed one's face. But they clung on, pulling his coat, grabbing his legs.

"*Onkel* Baer, *Onkel* Baer!"

They began climbing him. He kicked and fought. He managed to rip one off, to hurl her away. The others kept crawling over him.

Baer screamed. Blood spurted from his arm.

"You bit me!" he shouted. "You little mutated monster!"

Then another clone bit him. And another. Their eyes had gone savage. Their sharp little teeth ripped through his flesh. They had become like piranhas, covering him, eating him alive.

Stowy finally snapped out of her paralysis. She ran a few steps and found her gun between two massive gears. It was jammed between the steel teeth. Stowy tried to pull it free. She had to strain, to press one foot against a gear, to pull the gun with both hands (while careful not to accidentally shoot herself). As she worked, she must turn her back to Baer. But she heard his screams. Screams of rage. Then of anguish. Then bubbling, wet screams.

Finally she freed the gun. She walked back toward Baer and did not see him, only a pile of clones. They covered him like hyenas over a carcass.

"Sisters?" she whispered.

They pulled back, revealing their victim. A mutilated wretch. He was still breathing. Oh God, somehow he was still alive.

"We made him one of our own," said a clone. She wiped blood off her lips.

"We turned him into a freak like us."

"He will live with us now in the basement."

Tears ran down Stowy's cheeks. She looked down at the . . . whatever it was. No longer a man. Just a gurgling thing. An experiment. No, she could not let him live this way. Even after all he had done, Stowy pitied him. So she pulled the trigger. A gunshot rang out, echoing through the chamber. Before he died, with those very last heartbeats, he looked into her eyes. And he saw who had killed him.

She stood there for a moment, gun in hand, then turned away from him. She did not want to see or think about Dr. Baer anymore.

As she stood there in the machinery room, they gathered around her—the clones. None could stand. They crawled, gasping for breath, and surrounded her. Those who had hands reached up to touch her, and their eyes gazed into hers. She feared they would devour her too, but there was tenderness to their touch. They had never known a mother. Stowy stood there among them like a lighthouse rising from a rocky shore before dawn. She stroked their hair, touched their fingertips, and marveled at their tenderness, at their hearts that were still good.

One of the clones slumped onto the floor.

Another gasped for air.

One's eyes rolled back, and she leaned against Stowy and her breath grew shallow.

Stowy gasped. What was going on?

"We're dying," one whispered.

Another smiled softly, and her eyelids fluttered. "We . . . could not take our . . . IV stands through the ducts."

"We could not take our oxygen tanks."

Stowy wept. "I'll bring you back to your basement. Hook you back up to the machines that keep you alive."

"No, there isn't time," one whispered.

"We can run!" Stowy cried, tears falling. "We can make it!"

"No," whispered a clone. "No, it's better this way. It's

good this way." The young, deformed girl smiled. "We got to meet you. The real us. We are pieces of you, Stowy. But we fade away now. You gave us life, and we give our lives to you. Make yours a good life, Samantha Perry. Do not forget us . . ."

"Do not forget us . . ." whispered the others.

"I never will," Stowy vowed.

And she did what she could. She remained there with them as they died, comforting them until the end. She had thought them monsters, but they were the purest souls she had known.

The battle still raged outside this room. Dimly, like distant thunder through a dying rain, she could hear the booms and gunfire. A few distant voices sounded. American voices. They were winning.

Good, Stowy thought.

She wanted to run to the Amis. To ask for sanctuary. At least to thank them. But right now she was too overwhelmed to walk more than a few steps. She sat down by a rumbling generator, wrapped her blanket around her, and took out her plastic dinosaurs. For a good half hour, as gunfire clattered above, Stowy lined up her dinosaurs, snout to tail. Then she scattered them and lined them up again, this time in a different order. She was not playing with them. To her this was no game. She did not make up stories for them, did not make them roar or fight. Over and over, she lined them up, bringing order to chaos.

CHAPTER TWENTY
To Endure the Caterpillars

St Mary's Hospital
London
Earth
September 12, 2207

Standing in the hospital cafeteria, Bastian swept his arm across the tabletop, knocking down trays, cups, and napkin holders. He rolled out a giant map of the hospital and slammed a salt shaker down in the middle.

"We are here. The cafeteria."

Spitfire pointed. "The same map is hanging on the wall, Bastian."

He raised his chin. "I wanted a map closer to us."

"You just wanted to dramatically sweep everything off a table, then unroll a giant map again, didn't you?"

"Will you let me enjoy my maps?" he snapped.

Alice stood there with them. Her blond braids fell across her strong shoulders, and the blood of her enemies still stained her battle armor. The tall, powerful marine smiled at Spitfire.

"Spitfire, I know my husband," Alice said. "Let him have his toys or he gets cranky."

"Damn right," Bastian said, crossing his massive arms across his barrel chest.

As the young ones bantered, King stared at the map on the tabletop. It showed the hospital floor plans. A hospital swarming with the SS. They had found no generals here. No high-ranking officers at all. Some of the corpses, however, were hard to identify. Or to explain. Such as the corpse they found in the machinery room. It looked like something had eaten it. And those dead, deformed girls around the remains . . . A chill ran down King's spine.

"What the hell was going on here?" he whispered. His voice came out as a rasp. His throat was aching again.

"Damned if I know," Bastian said. "They were conducting some evil experiments. Sick bastards. I just wish we had caught some Nazi generals. They must have run away."

"It was a trap," King said. "There never were generals here."

Bastian stared at him from across the table. "The Wehrmacht soldiers we interrogated—"

"Told you what they had been told," King said. "To lure us into a ticking time bomb."

Bastian shuddered, his armor clattering. "Thank God they never detonated those explosives. Dad, they wired up enough to blow the entire hospital to the moon. I'm glad we killed them before they could set off the bombs."

King thought about that hideous corpse in the machinery room. Not far from that big electric switch.

"I'm not sure that was our work, son," King said, wondering what kind of monsters might have left the injuries he had seen. Whoever that poor bastard by the switch had been—they had done a number on him.

Do we have a guardian angel on our hands? he wondered. *Or a demon on the loose?*

Whatever the case, St Mary's Hospital was secure. By dawn, the Freedom Brigade had conquered the building. Leaving one company in the hospital, the remaining marines kept sweeping south through the city, mopping up the German resistance. After losing their spinnenmutters, the will of the Wehrmacht broke. Give them another day or two, and the Freedom Brigade will have liberated the city. Before any reinforcements could even arrive. That was the Freedom Brigade King had always known. That was the brigade King had deployed on alien worlds. It was still here, even without a mothership, as mighty and proud as always.

"Bastian." King reached across the table and clasped his son's arm. "I'm proud of you."

Bastian blinked, clearly surprised. He had been speaking of his battle plans, but his speech faltered, and he blushed. "I . . . Thanks, Dad."

King walked around the table, and his eyes were suddenly damp. He pulled Bastian into a hug. "I love you."

Ah, he was getting sappy in his old age.

Bastian held him close. "I love you too, Dad." The big man's voice choked, and his eyes dampened.

King was a large man, but his son was even larger. He thought back to that premature baby. So tiny. Nearly too small to live. Bastian had fought hard those first few months, and King had been there to fight with him. Now here Bastian stood, a giant, a leader of men, a liberator of cities. How that tiny baby had grown.

"It doesn't matter how old you get," King whispered. "It doesn't matter how tall you are. You're still my boy."

Huge sniffles sounded behind them. Alice and Spitfire—one a proud marine, the other a daring pilot—were both teary-eyed and blowing their noses. They were both tall and strong women, both high-ranking soldiers, both leaders, both decorated warriors, and both sniffling like babies. Ha!

Ah, hell, now King was sniffling too. Not that he'd ever

tell anyone. He quickly turned away to hide it.

Then, as he was drying his eyes, King noticed him.

Commander Larry Jordan had entered the cafeteria. The tall officer had been scouring the hospital, searching for more hostages. For hours now, the Freedom Brigade had been exploring St Mary, discovering new crimes in every room. The morgue was full of bodies. Tortured bodies. The surgery rooms were full of mutilated patients. Experiments. Many hostages had been found chained throughout the hospital. Some children had been hung on meat hooks from the walls. Living human shields. Truly, there was no limit to the cruelty of their foe.

"I looked everywhere for her," Jordan said softly. "I searched the operating rooms. The morgue. I don't know where Annie is."

The Freedom Brigade had saved many lives. But not everyone. The Nazis had murdered hundreds of innocents here. Maybe thousands. All in just a few days.

If only I had gotten here sooner, King thought. *If only I had fought a little harder, a little faster. I could have saved so many.*

Was Annie now one of the dead?

King tapped his temple, trying his MindLink again, trying to reach Annie. Nothing.

"Larry, I'm sorry." King stared at his friend in silence. He didn't know what else to say. How could he comfort a man searching for his daughter? How could—

The cafeteria door banged open.

In ran a doctor. A doctor with the dark skin of her father and the green eyes of her Irish mother. Dr. Annie Jordan.

"Dad!" she cried.

Jordan spun around. His eyes flooded with tears. "Annie? How could this be? I looked everywhere. Are you a ghost?"

She approached him, leaped into his arms, and they embraced. "It's me, Dad." Tears flowed down her cheeks. "I was in surgery. So many urgent cases. I couldn't leave them. And you know how surgery rooms have telepathic dampeners."

"Oh, Annie." Jordan held her, his face twisted with emotion, his tears falling, and he could not speak anymore.

King took deep breaths of relief. For a long time now, he had vocally insisted Annie were alive. But deep inside, he had worried, had thought her most likely dead. Thank God, she was alive!

"Annie!" King stepped toward her. "It's good to see you."

The doctor looked at him up and down. "Jim, you look like shit."

"So I've been told," King muttered.

Annie laughed and pulled King into an embrace. "Hug me for a moment. Then get your ass into a med-room. We're going to patch you two old boys up."

It was a day of reunions and of grief. A day of zipping dead comrades into body bags. A day of comforting the dying. A day of healing the wounded, those who had lost limbs, who had lost faces, whose lives were forever changed. An emotional day. A haunting day. A day of victory.

Yes, victory today. But the war was not yet won. This would be a long war, King knew. A war that might last months, even years. Maybe decades. But today at least—he was with his son. And Jordan was with his daughter. Those they loved were safe.

I wish you could have been here with us, Stowy, King thought. He missed his little adopted granddaughter more than ever.

Then the cafeteria door opened again, and this time King knew he was dreaming.

This could not be real. Just a dream. Or a MindWeb hallucination. Because he could not believe his eyes.

"Who hacked my MindWeb?" he whispered.

He shut the neural implant off. But she was still there. Standing in the cafeteria doorway.

Stowy.

"I see her too," Bastian whispered, eyes wide.

"How is this possible?" Spitfire whispered.

King took a step closer, still not able to believe his eyes.

A girl. A girl with messy, light brown hair, elfin features, big ears, and freckles. A girl wearing a tattered old dress covered with many pockets. Like always, she wore only one stocking, and she held a tattered old blanket, barely more than a rag. It looked just like her. Even the same clothes.

But no. There was a difference. Stowy—the girl King had known—would be grinning, frolicking around, as happy and carefree as a fairy. *This* girl was timid. She stared at her toes, trembled, and hugged a blanket.

King took another step toward her.

"Stowy?" he whispered.

She glanced up from her toes. Their eyes snapped together. The blood drained from her face, and her mouth opened in a silent scream.

*****

Stowy wanted to scream. Terror surged through her, constricting her lungs, locking up her throat. She could not make a sound.

She stared at him.

The old man. The tall old man with gray hair, a hard face, and steely eyes.

It was him. He was actually here.

The führer.

Führer Helmut König. The Butcher from Berlin. The Honored Father. Supreme Leader of the Fatherworld. The spiritual successor to Hitler himself. He was known by many names and titles. Each one shot fear through the heart.

He was said to be paranoid, a germaphobe, that he never left his fortress in Berlin. Yet here he stood! Here in St Mary's Hospital on Unreineland. He wore the uniform of an American soldier, but Stowy would know the führer's face anywhere. She had saluted him a million times. Every room in the Fatherworld, by law, must contain two portraits. One of Hitler, the Eternal Führer. And one of the reigning führer—currently Helmut König. Stowy's bedroom at home, her classroom, her living room, her hospital room . . . All had the same two portraits hanging from the wall. (The law did make exceptions for bathrooms.) Every morning, every noon, every evening, whenever she saw their stern faces, Stowy would rise to her feet and hail the führers. It was drilled into her. An instinct as powerful as yawning when tired or sneezing after sniffing the ashes of dead children.

Standing here in the cafeteria, Stowy froze. Unable to flee. And as the führer walked toward her, she reacted as she had been taught. She had been training for this moment all her life.

She squared her shoulders, straightened her back, and raised her palm in a Nazi salute.

"Hail the führer!" she whispered. (You were supposed to yell it. But for Stowy, even a whisper was a huge accomplishment. Yes, she had trained well for this.)

The führer halted a few steps away. His face paled, and his eyes widened. He was wounded, Stowy noticed. Bandages bound his shoulder and leg, one of his eyes was black, and scratches ran down his cheek. And oddly, he seemed to have shaved his thick mustache, one of his trademarks. He stared at her, eyes wide.

"Doppelgänger," he whispered.

The word shot through Stowy like a bullet.

Doppelgänger. She knew that figure from folk tales. A copy of a person from a dark world. A creature like a shadow come to life. Of course. This was Unreineland, the strange world beyond the sea of time and space, a realm of shadows and doppelgängers. Long ago, in one of her forbidden books, Stowy had read that every man, woman, and child had a doppelgänger. Even her. Even the führer.

There he stood. Not Führer Helmut König. No. A doppelgänger of Unreineland. Stowy read his name tape. ADMIRAL JAMES KING.

She lowered her hand, stared at him, and whispered, "Doppelgänger."

* * * * *

She didn't speak a word after that.

King kept trying. He would kneel beside her. Say hello. Ask her if she were hungry or thirsty. But she would look at her toes and ignore him. One time he briefly touched her arm. She recoiled, trembled, and finally scurried away to hide behind a chair. Whenever he drew closer, she would slink farther away, trying to disappear into shadows.

What happened to you, sweet child? King thought, gazing at her softly. She sat behind an overturned table, hugging her blanket, and if he got too close, she trembled until he backed off.

This wasn't his Stowy. King realized that now. She wasn't the Stowy from the starship *Freedom*, the plucky little stowaway who lived in the ductwork. *That* Stowy had looked the same, perhaps, but had been boisterous, rambunctious, loving to everyone. Still autistic, yes, but in a different way. *That* Stowy had been like an energetic kitten. *This* Stowy was more like a kicked puppy.

Of course, King thought, gazing at the pitiful girl. *You grew up autistic in a world that saw you as subhuman. Oh, sweet child, how did they hurt you?*

He wanted to comfort her. Yet whenever he tried to speak, to get closer, she shivered and fled farther away.

Of course, King thought. *I look like the führer. I terrify her.*

She could have fled the cafeteria. The door was wide open. She could have escaped St Mary's and vanished down the streets. Yet Stowy remained. A part of her, perhaps, trusted King. Or wanted to. She was like a poor dog who had never known love, eager for its first pat yet too frightful to approach.

"Sweet girl, they hurt you so much," he whispered.

She cowered under the table. When King stepped back, Stowy calmed enough to reach into her pockets. She pulled out plastic dinosaurs and began lining them up. She would not make eye contact or a sound.

King returned to his fellow officers, who sat at the back of the cafeteria, drinking tea and coffee. The place was quiet now. For the past few hours, the cafeteria staff—with the help of eager soldiers—had been cooking up a storm, feeding thousands of people. But it was late. Most of the Freedom Brigade was in the underground parking lot now, sound asleep. Most of the hospital staff had gone home (those who still had homes standing). Only a few of the senior officers (like King and his friends) were still here this late. Dr. Annie had gone to perform surgery, but Jordan was still in the cafeteria, along with Bastian, Alice, and Spitfire.

"I don't know what to do," King said. "She won't talk to me. Or look me in the eyes. I asked her to come eat. She won't budge. I can see her glancing at the food sometimes, and I heard her stomach growl, but she's scared."

"Bring food to her then," Bastian suggested.

King nodded. He took a plate and topped it with a bread roll, sausages, an apple, and some cheese. He walked back toward the table under which Stowy hid. She was still lining up her dinosaurs.

"Hey, Stowy," King said, careful to keep his distance.

She wouldn't look at him. It was as if Stowy wasn't even aware he was there. She just kept lining up her dinosaurs.

King placed the plate on the table. "I brought you some food. You can eat whenever you like."

He returned to his companions across the cafeteria. From there, he watched. For a long time, Stowy ignored the food. She hid under the table, wrapped in her blanket, lining up her dinosaurs over and over in different order. Finally a little hand peeked above the tabletop. Stowy grabbed the bread roll, pulled it under the table, and stuffed it into one of her many pockets. A moment later, the little hand peeked again. She grabbed the apple. That too disappeared into a pocket. The sausages and cheese got the same treatment.

"She's too scared to even eat," King said.

"No she's not." Spitfire shook her head. "She's not scared to eat. She's hoarding food. She's known times of starvation before. So she instinctively hides food."

King turned toward the tall pilot. He raised an eyebrow. "You're familiar with this psychology?"

"Not personally," Spitfire said. "But I heard stories from my family. My ancestors survived the Holocaust. They had almost starved to death in the Nazi camps. After they regained their freedom, they hoarded food for years. They hid it under mattresses. In pockets. Anywhere they could. Like nervous squirrels." Spitfire gazed across the cafeteria at the little girl under the table. "This girl is like a Holocaust survivor. A girl who survived the hell of Nazism. She's broken."

King pursed his lips. "How can I help her if she won't even let me near?"

"Maybe try offering her something sweet," Bastian said. "Like chocolate. To build trust."

King shook his head. "No. She's not a dog for us to train with treats. That's Stowy over there!"

"But not our Stowy," Bastian said. "That's not the little girl who stowed away on our starship. That's not the Stowy we knew and loved, who became the mascot of the *Freedom.* I loved her too. We all did. That girl is gone."

"But this one isn't!" King said. "And dammit, that's still Stowy. To me, at least. Okay, so she's a doppelgänger. But she's not like . . . not like *our* doppelgängers, all right? She's good." King's eyes burned. "Bastian, your doppelgänger, mine, my wife's, my granddaughter's—they're all Nazis. All goddamn Nazi sadists. But not that one! Not that girl under the table over there. That one is *good,* dammit. That one is Samantha "Stowy" Perry. She even has the same name! She's not like us."

"Not like us?" Bastian tilted his head. "What do you mean?"

King took deep breaths, calming himself before continuing in a low voice. "Inside every man and woman is a shadow self. An evil that lurks, chained up deep in the subconscious. An internal shadow of our soul, untrammeled by civilization, etiquette, or fear of the law or of God. A sort of Mister Hyde we keep chained up and hidden from polite company. Some ancient cultures believed that darkness inside could detach from the body, could become a new life-form. That is the legend of the doppelgänger. And out from the Fatherworld came our doppelgängers. Corrupted, violent versions of ourselves. Beings with no mercy. No compassion. Nothing but distilled evil. But they're still us. They're us as we might have been. Us after a lifetime in the Fatherworld. Carl Jung spoke of man facing his own shadow. And we faced ours in this war." King looked toward the table under which Stowy still hid. "But that one is different. Stowy, even the Fatherworld version of her, is not cruel. Not like our doppelgängers. Because there was never any shadow in her soul. There was never any Jekyll hiding inside her. No wickedness to manifest as some mirror universe villain. Stowy was always pure. In our universe and in that one. One who is pure casts no shadow, only more light."

Bastian wiped tears from his eyes. "That's our Stowy. Not a stain to her soul. Even in a world of pure evil, she's good."

Spitfire grabbed a jar of pickles. "Let me try."

She began walking toward Stowy.

"It won't work!" Bastian called after her.

The big man's booming voice was clearly loud enough for Stowy to hear across the cafeteria. But she just remained under the table, eyes lowered, playing with her plastic dinosaurs.

The old Stowy loved dinosaurs, King remembered. After the starship *Freedom* had been decommissioned, the top brass turned her into a tourist attraction. On one deck, they had set up a Jurassic-themed minigolf course, featuring animatronic dinosaurs. Stowy loved to play among them. It was probably her favorite place on the ship. King wished that minigolf course still existed. Would this new Stowy love it too?

She's younger than the old Stowy, King thought.

His Stowy would be twenty-four today. This new Stowy looked a decade younger. It was definitely *her*. Same clothes, same face, same name. Just different. Younger. On the Fatherworld, a cruel world, many families would have children later in life.

Spitfire approached the girl under the table. King followed, keeping a few paces behind, painfully aware of how much he terrified that little girl.

"Hey, Stows." Spitfire sat down on the floor. She was too tall to fit under the table. And that might have terrified Stowy anyway. So the tall, willowy commander sat down beside the table and pulled her knees up to her chin.

Stowy kept lining up dinosaurs. But she wasn't escaping. That was good.

Spitfire unscrewed the jar. "Want a pickle?"

Stowy seemed not to hear. She kept playing with her dinosaurs. Her face was blank.

Is the girl mute? King wondered. No. She had spoken earlier. She was terrified. Traumatized. As if autism weren't difficult enough on its own.

Spitfire pulled a pickle out from the jar. She took a bite, then grimaced. "Ugh! This isn't a pickle!"

Stowy's hands froze over the plastic dinosaurs.

"It's a brontosaurus tail!" Spitfire said. "A baby one. Tastes awful!"

Stowy's lips curled up in the faintest of smiles.

"You know what?" Spitfire said. "I think I'm going to gobble up all these brontosaurus tails. Because I'm a T-rex! Look at my tiny arms."

She held up two pickles, manipulating them like tiny arms.

Stowy's smile widened. Her eyes flicked toward Spitfire. "No you're not!" the girl said in the smallest of voices. "You're a—"

Stowy fell silent at once. Her hazel eyes glanced toward Spitfire's pendant. A silver Star of David.

Spitfire smiled. "Do you like my lucky star?"

"You are . . ." Stowy whispered. She reached out to touch the pendant, then pulled back her hand as if stung. "You are . . . subhuman?"

King winced, expecting Spitfire to rage. Stowy had been

raised in the Third Reich. All her life, she must have learned that the Star of David was evil. The most evil of all symbols.

But Spitfire remained calm. "According to Nazi ideology, yes, I'm subhuman."

And the dam broke. Stowy leaped into Spitfire's arms and wept onto her shoulder.

"Me too," Stowy whispered. She rolled up her sleeve, revealing a tattoo of an inverted black triangle. Symbol of the disabled, doomed to euthanasia. "Me too."

* * * * *

That evening, Stowy stood outside the hospital, gazing upon a field of rubble. In the southern distance, she could still hear dim explosions. The Alliance was still fighting in the south of England. They were fighting all over the world.

A cold wind blew, billowing Stowy's messy hair and dress of many pockets. Her assorted treasures jangled. A shiver ran through her, and not only because of the cold. Night was a dangerous time for orphans. Especially impure ones. Night was when the Gestapo could hide in any shadow. When their trained wolves sniffed and howled. Night was when the orphans emerged from their beds, scoured the city, and often never made it home. Night was death.

Stowy gazed at the city under the sunset. A mist hung over the fallen buildings, rubble-strewn streets, and artillery craters, and in the distance, light still shone in towers. Some parts of London still stood. She heard no wolves. All the monsters lay dead under the rubble. This was Unreineland, the impure land. Her castle on the clouds.

"We made it, Luna," Stowy whispered to her blanket.

Tears flowed down her cheeks. "We climbed all the way to our castle on the clouds by the moon and stars. The demons chased us here, but we found angels too. And the angels keep us safe." A sob racked her little body. "Luna, for so long, I thought I was impure. I thought I was broken. I thought that here, in my castle on the clouds, I would be cured. But I know now. I understand. I was never impure. I was a broken Aryan girl. But I was always a perfectly good autistic girl. My voice was always the perfect volume for speaking to mice, blankets, and other forgotten things. I never needed to be cured. I just needed to go home."

She stood in silence for a while, gazing at the dark ruins beyond, and they seemed beautiful to her, and the night seemed safe. She stood among angels.

A raspy voice sounded behind her. "That was beautiful."

Stowy started, spun around, and saw him there. The führer's doppelgänger. This so-called James King. His face was weathered, covered in dust, bruises, and white stubble like sandpaper. His uniform was tattered, his body bandaged. Yet Stowy still saw that imposing man who stared from murals, banners, and zeppelins across the Fatherworld. A tremble seized her.

King held out his hands in a placating gesture. One was a real hand, broad and callused. The other was a metal hand, a prosthetic that looked like a knight's gauntlet.

"Don't run away." His voice was raspy, and each word made the scar on his neck dance. "I know I look like the most evil guy in two universes. But I'm not him. I'm not Helmut König. And despite how scary I look, I'm a man of honor, and I like to think that I'm a good man. I'm James King. A man who once knew you. This world's version of you, at least. You were like a granddaughter to me. And you're not alone here. There are many of us who loved you, who prayed for your return. And here you are. You're home."

She looked at the ruins, then at the old man. Finally she looked past the old man at the others. At Bastian, the big marine with a big smile and big heart. Alice, his wife, a proud warrior and protector. Spitfire and Jordan, considered "subhumans" too, but in this universe they were brave and strong.

I wonder if I can grow up to be brave and strong, Stowy thought. *I wonder if I can grow up to speak confidently. To look people in the eyes. To grow from a meek girl to a proud woman. Like the Stowy who lived in this universe before me.*

She didn't know. Maybe her trauma lay too deep. Maybe her autism would forever block some paths in her life. Maybe she would never be like Spitfire and Jordan. Maybe, even as an adult, she would wrap herself in a safety blanket, line up dinosaurs, not make eye contact, and sometimes go mute. And if that was so—then it was so. And she would accept it. And she would love herself as she was, maybe an imperfect Aryan in the Fatherworld. But a perfect Samantha "Stowy" Perry in her castle on the clouds.

She thought back to *The Little Prince* (a book Spitfire had given her) and the words of the rose. One must suffer the caterpillars to enjoy the butterflies. For many years, those caterpillars had nibbled on Stowy. She hoped their time had passed. She hoped only butterflies filled her future.

Stowy reached into one pocket. She pulled out one of her plastic dinosaurs. Her little ankylosaurus. She stroked the dinosaur's armor, then held it out to King.

He took it from her.

"For you," she said. "To keep you safe."

Maybe Stowy was imagining it, but the strong admiral's eyes suddenly seemed damp, and his hand shook slightly as he placed the dinosaur into his pocket.

"I'll treasure it," he whispered, his voice sounding even

raspier for some reason.

Just then, a mouse emerged from the rubble around St Mary's Hospital. The little rodent ran toward Stowy, scurried up her leg, then hopped into one of her many pockets.

Huh. She patted her pocket. So Algernon wasn't dead after all.

King blinked at her. He rubbed his eyes.

Stowy gave him a shaky smile and shrug.

King stared for a moment longer, then burst out laughing.

"Stowy," he said, "it's good to have you back."

CHAPTER TWENTY-ONE
The End of the Beginning

The Reichskanzlei
Berlin
The Fatherworld
September 15, 2207

The Fatherworld.

A world once known as Earth.

It was the center of a galactic empire. An empire that must, Helmut König knew, forever expand. Or it would shrivel up and die.

Führer of the Fatherworld, he stood in the tallest tower of the Reichskanzlei. For hundreds of years, the chancellor would live and work here. When Hitler first moved in, the building had been humbler. During the 1950s, the ruler of a smoldering world, Hitler began a massive campaign of construction. Earth lay in ruin. And Hitler would rebuild it in his image. By 1960, the Reichskanzlei was the tallest building in the world, and it had grown since. Today its towers rose a mile high.

"What a time it must have been," König said softly. "To destroy a world and build a new one. What a man he was. What an opportunity we have."

From here in his offices, a mile high, König gazed upon his empire. It was midnight but Berlin shone with lights.

Thousands of towers soared, all draped with crimson swastika banners. Zeppelins hovered above, casting their beams of light upon the city. There was no place for the impure to hide in the Fatherworld. The Gestapo lit every shadow, exposed every impurity, and cleansed it. In the Pariser Platz, right by the Brandenburg Gate, rose a statue of Hitler. Known as Hitler Triumphant and forged of steel taken from the ruins of the Empire State Building, it was the tallest statue in the world. Had the Statue of Liberty still stood, she would barely reach Hitler's knees. Around the statue rose cranes with hanging bodies—the traitors collected the night before, hanged here for the crowds to see and jeer at.

Forty million people lived in Berlin. And all of them were Aryan. Well, nearly all of them. Every once in a while, the Gestapo found some crippled child or two. And a few subhumans still lived in the zoo, dressed in furs and leaves. The crowd liked to see them, to toss them treats. And every once in a while, the SS rode around the city in a Volkswagen with a few last subhumans inside. They were kept alive through the generations for the noble Aryans to jeer at. A reminder of the disease the Fatherworld had cured.

Yes, that was the problem. What did a doctor do when nobody was sick? There had not been a great challenge for years now. Not since the Fatherworld went to war against the Rah Empire among the stars. The Fatherworld had won, and for years now, the empire had not faced a worthy foe. And without war to harden the soul, Berlin was becoming a city of decadence. Cabaret bars as far as the eye could see! Everywhere in the city, they enjoyed the good life. The opera halls, the bars, the gladiator arenas where genetically modified beasts ripped criminals apart to the cheers of crowds . . .

"Rome became decadent and fell," König said. "We must never rest on our laurels. What we need is another war. Conquest!

We must reclaim this new world, this Unreineland. And build it in my image. I sent you out on this task. And you failed."

The two women in his office remained silent. Good. Smart girls. König had taught them well.

He gazed out the window. Down there, in the city, rose another statue. Smaller than Hitler Triumphant. A statue of himself. Führer Helmut König.

He was a tall man. A powerfully built man. A soldier. Even today, sixty-eight years old, he still trained every day. Still fought. Could still kill any man in a fight. His face was broad, his jaw square. A thick mustache adorned his upper lip, and his bionic red eye reflected in the window, peering back at him.

Finally one of the women spoke.

"Will you stop pontificating, Opa? I'm perfectly capable of conquering Unreineland. Send me back, and—"

"Silence!" König roared.

He spun around, lips peeling back.

Eva König stood there, munching on an apple. His demonic little granddaughter. Like all teenagers, she thought she ruled the world. She wore the uniform of the Waffen-SS, complete with steel-tipped boots and brass knuckles. Her armbands sported swastikas, while lightning bolts blazed across her chest, forming twin Sig runes. The sadistic girl seemed untroubled by his roar. She kept happily chewing her apple.

It was a mistake to let her rule the Waffen-SS, König thought. He had wanted the unit in family hands. But Eva was not ready. Too young. Too stupid. Too weak.

"I'm telling you, Opa." She swallowed another bite. "I got this. I just suffered a little setback." She took a final bite from her apple, then tossed the core onto the floor. "Pick it up, slave!"

One of her prisoners, some dark-skinned girl from

Unreineland, crawled across the floor to retrieve the apple core.

"Eva, get rid of your pet," König said. "We're talking. I don't want your impure little freak with us."

Eva patted her prisoner's curly dark hair. "But she's harmless! Like a puppy."

König drew his sidearm, aimed at the slave's head, and pulled the trigger.

Eva let out a yelp. She pulled her hand back, gasping. Chunks of gore covered her uniform. The slave collapsed onto the floor, head blown open.

"You nearly blew my hand off!" Eva shrieked, face contorted in fury.

"Next time, I'll shoot you in the head too!" König roared. "How dare you disobey my orders, you impudent little dog?" He slapped Eva. Hard. Cracking her bionic eye. She fell to the floor, and König kicked her in the stomach. She groaned.

"I'm sorry!" she gasped.

He kicked her again, this time in the ribs. "What kind of weak, pathetic worm apologizes? Stand up! Stand tall! You are a König, dammit. Stop groveling like a worm."

Tears filled Eva's eyes. But she dutifully rose to her feet, straightened her body, and raised her chin. Her cracked adlerauge sparked, searing away the tears. She must be in tremendous pain. One of her ribs might be cracked. Yet König had trained her well. Her pain tolerance increased every year.

"*Ja, mein führer!*" she said.

Blood dripped down her chin. Good. König stroked her bloodied face.

"Such a beautiful child," he said. "What is it about blood that makes women and children so much more beautiful?"

"I'd rather see the blood of my enemies," Eva said. "Especially the one who defeated me in battle in the sky of Unreineland. The only one who could. You!"

"That was not me!" König roared.

Eva winced, recoiling from another blow.

"That doppelgänger is nothing like me," König said, teeth bared. "James King is weak, sniveling, pathetic."

Another voice rose, coming from the shadowy corner of the office. "He's not as weak as we thought, my beloved husband. He was strong enough to defeat me as well."

She came slinking from the shadows, moving with the grace of smoke unfurling over a forest fire. Her adlerauge shone red, and her blue eye shone even brighter. Her lips cracked into a deranged smile that showed too many teeth. She was, if you asked König, the most beautiful woman on the Fatherworld, but hers was not a radiant beauty like the sun or stars. Hers was a dark beauty. The beauty of death, of the River Styx, and of the storm that had hovered over the void at the dawn of time.

She still looked as beautiful as the day he met her. Hard to believe it had been twenty-three years. Dr. Anneliese, a young and brilliant engineer, had used an elaborate machine to break into his home. And then, with a terrible weapon that wilted flesh, Anneliese had murdered König's wife. When he caught her, she had only grinned.

"Now you're mine," the young assassin had said. "By the ancient customs, I demand it!"

In truth, she had done König a favor. His first wife, mother to Wolfgang, had been a matronly woman with the personality of a mule. Her father was a rich industrialist. The only reason König had married her. Even emperors needed money and connections. Magda had served her purpose, had given him a son, and he had been relieved to see her corpse. Instead of killing young Anneliese Heisenberg that night, König made love to her. A month later they were wed. The entire Fatherworld celebrated.

She walked toward him now across his office—older, wiser, deadlier. Anneliese wore her black bodysuit, a sophisticated garment covered with cables, motors, and hidden blades. As she walked, a fly landed on her chest. Her suit's force field ignited, frying the insect. She stepped on the twitching bug, crushing it, and a smile spread across her lips.

"There is pleasure in killing even the smallest creature," said Dr. Anneliese Heisenberg-König. "Small pleasure but pleasure nonetheless."

"You could have derived great pleasure from killing James King," said König. "Yet you failed."

"Indeed." She lost her smile. "I failed. If it were any other doppelgänger, I would have been ashamed. But I'm not ashamed to lose to your doppelgänger." She ran her hands over König's arms. "He's strong. Like you. But there is one weakness that will be his undoing: Honor!"

König snorted. "This shadow self has honor?"

Anneliese stroked his cheek. "The doppelgängers have their own code of honor. Not like ours. Their honor is not about conquest or glorious purification. They seek honor in protecting the weak."

König couldn't help it. He laughed. "Protecting the weak? Weakness must be crushed! Driven out of society!" His laughter grew. "Protecting the weak! What next? You'll tell me they adopt cockroaches instead of stepping on them?"

"I adopted a pet," Eva said. The girl was pouting by the fireplace, gazing at the corpse of her maid. "Then Opa shot her."

The two adults ignored the petulant girl.

"My son is the only one worthy of carrying the family name," said König. "Wolfgang still fights at *Unreineland.* He is winning battles—while you two slunk back here with your tails between your legs, both defeated by this James King."

Eva raised her chin. "My papa is a great warrior! But if he

faced James King, the brave Wolfgang König would be here too. Defeated. Like me and that deranged engineer you married after Oma died." She pointed a gloved finger at Dr. Anneliese. "If you ask me, she's working with the doppelgängers."

"Enough!" König roared. "I won't have you two at each other's throats again. We're all part of the same family now. And the family must survive. There's a reason they don't call us Eternal Führers. We're not Hitlers. We're not holy. We are mighty yet we are mortals. If we show weakness, elements within our party will slash our throats. We must win this war. The Fatherworld must conquer—or it will rot and perish. And the same goes for our family."

Amazingly, that actually shut Eva up. His mouthy granddaughter stood silently, gazing out the window, contemplative.

"Husband, send me back," Anneliese said. "The girl too. I'll look after her, mold her. And I'll take . . ." Her voice dropped. She stepped closer, pressing her body against his. "I'll take the eisengolems."

The words hung in the air.

"The eisengolems," König said softly.

Anneliese's eyes lit up with the fires of madness. Her savage grin returned. She licked her teeth and grabbed König by the arms.

"My most marvelous creations! Men of metal. Soldiers who do not tire. Do not eat. Do not drink. Are not tempted by booze, gambling, or whores . . ." She glanced toward Eva, then back at König. She pressed herself against him, bringing her lips close to his. "All they do is march and kill. Forever."

König clutched her wrists, pulling her off him. "You told me the eisengolems weren't ready. That they were too fickle, too likely to get confused in battle and attack our own troops."

"So?" Eva said. She reached for the fruit bowl and grabbed some grapes. "We have lots of troops. If Oma Anneliese's robots kill some, we can replace them."

Anneliese glared at the girl. Her gloves sprouted steel claws. "I told you to never call me *Oma.* I am not a grandmother." She raised her chin. "I am only fifty years old."

Eva popped a grape into her mouth. "Wow, the prime of youth."

"Enough!" König snapped. "Save your bile for the enemy. Very well. I'll give you both another chance. Return to Unreineland. Take the eisengolems. And this time—don't come back without the head of James King!"

* * * * *

London
Earth
September 17, 2207

The Battle for Britain continued. For three days, the Freedom Brigade kept Britain standing. They had begun their assault on London with five thousand men. Within three days, they were down to four thousand brave marines. And those marines stayed standing and kept fighting for a nation. For a world. For civilization itself. Rarely in history, King knew, had so few saved so many.

Two days ago, reinforcements had arrived in Alliance dropships. The Tiger Division from India rampaged across southern England, while a courageous South Korean division fought to liberate Wales. By today, September 17, London was back in Alliance hands, and the Germans were driven down to Dover.

King wanted to fight those battles. Dr. Annie wouldn't let him. He remained in St Mary's Hospital, treated for a knife wound, two u-bolt wounds, and a whole variety of other maladies ranging from dehydration to simple exhaustion.

"I've had worse," King said.

Annie snorted. "Liar."

He raised his prosthetic hand. "Do you see this? I lost a hand once."

"When you were young. Well, young*er.* You're turning sixty-nine this Christmas. You need time to recover, old man. No fighting for a month."

"A *month*?" His eyes widened. "But—"

Annie crossed her arms. "You heard me." Then her eyes softened. "It'll be a long war, Jim. It might last for years. I want you to survive it. Pace yourself."

While he was here, he thought about Kim a lot. He missed his wife.

She had left him a message. During the Battle for St Mary's, Kim had undertaken a secret mission with Godwin. Where had they gone? King had no idea.

My boss and my wife, off on an adventure together, he thought.

He kept trying to reach Kim, but her MindLink was turned off. That could mean she was dead. Most likely, she had just turned the implant off. For safety. Yet how could he stop worrying?

While he recovered in bed (Annie kept checking to make sure he remained in bed), he watched the news. Snippets kept reaching them here in London. MindWeb was still on the fritz. Many news stations had shut down. But word still spread over radio, telepathy, cable, and plain old gossip. The war was still raging. Everywhere. In space. On land. At sea. Lines were being drawn, trenches being dug.

"Will you stop grinding your teeth?" Jordan said.

King turned toward the bed beside his. Larry Jordan lay there, his leg and chest wrapped in bandages. He was holding an open book. *The Unrelenting Struggle* by Winston Churchill.

"I'm not grinding my teeth," King said.

"You are, and I'm trying to read," Jordan said. "Can't you put your teeth in a cup for a while?"

"Just my luck they stuck me in the same hospital room as you." King snorted. "As if being your neighbor back at Nebraska wasn't bad enough."

"They were going to take you to the veterinarian hospital," Jordan said. "I had to convince them you weren't an ape."

"I'd have been better off at the vet," King muttered. "Your daughter is a slave driver."

Annie stuck her head around the doorway. "You two boys stop bantering and get some rest!"

King looked at Jordan as if to say: *See?*

The next day, George Godwin appeared on one of the popular telepathy channels, sending a community broadcast to anyone who'd listen. King was surprised. He put down the book he was reading (an old Louis L'Amour novel) and accepted the hallucination. George Godwin seemed to materialize in the hospital room beside King. His actual location was unknown. From wherever he was, Godwin was broadcasting across MindWeb to anyone able to connect.

As always, the high commander wore his three-piece suit, complete with coattails, a top hat, and a cane. His face was jowly, yet his eyes were as hard as any general's. He took a puff on a cigar, then stared into the camera. Right into King's mind and minds across Earth.

"Nineteen days ago, the enemy, who refer to themselves as the Third Reich of the Fatherworld, launched a surprise attack against Earth and her colonies." His voice was deep, gruff, biting through the cigar smoke. "They did not hesitate to slaughter women, children, even babies. They came to murder civilians. And they met soldiers! The brave soldiers of the Alliance, along with our allies in the Red Dawn and Desert Thorns, fought the enemy with honor, courage, and ferocity. For nineteen days now, our starships have been striking the enemy in space. We have driven the foul Weltraumwaffe farther from our sky, nearly halfway to the orbit of our moon. Meanwhile on the ground, our lines of heavy armor, artillery, and infantry continue to resist the enemy's advances. At sea, we have reclaimed many waters and continue to engage the enemy wherever he sets sail. Führer Helmut König, tyrant of the Fatherworld, hoped that a surprise blitzkrieg against our world would crush us. Which it very nearly did. Millions of us died in the surprise attack. Maybe tens of millions. Cities smolder. Many of our soldiers have fallen, and many of our grand starships are gone. Yet still we stand! Still we refuse to break!"

Godwin raised his fist, defiant, jowls swinging. Then he took another puff on his cigar, calming himself. After a moment he spoke again.

"At a dark moment during the Second World War, Winston Churchill, an ancestor of mine, said: 'This is not the end. It is not even the beginning of the end. But it is, perhaps, the end of the beginning.' And so it is now. And so we march onward. Into danger. Into darkness. Into the unknown shadows of our struggle. We will keep fighting the enemy. We will fight him on land. We will fight him on the high seas. We will fight him in space. And if we must, we will fight him in his own universe. We will fight to victory!"

He stared into the camera, eyes penetrating, then ended

the broadcast.

As the hallucination faded away, King noticed the smudged figure standing behind Godwin.

It was Kim.

"Where the hell are those two?" King muttered.

* * * * *

By October, King was itching to return to battle. He was still wounded. Dr. Annie wanted him to spend another few weeks recovering. King would not wait that long. The umbrion wounds still stung (those particles clung onto flesh like bulldogs onto bones), and his left leg still ached. But healing could wait. He still had a war to fight.

"Let me back at 'em," he told Annie. "That is an order."

The doctor placed a hand on her hip. "You may be an admiral, but I'm your doctor."

"Which is why I'm asking you first instead of stomping out right now," King said.

Annie heaved a sigh. "I'll discharge you. But be careful, Jim. You're not a young man anymore."

"Trust me, I know. I feel it every time I roll out of bed. Much like my breakfast, I snap, crackle, and pop."

She didn't even crack a smile. She placed a hand on his arm. "Have you considered it, Jim? Taking Rejuvenex?"

"I'm not taking any more drugs than I need to."

"I know men who've taken it," Annie said. "It takes ten years off their lives."

"That's what I'm worried about!" King snapped.

Annie smiled thinly. "I phrased it badly maybe. It makes them ten years younger. Godwin took it, and look at him. Halfway into his eighties and spry as a fly."

King crossed his arms. "That drug has a ten percent

chance of killing you. I'm not ready to take that chance."

"You face a greater chance of dying every time you go to battle," Annie said.

"That's different. That's . . . honorable."

"You and my father." Annie heaved a sigh. "Your honor will get you killed someday. I hope not until you're well past a hundred. Be careful out there, Jim."

That morning, he pulled on his military uniform. He did not don the fine dress uniform of an admiral, glittering with service ribbons and polished cuff links. No, he wasn't dressing for the bridge of a starship today. But for battle. He wore simple fatigues today. Good old olive drab. A gun hung at his side.

King wasn't sure where he would be stationed. Where he would fight. The war had swept him up like a wave, and for a long time, King had simply swirled in the current. Soon he would receive his first official mission. Where would he be stationed? What would be his role to fill in this war? King didn't know. He no longer had a starship. The *Freedom* was gone. Would they give him another ship? Maybe give him a desk job on Earth? Hell, if they sent him to the front line as a grunt, King would gladly go and fight alongside the boys. He was a soldier. Always was, always would be. Ready to fight, even die for his world. Soldiers got old, but they never stopped being soldiers.

He checked his watch. Godwin was scheduled to meet him in ten minutes. Last night, while King was sleeping, the high commander had sent him a MindWeb message. King replayed the message once more.

A little hallucination materialized in the hospital room. Godwin was sitting in a rock garden among mushrooms and flowers, smoking a pipe, looking like a sophisticated gnome. The rock garden wasn't a real place. King recognized it. A common background you could choose for MindPlay broadcasts. A figment of the imagination, triggered by tiny electric signals to the brain.

"Ah, King, old boy!" Godwin said. "Sorry for not keeping in touch. Your wife and I have been having quite an adventure. I know you're curious what we've been up to. Well, I can't say. Not over MindWeb. Too dangerous, old boy. Could be hacked, you know. This is in-person news. You're still at the hospital? Feeling better and ready to get back at the Jerries? Well, I got a job for you! Meet me in the courtyard tomorrow at the crack of dawn. I'll bring the tea."

With a puff on his cigar, the old man vanished.

That was it. That was the message. King had watched it three times already.

Meet me in the courtyard.

He must have meant St Mary's Hospital courtyard. Godwin was returning to London.

King stepped into the courtyard. Trees had once grown here. Only charred trunks remained. Bits of coal still littered the cobblestones, and bullet holes pierced the hospital walls all around him. Many of the windows had shattered. But the swastikas had been painted over, and the foul SS was driven south across the English Channel. The hospital once more became a place of healing. Some victims of the Nazi terror were convalescing here. Many had been buried in Regent's Park. They had to use mass graves.

The courtyard was empty today. No faces peered from the windows. Strange. Normally patients (those well enough to leave their beds) played chess here or simply sat and watched the sky. King looked down at a dead bird. A starling. The poor thing must have choked on the smoke in the sky. It lay still and silent on the cobblestones among the ashes. So many innocent creatures paid the price for the wars of men.

"Jim?"

The voice came from behind him.

He spun around, and there she stood. The woman of his life. Kim.

Her hair was collected into a neat, prim ponytail, the golden strands streaked with silver. She wore the dress uniform of the Alliance. The navy-blue fabric was neatly pressed, adorned with a golden aiguillette. Little steel gears adorned her lapels—symbol of the engineering corps. Five golden bars shone on each of her shoulder straps, denoting her a colonel.

She saluted him. "Sir."

He returned the salute, then rushed toward her. She crashed into his arms. They stood in the middle of the courtyard, embracing.

"You look good," she mumbled into his embrace. She stroked his cheek, her eyes damp. "You look strong."

He kissed her. For a moment, he forgot about the war, about his pain, about his fear. And all the universe was just their kiss.

Finally, when their kiss was over, he looked into her loving blue eyes.

"Where were you, Kim?"

Now more than love shone in her eyes. Excitement too. A nervous smile fluttered across her lips. "You're not going to believe this."

"Believe *what*?"

Her smile faded. "I can't tell. Not me. Not here."

"Kim!" He couldn't help but laugh. "What's going on?"

A deep, rumbling voice sounded from behind. "Military secrets, old boy. Ones not to be revealed here. The windows have eyes. The walls have ears. Even our very thoughts can be prey to detection."

King spun around, and there was George Godwin. The old Englishman was walking across the cobblestones, cane tapping. As he passed by the dead bird, he paused.

"Ah, pity." Godwin shook his head. "A weak, defenseless creature, victim in a war he does not understand."

"That's how I'm starting to feel," King said. "Sir, will somebody tell me what in God's name is going on?"

Godwin reached him. "I can't tell you here, old friend. I must take you with us. And *show you.*"

"Show me *what?* Sir, I'm sorry for being so insistent. But since this war has begun, I've been kept out of the loop on everything. I've been fighting in the dark, literally and figuratively. If I'm still an admiral, if I'm still a senior commander in the Alliance Armed Forces, I must know everything."

Godwin nodded, eyes shrewd. He leaned closer toward King, and his voice dropped. "It has something to do with the starship *Freedom.*"

Godwin leaned closer until he was whispering in King's ear. As King listened, the courtyard spun around him, the entire world flipped upside down, and he could not breathe.

The story continues in…

The Fires of Freedom

Freedom Fleet II

NOVELS BY DANIEL ARENSON

Starship Freedom

Starship Freedom

The Cost of Freedom

We Fight for Freedom

For Death or Freedom

Let Freedom Ring

In Pursuit of Freedom

The Guns of Freedom

A Time for Freedom

Freedom Fleet

The Freedom Fleet

The Fires of Freedom

Guardians of Freedom

Mintari

A World of Dinosaurs

Where Dinosauars Roam

March of the Dinosaurs

Alien Hunters

Alien Hunters

Alien Sky

Alien Shadows

Earthrise: The Original Series

Earth Alone

Earth Lost

Earth Rising

Earth Fire

Earth Shadows

Earth Valor

Earth Reborn

Earth Honor

Earth Eternal

Earth Machines

Earth Aflame

Earth Unleashed

Earth Remembers

Earth in Darkness

Earth, Our Home

A Prayer for Earthrise

Hear, O Earth!

Earth of Gold and Light

East of Earth

The Shores of Eternity

If I Forget Thee, Earth

On the Milky Way Rivers

Soldiers of Earthrise

The Earthling

Earthlings

Earthling's War

I, Earthling

The Earthling's Daughter

We Are Earthlings

Children of Earthrise

The Heirs of Earth

A Memory of Earth

An Echo of Earth

The War for Earth

The Song of Earth

The Legacy of Earth

Kingdoms of Sand

Kings of Ruin

Crowns of Rust

Thrones of Ash

Temples of Dust

Halls of Shadow

Echoes of Light

The Moth Saga

Moth

Empires of Moth

Secrets of Moth

Daughter of Moth

Shadows of Moth

Legacy of Moth

Dawn of Dragons

Requiem's Song

Requiem's Hope

Requiem's Prayer

Song of Dragons

Blood of Requiem

Tears of Requiem

Light of Requiem

Dragonlore

A Dawn of Dragonfire

A Day of Dragon Blood

A Night of Dragon Wings

The Dragon War

A Legacy of Light

A Birthright of Blood

A Memory of Fire

Requiem for Dragons

Dragons Lost

Dragons Reborn

Dragons Rising

Flame of Requiem

Forged in Dragonfire

Crown of Dragonfire

Pillars of Dragonfire

Dragonfire Rain

Blood of Dragons

Rage of Dragons

Flight of Dragons

Misfit Heroes

Eye of the Wizard

Wand of the Witch

Standalones

Firefly Island

The Gods of Dream

Flaming Dove

Utopia 58

Star Stuff

KEEP IN TOUCH

www.DanielArenson.com
Daniel@DanielArenson.com
Facebook.com/DanielArenson
Twitter.com/DanielArenson

www.ingramcontent.com/pod-product-compliance
Lightning Source LLC
Chambersburg PA
CBHW030846030726
47495CB00005B/1389

9781927601976